THREE
LEAVES

Also by Steven LaVey

The Ugly Spirit
Shorts

@S_LaVey

@stevenlaveyauthor

www.stevenlavey.com

Cover design by Lauria

www.fiverr.com/lauria

STEVEN LAVEY

THREE LEAVES

Three Leaves first edition 2017

ISBN-13:
978-1539324072

ISBN-10:
1539324079

LEAF I

I

I am obsessed with the delirium induced between wakefulness and sleep. Through the night, I hide away quietly in my bedroom, hanging out of the window smoking cigarettes – blue/grey plumes of smoke against a black, veiled sky – I think of it as an upturned darkened bowl, a lid clasped over the red, slated rooftops of the estate. Sometimes I might sit on the floor with my headphones on and listen to experimental electro, or haunting Pagan/Celtic alt. 80s rock. There are things I must consider and think over in the long stretch to dawn.

I think little secret, selfish thoughts that do me no good. As the grey wash of morning arrives, I turn on the big, old computer and listen as it creaks and whirrs into life. Sleepy and confused with exhaustion, I clack away at the keys, letting whatever nonsense comes to mind spill out on to the screen. I don't look up to read, I just keep hammering away, throwing out random images, letting my automatic unconscious dream out through my yellow, nicotine-stained fingers. I stop to light a sandalwood incense stick, and to fetch a cup of coffee – the aroma of both mixing in with my tired senses. I type until I hear my mother, step-dad, and brother, getting up. At this point, I must dress and put in an appearance – there is a pretence to keep up. Every day my mother comments that I look tired. I tell her it's nothing – I'm quite all right. Once my parents have left for work and my brother for school, I sit in the quiet of the morning eating a slice of toast with peanut butter. In the hypnagogic blur of sleepy delirium, my auditory

7

senses are acute – there are birds in the tree outside – their chirps like the roar of tiny dinosaurs – the sound of the pond water filtered through a little waterfall, gushes like a tsunami. At ten a.m., I take my clothes off and get into bed. It will be five hours before they return.

In the afternoon, my mother has inquisition on her lips. 'What have you done today? Have you heard from any of the jobs you have applied for? Isn't it time you did this or that? Why do you look so tired?' She tells me I should have an early night.

I mumble off-the-cuff uncertainties and blatant lies to pacify her and to buy more time.

'Still haven't heard anything. I hope they get back to me soon. I posted this letter/ I phoned this company/ so-and-so should have received my CV by now.'

For an hour, I sit uncomfortably with my younger brother in the living room while I eat. Then I return to my room and look over the gibberish written that morning. I move the words around on the screen, chop it up, cut it to bits, and hammer the images together to create bizarre juxtapositions that satisfy immensely. Before everyone else goes to bed, I take the opportunity to play bass guitar for a while. Much time spent fiddling with the Zoom FX box, a process of moving reverb, chorus, echo, drive, and distortion to blend effects that are equally pleasing and nasty to the ear. I fire up the computer and work on drum loops and synth parts, adding and cementing beats and sounds to accompany the bass. I pile the noises on top of each other like a sloppy sonic sandwich. On a notepad, I scribble lyrics – I sing along, and pluck away at the bass – but this isn't a song – like all my music – this is the dirge of a musical swamp; it is the sound of an ocean of audible shit.

It is unavoidable that I may have to venture downstairs to get something to eat or drink. This task involves going undetected through the living room, where my mother and step-dad are watching TV. I try (and usually fail) to achieve this without either of them engaging me in conversation. Once I have passed this tedious trial, I walk up the creaky, green-carpeted stairs to the top, then stealthily and quietly as possible return halfway down so I can hear what they are saying about me – always, it is painful, snide comments. I return upstairs with a sadness stinging me in my deflated ego and diminishing self-confidence.

They are asleep now and so I can breathe. I while away the dark hours lost in beat-lit. books, experimental films, adventure and fantasy video games and with eyes closed, I escape under the waves of every genre of musical expression. The ashtray becomes a stinking mountain of tab-ends – I smoke and daydream.

Thursday brings with it the job section of the *Chronicle*. My mother circles all the jobs she thinks will be suitable for me – each biro ring is a noose around my creative heart. With fake enthusiasm I make enquiries to appease her – a CV sent out, maybe a phone call – I tell her I am hopeful about hearing back about this or that – it fills me with delight that no one has yet invited me for an interview.

But Thursday precedes Friday, and Friday is Giro

day. With building anticipation, I await the thin brown envelope with the big square Giro cheque. I skip sleeping through the day on a Friday and immediately take the Giro to the post office to cash it in. Eighty pounds – twenty to mother. Sixty pounds – the little grocer's on the estate sells under the counter snide cigarettes and baccy – a large pouch of Golden Virginia will do me a fortnight, maybe a box of twenty Lambert too. Forty-five pounds – the corner shop, skins, filters, a bottle of Jack Daniels, vanilla coke. Thirty pounds – to town, and a rummage through second hand CD, book, and game shops. Three discs for a tenner from Steel Wheels – I mix up the genres, one from death metal, one from electro, then, maybe a lucky dip. Twenty pounds – a good while spent in the Oxfam bookshop looking for the missing titles from the works of the writers I admire. I check R for Rhinehart, B for Burroughs... then the horror and sci-fi section – W for Wells, B for Barker... sometimes I find a precious treasure of a book that I have longed for. It may be old, a first edition perhaps, with browned or yellowing rough pages. I flip through the book and the smell of time leaps out – a hand written inscription on the first page invites a fantasy of its former owner.

Fifteen pounds – just enough for a second hand PlayStation game from Charlie's Games. The little booth in the Green Market has the games up on the wall behind the counter in an unreadable mosaic. My eyes flick around the titles.

'Are you looking for anything in particular?' the woman with the big square glasses asks me.

I've been standing staring at the games for so long

that I'm entranced.

'Any good RPGs?' I ask quietly.

She points out some titles and I pick one that looks most interesting.

As I step off the bus on my street, a bizarre sensation reminds me once again of the strangeness of Fawdon. On Fawdon Park Road where I live, the cloying smell of chemical-chocolate from the nearby Rowntree's factory fills the air. On the left side of the road, the row of bungalows exposes the skyline and the large industrial pipes and silos from the factory stand out like colossal silver monuments. As always, I wonder if Fawdon exists on an ancient ley line. On the right side of the road is the row of white semi-detached houses, and half way along is home. As I near the house, I look forward to a quick kip, then the rest of the afternoon playing my game, alone in an exhausted internal quiet.

II

Every second Wednesday afternoon I have to visit Mrs Skeleton at the dole office. I take a ticket from the horrible machine; it is greasy and revolting, and the buttons look diseased with the presses of grubby fingers. I sit with my ticket, waiting for my turn, nervously watching the electronic numbers tick over.

Mrs Skeleton has a kind oval face, grey eyes, and mousy, light brown hair. She is in her late forties and quietly spoken. I feel as if she is my ally, and when I present her with my job diary, she does not judge me on the fact that I am obviously lying about my search for work, nor has she ever stopped my benefits or treated me curtly like some of the other benefit bastards have.

'Like I explained before,' she said, 'you are eligible to sign up for a New Deal training scheme after six months of unemployment. Are you still interested?'

I nod enthusiastically.

'And you still want to do New Deal for musicians?'

'Yes,' I reply quietly, erupting inside with happiness.

'Well the next time you come in to sign on I'll begin making arrangements for you.'

My mother has decided to get the internet installed. It is the most exciting thing I can imagine. She informs me it is to help me search for work. I tell her that I am starting a college course through the Job Centre soon and that I won't need to find work. She seems appeased by this, and I feel relieved that I can relax and not feel pressured into taking on a job that will kill my creativity. I tell her that the internet will still be useful in that I will be able to use it for my college work, although in reality I have other reasons for wanting to get into cyberspace.

My mother, who has no technological knowledge, gets our neighbour Sean to set up the net. The computer boots up, whirring into life, and the modem squeals – it sounds alien and bizarre to me. Over the next week an unconscious, silent war breaks out over who gets to use the computer in the living room to go on the net. It is uncomfortable for me to be in any other part of the house other than my room. I can feel the burning eyes of Jack, my step-dad, in the back of my head, as he counts the minutes I spend on the internet. I decide to wait until they are all asleep and I creep downstairs to go hunting.

The World Wide Web offers me the opportunity to do something I cannot in real life; talk to the opposite sex. I log into some of the chat rooms of the bands I like: Pantera, Deicide, Fear Factory – there are obnoxious, arrogant Yanks in the chat rooms who hate Limeys.

One night I begin to talk to a woman called Ali. She is eight years older than I am and lives about twenty miles away. I type away into the encroaching dawn. When my fingers ache from typing I walk silently and half-asleep around the living room – a somnambulist perambulating an itchy green-carpeted sea. After hours of screen-chat, I am delirious and washed over with sleepy waves of hypnagogic confusion. We have spoken about everything; I have told her more than I have told anyone in my whole life – I feel emotionally weary and drained with it, but it has been cathartic to have a real conversation with someone, albeit

13

electronically. Near six in the morning, she says she has to go and tells me what a lovely person I am and how much she has enjoyed chatting to me. To receive an expression of warmth from someone when I feel nothing but resentment from everyone in my life is almost too much to bear. I lie in bed, feeling swept away and drowned by my emotions.

Half awake-asleep. Sitting on the edge of my bed mid-afternoon. Too much light, tired eyes. I vibrate with delirium through lack of sleep. My body feels like it weighs a tonne, and I am irritable with fatigue. My mother knocks on the door then enters.

'Your gran is poorly,' she informs me, 'the doctor thinks she has a stomach ulcer.'

I have been thinking about Ali. I decide to ask her to meet up with me. I wait in the Pantera chat room for her to log in. I have already thought of the time, date, and place: noon this Saturday, Trillians. After I ask her, I wait with nervous fingers hovering over the keys. When she replies, I discover she has just been having me on, that the whole night we spent discovering each other was just a joke with her friends, while they were drunk, taking turns to talk to me.

I'm crushed, devastated, humiliated.

Mrs Skeleton arranged for me to start my New Deal for musicians, AKA an HCFE in music technology. At Newcastle College, I fill out the appropriate forms. Starting this course means that for the next nine months I am free from the tyranny of my mother and her insistence that I take on any old job. My creativity is safe for a while and I am excited about receiving my dole while engaging in something I love. It also means a relief from the job centre for a while. Mrs Skeleton seemed pleased for me and wished me good luck.

At the induction at The John Marley Centre, I meet my tutor, Paul Balls. I notice his egg-shaped head, and that his manner is nervous, confused, and bumbling. His mouth looks stuffed with a frenzy of pointy teeth. Balls shows me around the college – the instrument stores, staffed by Stu the dick and his dry irritating sense of humour – the six different studios, kitted out with control and live rooms. I am already looking forward to making some noise. Via the cafeteria, Balls leads me to the computer lab. Three long rows of big fat computers with chunky monitors – it all seems so high tech – Balls hands me a wad of paperwork to fill in and plonks me in front of a computer. He gives me a password and login name so I can use the machines whenever I like.

'I've got to do my next induction,' he mumbles, 'I'll be back in a while.'

Later that day, after Balls has finished his inductions, I meet the other reprobates on the course. These include guitar-widdle Nicky, MC Binman (always friendly, always stoned), silent Tony, and Lee. Both Binman and Tony have been in jail for drugs related misadventures and within five minutes of meeting both of them, they are regaling me with stories of life inside. Strangely, I am already acquainted with Lee, as we were childhood friends. I have an ambivalent reaction to his presence; I resent him as a figure and memory of a horrible childhood yet a familiar face is comforting to my social anxieties.

My mother points out that I am related to Lee (his dad is my great uncle's son) and I realise I knew this already but had forgotten. As the course begins, I find that I am babysitting Lee, and I realise he is lacking in all musical ability, other than being able to play the first few chords of *Wonderwall* on guitar. He has a long beaky face like a bird, a pale complexion spattered with brown freckles and his eyes are cold and empty hard-blue. When I look at him, I sometimes think he might lay an egg.

With excitement, I begin knocking off tracks in the studio and finishing all the units on the course too quickly.

'You need to slow down,' Balls tells me, 'you're whizzing through the course too fast. You've still got eight months to go!'

Lee sits in the studio with me all day while I fuck around with Akai samplers, drum machines, and synthesisers – I knock up a drum and bass version of Billy Idol's *White Wedding*.

Balls marks it as excellent, using the word 'trippy' in his professional analysis.

Going to college four days a week has altered my sleep patterns. Having to arrive for lessons at nine in the morning has naturally reverted my schedule of slumber back to that of a normal person. It is with regret though, as I miss my nocturnal activities. Still, when I am not due at college the next day I remain awake at night smoking cigarettes and being creative in whatever way my fancy chooses.

Burning eyes, fighting tiredness mid-afternoon – my mother enters my room.

'Your gran has her results back.'

Her eyes are wet with tears, a crack in her voice.

'It wasn't an ulcer. She has cancer.'

III

The word cancer has left me feeling numb. The thought of my gran becoming ill is impossible to me and I shut myself off to the reality of it. All the talk in the family of the malignant growth in her stomach and the impending hospital procedures, chemotherapy, fluid draining, hair loss, it bounces off me like rubber stones.

Throughout my life, my grandmother has stood in reverence to me – her unlimited kindness, warmth and comfort has always sheltered me from the tyranny of my inner tortures. The idea that she be snatched away by some black, 'alien' (as she describes it) tumour inside her is a concept I cannot swallow.

As such, I deliberately avoid going to visit her, so I do not have to acknowledge her illness.

In the chat room for the band The Red Hot Chili Peppers, I've met a nineteen-year-old girl called Emma from Canada. She is dirty. She likes to have cyber-sex. In the middle of the night, I sit at the computer contemplating the time difference between our two countries. We describe in explicit detail what sexual acts we would like to perform on each other.

Emma is desperate for me to fly over to Canada so I can fuck her. I explain that the reality of that happening is unlikely, but I appease her by telling her that my gran is sick and that if she dies I receive a little something in her will, and that it might be enough to fly to Canada so I can fuck her. I feel disgusted with myself for having this thought.

It takes me almost a month to build up the courage to visit my gran. She has already started chemo and she has lost her hair. I find her and my granddad sitting in the June sun on the green square of lawn in their back garden. She is wearing a bandana to hide her baldness.

Sensing my discomfort my gran shows me the bag of fluid attached to her stomach.

'I'm going to be all right, you know,' she smiles.

It is a smile of hope and despair.

Having finished all the work and units on my course in just three months, Balls has given me permission to do whatever I like at college. Therefore, I spend my time loading the Akai sampler with farts, coughs, the sound of doors slamming, burps, whistles, keys jangling – I've constructed an entire electronic drum kit out of these random noises and spent weeks putting together a drum sequence. Balls is impressed.

On a daily basis and with almost guaranteed certainty, Balls will regale both Lee and I with his tales of drumming in various soft-rock bands from the 1970s. He seems confused about the actual details of his anecdotes and I wonder if he is filling in the gaps of missing information with his imagination. The most important aspect of these tales is often the point that at one time he had hair. Precious, precious hair.

Talking to Emma on the internet has led us to declare that we are boyfriend and girlfriend. Although this is something that has strengthened my self-confidence, the realisation that we will probably never meet in person is beginning to dawn on me. Also, I am aware that I may be creating a myth out of someone

19

thousands of miles away and pretending and imagining that they are someone that they are probably not. You can only derive so much from a computer screen. There is no experience of their mannerisms, the way they talk, the movements of the body.

Therefore, in the hope of making our relationship more concrete and real, I make a video tape of myself messing around in my room and send it to her, asking her to send me one in return.

On my way home from college I stop by to see my gran. Her illness has stabilised but she has not improved. She looks tired. My granddad is watching the television. During the programme, a voice cuts in for a report from the BBC news – my heart leaps, you only ever see programmes interrupted by news in films.
Planes slamming against buildings. Dust and chaos. Everyone is silent, jaws open.

For days, it seems no one can discuss anything else other than planes, buildings, bombs, and people on fire jumping out of windows.

In the post, I receive a heartfelt letter from Emma. She is confused about her sexuality – her concerns are that she is bisexual and that all the kids at her college know it. She also says that she loves me. Inside the letter are three large maple leaves from her home town of Tecumseh.

A little sadness has come over me because I know we will never meet – I have to wonder if it is worth it to continue something that is in reality never going to be a physical relationship.

In a moment of hysteria, my gran has come to terms
with her cancer and her slow crawl towards death.
She wailed and cursed – begged a god she had only
just started to believe in again to save her – then sunk
in to a resigned self-pity in the knowledge of an
ephemeral world we cannot escape. As such, in her
acceptance that the cancer inside her will not
disappear, she has begun to make plans for her
posthumous assets, even though, as she journeys back
and forth to the hospital to have the fluid from her
stomach drained, she retains to me the façade that she
will survive.

At the same time, she has made my mother promise
to cease smoking should she die. That promise is
likewise forced upon my step-dad and myself. I feel as
if giving it up is the least I can do.

Yet still the word cancer has no meaning to me. I
refuse to let it penetrate into my mind. My mother,
however, spends much of her free time on the net
reading endless articles about the big C, and filling her
head with misinformation. With the likely demise of
my grandmother, my mam has become increasingly
tearful and lugubrious. She lacks hope.

I consider my ignorance and disbelief in the
impending death of my gran to be the only way I can
remain stoic.

To lose her to the black 'alien' fills me with an
already loaded sensation of wilderness and loneliness.
Like a dog tied by a rope all its life – her death will be
the noose cut free from around my own throat.

It is not that she forcefully imprisons me – it is her

enduring delusion that I am something that I am not. Her thoughts of me as a good, respectable boy are something I try hard not to shatter. She expects I will do well in life, and that I am innocent in action and thought – in playing along, and maintaining pretence, I don't let her down or hurt her feelings. Everyone else in the family thinks of me otherwise. On occasion when my uncle, granddad, or anyone else in the family calls me worse than shit, she has always stood in my defence.

To lose her is to lose my only familial ally – cast adrift upon her death. I am numb to cancer.

IV

Emma has decided to ask her dad if he will pay $800 for me to fly to Canada. I'm not sure what to make of this – I wonder if this means that she is either stupid, rich, stupidly rich, lying to impress me, or just so desperate for me to fuck her that she will do anything. I think it is most likely the latter. Not surprisingly, her father says no. I don't blame him either, what father would want to pay for someone to fly half way around the world to deflower his daughter?

I think about Emma all the time. I have her picture on the wall next to my bed – it pains me to know that I can't have a physical relationship with her. Online she calls me daddy and I call her baby, I tell her all that's left is to smack her ass, just like the Pantera song *Good Friends and a Bottle of Pills*.

However, I've made some other female friends online – it amazes me just how easily I can talk to them over a computer screen; it is something I fear to do in real life. My fear is simply through lack of experience and too much introspection, self-analysis and self-consciousness. At times, I find it crippling. I also just don't want to talk to anyone. I distrust everyone. I feel nothing but antipathy from all – I can hear the snide comments, bitching, and belittling comments smouldering beneath the surface of everyone – and I hate everyone because of it.

This distrust and misanthropy that I feel isn't borne out of nothing – growing up and dressing 'differently' and by that I simply mean wearing heavy metal band T-shirts, combat trousers, *Dr. Martens* boots and having long hair has brought upon myself a vast and unexpected torrent of hatred from everyone from old ladies to charvers. Countless times I've been spat on, burned with lighters, been forced to hand over cash and cigarettes or face violence; when I was fourteen I had my head stamped on by fifteen kids for wearing a Cannibal Corpse T-shirt.

My mother, in her vast ignorance and misinformed paranoia, has only managed to exacerbate my life further with her meddling. She will quite happily tell people that I 'have no confidence.' I wonder why.

I am only nineteen years old and already broken.

I have printed out a new picture of Emma. I spend a long time staring at it. She is very beautiful, with short blonde hair, a wide smile, thick lips, green eyes – she is slim, athletic, lithe, and has two huge nostrils like a dragon – and I want her so much it is painful. Torturous, even. To talk to her I have to stay awake at least until midnight due to the time difference. I'm verging on returning to full nocturnal hours again. Luckily, as I have finished all the units on my course, I am able to snooze my way through my days at college. Balls is happy for me to mess around on the computers. If I can be bothered, I open Cubase and work on some drum loops – I have created, performed, and produced an entire album on my own. Balls insists that I should apply for the foundation degree course next year and that he will be more than happy to give me a reference. I tell him I'll think about it.

But with only a few months to go before the end of the course I realise that I will be faced with the prospect of signing on again every fortnight, and being under the persistent nagging of my mother to take on any old job.

In order to get a real sense of what each other looks like, Emma has sent me a return video. Along with her tape is a letter.

Hey you,

I hope you get a good laugh out of this tape because I look and sound like an airhead!
I don't act that way in person, I was just very nervous because this tape is the first time you see how I look. Because the tape I used to record it on is old my voice sounds different and after there is an old football game. And my face looks shiny but that's just because of the lighting. I think it's about an hour long. Through the whole thing, I just mumble 'cos I didn't know what to say. I hope you focus on the way I look and not on how I act, 'cos I was just nervous.

Emma

PS I love you.

I love the tape. I watch it repeatedly. I want to climb into the screen and hold her. I tell her she is cute and gorgeous.
For the next tape I send her, I record a nocturnal walk around my estate and talk nervously and shyly in to the camera for about ten minutes. I take the time to plan what I want to say so I don't just ramble on.

Emma received my tapes but couldn't watch them – I

hadn't taken into consideration the different formats of VHS in our countries. So, she takes them somewhere in her town where they can be converted from PAL to NTSC (I had no problem watching her tape though). I feel a bit ill thinking that some random people somewhere in Canada are looking at my tape as it converts.

My gran's illness has deteriorated to the point where she is now immobile in bed. Her stomach is bloated and huge with fluid. She has given me £100 from her savings; I am disappointed that it isn't enough to travel to Canada. Looking at her lying in her bed, her entire body covered by the quilt, I realise the poor woman has lost her vitality, the shine and light has gone from her eyes – she is alive yet dead in spirit. Defeated by the alien inside her. Like a piece of fruit left in the sun, her cancer has shrivelled her up, drained her of her essence. Nothing of her is recognisable – not a trace of her auburn hair, eyes deep, hollow in crater-sockets. Her voice tired, weak, yet she maintains:

'I'm going to be alright, you know.'

I can't decide if she is just afraid to tell me she is going to die, or if she genuinely believes she will survive. When she talks, I notice the cracked, coffee stained tooth in her mouth, an unchanging reminder of her pre-cancer self.

'What will you spend your money on?' she asks.

'I dunno,' I shrug, not wanting to tell her that I want to go to Canada… 'some CDs or something.'

My granddad laughs at this, as if I were supposed to keep the money for something I've failed to comprehend.

'You spend that money on what you like, pet,' my gran asserts.

As children born during World War II, both of them have lived their lives with incredible thrift. As a child, they would offer admonishment to me for spending my pocket money on junk; cheap plastic toys, comics, trading cards, stickers, etc. They believed I should save my money. In my teens, not much had changed, and I found myself questioned for spending all my cash on music.

Emma is not the only friend I have made online. I regularly chat to 'Soul Stealing Wench,' (or Bunny, as she is known in the real world).

Bunny lives in London and is seventeen years old. On a daily basis, she surprises me with how cultured, interesting and sharp her mind is. She writes poetry, stories, and scripts. We also like the same music (we met in Fear Factory chat).

We've quite quickly become good friends and even spoken on the phone a few times:

'I'm bitter,' she tells me in her southern accent, '*I am* bitter!'

'Over what?' I nervously laugh.

'Everything!'

When the phone rings, the internet cuts off, so no one can get through to anyone at home. This is annoying my step-dad because he runs a building maintenance company, and because someone is at the computer all the time he can't accept calls from his customers.

My mother is on the net reading about cancer again – the net cuts off, and then the phone rings. It is my granddad – my gran collapsed on her way to the hospital for chemotherapy – they are keeping her in. It doesn't look good.

My mother urgently rushes off to the hospital. Later, she sits in the armchair at home, a tissue held under her brown eyes, soaking up tears.

'She's full of morphine,' she sobs, '…eyes rolling in the back of her head. She's just not there. She looks like a skeleton with a swollen belly.'

I am numb. No sadness rises up in me. I want to go to the computer to talk to Emma. However, I don't, I just sit on the settee opposite my mother in a cold, internal silence and listen to her sniffle and softly weep.

When my parents are finally asleep, I log on and begin to chat to Emma – it is all the usual craic – how we want to fuck each other – will I be able to come to Canada sometime – maybe she could come to England after her graduation from college. The situation appears to me to be futile – it will never happen.

As we are talking the net cuts off – the phone rings. My mother has the receiver upstairs and I hear her shout, run around the room, and then bolt downstairs.

'Me mam has died,' she cries, entering the living room.

I put my arms around her. Tears drip from my eyes – hot, running rivulets down my face – salty as they touch my lips.

'You were the apple of your her eye, you know?' my

28

mother tells me.

I say nothing, but inside I realise I've lost the only person who had ever seen any good in me.

At midnight, we walk up to my granddad's house. My mother links arms between my brother and myself. The stars are out, shining diamond-eyes in a black lid.

My granddad sits quietly in his armchair smoking his pipe. The thick smell of tobacco filling the room with a blue/grey plume of smoke. The house is full of my aunts and uncles. No one speaks, but all sit around my granddad, each with a cup of milky tea perched on their knees.

There is nothing to say following death. A silence that takes over, and rests in the mind – it is a silence of finality – a reminder of the impermanent, ephemeral nature of life. It is the silence of knowing that we all have to face that ultimate, final blackness.

V

I abandoned the computer in the middle of talking to Emma, and with a weeping, lugubrious mother at home, I fear to go back online to talk to her, lest I look like I'm being insensitive.

At the same time, I feel worried that Emma may think I am ignoring her.

Some people from the crematorium came to my granddad's house to take some of my gran's make-up and nice clothes. My mother went to view the open casket – came home and wept in the armchair.

'It's just not her,' she cried, her face all puffy, 'it doesn't look like her – I wish I'd never gone to see her like that.'

At the funeral a few days later I'm emotionally cold and stiff, as if I've tied myself up in a knot so that any sadness or mourning could not be released from inside. So consuming is the numbness that during the entire funeral service I zone out into a long, protracted internal and external silence.

Afterwards – at The Jubilee – little ham sandwiches, chicken drumsticks, and pints of horrible lager – strained, forced conversations – I decide to abandon ship and go home, my younger brother coming with me.

I take the opportunity of the empty house to get back online to talk to Emma – she is relieved to learn that I am all right.

However, while talking to her, I notice something has changed in me.

A day later – Emma is explaining how she had to stop in the middle of her morning jog when the song *Merry Go Bye-Bye* by Mr Bungle came on the cassette tape that I had mailed to her – she nearly jumped out of her skin with fright upon hearing the second half of the song.

As she is typing, I'm also typing, telling her that we need to end this electronic relationship. I try my best to put it across without hurting her feelings – and to be honest about the reality that we will never meet – after reading my message, she doesn't type anything for a while.

Eventually she says she is hurt and upset, but that I am right in that we could never have a physical relationship.

In bed with a heavy heart – and suddenly I feel very sorry for myself, not a self-pity, but sorry that once an ally and a friend, of which I had so few, was cut loose from my life. As I lay awake, a river of tears pours from my eyes. The mourning that I held back from my gran's death has been lurking somewhere in the numbness inside me, waiting to break out – hours pass as I weep a strange flood – a simple leaking from the corner of my eyes. It trickles down onto the pillow that is growing in dampness. All night in the blackness until the yellow of dawn blends from the grey – I lay tortured, ashamed, broken, confused – my heart aching so much I think I may die.

Days following – the mourning, a cathartic washing out of my mind – I am changed, renewed. I realise that I have no pretence to keep up – it no longer matters to pretend to be a nice-boy to my gran – I can just *be,* and I make the decision to jump into an existential river and let it carry me to an unknown end.

I am spending a lot more time online talking to Bunny. I am still friendly with Emma – we still talk, but only in cool pleasantries.

My mother has informed me that we are giving up smoking at the start of April. I have no choice in the matter. She has taken measures to make up for the nicotine withdrawal by purchasing nicotine patches and lozenges. The day before we begin, all ashtrays and lighters go in the bin – any remaining cigarettes are to be torn-up and flushed down the toilet.

I am apprehensive as to how I will cope.

My relationship with Bunny grows. She is eighteen and from Barnet in North London. She is cultured in a way that Emma was not, and we have much in common. We love the same music and film – also, we both love to write, and share stories, poetry, and musings, back and forth over MSN messenger – each returning honest critique and analysis.

We start to play some writing games – she writes a line of a story, then, I write one – soon after we decide to write a surreal comedy script together.

The script centres around two hosts who tell each other nonsense stories as they try to resolve an argument – they fade out into sketches – one story concerns a very camp super hero and a missing pickle that mews like a cat. Another sketch concerns a lost man looking for his dog on the misty Yorkshire

32

moors when he encounters some nudist, time-travelling tourists – another sketch involves a half-man, half-goose who lives in a mobile bath tub with a goose...

Writing these stories with Bunny makes my day and I find myself increasingly endeared to her.

I love to discover writers by association. For instance through Burroughs I discovered Kerouac and Ginsberg and all the other beat writers – and their contemporaries. Through association of obscenity in beat literature, I discovered Henry Miller. Similarly, ideas filter though the works of these writers so that I have become interested in subjects that they mention. Via Luke Rhinehart, in a roundabout sort of way, I've become interested in philosophy, Zen – and through Kerouac and Ginsberg, Buddhism in general.
My interest in the black arts, the occult, and mysticism grows with each book I read – and each book is like a door to another writer. H.P. Lovecraft, Edgar Allen Poe, Aleister Crowley, Helena Blavatsky, G.I. Gurdjieff, Anton LaVey.

On my way home from the Oxfam bookshop I suddenly feel overcome with a horrible, consuming melancholy – just as the sun passed out of the clouds, when the light moved across my path and mopped up the shadow – I felt suddenly sick with a deep sadness. It was a nameless sadness, over nothing in particular – which made it even more unpleasant to bear.

To rectify my pang of sorrow, I buy a bottle of Vladivar vodka from Fawdon Wine Centre. At half past five in the afternoon, I'm drunk out of my skull and feeling sorry for myself. I lament over Emma – how terrible I could never taste her, touch her skin, and drink her in. I drunkenly scrawl out a letter in scruffy handwriting – the black ink of the biro coagulated on the nib – torn, rough paper from a lined notebook. I stuff the letter in an envelope, seal it, and promise to send it to her tomorrow.

I wake up on the floor to a cold darkness outside. I have a blanket over me, the bottle of vodka has disappeared, and in its place a pint of water – I assume this is the work of my mother.

My mouth is dry. My head is sick.

Bunny refuses to send me a picture of herself. I assume this is because she must be ugly. When we talk on the phone, I imagine her – build up a mental image of her, through her squeaky voice and through the things that she says.

Her high-pitched mouse voice, with its Cockney accent, swirls about in the earpiece of the phone. The way her words sound as they buzz around in my lug and the pressure of the plastic of the phone against my lobe tickle me with an odd yet pleasing electric sensation.

I get her to say an assortment of different words for my enjoyment and to her bemusement. I imagine the shape of her mouth.

Now the smoking cessation has begun – tension in the house. I left the front door open all night by mistake.

'Anyone could have just walked in,' my mother snaps, sounding irritable.

'It was a fucking mistake!' I scream at her, shocked that I could raise my voice so loud.

A while later:

'I'm sorry I shouted at you.'

No cigarettes and there is an atmosphere of silent hate looming, an elephant in every room.

All remaining cigarettes snapped up and soaked in water, lighters, and ashtrays, all in the bin.

A week past and my index finger already losing its yellow nicotine tint – I'm coughing up phlegm and my lungs begin to clear out. My skin itches and burns, the circulation improving.

I hate everyone.

My mother and I are on the patches. My step-dad has gone cold turkey. He and my mother are screaming at each other over nothing.

My step-dad's neurotic hatred for the internet is like a poisonous gas hanging around the computer in the living room – no one dare go near it while he is in the house for fear of suffering the remark:

'On that bloody internet again, load of shite man! Waste of bloody money.'

I take a walk to visit my granddad. He sits silently watching a war film on TV – I make us tea – long thin china cups with floral patterns – empty tasting, grey milky tea. He sits breathing loudly through his nose while smoking his pipe, not saying anything. The house feels like it is a great cold void without my gran there – her warmth colouring their home.

My granddad doesn't want to talk. He can be a cantankerous old git at times, and so I leave him be.

On my way home I have the sensation of release

from some mental prison that I did not know was enslaving me. Spring in the air – a little more warmth and colour splashed in the gardens on the street. The sun makes me feel different – a fleeting sensation I cannot name or know for long enough washes over me – somewhere between a deep sadness and an inner marvel at the vastness of nature and the universe – and a yearning for something unknowable.

My skin is burning and by the time I arrive home, I am raw with hives. I show my mother.

'You have urticaria again,' she comments, 'It's been a long time since that flared up. You'd best get some anti-histamines from the doctor.'

I agree and say I will make an appointment tomorrow. In the meantime, I slather calamine lotion all over my rubber skin and lie on my bed all creamy and itching.

I listen as my step-dad comes home from work and he and my mam have a row. I can't hear what they are saying through the walls and floor – just the muffled bass of raised, arguing voices.

The lack of nicotine is causing an inner family war. This whole place could crumble at any moment.

I have to escape.

VI

Bunny and I both print off the entire script of Monty Python's *The Life of Brian*, and over the phone re-enact the entire film. Between us, we distribute the characters evenly and attempt to mimic their voices while laughing hysterically at each other.
It takes forever to get through it and I feel exhausted yet happy by the end of it.
'We've got lumps of it round the back!'
  'Cheers for that mate,' she laughs at the end of the three hour phone call.
  With my face burning, ear aching from holding the phone, and jaw hurting from laughing, I'm giddy with the sensation of having a friend.
  I lie on my bed feeling strange, wondering if I want more from her.

In a long, roundabout way, I tell Bunny that I have fallen for her. I know this is stupid because I don't even know what she looks like. To my surprise, she tells me she feels the same. I ask her for a photograph of herself.
  I wait four days for the picture. Then on messenger, she sends it to me. It's poor quality, low light. All I can type is:
Nice skin.
And she does have nice skin; it is a deep olive-colour. She has green eyes set in a round face. Yet all I can think is that she is not as beautiful as Emma is.

Later. Drunk now – I tell Emma that I love her. I tell her that it is possible to love two people equally. I tell her that I want both her and Bunny.

I tell Bunny that I lied about her photograph. I tell her she is ugly. My fantasy shattered by the fact that she is dumpy and physically unattractive – I realise that I've been building up a complete illusion of her physical appearance.

I feel terrible yet justified. Over the internet feelings don't matter – none of this is real. I won't have to see these people in real life. So who gives a fuck?

Bunny calls me on the phone, crying and screaming at me:

'Do you know how difficult it was for me to take that picture and send it to someone? You've completely destroyed my trust!'

She stifles her tears and I say nothing in an uncomfortable silence.

'Aren't you going to fucking say anything?'

'I'm sorry.'

But, I'm not.

After lying awake all night, I decide to phone Bunny and apologise.

'It's just that the photo was blurry – it's dark and hard to see you properly – perhaps it would be best if we saw each other in person?'

She softens eventually.

'Alright, do you want to come down to London for a few days?'

I had never been so far away from home on my own. The thought of doing so made me giddy and sick at the same time. However, the horrible atmosphere at home was the push that I needed to fledge.

'Okay, where do you live exactly? What's the best way to get there? When shall I come? Will it be okay with your parents?'

'I live in Hendon in Barnet, so the best train station is probably... I'm not sure, I'm terrible with trains... King's Cross? I dunno. You can get the National Express to Golders Green, that's closer. You can come anytime you like, it will be fine with my parents.'

I didn't want to wait around thinking about it, because I knew if I picked a date to travel down that was too far into the future I would never go.

'How about next week? It's half term. I could come for the week.'

'A week?'

'Is that okay? I'm really sorry about what I said about the photo. I do love you, Bunny.'

'Yeah, a week is cool, and I love you too, but if you ever do anything like that again...'

Telling my mother that I am off to London to meet someone off the internet will not be easy. I inform her in fact, so that she can do nothing about it.

'You're nineteen years old; you can do whatever you like.'

Even though she appears to be giving the freedom she believes should come with adulthood, I can tell she is not pleased and does not want me to go.

A few days later, she says:

'I've been thinking about this London thing, I don't think it's a good idea. What if it's a trick and you get raped or something?'

Even though I have been taking a drug called Zirtek

39

(an anti-histamine) to control my hives, they at this moment, under the sweat and heat of a ferocious anger, burst from under my skin. They itch and burn all over my neck – a furious, manifestation of anger.

Through a dry mouth I say, 'Fuck off.'

'What? I'm your mother, you can't speak to me like that.'

'You never know what you are talking about,' I inform her before walking off.

After college on Friday, I head to the Gallowgate bus station to buy my tickets. They are in a long, slippery blue and red wallet. I leave on Monday. I am apprehensive yet excited. In my mind I begin to play through a host of scenarios and plan what I will do in London should any of them occur. My mother has been doing the same thing and has bought me a mobile phone and given me some emergency money lest I 'find myself trapped in a sex dungeon by some pervert.'

She is misinformed, and a deluded fool, but I love her.

I'm manic with a giddy nervousness about my adventure. I have it in mind that I may not come home. I can only assume that my step-dad has made comment to my mother about me going on this trip, and I assume those comments will be negative.

I am conscious that in part I am fleeing from underneath their feet more than travelling for love. When I lie awake at night, a burning core of hatred towards everything that surrounds me smoulders and chokes – I want to wash myself clean of the acrid

40

stink.

The night before, I pack my bag. I talk to Bunny on the phone – we are both very excited about my trip. I have to rise at five in the morning. All night, from blackness to the grey light, I am awake – even when I drift off; my mind won't shut down completely. I find myself checking the time every half an hour.

That morning feeling – the one that I stay awake all night for – that quiet of the world not yet going – the pleasure of emptiness and solitude – a sluggishness in my body, with sleepy thoughts not quite real.

With the sun coming up I board the Metro to town. I am jittery with nerves as I wait at the bus station to board the bus – the big sign on the front of it simply reads LONDON.

I have that empty feeling in my gut – a single slice of toast and coffee for breakfast – and the sensation of unrested bowels with undigested food.

On the bus, I take a window seat.

A little girl looks at me and says to her daddy, 'Why is that man all in black?'

'I don't know,' the father replies, 'maybe he's going to a funeral.'

The bus pulls off and I sink into my seat with a sense of high-adventure.

There is a feeling of terror in me past the point of no return – beyond Darlington feels like stepping over the edge of the world. Every view out of the window is a masterpiece as it splatters by green and blurred. When the bus slows, I observe more closely every little detail of my journey – fields, little villages, sheep, people in cars, farmhouses off in the distance, and the white fluff of clouds.

I try to entertain myself by reading, but a combination of tiredness and excitement prevents the words from making any impact – they are just unabsorbed meaningless scribbles on the page.

It takes six hours to get from Newcastle to London and as we close in late in the afternoon, I am sick with nervousness. I try to stand up in my seat but can't. I can't do anything. I'm trapped frozen, gripped with fear – I have hardly eaten at all for nearly a day. I begin to think I have made a crazy mistake.

At Golders Green, I get off the bus and look around for Bunny. I can't find her. I begin to wonder if she isn't going to show – and then it dawns on me that maybe this was all a ruse to pay me back for calling her ugly. I wait for half an hour in a sweaty panic. I begin to make my way over to the travel shop just to check out if I can buy a ticket to get home. However, just as I cross the road, she appears. The picture didn't lie, and the realisation that I am about to be trapped in London with someone I don't find physically attractive for a week grips me by the throat. I remind myself I've fallen in love with her personality – how she looks does not matter. Bunny has wiry black hair, purple lipstick, olive skin, green eyes, she is chubby, a ring through her lip, she talks with a slight lisp where her teeth are misaligned, her hands are fat and round with stumpy fingers.

Bunny has brought her mother with her.

'This is my mum, John,' Bunny introduces her.

I wonder if I've heard right.

John eyes me up. All sorts of mad shit racing through my brain. Is she a *he*?

John looks like a man; no make-up, a wonky

Columbo eye, dressed in a masculine way. She is short and rounded like Bunny.

We walk down the street for ten minutes, John asking me about myself. I can't relax or answer her questions properly without mumbling and stumbling over my words. London is warmer than I expected and I feel my skin burning with hives.

'This is it,' John says stopping in front of a huge mansion.

Open-mouthed, I try to look up over an ivy-covered wall at the top of this beautiful house.

'No,' John laughs, 'I mean the car.'

I feel embarrassed as I get in the pokey little car.

A short drive – a street lined with trees – in the middle of the street is their house. First impressions, it smells of cat piss. Two Siamese cats look at me with terrified eyes then dart away to safety.

'That's Kiki and Marge, Bunny tells me, 'don't worry, they hate everyone.'

I walk through to the dining room – every wall filled with shelves and books – I stand open-eyed.

'We've had to put cellophane over the bottom row of books,' John explains, 'those bloody cats have being weeing on them, little buggers.'

I laugh nervously.

'Would you like a sandwich or a cup of tea?' she asks.

I politely decline.

A strange mechanical noise enters my ears. I turn around to see a man on a stair lift struggling to get out of it and into a wheel chair. Bunny had already told me her dad suffered from MS.

'Hello,' he offers a hand as he wheels himself into

the room, 'I'm Ray.'

I nod and smile. It is immediate to me that Ray is the embodiment of pain – I see it etched on his face. The frustration of living is in all of his movements – a living corporeal hell.

'Bun tells me you're a musician.'

'Yes.'

'What sort of music do you like? Do you listen to all of that horrible stuff she does?'

'Yes,' I'm nervous, but manage to say, 'I also like other stuff. Jazz, classical.'

His face lights up. 'Oh, wonderful. Who do you like?'

'Erik Satie, Debussy.' I mumble.

A smile breaks out on his face.

'Come on,' Bunny pulls at my arm, 'let's go upstairs, you'll be here all night if he gets on about classical music.'

She leads me up two flights of stairs to her room in the attic. All the rooms in the house filled with books.

'Mum can't stop buying books on Byzantine pottery,' Bunny notices me looking at the books along the way, 'Dad is pretty bad too – always buying books on religion and music.'

I recall Bunny told me her mum worked at the British Museum – a specialist in pottery.

Bunny's room is a pigsty – stuff everywhere – drawings and writing on the wall – it is a sea of assorted crap.

'Uh, sorry about the mess,' she sits on the bed that has no frame and is just a mattress on the floor.

I dump my bag and clear a circle in the junk. I sit down cross-legged. A hunger nips at my gut. I wish I had said yes to that sandwich.

'You don't have to sit on the floor,' Bunny invites me to the bed.

I move over to her.

'I'm glad you are finally here,' she smiles.

'Me too… Should we kiss?' I blurt out.

She leans over and we embrace. A weary, sleepy sensation, washes over me. I feel horny and when the kiss parts Bunny notices the tent in my pants.

'Hmmm…' she muses looking at it.

She pokes at it through my jeans with a fat finger, dirty nail.

'I think you should get this out,'

I slip my cock out – it flips into life, pink, purple, and tumescent.

She takes it in her hand and jerks it, I lie back while she puts it in her mouth.

After sucking a moment Bunny asks, 'Is this alright?'

I murmur in agreement.

She works on it – until I go off in her mouth. She violently spits the spunk onto the carpet.

With disgust, she says, 'Tell me next time before you come. I'm not a fan of swallowing greasy spunk.'

I get her out of her pants and slobber all over her cunt. It smells, but I like it. I have my eyes closed, but when I open them, I notice a red strand of Xmas tinsel lodged in the folds of her labia.

It is May.

VII

My balls hurt, are blue and veiny and I can't piss because Bunny has been yanking and sucking my cock since I arrived. My bell-end is burning.

I can't have a shit because the toilet is in the middle of the house, so that any attempt to dump will mean my straining and grunting will be audible, and I'm embarrassed to let it out of my bum. I'm backed-up, constipated as a result and my whole groin and anus box is uncomfortable. Making things worse is that three days into being in London I haven't left Bunny's house. I had assumed that we might have got out; I want to see some touristy things – this is my first time in London.

Even worse, I haven't eaten since I arrived. For some reason she will not feed me. I've mentioned politely that I'm hungry.

'We'll eat soon,' she has said.

I'm losing weight. All I can do is sleep, so I sleep until mid-afternoon. Then treated to an afternoon of films and TV – this I enjoy, despite my genital and hunger pains. Vincent Price movies, *The Avengers*, Roger Corman's classic horror films.

However, the distraction doesn't last long – I've never been so hungry – and I keep mentioning that I want to get outside for a bit – even just for a walk – so that I might find a shop and buy some food.

My mother called and asked if I was having a good time, did I like Bunny, was I okay?

As Bunny never seems to leave the room for more than a moment (not even to wash or have a shit herself) I cannot speak openly to my mother and tell her how much I hate this and want to come home.

All I can do is try and ride it out until it is time to leave. I am getting my dick sucked, which is compensation enough.

Four days, no food, and no exit from the house. I sleep all day, dreaming of meals I've eaten, of meals I want to eat – all swirling round, my belly concaving in on its self. I dream while waiting to go home – it seems so far off in the future.

I assume that Bunny is eating while I have one of my many naps.

While sitting watching another episode of *The Avengers* with Diana Rigg in a sexy cat suit I over hear John talking to Bunny:

'What have you been feeding that boy?'

Then the door closes and all I can hear is a muted aggressive conversation.

Next day at eleven in the morning we go outside – a crisp, warm, quiet street – I'm quiet and don't want to talk to Bunny. Dash into a newsagents and buy a *Mars bar*.

The chocolate and caramel are warm and I choke it down without chewing, gulping it like a duck. I feel weak.

'Mum has given me money to take us out for pizza,' Bunny tells me.

'When?' I blurt out. 'Now?'

'In a little bit.'

We walk through Hendon Park.

'I'm sorry for not feeding you.'

She puts her arms round my waist, fat little fingers, dirty nails under my top, pressing the skin.

47

We have pizza at a little Italian. I wolf it down. The taste and sensation of food in my mouth is incredible. I've never been starving like this before – I feel changed from it – I realise I've been taking my meals for granted.

Looking at my face in the mirror later on that evening – I'm gaunt and tired.

John has cooked dinner and that evening we all eat together. I say nothing. I just want to leave and never return.

All week Bunny has been running around after her dad – something she never told me until I arrived here is that she dropped out of school to be his full-time carer. She doesn't have a GCSE to her name, and yet, is one of the most intelligent people I have ever met.

Looking after her dad is her job. Her mother pays her for it. I realise this is why we haven't been anywhere all week – Bunny has been working and I didn't even notice.

My last day – I finally get to see some of London. We take the tube to Camden and have a wander around the Lock. I fall in love with the place instantly. We're both wearing hoodies; mine *Pantera*, hers *Marilyn Manson*. Bunny holds my hand, her fingers slip between mine. I suddenly feel self-conscious about it and pull her hand out from the tangle of fingers, cover it up by pretending to want to pick up a T-shirt from a stall.

Later that night, Bunny goes weird. I'm sitting on her bed while she writes something on her bedroom wall. Suddenly she tells me:

'I tried to stab my mum.'

She seems lost, as if trapped inside a dream – she's humming while writing – eyes locked to the wall.

I wonder if she has perceived that I'm not happy here.

'Shall we go for a walk?' I ask.

'No. But you can,' her words are dry.

I take a stroll to the shop around the corner. Even though I've eaten the last two days, I'm still as hungry as I was before I'd eaten. I buy some peanuts, chocolate, and a milkshake and devour them on the wall outside the shop. Then I go back in, buy four cans of lager and almost buy some cigarettes but refrain in the end.

Bunny doesn't drink because she is straight edge. So, I sit quietly on her bed in silence and drink my booze. She disappears for over two hours. When she returns it is ten at night. She tells me she had been for a drive with her mother. No dinner that night – I'm pleased I ate all that junk from the corner shop.

As we have done all week, we share her tiny bed. Because she is fat I've had to perch myself on the edge of it to sleep. The thought that I will be home tomorrow, and in my own bed, with a full belly is comforting.

The fact that we've gone cold with each other will make breaking up easier – but I decide not to do it until I get home – I haven't the strength to do it here.

My bus leaves early – nine o'clock, meaning I will be back in Newcastle for three in the afternoon. Bunny is different now, she is crying because she doesn't want me to go – salty, teary kisses and dramatic hugs. I say goodbye to her parents. Bunny takes me to

Golders Green on the tube – tears as I leave. I won't ever see her again and as I get on the bus, a feeling of relief. The bus seat so soft, a comfort, and as it pulls away, a relaxing feeling washes over me.

My thoughts turn over the last week – I'm changed, hunger has changed me – and I'm still hungry, aching with it. Where before the desire to desperately eat was never a concern, a hole has now opened up in my body and mind, an insatiable, gnawing ache that won't go away no matter how much I stuff my face.

On the journey home, I begin to plan my break-up with Bunny. Even though I've learned a lesson about meeting people off the internet, I decide to get involved only with women who live in the North East.

At home, I open the front door – the house is immaculate – it is the tidiest, neatest home I've ever been in, and it's mine.

My mother greets me. 'By lad, you've lost weight! What happened, didn't she feed you?'

I laugh and don't give an answer.

'Did you have a nice time then?'

I force out a meaningless 'Yes.'

'Steak and chips for tea,' she informs, then walks into the kitchen. 'Cuppa?'

I dump my bag in my room, which also is incredibly neat and tidy. I guess that having lived in Bunny's messy room for a week has made me see how lovely my own house always is, something I could never see before.

After tea, I go to the computer to check my emails.

'You can't go on the net mind,' my mother says.

'Why not?'

'Because I've had it taken out.'

A furious anger comes over me.

'Why?' I demand trying to control my rage.

'Because Jack wouldn't stop moaning about it – and it's him that is paying it. Since you left all he has done is complain about it so I told him to get rid of it.'

Going from not having the internet to having it was like discovering a magical third limb that I had never used, now that I had it, I couldn't go back. It was a gateway for me – the door to information, to discovery and to the ability to converse and talk to people in a way I couldn't in real life.

Not having it ruins my plans to find a new girlfriend closer to home.

It occurs to me that I have one term left at college and no college work to do, so essentially I can go in and spend the day in open access on a computer.

My plan still has hope.

VIII

Balls is trying to persuade me to stay on at college.

'You should do the HND,' he insists, 'I'll write you a reference; you'll get on it no bother.'

It seems like a hassle to me. The thought of student loans and whatnot. However, doing the Music Tech course has made me think it might be time to join a band again and that maybe I could stomach other people.

I know that Bunny will overreact to me breaking up with her – it puts fear into me thinking about it. Nevertheless, I do it anyway – she cries and calls me names. However, that's that – I say:

'We live too far apart, it can't work.'

The next day I log onto a computer at college – my hopes of meeting someone else destroyed when I discover that the college computers won't allow me into any chat rooms.

Like a crawling, snivelling dog, I phone Bunny and patch things up.

'You won't get another chance,' she tells me.

'Why don't you come up to Newcastle in a few weeks?' The words tumble out of my mouth with a sense of terror masked over by the thought of having my cock tugged and sucked.

She agrees and I succumb to this relationship.

Through the beat writers and the work of Luke Rhinehart, my interest in Buddhism (Zen, in particular) has led me to purchase a couple of books on the subject.

Buddhism: Plain and Simple and *Zen Flesh, Zen Bones* to be exact.

Reading Jack Kerouac's *The Dharma Bums* has made Buddhism appear quite romantic and attractive to me. Zen seems crazy, mad, and exciting. I learn a word: Satori. It means to awaken or enlighten. It is that moment when your perception changes and you can't go back to how you viewed things before.

From Luke Rhinehart's books, I have discovered the ability to question my sense of self, and although I didn't realise it from reading his novels, his book *The Book of the Die* links all his work into Zen.

I read all of *Buddhism: Plain and Simple* by Zen master Steve Hagen in one go. I am buzzing with excitement by the end of it. I can almost feel my sense of what is concrete in the world, my perceptions, ideas and illusions pulled apart – I feel crazy with it – I am eager now to learn how to meditate.

In the Yellow Pages, I find the phone number for the Newcastle Buddhist Centre. I phone and ask about meditation. The woman on the phone tells me that there is a beginner's course, an introduction to meditation and Buddhism, starting in three weeks. It is eighty pounds – my heart sinks as I know I can't afford it – and she must sense this as she tells me that if I'm not working or on a low income I can pay half – or even whatever I can afford to give.

I tell Bunny over the phone and she is excited for me. However, I decide to wait until the day I actually begin the course to tell my mother.

Bunny arrives for the weekend. I meet her at

Gallowgate bus stop – she's dressed all in black, purple lipstick, a spikey dog collar, hair tied up. She seems nervous and apprehensive. I quickly take her bag and carry it for her; this way I don't have to hold her hand, should anyone I know see me with her. In Monument Metro station, someone makes a woof noise at her.

All the way to Fawdon, she won't stop talking. I don't want to talk in public, and she keeps asking me if anything is wrong.

'I just can't hear you above the noise of the train,' I tell her. This is a half-truth.

I introduce her to my mother. Later, my mother's reaction:

'I'm surprised; I thought she would have been stunning to look at.'

Bunny is staying for a long weekend. After she sucks my cock on my bed, and I reciprocate by licking her cunt, we spend the night watching Vincent Price movies – *Masque of the Red Death* and *The Abominable Dr Phibes*.

Love means never having to say you're ugly.

In the morning – summer encroaching – a silent breeze under the curtains – light spilling through fabric cracks – the sound of frogs, the water of the pond – birds busying themselves with tweets and chirps – I lay awake looking at Bunny's back. She has a hunch – a lump at the base of her neck. Her hair is wiry, like pubes, her back is wide, a mass of white flesh – indistinct corpulence, wobbly, soft – amorphous sack of gristle wrapped in skin.

54

A day before she has to return home. I can't wait for her to leave. We enjoy many of the same things – music, film, art. We have a laugh, she is my friend, I love her – but I cannot get over the sensation of our relationship being more platonic than romantic. We share a creative heart. We mix ourselves in writing. This is how we work – artistic strength binds us. The continual encouragement we give each other, the way we dish it out, in honest, critical support of each other's creativity – this is our love. Nevertheless, it only stands firm for so long, and after three days, I hate her.

The tension reaches a high point the night before she leaves. She wants to go for a walk, alone. I don't understand why.

'Can I go sit in the garden on my own for a while?'

'Whatever.'

I creep down and hide behind the wall. She is on the phone to her mother – I can't get the gist of the conversation – it ends – then Bunny spends five minutes farting while stroking our two border collies.

At the bus station, I feign sadness at her departure.

'I'll come and visit you next,' the words tumble out of my mouth, automatic and hot with regret.

'I'm taking a course in meditation and Buddhism,' I tell my mother.

'What? What made you interested in *that*?'

I expected just that response. She said it as if she believed it would be dangerous. With a fear of unknown religions due to recent terror attacks in the world, I get the feeling that my mother thinks I'm joining a group of religious maniacs.

'It's not like a cult, is it?'

'No. It's not.' I don't want to say anything else to her so I leave the room, once again bewildered at her ignorance.

I'm ill with nervousness as one by one the people attending the class on meditation and Buddhism take turns to say a little something about themselves. My ears close up – nothing of what they are saying is passing through my lug-holes – I'm stewing under a terrified blanket, concerned with what bumbling noises will pass my lips when it's my turn to speak.

'My name is… I got interested in Buddhism… Jack Kerouac… Beat writers… Zen.'

My words are a verbal jigsaw. My face turns red.

The course takes place over a period of six weeks, each part a combination of meditation and Buddhism. Two men lead the course: Vajrakuppa and Maitrepaksa.

To my surprise, everyone at the Newcastle Buddhist Centre is pretty much white and middle class. I had expectations of Orientals.

Every week I learn something new – although there is no direct route of knowledge – and I am piecing Buddhism together in my own way.

I find myself confronted with a genuine, open hearted and warm environment. When Vajrakuppa speaks to me, it is without judgement. In coming to these classes I feel myself starting to open up verbally – to start to talk to intelligent, broad minded people gives me a deep boost in confidence.

My final day at college – Balls says:

56

'It's been a pleasure teaching you and having you here. Good luck, you should join a band you know, you've got good musical intuition, but it'll never be at its best unless you play with other people.'

I think seriously about this. On an unoccupied computer, I make a 'band members wanted' poster – it has little tags with my phone number at the bottom to cut into slips. Influences: Pantera, Sepultura, Deicide, Cannibal Corpse, Six Feet Under, Machine Head, Fear Factory…

While attending my Buddhism classes I have come to the realisation that one of my favourite authors, Luke Rhinehart, AKA George Cockcroft, is in fact a teacher of Zen. From his books such as *The Dice Man,* it is not immediately possible to recognise Buddhism in any shape. What I understood he was attempting to achieve was to shock his readers out of their everyday assumptions and monotonous roles as they define themselves, and to arrive at the conclusion that everything, especially the ego and personality, are in constant flux.

As I am empirically beginning to learn and understand for myself, nothing in the universe exists in isolation; everything is ephemeral, constantly moving, changing and fluid without permanence.

I've decided to write to Luke/George via email to tell him of my conclusions, as from tomorrow I will have no access to the internet.

When I arrive home, a letter from the job centre is waiting for me.

'I have to sign on again,' I tell my mother.

'Time to start looking for a job again,' she replies.

A terrible sense of doom rises up in me.

'It's a shame we don't have the net,' I mention, 'it would have been good to use it to look for work.' This is a half-truth, and in that half-truth, I realise that I will have no way to access my emails to discover if Luke/George has replied.

A sigh from my mother, then, 'It caused too much grief having it in the house. You can use the internet at the library, you know.'

In Fawdon library – a pale, long-faced woman, straw hair, dead eyes. The library is like a cupboard, every available bit of wall space lined with books – a small rack of CDs – the tiny desk behind which she sits – two computers crammed in a corner.

'Hello. Can I use the computer?' I ask awkwardly.

'You have to book a slot,' she tells me, then opens her diary. 'Computer A is free on Friday morning at ten-thirty if you want it.'

I wait three days and I'm eager to check to see if Luke/George has replied to my email.

All the while, I'm noticing a change in my thinking; questioning my self – the nature of truth – of the meaning of words – on my sense of existence.

I meditate twice a day – forty-five minutes first thing in the morning and last thing at night – I have built a shrine – with candles, incense – fresh flowers represent impermanence – in the centre, statue of the Buddha – hand touching the ground in earthly recognition – hand across lap, open lotus – legs folded, back straight. To the left below the Buddha, statue of Manjushri – sword above his head, cutting through ignorance – to the right below – Amoghasiddhi – he whose accomplishment is not in vain.

I have given up anything that might cloud my mind – alcohol, caffeine, meat – not because Buddhism says so, but because I wish to challenge myself – to see with my own eyes – to question via empirical understanding.

When I think of it – my hunger in London was a blessing – it showed me something of myself – and through that experience, I changed what *experience* overall means to me.

On Friday, I log on to the computer in the library. A reply from Luke/George:

Thank you. Your letter is one of the most pleasing I have ever received. My ego is now so swollen I am barely able to walk through doorways. What is so pleasing is that you have experienced the connection between spiritual search and my work, work that superficially often seems to be anti-spiritual. One reason I wrote THE BOOK OF THE DIE was to try to draw readers' attention to the way THE DICE MAN was an effort to deliver a series of blows that would awaken the reader to his or her true nature.

MATARI is, paradoxically, at one and the same time both the most overtly Buddhist of my books and yet perhaps the least Buddhist in its overall vision. Oboko, the protagonist of that book, is, despite his spiritual quest, the most human of humans, although a very good human by human standards. I hope you're able to find a copy. If not I'd be happy to send you one.

So, again, thanks, and keep that door open.

Best wishes,

Luke and George

.

IX

Visiting Mrs Skeleton at the job centre. I feel a wave of uncomfortableness pass through my body – she smiles:

'Welcome back, did you enjoy your course?'

'Yes, I learned a lot.'

'Well let's hope those skills you've acquired can help you find employment. Now then,' she turns the computer screen so I can see the list of jobs on it, 'we'll type in music, and see what comes up.'

Nothing comes up. She thinks for a moment then says, 'have you put your CV into HMV and Virgin?'

'I did it ages ago, along with all the little record shops, instrument shops and just about everywhere in town that had anything at all to do with music.'

'Right, I'll just try something else,' she types, and the word musician appears in the search box.

'Military musician, in the RAF. I don't suppose you'd be interested in that though, would you?'

I have a sudden romantic vision of myself travelling the world, learning to play the fucking tuba or something and being away from everyone. It isn't just a job; it is a potential permanent escape.

'I could be interested in that,' I tell her.

'Oh. Right. Well it says… to visit the recruitment office, which is on… Collingwood Street. Do you know where it is?'

'I'll find it.'

On my way home from the job centre I drop into JG Windows and put up my band poster on the board at the bottom of the stairs. I also look to see if there are any posters advertising for a bass player. In amongst the flyers I find one that has only a couple of tags left on it, so I take one. Influences: Skunk Anansie, Pantera, Metallica, Extreme, Jeff Buckley.

At home:

'I'm thinking of joining the RAF,' I tell my mother.

She is overjoyed, but as her excitement grows, mine diminishes, and the romantic vision I have melts into a grey blob that consists of drills, some prick shouting at me at, and not being able to play the fucking tuba at all.

Fuck the tuba. However, it's too late now; my mother has the Yellow Pages open and is already on the phone making me an appointment to see a recruitment officer.

I feel sick as she takes control of my life.

'He's got no confidence,' I can hear her trumpeting down the phone to whoever is on the other end.

I find myself unable to undo what I've done, and now I'm going to die in Afghanistan while wearing a gay grey tunic in a bloody pool next to my fucking tuba.

Two days later and I'm in the recruitment office.

A seasoned man in his thirties is asking me questions:

'Do you have any GCSEs?'

'Yes.'

'That's good, well you can probably enter as an officer.'

Really? I think, are people in the armed forces all thick?

'Now you want to join as a musician? Can you proficiently play a brass instrument?'

'No.'

62

'What can you play?'

'The bass guitar?'

'Well, unless you can already play something that is a requirement of military musicianship you can't take that route, the music side is actually just a small part of it.'

'I need to think about it.' I blurt out.

He gives me some leaflets to take away.

Later:

'I can't join,' I tell my mother, 'because I can't play any of the required instruments.'

'Is there nothing else you want to do in the RAF?'

'No.'

'You need a job,' she moans 'you need to do something with your life.'

I say nothing and go upstairs.

Vajrakuppa has a mop of black curly hair and the mannerisms of a seventies sci-fi robot. He's almost automated, but with a smile and a laugh that sounds programmed, but has warmth. He said he once met Allen Ginsberg.

'Ginsberg asked me for my opinion about a poem,' he told me. 'The greatest poet of the twentieth century asked *me* for his opinion.'

When I meditate, be it the mindfulness of breathing or the metta bhavana, I find my legs lose connection with my body and take on a mangled spaghetti sensation – and through regular meditation I find myself constantly changing, albeit subtly. My posture is better, my back straighter – I talk with a little more confidence – I feel inspired by the life story of the Buddha and his knowledge and wisdom gained through experience.

All true wisdom, it appears to me, can only be known through the empirical understanding of events that take place in both my inner and outer worlds.

To monitor this change in myself, I decide to keep a journal of my Buddhist experience.

To London and back – like a loop – returning home then waiting a fortnight to return – Mobius strip. I travel to see Bunny once a month, and she comes to visit me on alternate months. I value my relationship with her – how she feeds and nurses my creativity – but I am aware at the same time of the convenience of long-distance love; how I only spend two days with her at a time – I've never dared a week of her company again – and the rest of my time is free for me. There is a romance in our relationship that I enjoy – it is the romance of separation – the romance of travel and the journey, the unknown – our love is a myth because we see so little of each other. Built upon that myth is an unreality – a dream I have of what she is like – a false version of her that I force into existence through our separation.

This false version of her is not on purpose, it is a natural phenomenon. It is something that has manifested without any conscious involvement from myself – because our time together is so brief, and so all problems vanish. The difficulties and underlying annoyance I feel towards her – like cracks painted over – so little time for love, the issues are put aside – but I feel them like a small fire – the heat just enough to singe my mind.

We never have penetrative sex – we suck, lick, and

explore in every other way. Bunny is still a virgin –
and prior to her, I've only had one terrible experience.
I decide to approach the subject delicately when the
time is right.

Three months and no one called me about my
musicians wanted ad – so I go back to Windows to
remove it. In my wallet, the stub from the bass player
wanted poster – but I haven't called yet – the ad is
still up on the grey board and acts like a prompt for
me to pick up the phone.

 Once I'm home, I take the phone from the living
room upstairs – I dial, a girl answers.

 A flutter of nerves in the pit of my belly.

 'I'm phoning about the poster in Windows, for a
bass player.'

 A moment of silence, then:

 'Ah aye, if you're interested I can drop you off a CD
to see what you think.'

 I tell her where I live.

 Then a machine gun fire of questions:

 'How long you been playing? You got your own
gear? What days can you rehearse? What sort of shit
are you into?'

 I answer. Then she says:

 'My name is Ellie, I'm the singer, by the way.'

 A day later, I meet her by the crossing at Fawdon
Metro station – she jumps out of the car – blonde,
curvaceous, round face, button nose.

 'Hiya, here's the CD,' she says.

 I look at the cover. The name of the band is *Parallel
Charge*.

 'Have a listen, and if it's your cup of tea and you

wanna come for a jam let me know. We usually rehearse on a Tuesday night. We have a lock-up under Byker Bridge.'

'Alright, cheers.'

'I like your hair,' she says looking at my lawn of black spikes.

'Cheers,' I smile. She seems canny.

I take the disc home and chuck it on. It reminds me of Skunk Anansie – sloppy, loose sounding, chunky drums, guitars washed with phase. The three tracks are cool to listen to and I like the structures of them.

I plug in my bass and start to play along.

After a day, I call Ellie and tell her I'm interested in trying out. She tells me a date and time to turn up at the lock up, giving me a week or so to nail the songs completely.

I do my best with the songs as I'm due to journey south over the weekend. I decide to take the CD with me to listen to on the coach.

'I'm not ready for sex yet,' Bunny says.

'It's fine, there is no pressure.'

'It's not that I don't want to, it's just that I couldn't relax for my first time with my parents in the house.'

'I understand.'

'But you know, in a couple of months Dad is going into respite for two weeks, and Mum is going to visit her sister. I thought that maybe you could come to stay with me, like a little holiday. Mum said she'd feel more comfortable if you were here while they were away.'

'Of course,' I say.

She kisses me, unzips my fly, pulls out my now

tumescent cock through the hole, and slips in into the pink of her mouth.

I've seen lots of London now, and I've never starved. The British Museum, The V & A Museum, Soho, Kew Gardens with its wild peacocks, wasps, and continual run of planes overhead, Brent Cross, The Imperial War Museum, all of Camden.

On the bus journeying home – a bolt of sadness through me, itchy skin and sore eyes – I love her – a fleeting sensation – like a whisper in a dream – that panic of trying to hold onto a thought that was just inside your head before you woke. I've been on this route home so many times – winding slow through Golders Green, Jewish shops along the streets, clouds low, white and puffed three dimensional in the sky – blue and arched, scratched with white.

Past the introduction course, I can attend the main Buddhist sangha night. My first evening.

I enjoy the ritual of meditation.

> *Namo buddhaya*
> *Namo dharmaya*
> *Namo sanghaya*
> *Namo nama*
> *om*
> *ah*
> *hum*

Reverence to the Buddha, dharma (teaching), sangha (community).

Swirl of breath, breathing changes – filtering through nose, throat, lungs.

To stay in the gap between meditations; a sky-like mind.

X

I turn up for the rehearsal and meet the rest of the band. Jürgen, the sloppy drummer with his mop of black hair and sad-dog face, and high cheek-boned-male-model-looking guitarist, Dan.

We go through the four songs that are on the CD. No one says anything positive or negative, but I feel as if I've played the songs proficiently.

Ellie says, 'We have a gig in two weeks at the Tap and Spile. Do you reckon you'd be able to do it? It'll just be a short set, just the four tracks on the CD.'

'Yeah, of course,' I tell her.

I decide to type out the four noble truths as stated by the Buddha and put them on my wall.

Duhkha
The truth of suffering. Birth, sickness, old age, death. Pain, grief, sorrow, lamentation, despair. Association with the unpleasant. Disassociation with the pleasant.

Samudaya
The truth of the arising of suffering. Thirst and craving, re-birth. Continual grasping for fresh pleasure.

Nirodha
The truth of the cessation of suffering. The end of craving, withdrawal, rejection, liberation, non-attachment.

Magga

The truth of the eightfold path. View, resolve, speech, action, livelihood, effort, mindfulness, meditation.

I look at this all the time now, and reflect on my behaviour, thoughts, and actions. As I change, as my view of myself is shattered, the world and other people evolve. Not through what I believe the Buddhist view should be, but through my own eyes – through eyes unclouded – through watching my mind, then I slowly begin a metamorphosis – a transformation so subtle, observing myself, almost in a mind separated from the one that reacts to external stimuli.

The separated mind – thoughts like clouds, so empty and frivolous across a blue of relentless consciousness. The eyes look but never see, and so the mind thinks without conscious effort. Like a monkey swinging from branch to branch, the inevitable next thought is there, automatic, waiting.

The gig, downstairs in the old rickety Tap and Spile. My mother and step-dad turn up. I'm nervous, but not as nervous as Dan who is sitting slapping his knee and jiggling his leg up and down non-stop.

I haven't had so much as a sip of alcohol for months now and I don't miss it. Having a clearer mind means more to me, and I was under the impression that the fact that *I* no longer drank, wouldn't mean anything to anyone else. After all, what business was it of theirs? However, Jack, my step-dad, had decided to make it *his* business. Not in a direct way – but through a continual string of facetious remarks – as if to suggest there was something wrong with me because I wasn't drinking booze.

'Having a pint of water are you?' he sneers.

In the past, I would have internally curled up into a ball, and said nothing, then wilted like a flower, like burning plastic shrunk into nothing. Now, I watch the anger rise in me, it sits somewhere between my chest and my head, a hot sensation – prickles the skin – like my urticaria – anger is physical. I watch it move around inside me, and it eventually dissipates, but I wonder if it actually vanishes altogether. My anger leaves a dirty taste in my mouth.

I have to explain my non-drinking to the rest of the band who also seem put off by it. I don't want to say 'I'm a Buddhist,' because that isn't exactly true. I'm an explorer, and I'm testing myself, testing my inner experience against my outer experience. I doubt anyone understands, and so I play down everything.

I don't want anyone to think I've stopped drinking *because* of Buddhism. This is my choice – and how funny that the choice not to intoxicate and poison oneself is considered unnatural.

As with everything that happens inside me now, my emotions and thoughts, both ugly and beautiful, are clear before me – and with them a contempt and anger for these low-thinking idiots swirls around inside my head. It is a sensation, like anger, that is difficult and awful to acknowledge with honesty – and so into the mix comes a guilt that I hate, and a hate that I have to battle with.

On stage, we get through the songs – although my bass guitar strap fails me and I have to play the last song kneeling down like a fool – there are lots of compliments about how good we sound and look.

I expect to receive an invitation to join the band permanently – a week goes by and I hear nothing. I wonder what the deal is.

My two-week holiday in London with Bunny is a sharp contrast to my first visit. That first adventure now almost a year ago still haunts me with a pang of hunger. But the contrast is in the gluttony I'm now indulging in. Bunny's mother has left her credit card for Bunny to use as she wants, and Bunny is doing just that. An online shopping order from Waitrose – more than enough food for two people for two weeks, and all the best stuff – cakes, chocolate, expensive cheeses, luxurious fruit – I feel heavy in the gut and rounder in the cheeks.

There is a quiet here – the smell of nag champa, the warmth and light through the sky light in the roof – a stillness – long endless days that drag with a slow pleasure.

'Should we have sex?' I ask.

'I think so, I'm ready.'

On her mattress, she's gone cold, laying there like a cadaver, waiting to be unzipped, cunt frozen. I can't get my dick into her.

'It hurts. It nips,' she cries.

I'm wilting. 'It doesn't fit!'

I'm laughing – it's a laughter I can't control – I force my meat into her dry hole – she yelps and is now sobbing. I'm giggling – then my laugh, uncontrollably, melts into tears.

'Why the fuck are *you* crying?'

'I don't know.'

'Excuse me a minute.'

She gets up, pulls up her knickers under her black gothic dress and storms off – that horrible little madam walk that I can't stand. I follow her, she's in the kitchen – a hand full of dinner plates, and she goes into the back garden. There is a covering of green everywhere – huge trees where grey squirrels live not frightened by humans.

She stands there and smashes the plates one by one. White shards everywhere. I watch and a feeling arises, it sticks in my throat, I swallow it, but it's there in my fat gut.

We can never be lovers.

I meditate in the morning – in a circle surrounded by her mess in her room. Blue paint peeling off the walls – I ask her to join me, she says:

'It doesn't do anything for me!'

I wonder how she knows that if she's never tried it. Lately, Bunny has been putting up a religious wall against me, as if my interest in Buddhism is offensive to her. She has suddenly become very Christian; going to church on a Sunday, reading books about it – doing things she never cared about before and finding little ways to pump up her Christ over what I'm doing.

This holiday – I'm a non-reaction – all thoughts pass cloud-like.

On the coach on the way home, I'm reading *The Tibetan Book of Living and Dying*.

I write down this quote:

"Isn't it absurd, then, that we all long for happiness, yet, nearly all our actions and feelings lead us directly away from that

happiness.'

At rehearsal, Ellie says:
  'We've got these gigs coming up, if you're up for it.'
  'Of course.'

The Chester Moor. All goes well, sounding great. A new song – everyone is pleased. I get on with everyone in this band. Yet I don't drink – and I can feel the antipathy towards me because of it.
  Jürgen spends half an hour drawing an elaborate penis over the top of the queen's nose on a fiver. I sit and watch in silence.

It is difficult to explain to people, especially my mother, that I'm not simply swallowing ideals – I'm testing theory against experience. She has made the effort to embrace my investigation into vegetarianism, however drunk off her face she decides to pour hot, meaty gravy all over my dinner on Sunday. I look at her and she blurts out:
  'I thought you might have just fancied some meat gravy.'
  When anger or any other emotion arises, I have the opportunity to view it, and choose my reaction or non-reaction, instead of instantly grabbing onto that emotion and expressing it. This is the result of meditation. It is also why I find the people at the Buddhist Centre inexpressive and passionless on the outside.
  Vajrakuppa invites me to his house for lunch one afternoon.
  'He's not trying to shag you is he?' is my mother's

73

reaction.

The Friends of the Western Buddhist Order is an amalgamation of the various schools of traditional Buddhism, but with its own Western flavour. Many of the members, both ordained and lay, are converted Christians. Many are people looking for a refuge from a world that doesn't accept them. There is an overly homosexual atmosphere at times, as many of the members are openly gay – and make remarks about the acceptance that the FWBO offers them.

There are also, like myself, many explorers. People with no religious commitment to the FWBO, people who do not intend to call themselves Buddhist – but who are on a path in search for themselves and some truth about what it is to be human.

I think of what great beast Aleister Crowley said: *'Do what thou wilt.'*

XI

Lost in Heaton for forty-five minutes while trying to find Vajrakuppa's house. When I finally realise where it is I notice that I've walked past it three times already, and that my confusion has arisen due to the street name being obscured by a tree.

'I thought you weren't coming,' a warm smile on the threshold.

'I got lost,' I mumble embarrassed.

A tour of the house – no living room – it is a shrine.

'This is a Buddhist house,' he tells me.

Fresh flowers by the Buddha, smell of sandalwood incense. There is a deep quiet – I want to live here.

Tomato soup for lunch, crusty warm bread.

'Have you read any of Sangharakshita's books?' he asks.

'I've started reading *What is the Sangha?*'

He nods over a slurp of soup.

Sangharakshita is the founder of the Friends of the Western Buddhist Order. An English man, born Dennis Lingwood, he spent many years in the East studying Buddhism, and was responsible for developing Western-flavoured Buddhism.

Buddhism, as I had learned, develops its own unique style, depending on where it lands in the world. From its origins in India, it has mixed with whatever cultural flavour it has found itself with, to create a new blend, usually incorporating already existing philosophies and a pantheon of mythical deities into it.

'You know the Buddha said that the Sangha was the most important element of his teaching,' Vajrakuppa split his bread, 'he emphasised spiritual friendship as one of the most important elements of practising the dharma.'

(The Sangha is the community that practices the Buddha's Dharma or teaching).

I nod.

'Do you know about going for refuge? The three jewels – Triratna?'

He answers before I say anything:

'As Buddhists in the FWBO, we go for refuge to the Buddha, dharma, and sangha… do you consider yourself a Buddhist?'

'I don't know,' I pause, 'I don't like *isms*. I don't like labels. I find them narrowing – life is too complex to allow ourselves to be forced into thought and action because of a label.'

'Yes,' he smiles, 'most Buddh*ists* disagree with *ists* and *isms*. A practitioner of the Buddha-Dharma is more logical.'

Silence. Then:

'There is a mitra ceremony in a few weeks,' Vajrakuppa informs me.

A look of not understanding on my face. He explains:

'Mitra means friend. It's a ceremony for those who attend the centre who wish to take that next step, for those that want to take a deeper personal commitment towards Buddhist practice. It will be during the regular Wednesday sangha, so you'll be there anyway.'

After lunch, we go through to the shrine room – a long meditation on the mindfulness of breathing. Vajrakuppa leads the mediation, his voice soft, and calm. The bell, floating with a long ring between each stage of the meditation.

Nothing happens during meditation – a *nothing* that is *something*. Meditation reveals the mundane obviousness of mind – not, as I had once expected, magical false enlightenment. Meditation is everything that already *is* – everything I already know – a sensory engagement that is already there, just heightened, retuned, and opened-up. It is as if a fist forever tightly shut opens for the first time, revealing an obvious treasure inside.

The change in me has been subtle – over time my senses have opened up. On my way home – the colours of flowers brighter, vibrant as if the universe had only just then brought them into bloom for my eyes alone. All sounds have beauty and rhythm – the swaying clank of the Metro, the sound of birds, frogs croaking – a beautiful universal symphony everywhere.

I am lighter on my feet – my breathing is deeper, my life flows. Then the silence – I yearn for it, it is the greatest thing I have ever heard. Infinitely deep, layer upon layer of it. I realise that in the modern world I would have to travel far to find perfect silence – for even in normal silence, a deeper listening still reveals background noise that wouldn't be noticed unless you were attuned to it – pipes groaning, cars in the distance, the world is still there, always audible.

The mitra ceremony – a young kid called Will – only fifteen – becoming a mitra. I wonder how he could want to commit himself to Buddhism at such a young age. I think it foolish.

He says to me:

'Have you read the FWBO Files?'

'What?'

'It's a website, the FWBO Files. Have a look at it.'

The ceremony is beautiful – a puja, offerings of incense. The words enigmatic, the meaning is in the sounds of the words, not in the words themselves. In Pāli then in English.

Namo tassa bhagavato arahato sammasambuddhassa

I look at the website. It is slander against the FWBO. From what I can gather, it relates to stories of sexual assault by the founder of the FWBO, Sangharakshita, in the nineteen-seventies, as well as various testimonies by assorted disgruntled ex-ordained members on various things.

One of the main gripes: that the FWBO forces a homosexual, spiritual friendship down your throat, that its gay founder didn't believe in the possibility of spiritual connection between men and women, the FWBO is a cult and that Sangharakshita is a liar.

A gig at the Dog and Parrot with Parallel Charge – Bunny up from London. I sit with Dan and his girlfriend, Lisa. She seems distant and I'm not sure why. In front of her, a large, bizarre cocktail that looks like a jungle – it has plastic monkeys, trees and all sorts poking out of it.

'Isn't that impossible to drink?' I ask.

She shakes her head.

Later Dan says to Ellie:

'She's doing that thing again where she isn't speaking.'

I notice my feelings changing all the time – I love Bunny, I hate Bunny. The convenience of a long-distance relationship is both a blessing and a curse. After a year, the novelty is wearing thin. In a moment of decision, I decide to break up with her just as she is getting on the bus home.

'You're coming to see me in three weeks, yeah?'

'No. I'm not.'

'Oh my god! You're breaking up with me! I knew something was going to happen you've been funny with me all week.'

She throws a strop and in a frumpy rage tries to walk away from the bus.

'No, listen,' I say to her, 'you've got it wrong, we're not breaking up, I just need a break from us.'

'A break?' People are watching us now. 'We hardly see each other!'

The line for the bus has gone down.

'Are you getting on the bus?' the driver asks.

'We'll talk about it when you get home.'

She gets on the coach – her fat, tear-streaked puffy face in the window, framed through the glass like a painting of a domestic nightmare.

A month later, another gig, this one at the Live Theatre – the stage is impressive. During sound check, Dan's amp packs in, making his distortion lack depth – it's now jangly and tinny. He looks agitated. While they sit and drink, I find a spot on my own and read my copy of *Howl* by Allen Ginsberg. I'm wearing my glasses – not that I have to, they are for distance, but just because Ginsberg did. Sometimes I like to see myself as post-beat – writing, poetry, Eastern philosophy, Burroughsian cut-ups, audio experiments... embracing what the beats were about. *I saw the best minds of my generation destroyed by madness...*

'Haven't you got contact lenses?' Dan asks me.

It's a full house. Something is wrong on stage, Dan's guitar sounds like a swarm of bees in a biscuit tin and I'm somehow out of tune with him – it all goes wrong.

In the dressing room after the gig, I watch as Dan smashes all the lights, puts a hole in the wall and has a paddy. Ellie tries to calm him down.

I'm frustrated with their inability to confirm if I am actually a member of this band. After five months, they haven't said anything about it. No mention on their website of me, but still the 'bass player wanted' ad.

I head south. A walk through Hendon Park.

'I used to come here a lot when I was little,' Bunny tells me, 'when Dad could walk. I have this memory of him carrying me around on his shoulders. I must have only been two or three years old. I don't really have any memories of him walking much after that.'

There is a deep bitterness in her. One that hates how she had to leave school before finishing her GCSEs because of her Dad's illness.

'Mum kept me off school to look after him,' she explains. Much of this I already know.

'Plus I was being bullied.'

Bunny is the most intelligent girl I have ever known.

Friday night – we are on the street team for the Pitchshifter gig at the Astoria, which means we get backstage passes. I have a chat with Mark Clayden

80

about his bass rig.

We watch the show – Bunny gets up front, in the pit – she has a lovely smile, singing along. The band is incredible to watch – pure sonic energy.

Homeward – once again trapped with a desperate need to visit the toilet (having a shit in London is not something I can do easily) and so I'm eagerly waiting for the coach to stop so I can have a dump.

Green splattering by in the frame of the window – I can hear my heart beating inside my chest, a little sadness there.

Thinking little thoughts – how I am tired of explaining myself. They ask:

'What do Buddhists believe in?'

'Nothing.'

'Nothing?'

'Yes. No-thing.'

Belief has nothing to do with truth. There are no ultimate truths; all things are conceptual. The only truth I know now is impermanence. I feel closer and in touch with the only thing I will ever know for sure, my forever-changing mind and body, and how they will inevitably perish.

I fall asleep, my head rattling unconscious against the window. I have a dream that I am Angulimala, the finger thief. I am murdering people, chopping off their fingers and wearing them, thread as a necklace, around my neck. Each finger represents something that I cannot discern – image of lotus – dusty feet, wheels.

I return home to a quiet house. I meditate, in cool silence, until disrupted by my mother with the vacuum downstairs – I try to sit through it, but my concentration is broken.

That week I join the men's evening at the Buddhist Centre – a discussion group at which we work through a particular topic for the evening.

In my mind a creeping sensation. The words on the FWBO files website...

XII

Without realising it, I have overcome my silences. My ability to talk, and to engage people in conversation has surfaced, thanks mostly to my involvement with those at the Buddhist Centre. It has amazed me how deeply Vajrakuppa can listen. His attention to my words is complete and he is taking in everything I say, and not simply waiting for his turn to talk.

At home, without even being conscious of it, I'm full of a confidence that my mother has remarked upon.

One night I hear her and my step-dad talking about me.

'He's got more confidence,' my mother is saying.

'Yes, but he won't shut up now, I preferred him when he was miserable,' Jack replies.

My mother laughs. They both laugh. I feel cut through to the bone. A black, horrible sadness wells up inside me. I want to scream at both of them. All I can think of is how ignorant and stupid they both are. Even though I have been practising the metta bhavana meditation, one that cultivates universal compassion, I struggle greatly with these horrible remarks. A little seed of hatred in my gut.

'Don't let him hear,' Jack continues, 'he might go and write about it in his diary.'

'I can't believe some of the things he puts in it.'

So, my mother has been reading my diary as well. Another laceration on my skin. I feel sick.

'Drinking pints of water at the pub,' Jack is laughing now, 'what's he like?'

From the stairs where I'm hiding, I go to my room

and pull my diary from the drawer. It has become precious to me, even though it is simply a cheap blue hard-cover note book; it contains all of my thoughts on my Buddhist quest. I take a black biro and with violence scrawl THE ROBOT DWELLS WITHIN… BE MISERABLE BECAUSE YOU TALK LESS on the front.

I open it and draw a cartoon of myself as an ugly robot with googly eyes and sideburns. All my confidence is draining away and being replaced by pure hate. I don't want to swallow it, I don't want to rationalise it or to convince myself that underneath all humans suffer and various other woolly Buddhist dribble. I want them to die in a car accident. I want to walk downstairs and smash Jack's face in.

In my notebook I write out BE MISERABLE BECAUSE YOU TALK LESS followed by I AM A ROBOT. I write it out over again with such anger that the pen is tearing the page.

Then I write:

I know you read me so have a good laugh you fucking bitch.

I decided to hide my diary under my desk. It means having to pull it away from the wall every time I want to get it out, but at least it will be safe.

A combination of sadness and fury swirling around inside for days on end. I feel like I've let myself down for giving rise to anger, yet at the same time a bubble has burst – that Buddhist bubble that has surrounded me making me think that I have risen beyond the control of my emotions.

I want to see Bunny. I want to run away. Instead, I

decide to write a poem and send it off to the local newspaper. The poem is about the moments before mediation, the incense, the flowers, and the ritual of it. I want it in print so I can wave it in Jack's illiterate face.

A week later I check the paper – it's there in black and white. I show it to my mother.

'Well done,' she says.

Jack looks completely unimpressed. His idea of a bloke is one that has a day-job working with bits of wood or bricks, someone who drinks ten pints of shit lager and whose main interest is football.

In his eyes, I'm a threat. He's a little, small-minded, bigot of a man.

I'm rather pleased with my little poem in print.

It's my little 'fuck you'.

I have Bunny up for the weekend. We have no money and so sit and play *Mahjong Tiles* on the computer. I'm bored and want her to leave – I can't help it and an unpleasant atmosphere is building. We try to have sex again – I get my dick into her and she's a sack of lumpy potatoes – eyes staring up at the ceiling as I pump away.

'Hmm…' she says in a strange voice, 'that was better.'

'You didn't do anything,' I suddenly snap, 'you just lay there.'

She's hungry and wants a sandwich. I make it, ham and cheese, and give it to her.

'There's too much butter near the edges,' she looks at it with contempt, then hands it back to me and returns her eyes to the tiles on the screen.

85

Click, click, click.

I take the sandwich away and eat it on my own in the kitchen. I make her another one, spreading the butter with annoyance.

I arrive at Dan's house in Denton Burn. We're off to Cumbria – Workington, to be exact – to play at a bar called Monroe's. I'm excited about the road trip. I assume that we'll all be in the same car, but for reasons of space and equipment, we split into two groups. Dan, Ellie, and Dan's mam in one car, myself, Jürgen, a bloke called Ian who works with Dan's mam in the other car.

Jürgen wants to ride shotgun on the way out, and so I sit back and watch the Northumberland scenery flash by, until it begins to rain and the window becomes blurred. I have my copy of *Howl* with me, and so I dip into it.

The sky is black when we reach Workington – the place looks desolate.

After loading our gear in, there is our sound check, then the other band's sound check, then the wait. The other band, from Manchester, are like most of the bands we share a stage with; affable and eager to exchange information so future gigs can be arranged.

We rip through the set – everything is tight – the compliments afterwards are many and overwhelming. With a two hour drive back to Newcastle we leave around half ten. I get to ride shotgun this time, with a very drunk Jürgen talking rubbish in the back of the car.

'If I'm drunk,' he slurs, 'it doesn't even matter if I or anyone else punches me in the face.'

I sit there sober while he goes on about it, as if he is trying to justify his drunkenness against my sobriety, as if my sobriety was an attack on his drunkenness.

My not drinking, now for well over a year, has nothing to do with anyone.

Next day – I want to know my place in the band, after six months I still don't feel like I'm actually part of it. I ask Ellie, she says she will get back to me.

A phone call.

'Yeah, we don't feel like it's working out, sorry about that, best of luck…'

I feel cheated.

Everywhere I go there are people who don't want me to think outside the box.

The perfect man employs his mind as a mirror. It grasps nothing, it refuses nothing. It receives but does not keep.
Chung-Tzu

A strange game has started with Bunny – our stories, where we alternate chapters, have begun to make me paranoid. Little Dennis, a friend of hers, has started to make, albeit disguised, appearance in her chapters, and so has she, and they are lovers.

I am not sure if she is trying to tell me she is cheating on me with him, and attempting to hurt me in some way, or if she simply wants to and is writing out her desires – I also have the thought that maybe I am overly paranoid and reading something into what isn't there.

Yet Little Dennis, who is never around when I am in London, is the main topic during my phone conversations with Bunny. There is a slyness in her voice, something hidden, an unknown something that makes me think of her taking revenge.

I have a job interview with Royal Mail for the position of Post Person. After meeting with a man called Pat (seriously) at the Central Station depot, I find myself both confident and terrified that the job is mine. A phone call later that afternoon confirms it. My mother is so delighted that she looks like she might explode – already she is years ahead of herself in assuming things; it could lead to management, you could do this and you could do that etc.

I'm required to do a week of classroom training at the Gosforth delivery office – just down the road from where I live. On my first day, I discover that I'm not alone and there are three other new recruits. Ex-army Andy, Old Bloke Georgie and Student-curly-hair-name-I-forgot.

Eddie Shaft, gut with shirt and tie, balding and gingery, is taking the course. Throughout the first day, I watch as the romantic, pre-conceived ideas that all the new recruits are having (including mine) about postal delivery are smashed by Shaft. It's not a leisurely, gentle, walk in the sunshine with affable people greeting you on your round, offering you cups of tea, while dirty housewives invite you in for a 'bit' and the rich constantly give you tips – it's hard graft.

Day two: curly student doesn't turn up. I'm apprehensive.

Friday, I have to visit the Central D.O. to do a shadow round. Greg, the gaffer, introduces me to Joe. Joe is all face, too much face – mouth like a massive slit in an orange, his nose is running, hair like a coconut. He is friendly enough, and keeps asking me:

'Do you smoke tac? Do you want some tac?'

The D.O. is loud and horrible – everyone shouts at each other, music blares from various radios – I can't concentrate. Little pigeonholes on the primary – a long bench, row upon row of slots, grey mailbags, and letters dumped in front of frantic sorters, a papery smell, the sensation of rough against the fingers, paper cuts. From the primary, I find Joe's round, scoop out the letters and small packets and take them back to his bench, a small version of the primary but separated in to streets and businesses. I can't see which slot to put the letters in from the enormous bundle in my scared mitt – I can't do anything for looking too hard – Joe takes the bundle from me and shoves the letters in the right place without even thinking about it. This is not going to help me learn the route, I think.

However, Joe explains, 'This turn is a float. That means that you'll be covering a different route every day to cover for people on their day off. I'm on holiday next week, so you better pay attention.'

Off on the round, whizzing round town – I quite like Joe, he's a bizarre character, but I'm panicking inside because he is trying to get finished on time. I can't memorise anything at all – it's a horrible blur.

At home later, I frantically scour the newspaper for any other jobs to try to get me out of the mess I'm now in.

I'm doomed.

By the end of the week, I don't feel at all confident and I'm unwell with stress – I have to miss my final day's shadow with Joe due to a bout of stomach cramps and the shits.

To make things worse (or better in my eyes) I have to tell Bunny that I won't be visiting her as often, and she won't be able to come visit me either due to my new job. She is disappointed and yet there is something nasty and sinister going on in our relationship that no one wants to mention. It is a slow toxic bitterness.

My first day on the job alone – I haven't a clue what I'm doing. Curly-hair-student-poof never returned and Army Andy has dropped out after a week, I'm guessing out of fear. I'm in a panic as all the other posties are leaving the office while I'm at my bench trying to sort letters for the round – they might as well be in Japanese because none of the information is entering my brain.

Greg (the manager for the NE1 section) from the start of my employment has been about as much use as an ashtray on a motorbike. Seeing me struggling, he decides to give me a hand. Finally, about two hours after everyone else has left, I'm wandering the streets wondering what the fuck I'm doing.

After four hours I've only managed to deliver half the bag, I'm tired, hungry and I've had enough. I take the bag back to the delivery office – Greg, who is about to go home isn't pleased. I feel like telling him that if he'd actually trained me properly this wouldn't have happened.

I leave the mail there and go home, embarrassed and feeling ill.

By the end of the week, I've fucked up the round I've been on in one way or another. I've angered both customers, staff, and convinced myself this job will be the death of me.

One of the two female members of the delivery team, Alice, has taken an interest in me. She's in her mid-forties, attractive, with a mushroom bell-end haircut and massive dreamy eyes. In a bizarre envelope induced delirium, I find myself having a repeated fantasy about fucking her on a pile of letters on the primary. I am considering that the fabric of my new dark blue Royal Mail work trousers rubbing against my crotch may have induced the delirium, and likewise the material of my sky blue work shirt with red Royal Mail insignia is doing something strange to my nipples.

Old Bloke Georgie has dropped out – I'm the only one left. This fills me with despair. Yet, after the terror of the first week things get better, I have the same round to deal with for two weeks to cover for holiday, and after a few days, I can get a better grip on things.

I have a wage – it makes me feel something unsuspected, a freedom. Money I earned, and the freedom from the job centre and from Mrs Skeleton – suddenly life has greater potential.

XIII

Out of curiosity, I decide to peek at the Parallel
Charge website while in Fawdon Library. Only two
months after leaving, they have fully replaced me and
announced their new bass player – I feel a little sore,
as I spent over six months with them and never
received a mention. To dig into my wound further,
they explain that their new man is a wild, drunken
idiot, who downs pint after pint and rolls around on
the floor after gigs and various other dipsomaniacal
stupidities.

In my head, I play out a scene where Dan and
Jürgen have explained to the new person that I didn't
drink and was, in their eyes, 'boring.' And so, under
peer pressure, this kid has done what they've asked
him, and the poor fool is left feeling terrible for
abandoning his values just to impress them. Of
course, this is all a fantasy in my head, but something
about it I suspect is true.

I feel that sticking to my period of cessation from
alcohol while surrounded by thoughtless boozers for
so long has been a proud achievement – and
something I have learned a vast amount from as well.

After work one day, I decide to drop into Windows to
look at the notice board. Among the many posters
advertising for band members I find one that stands
out – it is handmade, with weird spiral drawings all
over it. They are looking for a bass player and
drummer. Influences: Portishead, Nine Inch Nails, All
About Eve, Kate Bush...

Contact Ariella.

I write down the number.

A change in the air – slight hints of autumn encroaching – early September. After a phone call with Ariella, I discover she works not far from where I live. Her voice is light, and distinctly not local, although I can't place it anywhere other than middle England.

We arrange to meet at Fawdon Metro station so she can give me the band's demo CD. It's a warm day, sun striking through clouds, a breeze that I listen to like music. I'm groggy from my post work nap, and I can't get a grip on my senses.

I wait for her. I see her coming – she has a slender face, curtained long dark hair, lips, eyes, body – all alluring.

She waves, a childlike gesture from small hands.

'Hello, it's nice to meet you.'

It sounds like she is acting – there is a rhythm to her voice, a slow graceful plod.

I take the CD and read the band name: Sepia Tears.

'I like the name,' I tell her.

In an instant I've forgotten all about music – I'm mesmerised by her and I can't help it.

'Where do you work exactly? Rowntree's?'

She laughs. 'I wish! No, Sanofi.'

'Well I'll listen to the disc, and if I like it I'll learn the songs then maybe we could have a jam in a week or so?'

'Yeah,' a smile so lovely, 'just let me know when you're ready.'

I tell her bye for now, but then she says:

'Ignore some of the bass parts that are already on

there, you can just come up with your own parts if you like. My voice sounds terrible at times too so you'll have to ignore that as well.'

I find it funny that she is apologising.

'Okay,' I say.

At home, I set up my bass and amp – turn the volume low, slip the disc in the hi-fi.

The music plays, it is ethereal – violin sweeping back and forth, piano forcing the melody forward, bass and snapping drums holding it together – and then Ariella's voice. Warm, unique, aching with a tenderness and a strange sorrow – I'm captivated.

I learn the four songs on the CD, goose pimples running up my arms and neck with each track. I'm eager, and so after only a few days I call Ariella:

'Can we have a jam? I love your music.'

She seems genuinely surprised.

'Yes, of course. Meet me after work by the Metro station.'

I bring my guitar and small practice amp with me. It's a cumbersome pain to carry. I arrive and she's early – she's reading a book, it's Jack Kerouac's *On the Road.*

'You like Kerouac?' I ask excitedly.

'Yes – this is my dad's, I stole it last time I was home.'

I look at the book; it's an old edition, maybe even a first edition. It's in good condition, too.

'Where are you from, originally?' I ask her.

'Reading, although my dad lives in Dorset now. My mother still lives in Reading.'

'What are you doing in Newcastle? Uni?'

'No, I went to Uni in Durham. I moved here with

Natalie – that's the violinist – she's away visiting her parents now, she'll be back in a week or so for the start of term.'

We get off the Metro at Haymarket – she leads me up past Newcastle University to Spital Tongues. Her flat is a weird shape – raised off the ground – space for a car underneath. Outside the door on the wall a plaque, it reads: The Dairy.

I set up in the living room. With no drums, I have to keep rhythm on my own. Ariella sings and plays piano – I watch her – she closes her eyes, red lips part, voice like honey.

She seems impressed with me. After going through the tracks a couple of times we sit and talk some more about the types of music and artists we like.

'When Natalie gets back we'll go through the songs again. Hopefully we can find a drummer too, do you know anybody?'

'No, sorry. What happened to your old drummer and bass player?'

'Oh, they were never in the band really, they were just helping with the recording.'

Later, she walks with me to the Metro station. We talk some more about music we both like.

'Have you heard this, have you heard that?'

'That album is amazing…'

'Her voice on that is incredible…'

'You should check this out…'

'Well,' I say looking at her with an increasing sense of attraction that I can't put out of my mind, 'I'll let you think about it for a few days and you can get back to me.'

'Think about what?'

Whether you want me to join the band or not.'

'Oh I definitely want you! You're great!'

I feel my ego begin to glow and I smile at her.

'That is if you want..?' she sounds apologetic.

'Yes!' I say emphatically. 'Of course!'

'Natalie will like you too, she'll trust my judgement. Hopefully we'll be able to audition some drummers soon too.'

We say goodbye. On the Metro home, I'm excited about making music with Ariella, and at the same time a little concerned, but also somehow pleased, about how attracted I am to her.

A meditation – all my thoughts are wild and rampant of Ariella. I cannot concentrate. Recently, I have been experiencing a large amount of synchronicity – people appearing just as I think of them, finding books I have just read about in other books while browsing in second hand shops, precognitive thoughts of what people are going to say to me. The universe seems infinitely linked – I cannot explain it.

So my thoughts of Ariella, I determine that it is a path to follow – partly on a whim, partly through what I believe is a connection we already have – there was a spark there, I'm sure of it.

Yet, my conscience feels dirty and I must cleanse it.

I feel terrible about what I am about to do but I have lost control of my usual reasoning.

I phone Bunny.

'It's over. It's not working. We're drifting apart.'

She is typically angry and her anger irritates me. Horrible bitter words. When the conversation is all over, through long silences and the plastic of the phone burning my ear, I feel relieved and purged.

Next day, I call Ariella.

'Do you want to go for a drink, maybe?'

'Would love to, we should get to know each other.'

'Great!'

'Meet me at Fawdon Metro station? Four p.m., on Friday?'

'See you there!'

A day later and I'm burning with excitement. I take the box of condoms from under my bed, and slip one in my wallet. I realise I am being highly presumptuous, and that I have gone a little mad. I've thrown everything else that is going on out of the window – music, Bunny, Buddhism – all of it has been put firmly aside as I am lost in a crazy whirl.

I meet her at the station. She is wearing a brown jumper and I can smell her – a smell not of perfume but of herself, unmasked, pleasant in a strange way.

We sit in the North Terrace pub, her local.

'I've never been in here,' I tell her.

She's having a glass of red wine. I'm on the water.

'You're being good?' she asks.

'I don't drink. I'm a Buddhist, sort of.'

She smiles. 'My friend Paul is a Buddhist, he goes to the Buddhist Centre. He's gay, not that that has anything to do with it. Do you know him?'

I ponder for a second. 'I don't think I know anyone there called Paul.'

Her lips pursed to the glass – they are thin when pressed together, and the red wine stains them a little.

'I can't drink too much,' she says in her soft little accent, 'I go a bit doolally.'

97

There is something rather twee about her. She holds the wine glass with both hands like a child while lifting it to her face to drink. It makes the glass, with its swirling crimson interior, look enormous.

Talk of music and books we've read.

'*The Dice Man*,' I explain to her, 'is about exploring the many aspects of your personality through chance, giving all your desires and fears the opportunity to live. I tried it for myself for a while; it caused a lot of problems.'

'How do you mean?'

'Well the die told me to drop out of sixth form, told me to dump a girlfriend at the time…'

'Sounds interesting.'

'I'll loan it to you,' I smile.

I want to touch her, to slide my hand over hers, to kiss her.

'What are you doing over the weekend?' I ask, hoping to secure another date.

'I'm going to Durham to see my boyfriend.'

A bomb explodes inside me – I suddenly have to struggle as the life drains from me, replaced with a terrible sensation of foolishness. Now and immediately, I have to invent a pretence and now I'm acting, I move away a little, not so much that she would notice, but just enough to reduce the defeated deflating embarrassment that is clogging my throat.

'What does your boyfriend do?' I can't work out if I sound sincere or not.

'He's at uni, studying politics.'

I want to leave, but can't and so for another hour I struggle on, asking pleasant questions. In the back of my mind, I'm unconsciously reverting – slowly moulding back into my previous self that existed before I met Ariella and went loopy for a while. I feel like a fool, and all I can envisage in my mind's eye is the fool card from my Aleister Crowley *Thoth Tarot Deck* – the fool, the holy fool that I am!

Eventually enough time has passed to leave naturally.

'Thanks for a lovely time,' her smile, and then she hugs me.

'Likewise, it's good getting to know you.'

'Nat is back soon, so we'll have another rehearsal, maybe next week?'

'Okay,' I agree, warm with the impression of her breasts still pressed against my chest.

I take out my journal and scrawl in spaghetti
handwriting all the words that are bumbling around in
my head. Bunny's bitterness, my foolishness, my
momentary lapse in attentiveness to my awareness.
The words are illegible, but I'm unravelling myself.
There is the sensation that my relationship with
Bunny has a sense of unreality to it, as for the last
year and a half I have seen relatively little of her in the
flesh, and our relationship has existed mostly as an
essence without a corporeal shell. Within the sense of
involvement with someone who is never there, a
romantic, false, projected, and confusing feeling
exists. Being cleansed of it, even via my own
foolishness, is a relief.

I have the weird feeling that I don't know, and have
never known, who Bunny actually is.

I sit in meditation, the metta bhavana – the
cultivation of loving kindness. Generated in stages
towards self, friend, indifferent, and then difficult
person. Typically, I would not use someone with
whom I have been physically and deeply emotionally
involved with for the friend stage – and somehow, as
I sit on a cool summer morning, no incense burning,
the statue of the Buddha, hand across his lap, I find
I've used Bunny for all stages of the meditation after
the initial stage.

Looking at the scrawl of words in the notebook – I
begin to pull phrases out, as I often do with things I
write, and reconstruct them into a poem. I make two

poems out of it – strange juxtapositions, things that fit but are not quite right. A weird rhythm to the flow, all scrambled but with a meaning that is esoteric, almost perceptible, like a flavour that only lasts on the tongue for a second.

Phone call from Bunny, my mother passes the phone through the door.

'Why are you ringing me?'

'I miss you.'

That deep silence – the sound of me breathing though my nostrils.

'This was a bad idea,' she says. 'I thought we should try and stay friends. I'll just go.'

'I'm sorry, it's too early to start trying to make things amicable. I've got nothing to say.'

A pause, then: 'I still love you,' her voice cracked.

A single tear, burning like a razor blade slicing open flesh, slides down my face. A sensation of pity and foolishness for myself.

'I still love you, too,' I reply.

'If we still love each other, why did we split up?'

'Because… it isn't practical anymore. It never was.'

For an hour, she begins a slow campaign of whys and what ifs. It's a slow, determined, bullying, grinding, and relentless battle that she won't let go, no matter what I say.

In the end, with my head battered, emotions drained and to get her off the phone, I agree we can try again. Throughout the discussion and bargaining over the aspects of our relationship, I have managed to gain that she will only call me twice a week (as my point about sitting in silence on the phone has finally

101

hammered home) and that due to my job we will only see each other once a month.

She doesn't like this, but I'm so sick of her that I have to make these conditions. In my head, I know we will have to break up eventually; it is just a case of how long I can go on.

Later, I have the thought that our relationship is continuing because of familiarity, and a sense of relief at continuing with the comfortable norm.

Considering that all Bunny ever seems to do is talk about Little Dennis, with whom I was certain she had romantic interests, I find myself in a state of confusion over her persistence to rekindle our relationship. Maybe I was wrong.

I find my way to Ariella's flat, where she introduces me to Natalie. Nat is Asian in appearance, but I guess not quite fully Asian, and it gives her an exotic quality. She is dark, with a wide smile, and she is small. I find her cute, even though her mannerisms are strange – somewhat forced and acted.

'I brought you *The Dice Man* to read,' I tell Ariella as I'm setting up my gear. I take the book out of my bag and hand it to her.

She smiles, turning the worn book over in her hands. 'I'm looking forward to reading it. Will I have to get some dice to go with it?'

I'm not sure if she is serious or not.

'You can just enjoy the story. I think for most people the die is symbolic, a token representing the ability to change.'

'Maybe I'll get one anyway,' she giggles like a child, 'and do something crazy!'

We go through the songs and I have to tap my foot to keep rhythm due to the lack of drums. The ensemble is more complete with Nat's violin sweeping back and forth across the melody from the piano, and the thud of my bass holding it together.

We have a break. Nat says, 'Oh, we're auditioning a drummer later this week, Friday at five. Can you make it?'

I tell her yes.

Ariella makes a round of tea.

'Ariella was telling me that you are still at university,' I say to Nat.

'Yes, archaeology. Midden shells.'

'What's that?'

'Basically, following the movements of early humans moving around the British Isles via huge pits of discarded limpet shells that they've left after eating them.' She pauses. 'It's really more interesting than it sounds.'

'I miss uni,' Ariella chimes, 'there's something amazing about spending all your time involved in and discussing something you're really interested in, although philosophy can be boring at times.'

Ariella had mentioned that she studied philosophy when we had met for a drink the other day. I expressed an interest in it, Western philosophy that is, and likewise she wanted to know about my interest in Eastern philosophy. It was a nice little icebreaker.

'I love Wittgenstein,' she continued, 'I saw the world in a completely different way after studying him.'

A day later – I've finished work, on my way home, half-asleep, hypnagogic – I'm thinking about Ariella, with a sensation that she will appear at any moment. I'm becoming so used to these sensations of precognitive synchronicities that they no longer cause me concern.

Next to Mark Toney near the Haymarket, I pass her in the street.

'Oh, hello,' she smiles and talks in her funny, charming way. 'I'm having an ice-cream.'

'I can see that,' I tell her, 'at first I thought your hand was bleeding, but it's just the sauce.'

'I suddenly had the desire for Rocky Road,' she giggles and takes a bite.

There's a sudden sense of awkwardness, one of knowing each other but actually not at all, as if we had both snapped out of a moment of familiarity into one of being complete strangers. It's enough to make me want to cut this impromptu meeting short.

But then she says, 'I'm reading *The Dice Man*. It's funny. I like it. Next time you come over you should bring your dice, we can do something crazy.'

I laugh at this, and sort of agree but say, 'Maybe, my dicing days are over. It only ever got me into trouble.'

I feel dreamy, confused, and not quite on planet Earth as we part, and later I wonder sincerely if that meeting and conversation ever actually took place.

I turn up at The Dairy to help audition the drummer. There are bits of drum kit all over the place. Both Nat and Ariella look bemused. The drummer, Seth, seems to be in something of a flap. He's massive, a huge, big, fat, monster of a lad with a puffy face upon which round glasses are placed. I set my guitar down next to my little practice amp and begin setting up.

Plug in, tune up, it only takes a minute.

'Coffee?' Nat asks me.

'Please.'

He's still setting up. I'm trying to reserve judgement, but I can already tell this guy is going to be no good.

'I recognise you,' he says to me. 'Weren't you in Parallel Charge?'

'Aye.'

'Their new bass player is a right piss head apparently.'

'So I've heard.'

I sit and drink my coffee. I finish it and he's still not quite ready. It's not that his kit is big or complicated; it just appears to me that he hasn't disassembled and reassembled it very often.

Nat is setting up her violin while Ariella is plinking away on her electronic piano. There is a bluebottle floating around the room. Amongst all the noise of them tuning up, I'm trying to remember a poem by Blake:

> *Am not I*
> *A fly like thee*
> *Or art not thou*
> *A man like me?*

I can't remember much of it, or seem to get the order of the verses right and then Ariella interrupts me:

'We're working on a new song,' she tells me.

'Let's go over it if there is time,' I tell her.

Seth is finally ready.

'What shall we play?' Ariella asks.

'Should we go through the tracks on the CD?' I

suggest.

Seth looks nervous, 'I didn't get much of a chance to listen to it.'

Then you're doomed, I think to myself.

He's out of time, can't keep up, faltering on every change between verse and chorus. And while I'm sure he's nice enough, he's a terrible drummer.

We go through the songs twice and he's worse on the second time round. We call it a night. After an eternity to pack up his kit, he leaves.

'What do you think of him?' Ariella asks me.

'I think he was terrible. I think we can find someone else.'

'Yes, me too.'

'Let's play the new song,' Nat suggests.

I listen to the whole thing through before asking about the root notes Ariella is playing on the piano. They play again and I join in, improvising and experimenting. Listening to Ariella's lyrics makes the process beautiful, yet uncomfortable, as they are obviously deeply personal, something I had gathered from the CD.

'No one knows how I want you, you're beautiful,' she sings.

I could never ask her what her songs are about, all I can say is:

'What's this song called?'

She smiles, '*Turtle Dove.*'

XV

I have, for the first time in my life, an excessive
amount of disposable income. Mother gets a
percentage for board – the rest I sometimes don't
know what to do with. I don't drink or do anything to
waste my money, yet I fear saving it, should I
suddenly die and not be able to spend it. Books,
DVDs, CDs – they're the only thing that seem worth
spending my wages on.

 Unlike my days of unemployment where I only
bought second hand books, and having to settle for
the luck of what I could find, I'm using my cash to
buy the books that I want. I've raided Waterstones
occult section for everything that looks of interest;
similarly, I've purchased numerous books from the
little stand at the Buddhist Centre.

 I want something substantial with my money
though, and so from Window's I buy a Peavey combo
bass amp – not thinking about how heavy it will be,
and struggling all the way home with it on the Metro.
While in the shop I spot a beautiful purple Yamaha
bass – I decide to save up over a few weeks and
purchase it.

I miss an audition for a drummer, as it was on a
Wednesday and I was at the Buddhist Centre – But
Ariella and Natalie seem excited about the person
they have auditioned, and ask me to drop by the flat
for a jam. I turn up to find a ginger-haired, pale-
skinned, empty-blue-eyed man in his late twenties.
(This I realise, with Ariella being twenty-four and Nat
twenty-six, makes me at twenty-one, the baby of the

band).

'Lavender,' the man thrusts a hand at me.

I shake his hand. He is somewhat limp in the wrist. His lips are thin and pursed together, a tiny meat parcel. His head dodders a little, he moves it as he thinks and his eyes seem to be searching the floor for something. His head is a rusty, gingery, square.

He has obviously listened to the CD, and his timing is good. We get through the songs. It sounds like it could work. After he leaves, Nat and Ariella quiz me as to what I think.

'Yeah, he's good' I tell them.

'He's got a car,' Nat laughs, 'that's important as well.'

We begin working together as a band, and while Lavender, Ariella, and Natalie start to become friends, I find myself deliberately keeping myself from entering the inner circle. While everything is very amicable and nice, I will not cross over the threshold of polite acquaintance into friendship. They invited me to a night out to which I declined.

'We went out with Lavender on Friday night,' Ariella explains as I arrive for rehearsal, 'to the Jazz Café.'

'I've never been there,' I reply.

'It's run by this big Santa-Claus man,' Nat chips in.

Ariella, with a twisted face says:

'Lavender tried to kiss me, he was so drunk. I told him I had a boyfriend!'

This conversation makes me take an even further step back from them all. My reaction, one that swirls up inside me and sits in my mind's eye waiting for me to analyse it, is to focus on my meditation and continual studies of the dharma. It has become apparent to me that people living entirely on a stimulant-reaction based existence populate the world. That is to say, that there is no pause for thought amongst most people, things happen, they react. Their actions show me that there is no gap in the process between thought and action, such as the one that I have cultivated through meditation.

This may sound somewhat arrogant, for even *I* still have the desire to act whimsically and impulsively, yet my demeanour has evolved a great deal to allow me time to judge my emotions and thoughts before bringing them into the world.

The feeling that I should want to limit my involvement with the impulsive, and the unaware, is correct for my current state of being. The only place I feel comfortable is in the company of the Sangha.

Bunny is up for the weekend. It is now impossible for me to travel to London to see her. I work six days a week, and will have to wait until close to Xmas for the chance to get away for a few days. She arrives on Friday afternoon, I'll still have to go to work on Saturday morning, but we will have all of Sunday together and she will return home on Monday afternoon.

Things feel strained and difficult; there is a silence between us.

'What's wrong?' she asks.

'Nothing.'

There has to be *nothing* wrong – because I don't want to argue when there is no escape from each other. Under the surface, there is a sensation that our relationship will either blow-up or fizzle out.

We play a childish little game. She mentions Little Dennis in all his wonderful, enigmatic capacity, and I pour out my admiration for Ariella, her musicianship, incredible voice, and lyrics. My trump card is putting the Sepia Tears CD on. Bunny sits in silence.

She goes home, and I notice my relief at her departure with a little happiness and a little sadness that I should feel this way.

Autumnal romantic sensations, the colder air, browning, and yellowing leaves that are crisp underfoot – darker nights, a faint fiery smell, and a musical wind that rattles through the trees.

Into October. The songs are tightening up, although I notice that Lavender is lacking in zest and dynamics. I find his playing style, while mostly consistent and correct, lacks any real groove or energy.

I try to force him to add flavour to his lackadaisical drumming by playing with as much loose emphasis as I can. It doesn't work. If anything, it makes him worse.

'Do you think we are ready to do a gig?' he asks.

Everyone looks at me for some reason.

'Yeah… I suppose so.' I'm unsure.

'My friend Nigel is putting on a gig at The Cumberland Arms,' he explains, 'in November. Just wondering if we should do it?'

'Yeah!' Ariella giggles in her child-like way.

The fleeting moments of change in the seasons – summer into autumn – I catch it in the wind, the way it makes me feel something for a second – something

110

unknown and nameless, like a secret whisper of nature. These transitional periods between the seasons have a profound effect on me, and I think to myself how much these isles have gained in the way of poetry, art, music, and literature due to the variable nature of the seasons and weather. I imagine Blake strolling around enraptured by these transitional periods. They are my favourite times of the year, much more so than the actual seasons themselves.

By November, the transition from summer to autumn is complete and moving swiftly towards winter. I turn up at The Cumberland Arms for the sound check – Lavender is already here and looking nervous. His thin, pink lips pursed tight together, and his face is white underneath his flat ginger hair. He's setting up the kit, and I dump my amp on the little stage and quickly plug in and tune up. The other band is floating about the pub, waiting to sound check after we are done. Ariella and Nat arrive via taxi – I head outside and help bring Ariella's piano in. The thing is heavy and awkward to get up the stairs.

Nat hands me the set list, which consists of the songs from the CD, with the new song, *Turtle Dove*, at the end. In rehearsal we're currently working on numerous other pieces of music, none of them ready to perform live yet though.

Our sound check seems to take forever. Lavender is shaking with nerves, faltering on the kit, and he looks on the verge of running away.

We get through it, the other band sound check, doors open, the place begins to fill up with people.

Lavender in the corner – a practice drum pad – it's

an octagon with a black base and a creamy skin over the top. He's hammering away at it with drumsticks, head down, in a trance.

'Are you alright?' I ask him.

'I don't want to talk, I'm too nervous.'

I think he's being silly, but I leave him be.

Vajrakuppa and some other people from the Buddhist Centre turn up – the place is quite busy.

There's nowhere for me to sit next to anyone I know, and so I find a table and sit alone, waiting to watch the first band. Suddenly, at my arm, a girl.

'Hello,' she says. She's a mass of blonde curly hair, grey eyes, lips folded top over bottom. There's something familiar about her.

'Harry said I should talk to you, because you are a writer,' she tells me with a lisp.

I'm thinking, who is Harry? I don't know anyone called Harry.

I'm confused, and so stare at her with my mouth open.

'I'm Alice,' she introduces herself and sits down.

'Harry has been telling me all about you.'

'Harry? Harry who?'

'My sister, Ariella.'

The penny drops, and I realise she's been saying 'Ari' not Harry!

I'm not sure what to make of Alice; her funny little lisp means I have to concentrate hard to understand her over the din in the pub.

We talk about books and writing.

'I like the beat writers,' I inform her, 'Burroughs and Kerouac, you know?'

'I don't know them. Have you read Bukowski?'

112

'Not yet.'

We begin a ping-pong match of have you read this or that:

'Rhinehart?'

'Plath?'

'Crowley?'

'Thompson?'

It goes on.

We're finally on stage – Lavender is struggling – he's like a rusty automaton; no groove, just a flat beat. He slips up a few times – Ariella notices and laughs a bit while singing. I wonder how it looks to the audience.

The last song is *Turtle Dove*.

'Feathers falling… to where I stand…' she sings.

After the gig, back at The Dairy, a collection of people from the other band and from the pub.

'This is my boyfriend, Johnathan,' Ariella introduces me.

He looks like Art Garfunkel; a big mop of curly hair, a tweed jacket with leather patches on the elbows, pointy shoes. He's not what I had imagined at all, and I realise that I've unconsciously built up an image of him as something of an athletic, good-looking, very masculine man. I suppose I've assumed this form of him in my mind based on how attractive Ariella is – I've assumed he would be of comparable attractiveness – but he's not.

He doesn't say much to me. Johnathan played the bass on the Sepia Tears CD too – somehow, perhaps because I haven't played my bass parts the same as him, he seems off with me.

I am regretting coming to this little post-gig soiree – I feel out of place, yet I wanted to show that I like being in the band, which I do.

I stay as long as I decide has been necessary.

At the door, Ariella:

'Will you be alright getting home?'

'I'll get a taxi in town.'

'Thank you for coming back for a bit, I know you don't drink – sorry, we're all a bit drunk.'

'Don't worry about it.'

There is a cold, dark night out there – I'm already shivering a bit.

'See you at rehearsal, next week,' she smiles.

Then a hug I'm not expecting – just right, not too long to be uncomfortable.

In the black of the autumnal night, her warmth dissipating from my chest.

XVI

Time is the thing that seems to be slipping away from me – time to meditate that is – and there is a noticeable difference in my mind when I haven't had time to sit and breathe.

The only real time I have to meditate is four in the morning, two hours before I start work – as the darkness of night lengthens, and the temperature drops, hauling my backside out of bed is an increasing struggle. I go straight from bed to the bathroom – blast my face with cold water to wake up – then light incense and candles – sit for forty-five minutes.

There is a quietness as I step outside in my blue post-man's uniform. In the morning sky – stars, dust spattered across black velvet – like chalky specks.

My breath visible in front of me – through Fawdon, always the smell of chemical chocolate – round the corner to the bus stop to wait for the night bus.

Trees stripped of their leafy clothing – a sense of uncertainty as I wait in the dead-quiet. I watch up the road for the head-lights of the little bus – it comes into view – I board – it's always the same faces, all going my way.

There's always a funny smell on the night bus, of dry heat from the vents. Through the window, the winter moon staring like a blue-white eye.

December, our next gig arranged by Natalie, is at Durham students union. We're sharing the stage with Johnathan's band The Girls of Porn. They are terrible – deliberately so, just a lot of idiotic noise for the sake of it.

Lavender, with his doddery head, is panicking again, and rattling away in a corner on his practice drum pad.

I decide to go outside. Standing in the cold I look up at a naked tree – in it are four pure white pigeons and one crow. The contrast of black and white is striking – with a light frost on the ground, the orange of the streetlights.

On stage. The slow, uncomfortable thud and snap of Lavender on the drums – a man of no confidence, pale-faced and burning ginger. Natalie, swaying back and forth, the sweep of her violin, soaring, and plucking. Ariella, on the keys – and that voice.
Turtle Dove:
'Spin me a six, and I'll be good forever…'
My calloused fingers on the bass – thumb gently rested on the pickup.

Rehearsal a week later. Nat says:
'We've had a complaint from the neighbour about the noise.'
'Maybe we should go to a practice room,' I add. 'Besides, it will be better to hear ourselves at full volume.'
'We'll just practice here tonight and hope we get away with it,' Lavender interjects, 'we can rehearse at First Avenue, I'll book it.'
Later, Lavender offers me a lift to the Metro station.
'Have you met Pete?' he asks. 'He works at First Avenue.'
'I don't think so.'
'You'll totally get along with him. I was telling him

you're a fan of William Burroughs. He likes all that kind of stuff too.'

A week later at First Avenue practice rooms I meet Pete. He has a haze of blue cigarette smoke around him, eyes hidden behind dark glasses, grey-white hair, and a thick Scouse accent that is a slow dirge.

Twenty years older than me, he seems wise and worldly – his knowledge of all things Burroughsian and beat is fathomless. I find myself having a conversation with him that I cannot have with anyone else. We have a mutual understanding of an obscure subject.

'Have you heard the album Burroughs made with the Disposable Heroes of Hiphoprisy?' he asks.

'No.'

'What about *Dead City Radio, Call Me Burroughs, Poetry Systems, Break Through in Grey Room*?'

'No.'

'Bring me some blank discs in, chuck, and I'll burn 'em for you. You're in for a treat.'

I take an instant liking to Pete and look forward to talking to him again.

For the first time in months, I'm on the coach to London. It is cold and I'm huddled in my coat. It is six in the morning. As the bus moves slowly out of the city, I'm peering out of the window into the still dark world. I've taken a few days holiday from work. My bag filled with Xmas gifts for Bunny.

I am licking her vagina. Sweet with urine – folds, pink and pursed, kisses, frantic tongue to the nub. A sliver

117

of purple tinsel hidden inside the lip. How could this be? Again, how could she have tinsel embedded in her vagina? It is Xmas this time, so there is at least some explanation.

I feel the sensation that I have had my fill of this – that although we have broken up and reassembled our love, it has just been paint over dirt. I begin to think about ending it before I have even departed. I decide I am never coming back here.

I come home still disconnected – as if I had never went in the first place, a vast gulf of space between us – one filled with a platonic relationship, dirtied with a forced romance. Swirling around inside me a force that is propelling me towards change – a gnawing, desperate, inevitable, change that will come as surely as spring will succeed this winter.

Knowing Bunny, she will turn into a bitter, stroppy beast if I break up with her around Xmas time. I decide to wait until the New Year.

The weekend before Xmas, another gig at The Cumberland. Lavender gives off the impression of being depressed, a quiver in his voice – I wonder what is exactly wrong with him. I suspect he lacks a certain fortitude, not just in the face of performing, but also in everyday life.

'There's something wrong with Lavender,' I tell Nat and Ariella.

'We know,' Nat replied, 'but he's always like that, isn't he?'

The other band, friends of Lavender's – a folk ensemble, the singer wearing a queer sailor's hat.

Later, Ariella says to me:

'You always wear black, don't you?'

I'm staring at the floor, where a scrap of tin foil has fallen, somehow accidentally folded to resemble a silver rose.

Nat is away for Xmas, Lavender is unavailable, yet Ariella invites me over to The Dairy for a quiet song writing session.

'Have you any ideas?' she asks.

'Not really. We could jam around something though.'

'Play something.'

I begin moving around the frets – a steady, pumping rhythm while she explores the keys around it.

We stop. In the silence, some wind chimes outside play a tune that in time and key resolves the end of the jam. We both laugh.

'My sister had some wind chimes in her window when we were little,' she tells me, 'but it was missing a chime, so it always sounded funny.'

'One chime less.' I say.

Ariella begins to play the melody she had just been playing and sings:

'My sister's wind chime, one chime less.'

She giggles, 'I'm not sure if that works or not. I'll be visiting father when I head home tomorrow, so I might play around on his piano to see if I can write some proper lyrics for it.'

New Year's Eve, a puja at the Buddhist Centre. A set of call and response venerations in Pāli and in English. The sounds of the Pāli words are incredible and not easy to master.

119

At the end, the repeating Avalokiteshvara mantra –
the meaning implied in the sounds of the words, not
in the words themselves.

Om mani padme hum

Into the cold night – a strange feeling amongst the
drunks and revellers as I walk across frosted ground –
orange and yellow, streetlight spilled over it, glittering.

How odd and unique my life appears to me.

Gloom of the New Year – festive sensations faded.
The world returns to normal.

In my mind the realisation of what I have to say to
Bunny, and yet I cannot bring myself round to doing
it – and so I'm avoiding her.

'Tell her I'm asleep if she calls,' I tell my mother.

At work, delivering mail all around Newcastle City
Centre, I encounter all kinds of things. The blue and
red of my uniform invites all sorts of people, as I am
a walking attraction to which they can spontaneously
engage in conversation.

Drunken old man, incoherent, gibbering – dressed
in a green camouflage jacket, bald head with red
spots, grey beard. A set of keys on a tatty bit of string
around his neck, blue plastic bag filled with cans of
cider. His hands are brown and crinkled like old
paper.

He accosts me, mumbling:

'Girls dancing on poles. Why would anyone want to
do that?'

I think of reasons that I don't tell him.

Then he says:

120

'I admire you,' and walks off.

I wonder for a moment if I have just encountered a Rhinehartian actor, I wonder if this old man had cast a die this morning, telling him to spend the day acting the drunk.

It was possible that anyone could be anyone.

The old man who lives on St. Thomas Street.

'I'm ninety,' he tells me every morning as I hand him his post.

His shaggy old dog sniffs my crotch and nibbles at my black fingerless gloves.

'Calm down, Poppy!' he tells her. 'I was a doctor for many years,' he repeats daily.

The same routine. Then he shakes my hand.

Late January, today I'm not wearing my gloves. The handshake – for the first time skin to skin, his bones so fragile, my grip accidentally too strong. The sensation and the image of his soft, bony, lifeless hand with me all day.

It's raining, a letter from overseas, wet, and the ink on the envelope running a little. I push it through a letterbox. My phone rings – Bunny calling me at this time of the morning.

I answer.

'Where have you been? We haven't spoken properly for weeks.'

I hold a deep silence.

'Is something wrong? You've been avoiding me.'

The words in my throat.

'Hello? Can you at least talk to me?'

'I'm sorry,' my words are stern, voice straight as an

arrow, 'I want us to break up.'

Tears. Then, 'Why?'

Pause. 'Because I don't love you anymore.'

She gives no argument. It's over; I've won. I'm free.

Onward delivering letters, excited with the ambivalence of sadness and joy.

XVII

Into a wilderness – snow falling – the long dark of February. Ice threatens me everywhere I walk, and I creep through quiet streets in the cold of morning.

There is a feeling of numbness, post Bunny, and a relief. But also, a disconnection – a three hundred miles severance. She no longer calls, I no longer avoid, or sit in silence or feel obliged towards a false romance. In my head, I have the image of an unwanted, mangy, unloved dog put to sleep, no emotion in termination.

A gig at The Fish Tank in Durham. It is snowing and deadly ice lines the streets. The Fish Tank is on a bank – Lavender has driven us here, the four of us and equipment squashed up in his green Nissan.

Loading in the gear – Nat says:

'Give me your hand, I don't want to slip on this fall down bit, these heels weren't designed for this type of weather.'

I help her up towards the door, but we slip – her tights rip as she falls on her backside – her little skirt open, and I glimpse her satin knickers – the bend, curving and inviting.

She's embarrassed, but the rip in her tights adds to her attire and we both notice it.

I haven't had a drink for nearly two years. A little bit of desperation that comes with change grips me – and so I get myself a JD and coke. Lavender notices me buying it.

'Are you having a drink?' he's obviously pleased.

'Yes.'

'Is this because you've split up with your girlfriend? Are you alright?'

'Yes.'

He scoots off to tell Ariella and Nat.

'Don't get too drunk now,' Ariella laughs.

I hate them a little bit.

I only have one drink, a little bit of guilt creeps up on me.

Guilt over what? I think.

Gig over. They are going to a party at Johnathan's house.

'I thought you were driving me back to Newcastle,' I say to Lavender, 'I've got work tomorrow!'

'Sorry, you can get the last train.'

I'm annoyed, but as usual, accept the situation.

The platform is cold and frosted with snow. Two other people waiting for the train. The delay time on the screen keeps going up. Ten minutes delay... twenty minutes... it hits an hour and I panic a little bit. It's now half-eleven, there is no other way to get back to Newcastle other than this train. At midnight, the screen announces the cancellation of the train.

I'm fucked. The Fish Tank will have shut now, and everyone will be gone. I begin frantically weighing up my options. Phone my mother, phone Lavender and go to the party... walk... get a taxi and pay for it at the other end.

I turn to walk out the station when the other man on the platform stops me.

He's wearing a suit and a long black coat.

'Do you need to get to Newcastle? I'm stuck now too. Shall we share a taxi?'

I can only afford to share the taxi with him to Central Station. I have to walk the four miles to Fawdon. By the time I get home, my ears are so cold and numb they are bright red.

It is two in the morning. I have to be up at four.

'We're going out on Friday,' Lavender tells me at rehearsal, 'me and Pete are going to the Jazz Café. You should come.'

'Alright, aye, I will.'

There is already a regret building up in me from agreeing to this – yet since my split with Bunny I have felt thrust forward into having a new life – all the old seems tainted with a sour flavour.

I think of what Burroughs said:

Desperation is the raw material of drastic change.'

Friday night – I meet them in Tilley's Bar. The floor is sticky and the toilets are disgusting. There are alcohol-induced arseholes everywhere. I hate pubs.

I drink JD and coke.

Lavender: 'Tell me if you feel sick or anything.'

'I've drunk plenty in my time,' I tell him, 'I'll be fine.'

Onto the Jazz Café. Lavender asks:

'So your Buddhist people won't be angry with you for drinking, you won't get kicked out or anything?'

'It's not like that. It's not dogmatic. It's up to the individual to decide on what is morally acceptable and to consider the consequences of his actions.'

'So you can drink if you want?'

'I can do whatever the fuck I like.'

I'm a little shocked at myself. I can't decide if the

125

alcohol is having any effect. I still feel lucid and logical – yet there is the encroaching feeling of abandonment – the casting off all the reason and rationality that I have held so highly over the last two years – there is the desire to disregard my reason for immediate sensual gratification, even though I know empirically that it will bring me nothing but trouble.

I talk to Pete – over the din of the Jazz trio in the corner – about the Beat writers.

'Have you read this?'

'What do you think of the homosexual sex in Burroughs' novels?'

'Have you seen *Pull My Daisy*? *Last Academy Documents*? Cronenberg's *Naked Lunch*?'

On and on. The interior of the Jazz Café – old yellowed patterned wallpaper, rickety seats – cigarette smoke in blue plumes rising from the tables. Our food – that I had forgotten about – arrives. Five-pounds on the door and a free burger.

Behind the bar – a sexy young woman – Roxanne, as Lavender informs me. All of the drinks are from bottles and cans; there are no pumps.

Sickly-sweet sensation in my mouth, alcohol slowly penetrating my actions and words.

The owner of the Jazz Café – Bert Crumpets – a tramp-like Santa Claus of a man – with red neckerchief, blue beret, grubby demeanour – is pottering around, grunting at his punters.

Pete leaves. I suspect Lavender's intentions have been to bring me on side for some reason, to establish a camaraderie. He pops a question at me:

'What do you think Ariella's songs are about?'

I suspect he has been waiting to ask me all night.

126

'I don't know.'

'What do you think *Turtle Dove* is about?'

I think for a second. Then I say, 'It must be about someone dying. It has the words, "my dying dear," in it.'

'Who does she know that is dying? It's obviously someone she's secretly in love with.'

'I don't think it is,' I tell him, 'I've thought about it too. I think it's based on a book she must have been reading.'

'Really?'

'Yes, well, you know she loves Kate Bush? And Kate Bush sang a song about *Wuthering Heights*?'

'Aye.'

'Well, it's the same thing.'

'What book is it about then?'

That, I couldn't answer him.

Natalie, who I have started to discover, is socially inept and not at all sensitive to how other people feel, greets me at rehearsal.

'We've got bad news,' she tells me, 'Ariella has lost her job at Sanofi.'

Ariella is sitting behind her piano.

'That's awful,' I say, and wonder why she felt Ariella couldn't tell me herself.

Mid-week, my mother asks:

'Are you not going to your meditation class?'

'Not tonight.'

I have the feeling I won't be going back ever again.

Friday again – Tilley's and then the Jazz Café. On the

way to town, I buy a bottle of vanilla coke and a miniature JD, combine the two, and drink it on the bus.

'Is Ariella alright?' I ask Lavender.

'Not really, I had to loan her twenty-quid to buy food.'

'Will it take ages for her to get benefits?'

'She won't sign on. I asked her about it, but she won't do it. She's too proud.'

'Fuck.'

'Anyway, Bert Crumpets has given her some shifts at the Jazz Café.'

'Well, that's something, I suppose.'

At this point Pete chips in, 'Yeah, but that's only 'cos the dirty old fucker likes Ariella's tits.'

'Did I tell you about the photographs?' Lavender asks me.

'No.'

'Apparently, Crumpets sent some pictures to be developed, word got out from whoever processed them that they were of him doing weird shit in nothing but a stripy jumper.'

'What kind of weird shit?'

'I dunno. Rumour has it that he also has cameras in the bogs.'

'You're just paranoid, Lavender,' Pete says.

'I'm not, man.' Lavender turns to me, 'Have you read *Them*?'

'No... what's that?'

'Jihadists, neo-Nazis, the KKK... they're everywhere... they're controlled by a secret elite.'

I don't say anything but take a sip of my JD. Then he continues:

128

'I went for a job interview a few weeks ago. The bloke that interviewed me wore this ring; I've never seen anything like it, gold with a large red stone. I reckon he was a Mason. Then he gave me this weird sort of handshake.'

I decide Lavender is definitely paranoid.

At the Jazz Café, I go to see Ariella who is working at the little bar upstairs. She seems embarrassed to see me there.

'Are you okay? I'm sorry about your job.'

Crumpets walks over and mumbles something to her under his breath while looking down her cleavage.

'Yeah,' she says after he goes away, 'I'll be alright.'

'If you need to borrow some money or anything, just let me know.'

'Thank you,' she says, 'but mother has said she will help me out. Anyway, I have to go and get some more ice.'

I sense a little more sadness in her than seems apparent for the situation, and she walks off, lost in an unknown thought.

I have a hangover. Everything feels hyper-real. By giving up my reasoning and mental focus I have stepped over a threshold that is leading me down a path that can only be controlled by my emotions and not by logic. I know this empirically, yet I have no intention of reversing my decision.

XVIII

A phone call from Natalie to inform me that she's cancelled rehearsal because Ariella is ill. Then, moments later, Lavender calls me.

'Do you know that rehearsal has been cancelled?'

'Yes, Nat just told me.'

'Do you know why? What did she say?'

'That Ariella is ill.'

'Yeah, but it's more than that though. She's pregnant. I'm not supposed to tell anyone, so keep it to yourself.'

I find it strange that he is calling me to gossip. Sometimes I wonder about Lavender's agenda.

Still, we arrange to meet on Friday night.

In the Jazz Café – post greasy burger and chips, that ticking hour before closing, red wine drunk, cigarette smoke. Pete has left to visit his paramour, Carolina. Lavender and I sitting at a table.

'Is Ariella alright?' I ask him. 'I wanted to see if she was okay, but I didn't want to bother her. I didn't want her to know that I know. If you know what I mean?'

'She's having an abortion. She's actually more devastated at Johnathan's attitude to the whole thing.'

'What do you mean?'

'Apparently he's shown her no kindness or care over the whole thing; he's just left her to get on with it. She told me he's fucking off to London to a gig on the day she's having her abortion.'

'That's shit,' I say, and I have a feeling of sadness for her, for losing her job, and now this.

'So you must be after some new bit of skirt now

then, eh?' Lavender changes the subject.

'I dunno. I think I need a long break from women.'

'Nah, it's better to get back in the game, man. You don't have to get involved with anyone, but, you know… you can still take someone home.'

'I'm not taking anyone to my mother's house.'

'Well, you could go to theirs, then.'

'That is great as a hypothetical situation, dude, but to me the Jazz Café doesn't appear to be prime flirting ground.'

'Go on, man!' he urges me. 'What about her over there?'

There is a moderately attractive woman sitting on her own by the door. Red lipstick, short black hair, a cigarette nestled in the ashtray beside her.

'Ha'way, let's go and talk to her.'

He drags me over and I sit in silence as he talks to her.

'Don't you recognise my mate here?' he is saying. 'He's from that band Sepia Tears.'

I sit slouched in the rickety old chair not knowing what to do or say. Through a hazy, drunken fog, I begin to wonder how I have gone from the path of enlightenment to hanging around with this rusty-headed fool.

'I'm just waiting for a taxi,' she smiles politely.

Sunday after – Lavender invites me to join him and Pete for drinks at the Chillingham. I hand Pete some discs for him to burn me a selection of Burroughs' audio works.

That night we drop into the rehearsal rooms next door, Pete brings out some hash. I'm not opposed to

131

smoking dope; it's just been so long that I've forgotten the effects.

As he crumbles the brown hash into the Rizla, I'm aware of my old life slipping further away. He lights it up – that old familiar smell – inhale, burning at the edges of reality – audio pockets, missing time – things I may or may not have said and thought. Giggling like a fool.

Looking at Ariella during rehearsal – Lavender secretly tells me that she had her abortion today – I hate knowing something that I shouldn't – and now Natalie buzzing around her in an overbearing way. Ariella's face is eggshell pale, a terrible sadness there, under the surface. I feel terribly sorry for her. The pretence of not knowing what is going on is hard to maintain.

As Lavender explained, she is more upset at Johnathan's lack of interest in what she is going through, than the physical experience of the abortion itself. I find the fact that he went off to a gig in London instead of going with her rather deplorable.

Next day, the whole thing is weighing on my mind. I send Ariella a text message asking if she is okay, pretending I know nothing, just that she looked poorly the other night. She calls me immediately.

'Yes, I'm fine,' she tells me. 'Do you know what happened?'

I hesitate, 'Yes. I'm really sorry, Lavender told me.'

A hard anger in her voice, 'Did you ask him, or did he just tell you?'

'He just told me.'

'I thought so; I didn't think you were the gossipy type. You know what? I'm fucking sick of him. He's been poking his nose into my life since the moment we met.'

'Maybe he has a thing for you.'

'Do you think so? Well, he has no fucking chance. Anyway, thank you for your concern my darling.'

'It's alright, I hope you are okay. If you need anything, let me know.'

Three weeks later and spring encroaching, different skies, lighter rains. That strange sensation of being in-between seasons – the dark residue of winter and the teasing bright of spring amalgamated.

My emotions are heightened as a result of this change, and also my defences, the rational thought-watching-separated-mind created via meditation, is vanishing.

I notice synchronous events everywhere. Pre-thought, precognitive images, before the actual thinking mind commits to the concept, appear in my mind's eye.

Rounding the corner on St. Thomas Street, sunlight breaking over the cool ground – I have a powerful sensation of a synchronous event about to take place – though I can't discern what – just the feeling of someone – an old girlfriend from school. The sensation stays with me as I walk towards Haymarket – and she's there, we bump into each other, exchange pleasantries. It's all over in seconds – yet, something profound has happened to me, something life changing – it is deeper than I can explain, and a well of buried, confusing emotion erupts inside me.

133

Through meditation, removed from my emotions, not callous or cold, but choosing to see reality without the clouded haze that emotions can bring – with all my defences down, they flood through me all at once, and I'm drowning under it, gasping with the full-weight of the human experience.

I keep going, propelled by something, I do not know what – into the newsagents, I buy a copy of *Fortean Times*. On the cover, a blue-grey picture of an old man with spectacles, beard, balding.

On the Metro home, I open the magazine, an article on synchronicity – answers presented to me – I discover the image on the front is Carl Jung. My heart is beating so fast I think it will explode.

Everything understood by the story of a scarab beetle.

Later that night I am awake watching the telly – *Disinformation*, the writer and artist Grant Morrison, in his excited Glaswegian accent, explains sigil magic.

You write down something you desire. Remove the vowels and the repeating letters. Then create an image, as esoteric and distorted as possible with the remaining letters – skewed, backwards, upside down, broken up, rearranged. The image kept on you at all times until an appropriate time to charge it arises. To charge it, an orgasm, drugs, dancing to the point of frenzy, meditation – at the peak of these experiences, visualise your sigil. Keep it secret, when accomplished, burn it.

I decide to do this – I see it as a way of focusing my will – I'm overpowered by my synchronistic experience that I decide to throw everything I have into destroying my rational mind – to move away from reason, from the endless watching of thoughts, to go full-force in the other direction, to be fully hedonistic and Dionysian.

Lavender on the phone:

'Ariella has split up with Johnathan,' he tells me.

I'm quite tired of his gossiping.

He adds, 'She wants us all to go out on Friday night.'

That Friday we smoke a joint at The Dairy, then round the corner to the North Terrace pub. Ariella is drinking red wine – red stain on her lips. Nat is drinking Glenfiddich straight and smoking a cigarillo, Lavender has a pint of some horrible lager and I've opted for my usual Jack and Coke.

Everyone is high, Ariella is giggling like a child – it is endearing and a little bit worrying as she has lost some control.

Towards the end of her glass, she admits, 'My alcohol tolerance is so low man!'

She bursts into another bout of hysterics.

We get into Lavender's tatty green Nissan.

'Right,' he says, 'where are we going?'

We decide on The Free Trade.

While driving, Ariella in the back giggling, a high-pitched squeal – and she's talking nonsense.

'Yumkins, bumkins, pumpkins!' she laughs, followed by a long and satisfied, 'hmm…'

We all laugh at her and she laughs back at us, and this cycle of hysterics continues until we reach the Trade – my eyes filled with tears from laughing – Lavender begs her stop lest he crash.

In the Free Trade, things calm down a little. I admire

the graffiti in the toilet – every bit of wall space covered in scrawl.

At a rickety table near the open fire, Ariella begins prodding my leg with hers. I'm not sure what's going on at first and so I poke my head under the table to see what it is.

'Is she playing footsy with you?' Lavender asks, then adds proudly, 'She was doing that with me earlier too.'

I'm not sure what to make of this, but then, Nat gets a go of Ariella's feet as well.

Later that night at the Jazz Café, I tell Ariella, 'I'm sorry to hear about you and Johnathan.'

'I'm guessing Lavender told you about that?' She purses her lips in anger.

I realise I've dropped him in the shit.

'Yeah. Sorry.'

'I'm going to stop telling him things. I should have listened to Natalie.'

Her good mood seems to disappear a bit, and she seems lost in thoughts.

'Are you okay?'

'Yes,' she waves it off, 'I think I might go home now.'

I look at the yellowed, nicotine-stained clock on the wall.

'It's half-one. It'll be closing in half an hour anyways.'

She hugs me and kisses me on the cheek.

She disappears off to find Nat. As they are leaving, Lavender scuttles around after them, insisting on sharing a cab. He's like a fly around a honey pot.

I join them outside, bid farewell and head towards Central to obtain a cab myself. Seconds later

136

Lavender is running after me.

'I think I've pissed her off,' he explains.

XIX

My phones buzzes – a text from Ariella. My eyes widen as I read:

I want you, you sexy fuck.

I reply asking if this is a joke. Apparently it isn't. I feel a bit giddy and unsure as to what to do about this – I'm shocked and surprised. I wonder if she has gone a bit strange since losing her job, having an abortion, and breaking up with Johnathan.

I don't reciprocate, and yet I don't turn her away.

Next day, Lavender on the phone, 'Ariella has a new job,' he tells me, once again not comprehending that I'm not interested in his gossip. 'I drove her to Ponteland, or "Ponty Land" as she called it, for the interview. She was talking about you the whole time mate.'

'Really? What did she say?'

'That she's after you. I told her it was a bad idea of course, and that you wouldn't be interested, because we're a band, and you two getting involved like that will just ruin it.'

I hesitate for a moment. He's right of course, but part of me wonders if that is really the reason for him saying this – I suspect his motivations may be to do with his own feelings towards her. It makes me despise him for being so feeble and pathetic.

I arrange to meet Ariella to talk to her about it. Walking through Leazes Park, shadows cast here and there from trees and various stone statues. We sit in the gazebo, the sun behind us.

'I hear you have a new job?'

She twists her face, realising that Lavender has been gossiping again.

'Yes, it's at a care home. It's a pain to get to, but it's a job at least.'

'Are you serious about what you said?' I ask her. 'Do you just want to shag me? Because we're in a band, and as much as I would like to,' I pause, 'it could ruin things. Is it worth it?'

'I want more than to just shag you,' she blushes, 'I want you.'

'What about the band?'

'The band won't suffer.'

We walk some more. My heart is beating fast and I'm giddy with nerves. I feel that I can't help myself – I feel drawn in by her, and regardless of my brain telling me to be sensible, I find words falling out of my mouth.

'Well, then,' I begin, 'maybe we should kiss?'

She giggles. 'Okay, but not here, let's go somewhere where no one can see.'

We walk into the University Campus and hide behind a concrete pillar. I put my hands on her slender waist and move towards her. To my surprise, she crumples to the ground and giggles before I put my lips near her.

'I'm sorry,' she's laughing, 'I'm not as sophisticated as I try to make out.'

We try again. We kiss; her lips are like crushed velvet, red, pursed, soft. They are depthless and infinitely warm beneath my own lips. The kiss folds into a hug, she clings to me, pressing her body tight, tucks her head in under my chin – I wrap my arms around her. We hide together.

'We should keep this a secret,' she tells me.

Friday, and I've lied to Lavender about why I'm not coming out for the evening. The truth is that Ariella is on her way over. I meet her at Fawdon Metro station. I notice her bag that seems overly large. We buy a bottle of JD from the shop. She opens her bag – it is apparent she is planning to stay the night, even though we didn't actually discuss it.

'You've come prepared,' I laugh.

We kiss – when I pull away to look at her, I'm struck by just how beautiful I think she is – and although I don't intend to, I find myself comparing her to Bunny. The contrast between the two is great – compared to Ariella's slender face, her shining green eyes, her very *being* and form – Bunny is a troll.

With each kiss, I find myself a little intoxicated, and my head begins to swim, my pulse races – electric shivers through my body as we press together.

In silence, with curtains drawn, a soft song of spring somewhere beyond the open window, we undress. Her body, hourglass, perfect, everything perfect to the touch and to the taste – her flesh against my lips – the way her nipples erect – her juices flow onto the bed, stains here and there – and the smell of it.

Myself in her mouth – the warmth moving from my tumescent cock through the rest of my body – the taste of her cunt, rubbery, velvety, oceans.

Inside her, a great tide washing back and forth, bringing myself to orgasm – she begs I hold it in her, and I'm on top of her, breathing, still hard inside – an earthquake in her folds, ripples along my shaft as she rises, arches her back with her come.

In silence, naked, the red curtains blowing gently, a breeze over our bodies. Entwined, legs and arms like a mass of snakes.

A long and slow deflation.

We dress and I open the JD – I go downstairs and inform my mother not to disturb me, I have company. She wants to know all – I give her little.

I slam a pizza in the oven and once cooked we share it – the television in my room is on, but we're not watching it.

'I'm going home next week,' she tells me, 'Mother is driving up from Reading to pick me up on Wednesday. You should come and meet her.'

'Okay. What about your new job?'

'I don't start for another three weeks. I'm spending a week with mother, then going down to Dorset to stay with my Dad.'

The thought of her going away for two weeks kills me. The thought of her ever leaving my presence is enough to make me wince.

'What made you want me?' I ask her.

'You're a beautiful boy,' she explains and blushes.

Later, and we're drunk. I'm acting strangely, wandering around the room, pacing back and forth. Saying odd things – as if a sudden disbelief that such a beautiful creature as Ariella could be in my bed. I feel that there is a blossoming romance already, that there is no turning back. Yet, I am all doubts in my head. In bed, we hold each other, my head spinning with a mix of alcohol and emotion.

I feel my clarity, my ability to rationalise, is slipping away from me.

141

In the morning, we're fucking again – after I pull out of her, the sight of the condom broken, and my white gunk on the inside of her thigh, running from her cunt.

Her face turns grey.

I phone work and tell them I am poorly. I walk Ariella to the Metro station, via the chemist, where she is upset that she has to buy the morning after pill. The abortion brought back to her mind, and I feel guilty – so I give her the money for the pill.

'I know you are skint at the moment,' I tell her.

She boards the train, and watching her go is a pain such as I have never felt – I feel a little mad, not myself at all, like it is taking all my will to prevent myself from going loopy. I feel intoxicated by her.

I cannot think about anything other than Ariella.

Mid-week, I decline Ariella's offer to drop by and meet her mother. Lavender will be there though, she has informed me, by his own invitation.

I've declined to go due to a worrying thought that it would be awkward, that maybe Lavender will realise something is going on, that maybe our secret could unearth. I'm giddy inside, I don't know if I can be relaxed and normal.

Next day, she calls me in the evening from her mother's house in Reading. All of her thoughts are of me, she tells me. In bed, I ache for her.

Two weeks of pure agony – I feel swept up by a tornado that is making me insane. Not one thought has been of anything other than her – I feel her essence shifting about inside me, like a liquid, hot and moving, volatile – and the words that I fear to admit to myself, that I love her and I'm crazy with it, keep returning to the front of my brain with disturbing alacrity.

Nothing matters; I can't care about or concentrate on anything but her.

Friday night, in the house I sit and drink more JD than I should and so I'm drunk – and I'm drifting in an awake-dream. A somnambulist, on automatic, living in the lines of a strange poem. Everyone is dead. All the love in the world resides with the dead – love buried in the earth. I'm supposed to meet Lavender in town for drinks. I reply with weird text messages, not correcting the auto-speller on my phone. *Cock chocolate. Oblong in my turrets. Monocle Tuesday.*

He asks if I'm okay.

I'm on the Metro to town, but I get off at Regent Centre, and walk down Hollywood Avenue to the cemetery where my great-grandfather is buried, and where the ashes of my uncles and aunts are scattered over.

I find the grave and sit in front of it. I'm wearing my long leather trench coat, hair glued back with gel, fingerless gloves, DM boots, and wristbands with spikes. On my mini-disk player, Katatonia, Opeth, Six Feet Under, Deicide.

You are dead – my relatives that I've never known. Dead, all dead. Something in the earth – like answers to questions I've never asked but need to know. Deep in the crumbling soil, skeletons with secrets.

I leave the cemetery and head into Asda where I buy a pack of weird alcoholic fruit shots, hide them in my pockets, and slug them off in a corner on the train. I'm driving myself along, not in reality, but in a hypnagogic state. Into Tilley's, Lavender sitting at the bar with Johnathan. I get my drink, a JD with coke.

'Are you alright?' Lavender asks me.

I nail my drink in one.

'There, I've had my drink.' I tell him in fact.

I want to turn to Johnathan and tell him that I'm fucking his ex-girlfriend. However, I don't I just turn around and walk out. I get in a taxi by Central Station and I'm on my way home. Lavender is pestering me via text. I turn my phone off.

Home, and I'm polishing off my bottle of JD. Blind drunk, an anger, burning, red, exploding, ripples through my skin. I pick up my four-track and throw it across the room. Part of it smashes off, the pieces scattered across the floor. This act of violence, in its instance, cleanses me of something, and I like it – this drunken rage, this feeling of bravado and power that is rumbling around in me. I stamp on the four track, over again until it is in bits.

The next day, and a guilt and terrible remorse, the flavour of my actions stale in my head. I sit outside, listening to the water from the pump in the pond, a grey haze of booze and sleep still lingering before my eyes.

In my notebook, I try to write something, but I feel sick.

All I can scribble is:

Mr Hyde was here.

XX

The wait for Ariella to return is agonising. We talk on the phone a little bit and send each other text messages – yet I try to refrain from doing both of these as it increases my desperation for her.

After my weird bout of drunken behaviour, I've aroused Lavender's suspicions, and so I'm avoiding him as much as possible.

I visit Pete while he's working at First Avenue on Sunday. I'm wearing my long leather coat; the inside pocket is just the right size for a paperback, and so there's always one in there. I stuff Burroughs's *The Soft Machine* inside it to read on the train.

'Ah, Mr Noir,' Pete jokes behind his dark glasses. He opens the little fridge behind the counter and plonks a can of Fosters in front of me. We indulge in the usual beat talk – Burroughs and cut-ups.

'Have you ever read *The Life and Opinions of Tristram Shandy?*' he asks me.

'What? No.'

'Get a copy of it. The death page is right up your gothic street, chuck.'

We smoke a joint, and I head home. Baked out of my head on the Metro, an idiotic thug is sitting beside me making threats. I just laugh manically at his words. Beyond my drug-haze, the other passengers on the train immersed in a fear of this dick. I stare at this kid with cold, dead, stoned eyes. I say nothing as he promises to 'Chin me for being a stinking Goth.'

It's like watching a film, the threat unreal, behind a screen.

I don't react; I'm numb, and so when he gets

nothing from me he goes away. At home, I get into bed and under the covers, cocooned in a stoned bubble.

The day of Ariella's return. I'm ill with excitement. She tells me she has to go straight to Ponteland to her new employer to fill out some forms, and so I meet her in town in the afternoon.

Late April – warmth under a lid of cloud. When I see her coming, my heart explodes. She is wearing a soft white shirt, our arms around each other, desperate kisses, the feeling of her shirt, breasts, and essence against me.

Back to The Dairy, talking of all her adventures at home.

'I had lots of pea fritters at my Dad's,' she explains, 'you can only get them in Dorset.'

'I thought a lot about you,' I tell her.

'I thought a lot about you too.'

We undress and lay on her bed, she rides my cock, skin rubbing, gooseflesh – when I come I see my sigil, the intention of my will projected into my mind's eye.

I realise I will have to burn it.

It has come to my attention that All About Eve are playing at Trillians next week, on the fifth of May. At rehearsal, I explain this to Ariella, and that I will get us tickets.

'Who is it that's playing?' Lavender asks, his head lopping, his demeanour soft.

'All About Eve.' I tell him.

'I might come to that, if that's alright?'

I wish I had never said anything in front of him.

146

'Sure, of course,' I lie.

Next day, I drop into Trillians to buy tickets. I don't get one for Lavender though, hoping to put him off by telling him I only had enough cash for two.

Day of the gig, he hasn't forgotten – he insists on coming, and has to pay on the door. He is watching us with his grey, jealous eyes.

As the band play, Ariella holds my hand, rests her head on my shoulder. Caught up by the sound and sentiment of the music, and the joy of having her close to me, we kiss, just briefly.

Lavender at my shoulder, 'Can I talk to you mate?'

'What?' I snap at him.

'Can you just come outside for a moment?'

I go outside and stand glaring at him. I'm fucking sick of him.

'I know what's going on with yous two, I can see it happening,' he lights up a cigarette.

'And..? That's between us, isn't it?'

'Yeah, but what about the band?'

'What about it?'

'If yous two get together it will ruin it.'

'No it won't. At the end of the day, Lavender, what Ariella and I decide to do is nothing of your concern. So mind your own business.'

He looks hurt by this.

'But, don't you think the dynamic of the band will change?'

'Yes, but only because of the way you're going on, mate.' I snap at him.

'You should think carefully about what you're doing before it's too late.'

'It is too late.'

The pain on his face from this last remark is great, and I'm pleased I've inflicted it upon him.

'What is it that you think I was doing the other Friday night?' I add just to finish him off.

I turn to go back inside.

'Are you alright?' Ariella shouts at me over the band.

'Yes. The man is an absolute worm.' I tell her.

We kiss, music swirling around us.

Lavender does not reappear.

Due to Natalie having to do some invigilating for an exam, we switch our rehearsal time around, and so we decide to attempt to have a quiet jam at The Dairy. No one has heard from Lavender for a week or so.

An hour after he should have arrived and no sign of him. Eventually I call him and he answers.

'I've been sitting outside in the car, wondering whether I should come in or not.'

I look out the window at his car parked directly underneath.

'Just come in, man.' I tell him.

He sheepishly enters, bringing bits of his kit with him.

'Do you want a hand?' I ask him.

He shakes his head and mopes off back to the car.

Ariella and I share a knowing glance.

He begins to build his kit.

'Are you alright?' I ask him. 'Listen, I'm sorry about the other night.'

'I don't wanna talk about it.'

'Well, we'll have to,' Ariella interjects, 'because I'm not playing music with this sour fucking mood in the room.'

'I'm just not happy about yous two getting together,' he replies without looking either of us in the face.

'Aye, but it's got nothing to do with you.' I tell him.

At this point, Natalie tells him, 'I admit that I was a bit worried about how it would affect the band, however, they are both adults, and I trust that they will keep their relationship out of the music.'

'If things go tits up,' Ariella tells him, 'then you can moan like a bitch, and say I told you so.'

'I already know how it's going to end up,' he says quietly.

Ariella, now very angry, snaps at him saying, 'Do you, now? You don't know fucking anything at all! From the moment you joined this band you have been following me about like a little puppy. You've told people things that I've told you in confidence… You need to grow up, Lavender!'

'I'm just trying to be a good friend,' he tells her.

'A friend?' She laughs. 'If you were a friend you'd be happy for us.'

'You know what, mate,' I jump into the conversation, 'if Ariella had come onto *you* instead of me, I don't think you would have turned her away. That's what this is all about isn't it?'

'No. It's not.'

Ariella: 'Yes it fucking is!'

Natalie, who has been quiet up until this point, adds, 'I have to agree with Ariella, you come across as obsessed with her.'

'I've just been trying to look out for her.'

A long, awful silence.

Then, Lavender: 'I think it might just be better if I

leave the band.'

'I don't want you to leave, mate,' I tell him, 'but if you stay then you'll have to accept me and Ariella being together.'

His pink lips twisted, not once has he removed his gaze from the floor.

'I'd better leave then,' he answers.

In silence, he packs his stuff up, loads his car, and drives away.

'I need a drink,' Ariella says, and pours herself a glass of red wine.

'What are we going to do now?' she adds after taking a drink.

'Advertise for a new drummer I suppose,' I say. 'I can make some posters, get them put up around town.'

'Thanks. That would be great.' Natalie smiles.

'It's a shame that we have to take a step back though,' Ariella sighs. 'We've got all these new songs sounding really good; it's going to be hard working on things with no rhythm.'

Then a thought occurs to me. 'Well, I could programme some drums, just for us to jam along to for now, until we find someone else.'

There is agreement to this idea, and I promise to have some done for our next rehearsal.

Ariella walks me to the Haymarket Metro station. She hugs me and won't let go. Kisses, lengthy embraces, against the wall.

'So this is us now then, is it?' I ask.

'This is us,' she replies.

LEAF II

XXI

My interest in Buddhism now gone – and so with my recent experiences with synchronicity, a renewed study of the occult is underway. I'm reading Crowley, LaVey, and Burroughs (of course), I keep thinking about Ginsberg's Blake experience. I read up on Egyptian, Norse and Eastern mythology – study demonology, witchcraft, the black arts, grimores, sigils, and invocations.

The power of will, the ability to influence via the heightening of the senses, appears to me to have real direct application to promote change. A form of chaos, a breakdown and abandonment of the rational mind directly influences that application, so I have learned empirically. This chaos is the opposite of the thought-watching brought upon by my meditation – an activity that has now exhausted me.

This destruction of rational thought is like the art of the Surrealists, and Burroughs/Gysin cut-up experiments; there is direct involvement, yet an arbitrary element. It is at once joyous and terrifying.

In less than a month, I feel more for Ariella than I did for Bunny in two years. I'm insane with it. I eat and sleep less. My behaviour has become bizarre – I cannot take direct control of my words or actions.

Sunday afternoon in mid-May. I drop by to see Pete, my friendship with him is important, even though my friendship with Lavender has ended. Pete is sympathetic.

'You know what Lavender is like,' he says.

Yet, I get the feeling that I won't be coming back to

153

speak with him any longer.

I meet the girls next door at The Chillingham. We have a quiet drink.

Natalie worrying about Lavender coming in.

I find myself overcome with a terrible melancholy – I stand up. 'I have to go.' I tell them.

Ariella looks concerned. 'Are you okay?'

'I need to sleep,' this is a lie, although it doesn't feel like one, 'I'm tired from work.'

I hug her, but don't kiss her and head for the door.

I look back and she's standing watching me. Everywhere a sadness and gloom – rain meets me as I walk, light and misty. I shiver, love burning – overcome – silence, drifting along awake and asleep.

Here and there, shadows lick the ground, the rain spits on and off.

That sudden noticeable change in oneself – and the old ghosts of who I was flickering over me. Skin peeling. All my thoughts are of the sensations that accompany Ariella – the way our tongues touch when we kiss – like silk snakes. The roundness of her curves, the way my hand follows them, flowing like the natural path of a river. A dangerousness about her, something in the eyes. *Les yeux sans visage.* My world stops in those orbs.

We click and 'schlupp.'

I detect a pre-meditative scheming in her motivations.

Another gig offer at Durham Uni – without a drummer we almost pull out, however Nat suggests we just do the gig anyway, using the pre-programmed drums I have put together.

'Johnathan will be there,' Ariella informs me, 'he's been pretty hurt by us splitting up. Maybe we should pretend not to be together for the night, he doesn't know about us yet. Plus, he's busy doing his exams. He's already told me that he's struggling with them, because I dumped him.'

This makes me angry. 'Didn't he just fuck off to a gig when you were pregnant?'

'Well, yeah. I'm not angry about that anymore though. I still don't know if I should tell him about us or not.'

'It's your decision,' I tell her, 'if it were me I would tell the truth. But, it's up to you.'

'He's moving back to London soon,' she ponders, 'I'd rather tell him to his face.'

It's a warm evening at the gig – endless blue skies that go on late into the night, blending and merging with the veil of dark that closes over like a lid.

Sitting outside on the grass, talking to Alice, listening to the funny way she pronounces her words.

'It's good of you to be okay with 'Arry talking to Johnathan all night,' she says.

She's been talking to him for the last two hours. I look over my shoulder and can see them in the distance, chatting.

I'm a bit green about it.

I decide to go for a piss – as I'm leaving the toilet Johnathan walks in.

'Hello, mate,' I say.

He ignores me and stands there having a piss. His ignorance of me makes me assume Ariella has told him everything.

Looking at the back of his curly haired head, his tweed jacket, brown shoes – a scene plays out in my head where I grab him by the hair and smash his face against the wall.

I've done nothing wrong, after all. She came on to me. Why am I the bad guy all of a sudden?

I find myself struck by the brutal violence of my vision. For so long, I've been calm though meditation, but there has been a slow trickle of darkness encroaching – a disturbing manic chaos growing inside.

For all the horror that would come from breaking his face against the tiles, I find myself wanting to do nothing more than just that.

Shaking with the violence of it, a cold grey screen of static rising over my vision, I turn and walk out of the toilets.

I find myself feeling like an actor in a film reedited to have different meanings to the actions – different words dubbed over, new music.

I feel like I stink of secret thoughts.

Later, back at The Dairy, Ariella explains:

'He took it really badly, says I've ruined his chances of doing well in his exams. I feel terrible about it now, what have I done?'

I hate him.

'You had to split up though, didn't you?' The question sounds rhetorical, but I mean it.

'Yes,' she replies, 'Johnathan is a good friend, but he was never right to be my lover. I've just hurt him really badly.'

Fuck Johnathan, I think.

'I don't suppose it will matter soon, he's moving back to London after his exams,' she sighs.

We go to bed and screw. Glimpses of her face aroused, flushed red, rolling in passion – wet stains on the bed. Shuddering orgasms – white tendrils of cum on her inner thigh.

She falls asleep and I'm awake feeling mad.

I hate my job. Leaving the warm bed sheets and her body, through the litter and early-morning. Pollock-looking vomit on Northumberland Street, down Central to the D.O.

Sun bursting, moon still visible, flames lick the horizon.

The noise and chaos of the office – blokes, they seem to me immature giant children – making stupid noises and talking about insubstantial, irrelevant twaddle. Bickering, schoolyard craic. I move about like a ghost, avoid everyone, and don't talk to anyone. A misanthropy frothing at the surface – I refuse to get up onto the primary. I buy a Mars bar, a cup of coffee in a beige plastic cup and sit on the toilet. Someone comes in and turns the light off. I'm shitting in the dark.

Out on the streets delivering letters – there is a rift and a pain inside me – in my tongue, in my aching violent teeth.

I'm in love, and it hurts. Doom, sadness – a connection that is animal, raw, and white when we fuck.

Days later, we're fucking. No voices, just grinding, I grind downwards. Afterwards, I mumble, incoherent,

157

lipless, and numb.

Struck heavy with terrifying feelings.

Her long black witch hair, sleek over her pale face.

All talk of poor little Johnathan. Now, I feel second best.

I begin to wonder. There is a new song, 'Saccharine.' She sings:

'…*Sugaring my tracks, mistress in the art of spinning pretty little traps. This is saccharine, and rest assured, she's choking, knows exactly, what she's doing…*'

I want to ask her its meaning, if it is about her luring me into being with her, because, so I assume, Johnny-boy is moving away. The thought of it is horrifying.

I swallow that ugly thought; I can feel it eating me like a cancer. Already a scab only picked from the inside.

Post orgasm, naked while our tongues flick in and out of each other's mouths.

I feel mad with our sex.

XXII

Drummers auditioned, not suitable. Mostly, they are poor; however, part of me doesn't want anyone else in this band.

Post-auditioning, Natalie voices what we're all feeling: 'The band is working really well with just the three of us. Can't we just play live using the electronic drums?'

I agree, yet I have the sensation of not caring about it all as much as I should, for the burning inside me for Ariella is incinerating everything else in my life.

'I'll go around town,' I offer, 'and visit some of the pubs that put on gigs, see if I can get in touch with the promoters.'

It turns into a little pub crawl on my own. I visit all the places that I know put on gigs, Trillians, The Tap & Spile, The Dog & Parrot, The Archer, and The Telegraph.

By the time I get home, I'm a little bit drunk, but I have a list of numbers to call.

After making the calls, I've lined up gigs for the next three months.

Gig at the Tap & Spile, underground, I've played here before with Parallel Charge. Jason, the promoter, is a large, round, sweaty man. He's very affable and I like talking to him. He's impressed with the band.

'Thanks, for giving us the gig,' Natalie says to him, 'next time we'll play all our best songs.'

'They weren't your best songs?' he asks sounding bemused.

'No, we're saving those for our gig at Durham University next week, we're getting paid quite a lot of money for it,' she explains.

Ariella rolls her eyes and pulls me away.

'She's such a social retard, sometimes,' she tells me. 'Why did she say that? She's got no concept of other people's feelings.'

After playing the gigs I've booked, more come in off the back of them. People seem impressed with us, and we get to know some local bands and promoters.

July. In the middle of the pavement on Fawdon Park Road, with chocolaty air from the Rowntree's factory permeating my nostrils, I stop to look at a Xmas card that is laying there out of place.

It seems so strange, sitting there, as if it were desperately holding onto some half-forgotten sentimentality. The picture on the front depicts a snowman, black buttons up his body, sparkling frosty around the edges.

I stand and look at it. This out of place card represents how I feel; we both are anachronisms, out of place and time.

I noticed a little fold of sellotape on the corner where it once hung on a wall. I desire to peel the card open to see what is inside, but instead I kick it to the kerb.

I think about it all the way to The Dairy.

I arrive with the intention of explaining my little moment to Ariella, yet both she and Nat are flustered and busy having a serious conversation.

'You both alright?' I ask.

'Dalglish, our landlord, has been round,' Nat explains.

'He's not renewing our contract on the house,' Ariella adds, 'so we need to find somewhere else to live. So we were wondering, my darling, if perhaps you'd like to move in with us, when we find a new house of course.'

My heart jumps. The prospect of sleeping in a bed every night with her gives me no reason to think about it.

'I'd love to,' I smile.

'It will be good for us, for making music. We can simply rehearse when we like, and create all the time.'

I nod. While I do agree with her, it isn't the reason that I want to hear regarding living together. I want her heart to ache for me, as mine does for her.

I stand looking at them both as if framed in a picture, trying to decipher a meaning.

August. We've become a little family, so much more without Lavender, and because of the love between Ariella and me. The three of us on Tynemouth beach – I have my camera, snapping away, laughing, as Ariella jumps in and out of the water. She squeals, holding her turquoise skirt up around her milky thighs, as the surf laps around her toes – soft sand in between them.

The three of us at my mother's house, sand everywhere – in bed, the three of us, laughing – I'm in the middle.

A while later, Nat leaves. Ariella and I – sand in her toes, hair, mouth, cunt. She has a shower, her hair slick, and darkest black afterwards.

All these moments seem unreal. I'm pulling connections together, to synchronise, yet all there is, is a horrible green monster.

'Johnathan,' she mentions, 'did this, did that, Johnathan did so and so, he once said this, he once said that,'

It burns me, hard, and green and awful. I am

desperate for her to reciprocate the irrational madness that I feel – yet she is rational, equal, boring. There is one-sidedness that chokes me to death. Jealousy unfolding.

I'm at work and can't go to view a house – but I trust Ariella's opinion. Later, they're both excited about it and want me to see it.

'It's in Jesmond,' Ariella explains, 'it's got lots of character, you will like it. I can arrange with Sally, the girl who is living there at the moment, for a time for you to come and have a look.'

'Alright,' I smile.

From the outside, the house is rickety-looking, up on a bank off the road. It overlooks the vast trees of Jesmond Dene, and I'm excited about the view. The street is quiet, a nice atmosphere. Inside, Sally, a large barrel of a girl, lets us have a look around – the carpets are old, the walls need painting, old furniture, the wooden stairs creak loudly, the kitchen is cold and ugly.

'You're right,' I tell Ariella, 'it has character, we should move in here.'

Sally, overhearing this, pipes in, 'Have you met Mr Geezer?'

'Is that the landlord?' Ariella asks.

'Yes, he's a bit of a character.'

Nat makes all the arrangements and we decide on a date to move in. Mr Geezer is at the house as we arrive. He is a rat-faced man, pink beady eyes behind jam jar glasses, hook-nosed, white haired, skinny. When he talks, his words and voice are like cardboard. He is a taxidermy human.

My mother, who has helped us move, is barging around the house pointing out all the terrible things that are wrong with it and giving Mr Geezer a piece of her mind.

'You can't rent a house like this, look at that, how much are you charging? This is a disgrace.'

He's not charging much, is what I think. I'm beginning to boil under my skin listening to her.

I drag her outside.

'You can't live here,' she bullies me, 'the place is a dump.'

I have words swarming around in my mouth. I wash them around my teeth, concerned that they may never leave my tongue.

Then they tumble out, 'For fucks sake,' I snap at her, 'I'm a grown man, and I can make my own decisions, why can't you keep your fucking nose out of my business, stop speaking for me. You think you're helping me, but you just make things worse.'

Her face flush red, slapped with words. A tear down her face. I'm not sorry.

'This is my decision,' I continue, 'it has nothing at all to do with you, I don't want your help and I don't want your fucking advice. So keep your big fucking nose out of my business.'

I turn around and walk back to the house. I'm still not sorry.

A frenzy of unpacking and sorting begins. Ariella and I begin to organise our bedroom. The bed is under the window; exhausted and unpacked we lie on it – sun coming through and resting on us.

'I can't believe we live together, Mr Cat.'

'Mr Cat?'

'Yes,' she giggles, 'because you are always dressed in black, and you are sleek and prowling, like a cat.'

'Am I?'

'Yes, you are, Mr Cat.'

Later that night in bed, curled up together, snoozing – sounds and sensation of a new home – traffic, trees rustling, rain beginning, the strange heat of the old radiators.

I wake with a start as something spatters next to my head – a glob of rain, gathering at a crack in the ceiling above my head, and now dripping on to my pillow.

'Wake up Ariella, we need to move the bed, there is a leak in the roof.'

Sleepily shifting the bed.

'I'll speak to the landlord tomorrow,' I tell her, as I head downstairs to get a pint glass from the kitchen. I place the glass under the drip and get back into bed, listening as the glass begins to fill.

Silence in between the ping of water on glass, then, punctuated by Ariella's phone buzzing – sleepily she reads her message.

'It's Johnathan,' she tells me and I tighten up, green with jealous rage, 'he wants to talk to me, sorry my darling, I won't be too long.'

She leaves the room and I begin to bubble into a boiling froth of hatred.

It is a scab I endlessly peel.

XXIII

Asleep – Ariella at my cock, I fill her mouth.

'Mr Cat, we are anachronisms,' she tells me in whispers, 'we are actors in an old film, cut out, and re-edited into a different film.'

Her nocturnal embraces, black and white.

New journey to work, same night bus – different bus stop. Up the bank, round the corner, moon hanging low, circle of stone, an unblinking eye watching me.

Brown plastic coffee cups at my sorting desk, dark circular stains overlapping each other.

At home, we name the house 'The Beat Hotel.' Water leaks through the ceiling from the bathroom into the kitchen when anyone uses the shower. I drop a cup into the bathroom sink; a chunk of enamel falls out, like a jigsaw piece. Rain drips through the ceiling in our room, wind whistles through the front door.

Mr Geezer promises to fix everything.

Ariella and I explore the Dene – although I already know much of it. Trees, ancient, wise, grand, voiceless – little stone bridges across the flowing burn, waterfalls gushing, as if the water is shouting in places, an old stone mill, iron gate. The quarry, enclosed in stone, old tea light candles in the dirt. There are little cottages scattered here and there, old and eerie. At Pets Corner, we talk to a Mynah bird – he is a friendly little thing – jet black, orange ring around his eye.

Little graves of the pet cemetery, a picnic field – we sit in the September sun, autumn encroaching.

Somehow, the talk always ends up on poor old Johnathan and I fold up and combust inside, like a burning piece of paper.

While she is at work – empty house, Nat at uni – infinite silences surround me, and a new sense of self, one unrestrained – I find myself in a whirl of freedom from parental oppression. The ability to be, and to say and to feel without imprisonment – a strange, beautiful, overwhelming sensation.

I write, alone, frantic, smoking hash, taking penis-looking Indian cubensis mushrooms, smoking salvia divinorum – a blazing, furious headache.

The freedom makes me wild, the taste of it – the smell of autumn creeping through the window.

Alone, October, baked out of my head, listening to Darkthrone's *Hate Them* with the windows open – crusty black metal, the naked trees of the Dene. I'm eating canned, creamed mushrooms. Ariella has left her computer on, and so I snoop like a dirty private dick. A poem called *'Little Lemon Leaf.'* It's all about how she has hurt poor baby Johnathan, and now she has to look after him. I want the curly haired faggot to die.

I am feeling used, tired – like nothing but good for a fuck, to keep the music going, flowing.

Ariella's birthday – a trip to Metroland. The world's fastest waltzer, the swinging pirate ship, mini-roller coaster. At the end of the day, Ariella says:

'Thank you for a day filled with wonderful sentiment, and beautiful gifts. I think I will remember this day forever.'

In the transformation that truly being myself and alone brings, I find my skin shed from my former self. Wandering the Dene, long and empty autumnal afternoons. Using my minidisc player and microphone to record the sounds of leaves underfoot, trees, wind, the earth – all synchronising, pulsing.

I sit in the quarry on a large stone, smoke a joint, then trudge about, lost in a red haze of anger, it gains momentum, as if moving forward, all-consuming hate propels me.

I invite it; let it have me, no longer decide to fight it – all reason crumbling.

I am tired and insane with love, and all thoughts obsess – there is a terrible beast under the surface, cracked, bound to tear me apart.

In amongst the trees, I feel there has been a summoning of some unknown demon. I recall Crowley in the Egyptian desert – summoning Choronzon, the dweller of the abyss.

Zazas
Zazas
Nasatanada zasas

I am possessed with love for Ariella, and a hate so deep for Johnathan that I simply want him to die.

We decide to record our music – two days at The Cluny Studios. The electronic drums sound clunking and too rigid on the recording.

'I'll make them have more groove for new songs,' I explain, 'more of an electro feel.'

167

We send the disc out to magazines, sell it at gigs, and give it away on the street.

The album cover is black with a purple heart both flowering a tulip and bleeding into a cup below it.

At home, we listen to our music, and then her phone rings, Johnathan interrupting. I want to take the phone from her hand and throw it out of the window.

Upstairs, I'm having a violent, jealous sulk. Yet all I can do is paint a mask over my hatred, pretend it's all right, while the green demon eats me like a cancer.

Trying to inflict a wound on Ariella, I get back in touch with Bunny. We talk on the phone, and then I reiterate all that we talked about back to Ariella. She seems unmoved.

All I can think about is how I want the world to burn and for there to be nothing left but our love in peace – and how I hate that she doesn't want that too.

December – as I walk along Matthew Bank, a car pulls up beside me.

'You fucking Goth,' followed by a barrage of eggs that mostly miss and splatter on the pavement and wall, but one gets me, the yellow of the yolk against the black of my coat.

I grit my teeth so hard with hatred that I think they will explode.

There is the anticipation of snow in the air, and as I enter the house from the cold, I discover a house boiling hot. Nat has the heating turned up full, and the contrast from the cold outside to the heat inside brings me out in a rash of itchy hives.

I'm cold on the inside, overheating on the outside, and frothing with anger. I feel blind, manic, and insane.

'Some dick head, charver cunt has just egged me from his car,' I snap at Ariella who is quietly lying on the bed reading my copy of Henry Miller's *Tropic of Cancer*.

'Oh no, are you alright, Mr Cat?'

'I fucking hate everyone. They wouldn't have done it on foot, the spineless cunts.'

'They're just childish idiots,' she says in a soothing voice.

She puts her arms around me. I'm rigid with a violent misanthropy.

I want to drink, and so from the fridge I begin working on the eight bottles of Bud that are in there.

Later, we sit down to watch a film – *Princess Mononoke* – just as it starts her phone rings. It's Johnathan. She disappears. After ten minutes of waiting, I turn the film off and go upstairs.

Half an hour later, she follows me.

'Don't you want to watch the film?' she asks poking her head into the bedroom.

I'm in bed with the covers up over my head. I flip them back and stand up.

'No, I don't want to watch the fucking film,' I snap at her.

Her face fills with fear. 'I'm sorry I had to talk to Johnathan again.'

'You're always talking to fucking Johnathan! Every fucking night! What about me?'

She looks like she's not sure what to say. 'I'm sorry, Mr Cat. He's depressed, and I still feel guilty.'

169

'Fuck him, the curly haired prick. Why doesn't he get a fucking life man?'

'Oh, fuck you,' she calmly says, and turns to leave the room.

From under the bed, I grab the length of metal shelving that I keep as a weapon against intruders and point it threateningly at her.

'Don't fuck with me, bitch,' I say through gritted teeth, 'you're lucky that ponce has moved away because I'd like to wrap this fucking thing around his ugly fucking head.'

She turns and storms out of the room. I throw the length of metal across the room, leaving a hole in the wall.

Days and days of apologies – and I feel sick for having to grovel like a sycophantic dog. I shower her with gifts, kisses, compliments. We fuck, and I spray white cum on her face.

Snow falling – at four in the morning, I trudge up Matthew Bank, my prints the first to be left in the soft, white blanket. At the top of the bank I turn and look at my trail all the way back to the house, amber streetlights in the dark illuminating my path.

When I return seven hours later, the snow is sludge, black and grey. I'm disappointed that my beautiful, clean path, where footsteps were so crisp, is now lost beneath dirty slushy gunk.

When I get home, Ariella waiting for me, her fawn-like face, and I watch her thin arms with blue and purple bangles on her wrist, as she writes secretly in her notepad.

170

'I've decided to go home for a little bit,' she explains, 'I wasn't sure if I was going to, but I would like to see mother and then father for Xmas.'

'Okay.' I say trying to hide my disappointment.

'But don't worry, I'll be back in time for Xmas day,' she adds, 'I want to spend it with you.'

'When are you going?'

'This Friday.'

Three days – my heart begins to hurt already.

'How long are you going for?'

'Two weeks.'

I feel like I want to crumple up on the floor and die. I sit beside her and put my arms around her – the bones of her waist and the corduroy material of her maroon skirt against my hands.

'I'll miss you.' I tell her.

'Don't worry, you silly boy,' she kisses my forehead, 'it's not forever.'

To me it is, and I'm already insane with it.

XXIV

I take Ariella to the train station – her train pulls away, my heart is cracking. At home, left alone with Natalie – there is a gap opening up between us, a deep unspoken resentment. I find her in the living room with two of her friends, a couple, Pierre and Ali. Pierre, or Pee as everyone seems to call him, is the overly opinionated type – and likes to voice his opinion whether you want to hear it or not. I find him unbearably arrogant, and I would like to throw the cunt through the front window. His girlfriend Ali, however, is quiet and reserved. She is strange to look at; her shoulders are incredibly square, making her resemble a long, fleshy, human rectangle. Her eyes are large, blue, and glistening – brown hair falls about her face.

Pee is making comments about the band. He is neither a musician nor is he particularly well listened.

I sit in the old brown chair, listening to him waffle on. I stand up and make a point of leaving the room while he is talking, in particular, while addressing me.

Later, Nat says, 'You were rude to Pee and Ali.'

'So fuck. He's an annoying prick.'

'But they're my friends,' she has a look of disbelief at what I've just said on her face, 'and I want them to feel welcome.'

'Fair enough, I just don't see why I should listen to him talking about things he knows nothing about.'

'Well, maybe just stay out of the room when they're here,' she says, turning to go into her room.

I give her the middle finger behind the door and call her a bitch.

Two days later, Nat leaves to go to stay with her parents on their houseboat for Xmas. I'm alone – for the first time in my life, truly alone. The feeling that no one is going to walk through the door is overwhelming, and I'm not sure what to do with myself. I have ten days to spend in whatever way I wish, with no one to bother me, but when I sit in the silence of the house, I find that I'm missing Ariella – more than I can deal with – and I'm dying for her to return.

I notice Nat had been trying to affix a lock on her bedroom door. Naturally curious I peek into her room, as I've yet to venture inside it. It's neat and tidy, nothing weird, just typical girly stuff. On her bed, her violin in its case. Probably the reason she was fitting the lock, I presume, as it is worth a lot of money. I had initially thought her attempts to put a lock on the door had been to keep me out – which got me thinking about going in.

I open her drawers and paw at her knickers, then pull my cock out through my zip and begin to rub myself off with one of her stockings. There is a laundry basket in the corner and I rummage through it looking for dirty underwear – I find a pair of panties, I smell them, enjoying the aroma of her cunt as I bring myself off.

A few days before she is due to return home Ariella informs that she is planning to stay with Johnathan in London for a few days. I'm so ill with guilt, hatred, and jealousy that I can't articulate anything to her about how I feel, and so I simply say nothing about it.

A day later, I decide bring about synchronistic events to either physically destroy Johnathan, or to remove him from Ariella's mind altogether.

The Destruction Ritual – I'm high on adrenaline and hash – music, in the form of Dimmu Borgir, swells. I've converted our practice room – on the table, black cloth, dagger, statue of Baphomet, black candles, incense, a chalice filled with absinthe.

The invocation of infernal names – the dagger, held outwards, pointed to the four directions of the infernal princes – I consume the absinthe, read aloud the destruction ritual. I feel heightened – senses alive, buzzing – I'm manic and all I can think about is sticking the silver dagger into Johnathan's neck.

Next day I'm trying to forget about the whole thing, trying to rationalise everything – she wouldn't sleep with him, she loves me – trying to put him out of my mind, trying to cool my rage – but I go round in circles, the same violent thought eternally recurring.

Ariella returns – I'm almost in tears at the train station as she disembarks. I die a little when we embrace.

'I missed you so much,' she tells me, 'I've forgotten what a beautiful boy you are, Mr Cat.'

On Xmas day we walk to my parents' house in Fawdon, it is cold – Ariella is carrying the panther soft toy that I bought her, it is jet black and looks like a small cat.

'He reminds me of you,' she says.

Nat calls her on her mobile.

Merry Xmasses all round. I thank Nat for the new

174

minidisc player that the two of them have bought me. I'm overjoyed at this, as it means I no longer have to be precious about my other minidisc player, as I use it for the backing drums.

'You have to keep your new minidisc player for the band,' Nat tells me.

I tell Ariella what she said.

'Oh for fucks sake,' she sighs, 'she really is an emotional retard.'

After visiting my parents, we spend Xmas day alone, later, I'm violently drunk, shouting at the T.V.

'You're a pack of cunts!' I slur.

'For fucks sake,' Ariella laughs nervously, 'it's *Oliver Twist!*'

'Fuck off,' I tell her, seriously.

We sit in a horrible silence.

Four in the afternoon and I go to bed, a black and angry veil coming down over my eyes – I sleep heavy, cotton sheets, dehydration, the sensation of Ariella getting into bed, sleep and nightmares in sweat.

New Year, 2004.

I am ill with paranoia – I assume nothing but reverse psychology from Ariella. A violence in me – everything she says, there is double meaning.

Gigs, all around town – the bleakness of January, sycophants lurking around her.

'This is Dom and Gary,' Ariella introduces me to two young men.

Gary is fat and ginger like a teddy bear, Dom is short with long hippy hair and a mouth and chin that protrude out from his face.

We shake hands. They love our band. They are in a

band themselves.

'What's your band called?' I ask.

'No Division,' Dom says.

They are both canny – we discover we like lots of the same music, know the same people.

'We'll come check out your band,' I promise.

'They were nice boys, weren't they?' Ariella says to me later at home.

'Yes,' I reply, not able to hide the distrust in my words.

'What's wrong?'

'Well, because we always have to pretend not to be a couple when we are performing, you always get snivelling dogs sniffing around you.'

'Not everyone is after me in that way, and besides I love you, not anyone else, Mr Cat. It's all for the music, isn't it?'

I can feel my blood beginning to boil. What I would give to feel like our love was special, what I would give for the whole world to fuck off.

'I hate men,' I tell her.

'You hate men?' she laughs.

I get into bed, cold, hard, and full of hate.

Sunday morning in January, Ariella and I walk through the Dene to Rehill's. I buy a glass bottle of coke, holding it and feeling the weight of it in my hand.

'There's something lovely about it being in a glass bottle,' I tell her.

We're on the wide bridge with the red path, and black elaborate railings. On one side it overlooks a motorway, the other the green grass of a picnic area.

Three lads, early twenties, hanging over the railing, towards the Dene. One has a megaphone.

'Goths!' he shouts at us through the megaphone as we pass, 'stinking fucking Goths!'

I furiously move towards him.

'No!' Ariella cries, 'it's not worth it!' and she grabs at my arm.

I pull free and before he can do anything about it, I've rammed my knee into the stomach of the guy with the megaphone.

I watch him doubled up on the floor in pain while one of his mates is posturing like a boxer and the other one stands back, face white as a sheet.

Boxer-boy lunges at me and now we're on the floor, scuffling and trying to get punches in. He smacks me in the nose – blood smeared across my face, my long leather coat is torn. Ariella is crying – she tries to pull me away from him. I watch as she falls to the floor on her backside.

In a furious rage, I push past the kid – pick up the megaphone and crack him across the head with it. There is blood, a river of it across his face.

He's on the floor crying, 'I'm blind! I'm blind!'

But it's just blood in his eyes. The scared one is on his phone; it's time to leave. I drag Ariella off through the Dene at a pace.

'We should have just waited for the police,' she is whimpering, 'you've really hurt that boy.'

'Good,' I reply, 'I hope the cunt dies.'

'That's horrible,' she sobs.

'Stop fucking crying,' I snap at her, while dabbing at the blood still leaking from my nose. 'We need to get home.'

'Maybe you should see a doctor?' she suggests.

'I'm fine.'

At home, I spend a long while cleaning blood, snot, and gunk from my nose – It looks swollen already, but I don't think it's broken. I'm nervous and keep looking out of the window for the sign of flashing blue lights.

XXV

Everywhere there are leeches, psychic vampires – I try to make the world smaller, to crush everything beyond the realm of the bubble of our love.

Natalie lingers like a fart: stinking around, crying, and snivelling when Ariella and I show each other affection, and so we have to hide it. Smaller we recede, shrivelling up.

We are in bed, reading. 'She is fucking weak,' I tell Ariella, 'it's not our fault we love each other, I'm sick of her lonely stupid face.'

Ariella has been sheepish since the incident in the Dene.

'Her cunt must be all dried up,' I add, 'and I'm so sick of the way she yaks on and on.'

Later Nat comes into the bedroom and I hold my book up over my face to ignore her.

'That was really horrible,' Ariella says sounding sad, 'you just ignored her, what's wrong with you at the moment?'

'I'm sick of her, she's jealous of our relationship, I feel as if we are hiding our love. We can't be affectionate anywhere anymore.'

'We still can, when we are alone.'

February, my birthday. A gig at the Chillingham – we play really well, there is a good atmosphere – all negativity forgotten for the night, a little family again.

Outside, Ariella's warm body against me in the cold – her green/black coat, the way the lapels fold, rounded down her shoulders – the mole on her face, diamond eyes. The taste of red wine on her lips.

179

'I'm sorry about the lack of affection in public,' she says hugging me, 'I just want the band to make it so badly.'

Valentine's Day – the corridor by the front door in darkness, cold through the crack in the door. The living room framed by light – Nat sitting alone, crying.

Ariella and I about to head out for a romantic meal.

'Are you alright?' she asks Nat.

I know why she's crying – because nobody loves her.

Down the street, I say, 'Fuck her, man, she's a little vampire. Why the fuck should we feel guilty because we are in love?'

'She's just lonely.'

'So fuck? She was deliberately crying so you would see it.'

'Maybe I should go back and see if she is okay.'

'For fuck's sake, man.'

Moments of happiness come and are spoiled – always soured by Ariella's inability to keep anything sacred. A dead afternoon, a nowhere in the middle of existence.

'Will you piss on me?' she asks.

She takes her clothes off; they crumple on the floor, her skirt a maroon puddle. She climbs into the bath – blackish tide marks up the side, blue-sky paint peeling, floorboards exposed.

I take my cock out through the zip and piss on her.

My piss is clear without a trace of yellow. I finish, dripping, and she takes my cock in her hand, slowly pulls the skin over the hood – tumescent now, veins filling.

In her mouth. The serpent wet – a lubricated leviathan. Eruptions onto her skin.

March. London – three gigs over a long weekend. The 12 Bar, The Union Chapel and Jack Beards. There is a black cloud hanging over me already, as we pack the night before. On the train, I escape by listening to music – Dimmu Borgir.

We are staying with Nat's old college chums, Julia and Scott, in Hammersmith. They are both nice, yet I find myself full of misanthropic venom towards their middle-class house and values. Ariella and I will sleep in the enormous attic room – we will fuck here, we have decided. The room is white and creamy with a skylight, low ceiling, en-suite. I spread out on the bed for a while, hard pillows.

The 12 Bar in Soho – old and creaky. Zane the promoter is a slimy, greasy, suit-wearing snake. He ignores me and only speaks to the girls.

'What a cunt,' I tell Ariella once he is out of range, 'he refused to acknowledge me.'

'I know,' she sympathises, 'let's just focus on playing well; I'm nervous enough as it is.'

The stage is tiny and weirdly designed, so that I can see the feet of the people on the next floor, and not the audience watching us.

I have to mingle and chat. Londoners – gig offers in Morocco, compliments – blokes buzzing around the girls like flies on shit. I wonder if Ariella would suck someone's cock for a record deal.

The green demon rears its ugly head and I disappear

181

off on my own. The little seating area upstairs, I am alone – I kick a table over and smash a glass hard onto the floor, hate bubbling in my throat.

Ariella finds me, finds my destruction.

'What have you done?'

Next day, Ariella, 'I'm going to see Johnathan tomorrow night, I hope you don't mind?'

I hope he dies, I think.

'No of course not,' I lie, 'I had thought about going to catch up with Bunny actually.'

We head off to Soho together, mooch around the porn shops – a difficult silence given off by blokes in the shop, as Ariella and I openly converse about the cocks and cunts on the covers. We buy a VHS – a latex and bondage fetish movie.

'Nat wants us to go and have tea with her, Julia, and Scott at a pub in Hammersmith.'

'Fuck them.'

'Why are you always so nasty?'

'Because I want to be with you. It's never just us, is it? There is always someone else involved. We can never be alone, and I'm sick of having to pretend that we are not together when we do gigs.'

'Is that why you were angry last night.'

'Yes.'

'I'm really sorry, Mr Cat.'

'Can't we just have some food alone? Can't we even just spend one evening alone? Fuck Nat.'

'Alright, but I feel bad about it. Julia and Scott have been kind enough to put us up for the night.'

Fuck them, I think. Fuck everyone.

Back at the house, we all sit round and watch the

porn. Doctors in PVC, cocks and cunts, cut out holes in clothes – nipple pumps, spunk.

A funny atmosphere. Smell of stiff sex in the air.

Ariella is getting excited and she drags me off to bed. She sucks my cock and I'm up the wall. The bed is soaked in our juices.

Next day, Ariella goes off to see Johnathan and I hate her for it. I take the train from Hammersmith to Hendon. Bunny and I head to Camden, I get very drunk – talk to some bloke about dub music, I buy him a drink; he gives me a CD of him singing. I decide never to play the disc. I'm not interested in talking to Bunny – I'm drunk and I hate myself. I sleep in my clothes on the floor in Bunny's room – pencils, fag-ends, CDs all digging into my skin.

I wake up dry in the throat, bleary eyed, ill and reeling, hung over, sick. That feeling of alcohol like poison in my veins. I bid Bunny farewell – on the way to the station I buy a Mars bar and some Lucozade. At Hendon, I miss the train by a second and have to wait for another. On the next train it stops one station past Hendon at Golders Green and I have to get off for some unknown reason. Tube worker tells passengers there's been a crash up ahead, and so I have to get the bus back to Hammersmith. I don't know where I'm going, and begin to feel apprehensive with booze sickness and the unfamiliar drive on the bus. I'm worried I won't know where to get off.

Zombified – I make it back to Hammersmith. I lay down on the bed in the attic room. Ariella has been in the shower, her hair clinging to her shoulders. I notice

183

the way her breasts sit in her vest top as she sits down, her thin lips pursed.

'You reek of booze,' she tells me.

I have a shower. I lie in the towel on the bed next to her, rest my head on her shoulder. A silence. I show her my semi-tumescent prick under the towel. Then the grip of her hand around it, fingers over meat.

The Union Chapel – there is no bass amp for me, and so I'm to play through the p.a. system. It sounds terrible, like wet farts.

A foul mood creeping over me – I put no effort into the performance. After, I have a few drinks, put my headphones in, and ignore everyone.

The other band that night, the drummer was once in The Animals I'm informed. Grey clown-hair, dickhead suede rocker-jacket.

'You've got your own personal music?' he asks noticing my headphones.

'Fuck off.' I tell him.

'What did you say to me?'

'You heard you horrible old cunt, now fuck off before I push you down these fucking stairs.'

Later, Zane: 'I don't appreciate you speaking to Marty like that.'

'Well you can fuck off as well you southern prick.'

'I don't know what your problem is mate, but you'll not get any more gigs out of me with that attitude.'

'Here man, you're only after the girls, you slimy bellend. You couldn't even organise a bass amp, what sort of promoter are you?'

Nat is unimpressed. However, we have to put it all aside while we do an interview for a London fashion magazine. I'm so drunk that I don't care anymore.

Later, Nat: 'You've spoilt everything; we probably won't get any more gigs in London now.'

'Get fucked, pet.'

The whole world is my enemy.

'I'm sorry about the last two nights,' I apologise as we are setting up in Jack Beards, 'but you must admit that Zane is a lecherous, smarmy twat.'

Silence. I'm unforgiven. I don't care. We run though sound check. I'm a black cloud.

I mooch around the pub in a sullen mood. A funny old man, quick-lipped, jazzy-fingered, and interesting, he starts speaking to me, his words a funny southern rhythm.

'Hi, I'm John Clarke, the beat poet,' he informs me. 'I heard you playing before, I like your sound.'

'John Clarke?' I say. 'Like John *Cooper* Clarke.'

'No, no,' his white hair and friendly face under a little blue beret, 'that's the *other* John Clarke.'

'Do you like Burroughs?' I ask him.

'Of course, of course,' he says hopping a bit with enthusiasm, 'and Kerouac, and Ginsberg and all the other beats.'

I roll my sleeve up and show him the tattoo on my inner forearm of the front cover of *My Education: A Book of Dreams.*

'Wow,' he tells me, 'that's how I like my jazz!'

I swap him one of our CDs for a book of his poetry and he signs it for me.

Later, after we have played, he is on stage, freestyling jazz poetry.

185

'And if you see this guy here, he'll show you his Burroughs tattoo!' He drops into a poem.

On the train home, I think about him saying this, as I stare empty-eyed at the countryside splattering past.

XXVI

I make apologies for my behaviour in London. The sun through the windows in our room, spring sneaking in. There's no carpet on the floor, just the brown of painted wood, and rugs with dreadlocks. Ariella and I sit on the bed. She is fawn-like; her face sometimes reminds me of a deer; pursed lips, grey/green eyes.

'We'll never get anymore gigs through Zane now,' she tells me, 'and we need gigs in London. No one is ever going to notice us in Newcastle.'

'That's not true. We're making a name for ourselves; we've had good reviews in a few magazines and on the net. Even if some fucking dick heads hate the programmed drums.'

'I know,' her head on my shoulder, 'it's just, we have to make it. I can't keep washing old men's balls and wiping their arses for a living. Plus, you should let me help you with the drum programming for the new songs.'

I run a sympathetic hand through her hair and don't reply.

'Are you alright, though?' She asks me with a hint of sadness. 'You seem so angry all the time. I mean, I know you've told me all about how you don't know your dad, and your childhood traumas, and you hate your job too, but we have each other, Mr Cat. Don't we?'

'Yes, of course,' I tell her. I'm about to say more then she cuts in:

'We trust each other, don't we? You know I don't have any romantic feelings for Johnathan. I love you.'

'I love you too.'

Silence, traffic on the road, the green of the trees in the Dene. Afternoon emptiness.

She goes downstairs and I sit and feel like a little boy trapped in a man-suit. She trusts me to spend a night with Bunny, yet I can't even bear her mentioning Johnathan.

I am green jealousy made flesh. I sit and drown in anger and uncontrollable fury. This is hate in the form of possession, and I taste it, disgusting and vile, in my tight mouth.

The train that I narrowly missed in Hendon was derailed, killing five people. Arriving at the station a few minutes earlier, I could have been on it. I could be dead.

I take this as some kind of synchronistic sign. I'm explaining this to Triple-X Terry, the promoter for the gig night at The Telegraph. He is a wispy, smoke of a man. All yellow and nicotine behind foggy sunglasses that he wears even when indoors. He looks like a walking tumour.

Nat comes up and says, 'I've dropped my ring down the back of that sofa, do you think you might be able to reach it?'

I peer down into the dark, using the light from my phone as a torch. Fluffs, a wine glass, several coins, cigarette packets. I slide my arm in, elbow deep and fish around feeling for her ring. I pull up some of the coins, and then have another look for her ring. I spot it, slide my arm back in and try to bend it round to pick up the ring. I get hold of it – but when I try to pull my arm back out it is trapped at the elbow, and I can't spin it back round to pull it out.

'Fuck. I'm stuck.' I'm a little bit panicky.

'We're on in five minutes,' Nat tells me.

I try to force my arm out but it won't budge. The whole pub is watching now, and I try to wriggle my arm around looking for the best way to pop it out. The fabric of the sofa is burning and cutting my arm as I shift it about. It won't come, and so in desperation I yank it as hard as possible, pulling my arm out but also tearing the skin off all along my forearm.

I play the gig with a ripe-red wound stinging and dripping with blood.

After, I talk with Dom and Gary who have turned up to watch us. They are nice lads and invite us to go and see their band The Divide the following week.

Later, Ariella:

'They're nice boys. I know you say you hate men, but it will be good for you to have some friends.'

'I don't need friends. I've got you.'

'We can't live in each other's pockets all the time. It will do you good to have other males to talk to.'

Why can't the whole world just die and leave us alone, I think.

We go to watch The Divide at Trillians. They sound great, really heavy and tight. Gary's kick drum sounds like a bag of conkers every time it slaps the skin. They play a cover of Metallica's *Sad But True*.

We get drunk together afterwards. Outside Gary scoops up Ariella and she has a ride on his shoulders. I'm so ill with green that I want him to tumble into the road and fall under a car. I'm drunk; I decide not to fight my silly feelings. I'm angry that, in comparison to Ariella's sophisticated emotions, I'm a Cro-Magnon cave dweller.

Destroy all rational thought.

In bed that night:

'They really are nice boys,' Ariella tells me.

'Aye. I'm sure they're only sniffing around you for one thing.' I turn away from her to face the other way.

'Listen, men and women can be friends you know. Just because they want to be our friends, doesn't mean they want to fuck us.'

'You know nothing about men.' I tell her.

'Oh don't I? Really. Well you're friends with Nat, aren't you? You don't want to fuck her do you? Or do you?'

I laugh at this.

Silence, I turn off the lamp. In the darkness awhile.

'Will you put your cock in me?'

I flip it out, stiff. Slide up her purple nightie, finger her hole until damp. Slide it in and out, come.

'Hold it in me,' she instructs.

A moment then she shudders with her orgasm.

'I wish you could keep your dick in me forever.'

We're putting together a batch of new songs. Ariella wants to aid me in putting the electronic drums together. I have to work in a particular fashion – concentrate, edit, rearrange. The last set of drums I made were straight patterns to replace Lavender's beats. The new ones are purposely electronic and industrial. I'm emulating Orbital, The Prodigy, Nine Inch Nails, and Ministry.

190

Ariella is sitting behind me on the old brown settee. The living room appears to be subsiding and slopes downwards in the corner where I'm at the computer putting the drums together.

'Can you make, like a fish noise on this bit, but a fish that is flying.' Ariella asks.

I have no idea what she means, and I'm becoming annoyed with her lack of technical knowledge.

'It's just how I explain things,' she adds, 'I'm sorry if it makes me sound like a retard. Oh, oh, this bit should sound like volcano, you know, roaring and whooshing.'

I look at her in dismay. 'If you want me to change the tempo, or the speed of the high-hats, or the sound of the kick-drum or something, then I can do that. But, I'm not a fucking sound-effects wizard,' I snap at her.

'Sorry. I know I'm not explaining very well. Can I have a go?'

She's sitting on my knee making a mess of my work.

'I'd like to go to back to college and study music production again,' I tell her, 'I already have a HE access qualification.'

'Maybe you should then,' she replies.

We work on the new songs everyday over a month, while still gigging at the usual haunts in Newcastle, and lining up more gigs and booking in to record a five-track demo of our new songs in April. The thought of going back to college has become a reality, and I decide to apply to return that September to do a foundation degree in music production.

I want to have a vastly superior knowledge of

191

putting our electronic drums together, so that Ariella
will desist in asking me to conjure up bizarre noises.

A gig for Triple X Terry at The Stout on a wet, windy
Tuesday. We pay twenty quid to hire out his p.a.
system, hoping to pull the money back on the door.

No one but Gary and Dom turn up, and so we end
up paying to play. Ariella is upset.

'I'm not paying that greasy bugger to play in an
empty and dark room to no one,' Ariella tells me.

'I'm sorry,' I explain.

The night cut short. Ariella talking to some bloke
upstairs. I'm staring at him, dagger-eyed.

'You alright?' Dom asks.

'Aye, I'm just sick of having to pretend we're not a
couple when we play live.'

'Well, you know she's probably just being friendly.'

I bite my lip.

'At the end of the day mate, she's going home with
you.'

His words ring true, but a terrible monster in me
doesn't want to accept the truth. Trapped in my black
gut, I come to realise the nightmare that I'm on a
winding path of self-destruction. It bubbles under the
surface; I can taste it, green and red with anger and
jealousy. There is no question of succumbing to it; it
is in possession.

'We're going to see Killswitch Engage in two weeks,
if you want to come.' Dom breaks my sickness. And
then in May we're going to Download, you'd be
welcome to come along.'

I'm surprised and confused at this extended hand of
friendship. I agree to go to both.

Later in bed, I tell Ariella about it.

'You need friends,' she tells me.

'I have you.'

'You need more than just me, silly. It will do you good to have some mates.'

I say nothing. Just breathe. The soft smell of the washing powder on the sheets. Ariella's breasts hidden behind a thin, lilac nightie. My teeth pressed together so hard I think they will explode.

I go to sleep on a thought:

I want everyone in the world to die except for us.

I reach my arm across her foetal body, my front to her back. I hold on to her for dear life, hiding from my monsters.

XXVII

Inside a large white canvas tent in the middle of Leazes Park in the centre of Newcastle. Near the lake that is full of murder weapons and shopping trolleys. Island in the middle, where mallards, Canadian geese, and swans nest. Boats, men fishing for brown trout, and people staggering around drunk and high.

We're performing at the annual Green Fest. The p.a. system is massive – my electro-drums thunder through them and I love it. I've never heard them sound so enormous. A massive crowd is watching us. The sun is shining, and I have an angry wasp hovering next to my face. I try to keep still and carry on playing, hoping it will go away.

Even though I expressed that I didn't want to, we're playing *Turtle Dove*. I've told Ariella that it sounds exactly like *Cornflake Girl* by Tori Amos, and that she seems to write the same old plinky-plonky tunes on the piano. I didn't mean it to be offensive, but she has taken it that way.

The strange soft-hard sound of applause.

Gary and Dom are watching us.

'It's funny that you play this kind of music mate,' Dom tells me, 'considering you listen to death and black metal.'

'I like lots of different genres of music,' I tell him.

A few days later, we're rehearsing. I get sick of listening to Ariella and Nat working on one particular bit of a new song. I'm tired from work and decide to go to bed and read.

I can still hear them from upstairs. Nat is continually

retuning her violin. It begins to annoy me. Then Ariella starts to sing *Lemon Leaf,* her song about how she has hurt poor Johnathan. I've been thinking about what Dom said at the Green Fest.

I lose control; fling my copy of *Cities of the Red Night* across the room. A storm on the stairs, thundering feet. I kick open the door to the music room. The blue walls an ocean, beyond the red mist in my eyes.

'Will you two shut the fuck up!' I scream.

Their eyes filled with animal fear. Mouths sewn shut with terror. I am hate personified. I pick up my old bass, the silver one that I've had since I was twelve.

'I'm fucking sick of this pussy-music.' I tell them through bared, snarling teeth, and white-foamy spit.

I take the bass through to the little back garden, a messy jungle tangled with unnameable weeds, plants, and trees. I swing the bass down from the neck on to the first concrete step that leads up. It shatters the slab and the bass. I bring it down again, a repeated act filled with pure, pleasurable violence. I imagine the concrete is Johnathan. I imagine it is everyone on this stinking planet. Over again I bring it down in swings filled with hate and hurt.

The path is smashed. The bass destroyed, and there are cracks in my heart. I walk back up the stairs, their faces framed through the door like lost little girls.

Killswitch Engage at Newcastle University students' union bar. The ceiling is dripping with moisture. In the pit, sweaty bodies slam in to each other. Over-priced pints served in plastic cups that spill, leaving hands and shoes sticky.

I'm wearing my Cannibal Corpse, *Butchered at Birth* t-shirt. This is my home. This is my music. It is more than just an admiration, or an appreciation of an art form. It goes beyond respect, beyond acknowledgement of skilful musicianship. I feel metal in my blood. Raw, driving, violent.

I feel welcomed into friendship with Gary and Dom.

Dom says, 'Let's get together for a jam sometime.'

I say, 'Okay.'

It is the 8th of April 2004. Today it is one hundred years of the Crowlian new aeon. I smoke a joint and think about this. Flip though *The Book of the Law*. I think about my own *will*.

In the Dene, I find myself detached, stepping beyond myself. New leaves, spring born, and the sound of running water. The colour of ancient stone, the quarry, the old mill – green and yellow mosses. Somewhere far off, auditory hallucinations that are voices, whispering terrors at my ear. I walk head down, circling, directionless. The world folds in, red haze blossoms over my eyes in angry eruptions. All I can think is hateful thoughts.

In the blackness inside, an enlightening revelation stares back at me from fuzzy edges – I am dirt. I am earth. I am animal. I am the violence that no one wants to acknowledge, the rage swept away by politeness. The hate locked up, the fury choked quiet.

I want to hide yet I can't look away from my monster. I pick up a stone, smooth and palm-perfect fitted, and hold it, as if to distract myself.

I understand that deep down I want to be the monster, because I am deluded into thinking I am more than just an upright animal. I know that everywhere I run my demon is right behind me, waiting. I'm worse than most because I deluded myself into thinking that spirituality was real, that Buddhism and meditation and woolly thoughts led to salvation from the self. The self is a disease and you can't hide from or cure the horror that is this flesh.

I keep moving, red-eyed, and cotton-mouthed, repeating to myself, 'Zazas, Zazas, Nasatanada Zazas.'

Two weeks later and we're at The Cluny Studios recording a new demo. Ariella asks Dave Tony, the studio engineer, if he can make all sorts of stupid swishing and whirring noises.

'Like a fish in the sky.' She tells him.

Hearing Ariella sing in isolation, with the music stripped off.

'We are three butterflies/ we're blowing in a violent breeze/I have to be careful not to drink from the wrong bottle, I'll pay.'

I feel sick and sad in my gut.

'Our wings are made of powder and paint/you make the first move, we'll make the last move.'

I feel tears hiding behind my eyes.

Next day, Nat:

'There will be some A and R people at the Generator gig next week. They are looking to review demos at the gig, we should take ours.'

Next week, A and R men:

Our demo begins to play.

'This sounds too much like Kate Bush. Why try to be Kate Bush? Kate Bush is Kate Bush.'

Ariella's sad and irritated face.

There are local acts on, all trying to grab the attention of someone from a record company.

We play. Then I recognise the next act; it is Lisa, Dan Thujone's girlfriend.

I spot him in the crowd. 'Hello,' I say to him, 'I haven't seen you since my last gig with Parallel Charge.'

'You must be having fun with these two sexy bitches,' he laughs.

I nod. 'Your lass has an amazing voice mate,' I tell him. 'So what's happening with Parallel Charge?'

'Nothing now man, we split up.'

I tell him I'm sorry to hear that.

Later, I'm a little bit drunk. Dan is at the bar, a look of despair on his face.

'You alright man?'

'Aye,' he sighs, nods towards Lisa, 'she's just hard work sometimes. I see you're drinking anyways, what happened? You used to be teetotal.'

I shrug my shoulders. I have no real answer to that question. All I can say is, 'Fanny, mate.'

He laughs at this, and I can see we've broken some ice that we never managed while I was in Parallel Charge.

At the end of the night:

'Listen, mate,' I tell him, 'don't suppose you fancy a pint sometime?'

'Aye, alright.'

I give him my mobile number.

The girls are in a bad mood, the night didn't go as planned. The A and R men didn't like our demo and we didn't get spotted. For some reason, I don't care.

198

'I think we need to move to London,' Ariella tells me in bed. 'We'll never get spotted here.'

Part of me would like that, part of me wouldn't. I don't want to say yes or no.

'Yes,' I tell her. I mean maybe. 'You're right; we're more likely to get spotted.'

'Could you transfer your job to London?'

'I dunno, probably.' I lie. 'I would still like go to back to college though.'

'Maybe you could do that in London?'

'Maybe.'

The talk of London goes on. I start a conversation with Ariella about moving into a house in Newcastle together instead, alone. Like a proper couple.

'I'd rather buy than rent.' She tells me. I sense a bit of sad resignation in her voice. She says, 'I guess London will be too expensive for us. Maybe in a few years.'

We visit a mortgage advisor at the Halifax bank. Late April. The thought of not living with Nat excites me, and I hope I can create a little world for just Ariella and me. I hold Ariella's hand, tucking her little finger in, like a hidden worm. There is a bright sun in the sky; there is hope.

The advisor, after a few clicks at her computer, says we can have a mortgage of sixty-thousand. We arrange a few viewings. An afternoon spent traipsing from one grubby, horrible, one bed flat in the arse-end of Newcastle to the other. Home, deflated.

'What about trying to get something through the council?' I suggest.

'What about London?' Ariella replies.

199

Ariella is at work while I visit a council flat in Cruddas Park. It is a three room, depressing little box. The tiny kitchen and living room combined. I know these flats, as I've delivered post here a few times. The combined brown smell of cooking, coughs that emanate from cardboard walls. Drunks, the smell of piss in the lifts. Voices that echo, ghostly through corridors. I don't want to live here.

After explaining this to Ariella, she tells me that Nat is moving in with a friend from uni, so that we definitely can't stay on where we are now.

'We're just going to have to rent again,' she breathes with contempt, 'we can't fucking afford the deposit.'

I sit in silence. A gnawing terror at the front of my mind.

'Oh, by the way,' she adds, 'father wants to know if we want to visit him for a holiday in June maybe. I thought we could drop into see my mother along the way.'

Her father lives in Dorset, her mother in Reading.

'Yes,' I tell her, 'of course.'

XXVIII

Ariella's computer left on while she is at work. I rummage through her emails to Johnathan. His soppy letters saying he still loves her.

In the haze – a sleepy awake nightmare I am living in, I realise I truly want him to die. All my thoughts tinted with a ferocious red terror.

I am more than just man. I am animal upright. Selfish, violent, hate-filled, empty of empathy. My hate for Johnathan feels transcendent – taking me beyond the deluded idea that I am more than dirt personified and that my life has meaning and spirit because I am human. No spirit, no soul. Just the grit between my teeth, blood pumping, existential agony.

Walpurgisnacht. Witches Night. I am alone in the house. Another destruction ritual.

I shave my head down to the skin. Dressed in black. Focused.

A set of white drawers, the top the altar. One of Ariella's scarves laid out, dagger, statue of Baphomet, incense, black candles.

My senses heightened, raw, twitching.

Desire.

A sigil drawn for physical destruction.

The death of my monsters.

Release.

Thirteen steps.

Infernal names. Cardinal points. A deep meditative trance of hate.

Static whirring in my ears. Teeth aching. Skin crawling.

Downwards. Breathing heavy and hot, lungs rising and falling, massive waves. Reeling forward, insane. Stars and colours swirling under my eyelids. Dissolving.

Shemhamforash.

The first day of May. Ariella and I have been together for one year. We spend the day in the Dene. A picnic by the little pet cemetery. I'm smoking a cigar. Glass bottles of Coke, I take the lids off with my teeth. Sushi, little rice crackers.

'I'm really looking forward to visiting father.' She tells me.

'I'm looking forward to a holiday,' I reply, 'I think I need it. It will be nice to have some time alone for once.'

'Well, we won't be entirely alone, my dad and Dot will be there.'

The sound of trees swaying, warmth of the sun. The yellow of daffodils.

'What are we going to do about finding somewhere to live?' Ariella says to me.

'Maybe we should visit some letting agents and see what they say. We don't have much choice.'

'Yes,' she agrees. The sound of reluctance in her voice.

I can hear her heart saying, *let's move to London.*

A dog barks. The hum of traffic far off.

I wonder if she can hear the ache of suffering in *my* heart.

'Happy anniversary.' From my pocket a gift, wrapped in purple craft paper.

She opens it. A black necklace. Beads and teardrops.

She kisses me. Thanks me.

She didn't get me anything, but it doesn't matter.

A gig at The Stout for Triple X Terry. His words all smoke, eyes hidden. A vapour of a man.
Underground, a set of stairs that leads under the pub to a small bar and a hollow in the wall where the bands play. A good turnout this time. Afterwards Gary and Dom pawing playfully at Nat and Ariella.

I bite a chunk off my jealousy and swallow it. Green and bitter down my throat. Everyone standing in a circle telling jokes.

Dom farts. A squeaky little mouse from his trousers – the stink potent. The circle disbands at the horror of the guff.

'That's horrible!' Ariella shrieks.

I laugh. 'You can't complain, yours stink just as much!'

Her face drops and she pokes me in the eye. A playful poke, but enough to get the message across to me.

My face drops. The bile of jealousy and rage back up my throat, burning, acidic.

I go up the stairs and outside. Round the corner on my own. Stand alone, just breathing.

Five minutes. Ariella comes to find me.

'Are you alright?' she asks.

'Why the fuck did you poke me in the eye?'

'Look, I'm sorry, I shouldn't have done that. But you embarrassed me.'

'No one cares.' I tell her.

'Well, *I* fucking care.'

The red mist in my eyes, like red food colouring

dropped in water – the way it disperses, clouding the clarity of the liquid, eventually taking over, bloodied.

Anger snapping, exploding.

I whip my fist towards Ariella's face, deliberately miss, and slam my knuckles into the wall. I grit my teeth and walk away.

I'm sitting on the floor outside the pub in the dark. The taxis are pre-booked to arrive at 11pm. I hold one hand with the other – there is a vague sensation of pain beneath the alcohol in my system.

I'm silent. There is silence between Ariella and me. Horrible silence. Into the taxi, Nat, Ariella, Alice – I'm in the front with the driver.

Our street, they're giggling in the back, stupid jokes.

'Will you stupid fucking bitches shut the fuck up!' I snap.

The look in their eyes, scolded children.

'Hey,' the taxi driver turns to me, 'you don't swear in my cab, you hear?'

He is a little Indian man, in his fifties. Balding, fat.

'Fuck you.' I tell him.

He pulls into the kerb.

'Get out,' he tells me. 'I won't have swearing in my cab.'

'Here man, my hand is fucked you fucking cunt.'

He drives off down the street. I pick up my pace. It's not far to the house, and by the time he has pulled up and the girls are getting the gear out, I'm there. I grab the taxi driver by the shirt with my good hand and slam him against the cab.

'Speak to me like that and I will fucking murder you, you Paki cunt,' I scream in his face.

'I'm calling the police,' he tries to get his phone.

204

'No, please,' Ariella begs him, don't call the police, 'I'm sorry – he's just drunk and had an accident.'

I move away.

'You are banned from Five Star Taxis for life,' the taxi driver tells me.

'Fuck off, man.' I reply.

He drives off.

'Well, that's fucking excellent,' Ariella shouts at me. 'They are the only company that will take our gear to gigs without charging us. What will we do now?'

'Fuck off.' I tell her.

'What's wrong with you? What's with all the bravado all the time?'

I throw my bass over my shoulder in its carry bag and pick up my amp with my good hand.

I'm not saying anything more. I turn and head up the stairs to the house.

'I suppose you're going to leave us here to carry all this stuff?' Ariella fires at me.

I turn around and wave my damaged hand at her.

I'm in the house. I lock the door, put my key in the hole, and put the chain on.

I sit in the living room listening to them call me names through the letterbox, demanding that I open the door. My phone rings relentlessly. I go into the kitchen and get a bottle of red wine, open it, sit and drink it from the bottle.

The world a hideous haze.

Nat slamming her foot against the door to break it down. I'm unmoved by all this, serene in a buzzing vibration, letting my monster just be.

The quiet of my own psychosis.

'Listen,' Ariella begs through the letterbox, 'I

understand that I've pissed you off, but can you at least let us bring our gear inside? Then we will fuck off and stay somewhere else for the night and you can calm down.'

I pick up my boot and walk into the hall. I launch it at the door.

'Fuck. Off!' I scream.

I return to my wine. Five minutes and they're gone.

My world is swirling, yellows and browns, everything mashed. I'm insane and drunk with it, head buzzing static, descending downwards, becoming undone, unravelling.

I finish the wine.

A bottle of sake that I purchased on a whim. I try to open it, but the lid is stuck and I can't manage with my sore hand. I smash the top off with a hammer, green glass on the floor. The Japanese writing on the front. I pour it all into a pint glass and smash the bottle against the wall.

I am rage personified.

I sit in a stupor in the living room, looking at my mangled right hand. It is blue/purple across the knuckles, the little finger poking out at an angle, swelling around the metacarpal bone. I play with the finger; push it back and forth, trying to work out if there is any sensation.

The carpet is spinning, a mushy colour, like paints mixed.

I go to bed. Sleep in my clothes.

Next morning. The mess and debris of my violence. I look at myself in the mirror. Hungover eyes, tired face – a black buzzing sound in my head. My little finger mangled. The back of my hand, marbled shades of purple, black, yellow, and blue.

Apologies via text. They come home. Nat gives me daggers. I'm not bothered about that, she can rot.

I'm amazed that Ariella softens so quickly.

'I'm sorry I got upset and poked your eye,' she says, followed by, 'your poor paw,' she examines my hand. 'It looks broken. You need to see a doctor.'

I nod. A silent, sorrowful, little boy. 'I'm so sorry,' I say through half-tears.

'You really scared me last night,' Ariella now serious but softly spoken, as if not wanting to re-awaken the kraken, 'Alice was telling me to leave you and to call the police. I spent half the night explaining that you are a good person.'

'I'm sorry,' a hot tear down my face.

'But I had to tell them about all the other stuff that has happened.'

I nod again, quivering lip.

'And that poor taxi driver,' she adds dismayed, 'he was just a little man.'

Her words ring in my head. Repeatedly. Just a *little* man.

'I can't believe what you called him,' she continues, 'I've never heard you say anything like that before, you don't really think things like that, do you? Because I couldn't be with someone who has racist thoughts.'

I shake my head. 'Just angry.' I say, strands of spittle in my teeth, fighting back tears, red-hot eyes, burning throat.

Her arms around me. I feel my life is nicely painted dirt.

XXIX

I make an appointment to see the doctor at the
University Medical Centre. Young female doctor
looking at my hand.

'What happened?'

'Hit a wall when I was drunk.'

'Yeah, that's broken,' she sighs, 'you silly boy.'

She's on the phone. Hospital referral. Bandages-up
my hand.

Day later. At the R.V.I, the plastic surgeon runs
through the procedure.

'Two pins in your hand, cast for six weeks.
Operation in three days.'

I'm due to take a fortnight off work for holiday next
week. I drop into the D.O. and explain the situation
with my hand. I can keep my holidays for later in the
year. I'm on the sick now.

I buy a bottle of Jack Daniels, and a box of café
crème. I'm going to sit and play on my PlayStation for
six weeks. All the forthcoming gigs cancelled. The
girls are distraught.

'I suppose we can use it as time to write new
material,' Ariella suggests.

'It's a shame though, 'cos I really wanted to do that
gig at the Free Festival,' Nat adds.

'I can record electronic bass over the drum tracks,' I
tell them, 'so you can still do the gig.'

The operation. A cubicle, a nurse pulls the curtain
around and tells me to take my clothes off, get into a
white and green gown, my bare arse poking out the

back.

I'm nil by mouth. Wearing surgical socks. Lying on the bed, stiff sheets.

Ariella worried about me this morning, she'll come to the hospital later, when I come round. I'm not nervous. I almost hope that when the blackness of the anaesthetic kicks in I never open my eyes again. Just drift off into space. Carried off by the wind of eternity like a speck of irrelevant dust.

The plastic surgeon explains the operation again. The anaesthetist explains the anaesthetic, plugs me in – needle insert in the back of my good hand where the goodnight juice pumps in. The nip of the needle, white surgical tape. Post-anaesthesia, I'm drowsy, floppy, delirious.

They wheel me off. Plug me in. The image of the porter's face over me, fade out quick. Sinking, black. Gone.

I wake up, it seems like only a second later, and the nurse is beside me already. Eyes rolling in my head. She says something but I feel heavy in the head.

'Ariella?' I murmur.

'Is that your girlfriend?'

I nod. Eyelids come down.

I wake up again. Clearer this time. The nurse is there again, a kindness radiating from her. A kindness I feel I don't deserve. Still light outside. The bright lights of the ward in my face. Nurse brings me cardboard toast, a little pot of jam and warm butter, cheap orange juice and mud-coffee. I eat and drink it all. It is five o'clock. Ariella arrives. She has bought me a present from the shop in the hospital; a child's doctor set. I laugh at it.

209

'I thought it would cheer you up,' she laughs.

'Do you want to play doctors and nurses?' I mutter.

I can go home. It is darkening outside. Spring evening, the way the light takes forever to fade into black, clouds grey, pre-electric tingle of rain. I'm silent.

'Are you alright, Mr Cat?' she asks me on the Metro all the way home.

'Just tired.'

I hold onto her for dear life. As if I might crumble, should I let go.

On our street, Nat is ahead of us on her way home. We catch up to her.

'I've started doing kung-fu lessons again,' she tells us, while looking at me, as if to say, I'm dangerous now, don't fuck with me, don't get violent again, I'll make you regret it.

She might as well have told me she'd bought a hamster to protect herself for all it mattered to me. If I woke up tomorrow and she no longer existed, if everyone in the whole world except Ariella and me just disappeared forever, it would be a blessing to me. I wouldn't regret or care that their lives, their hopes, loves, desires, kindnesses, desperations, vitalities, religions, evaporated into nothing. My heart would not lament their vanishing.

The pain it causes me because I know it will not happen. Trapped in a world that will not decease. Therefore, I think the opposite, and everywhere I look there is kindling for the sparks that will create the raging pyre of my own self-destruction. Like a runaway train, heading for the inevitable crash when the track runs out.

The Free Festival next to the Civic Centre, it is cold, the last weekend in May. There is no real audience, just people scattered, passers by watching out of bemusement. The girls are on stage playing along to drum tracks with backing bass. Standing and watching when I would normally be playing is a surreal experience.

Dom and Gary arrive.

'We're going to Download next weekend,' Dom tells me, 'do you want to come?'

'Aye, that would be mint.' I tell him.

We discuss all the bands that are on, who we want to see the most. Slayer, Machine Head, Hatebreed, Damageplan, Metallica.

'You can get your ticket from Steel Wheels,' Gary informs me.

The girls finish playing and I nip off round the corner to get my ticket.

'Lads' night out tonight,' Dom says to me when I return. 'Fancy it?'

'Alright.'

Ariella and Nat are standing with them, a look of concern on Ariella's face at the prospect of me going on a lads' night out. I think for a moment, and realise I've never actually been on one before. I'm 22 years old.

We go home for a while, so I can eat, change clothes and stash my Download ticket somewhere safe. I decide to drop Dan Thujone a text to see if he wants to come out for the night. He declines.

'I'm surprised you're going out for the evening,' Ariella mentions, a slight annoyance in her voice, 'I thought you hated that sort of thing, I thought you hated men.'

'I do.' I shrug my shoulders. 'I'll stay in if you want.'

'No, don't be silly,' she softens, 'it will do you good. Besides they are nice boys.'

The rock night at Krash. Drunk, I buy 16 Marlborough Lights from a vending machine. My first cigarette in three years. Tastes like hot burning tar. I smoke half the pack – on the way home toss the packet over a wire fence leading onto the tracks by Ilford Road Metro Station.

Guilt.

I stagger down the street – I like living in this area, the houses, the Dene, the sensation of clean urbanisation – how the night sky meets the roofs of houses, how the trees sound, symphonic in the wind.

Ariella in bed. I get in, she sleepily loosens my cock from my underpants, strokes it, takes it in her mouth.

'I'm on,' she tells me, 'so we can't fuck.' She rubs her cunt agonisingly.

In the dark of the room, she jerks away at my cock until I come in her hand. She gets up and washes it off in the bathroom. I'm drunk under the covers, light from the hall hurting my eyes. She's back in the bed. A body of hills and valleys next to me, my hand over the dips and rises of snoozing flesh until sleep takes me.

Download. Gary and Dom pick me up in the morning. It's a three-hour drive to the festival in Donnington Park in Leicestershire. Dom in charge of the CD player, putting on discs of all the bands we are going to see. Gary is driving.

212

'I feel comfortable enough to fart in front of you now,' Dom tells me as he lets rip.

The stink is horrible in the hot car and I open the window.

'Who do you think would win in a fight between me and Giant Haystacks?' Dom asks.

'Well, you,' I tell him, 'Giant Haystacks is dead. It can't be that hard fighting a corpse.'

The craic goes on like this.

After a stop at a motorway service station, and back on the road, Dom says:

'I've brought a special CD.'

He puts it on. There's only two track on it. One is William Shatner singing/talking *Lucy in the Sky with Diamonds* and the other is Leonard Nimoy singing *The Ballad of Bilbo Baggins*.

My face hurts from laughing as Dom turns it up full blast.

'Check out the tuba solo,' he shouts over the song.

He puts it on repeat.

Dom is singing: 'Dildo, Dildo Daggins, the greatest little hobbit of them all!'

We hit the queue to get into the festival. It's moving slow. All around cars have their windows down with an assortment of heavy music blasting. I can hear Metallica, Manowar and Pantera. It is blazing hot and stuffy in the car; all the windows are down. We are blasting *The Ballad of Bilbo Baggins*. People in other cars are laughing along with us.

We park up. Join a long line to get a drink, which is an extortionately priced plastic pint of pissy Carlsberg. I buy a lanyard with stage times on. We sit and watch Soulfly and Il Nino.

We catch Korn and Machine Head. For Damageplan, I get right in the pit and jump around like an idiot, people are banging into my cast and it hurts but I don't care. We get right up close for Slipknot. I want to watch Hatebreed but they are on at the same time as Slayer due to some problem with the headliners, Metallica. We watch Slayer from the back of the tent and I can't see anything. Word gets about that Lars Ulrich is ill.

Later that night we're waiting for Metallica to come on. It's raining, but only a light rain that is refreshing. Then the piss bottles start – they come in from all directions, I take one right in the face, blood coming out of my nose. Then one in the back of the head. People are getting impatient; Metallica should have been on an hour ago. It's fucking horrible.

Finally the come on. James Hetfield explains that they have recruited drummers from other bands to cover for Lars. The night descends – I feel amazing.

We get back to the car at two in the morning.

'Let's sleep for a bit, before we head off,' Gary suggests.

I doze a little. At six a.m. Gary wakes everyone up starting the car.

I'm home by ten. Ariella is still asleep in bed when I creep into the house. The room is full of light.

'Did you sleep with the curtains open?' I ask.

'Yes, it didn't feel right without you. Did you have a good time?'

'It was one of the best days of my life.'

A day later. Ariella:

'I thought we could go down to see father next

214

week. We could stop and see mother in Reading on the way, she's been a bit lonely and down recently.'

'Alright,' I agree.

'She's got man trouble again. She's always been the same,' Ariella sighs, 'always has to be with someone, always terrified of being lonely or left alone.'

I listen to her words as they ring out, not in the living room on the rickety sofa where we're sitting, but in my head – they ring long and painful, and I die with them a little because I know, and have always known, that it's like mother like daughter.

I know I've had this thought before, that Ariella is scared of being alone, but it was never there, real and present in my mind, just lurking in the background, like a cancer, growing, gnawing, and eating away at me. Black, hideous, swirling thoughts that I've refused to accept because it will destroy everything.

I realise it wasn't lack of love, or the pregnancy that made her dump Johnathan and move onto me; it was his going away and her impeding loneliness.

When you know that you know, but you don't want to know, so you shut it out. Slam the door tight closed, let it bubble on the other side until the door is rattling, ready to explode.

Then, in one quick moment, it's open wide.

I could have been anyone. Anyone that just came along and was there at the right time. Just a man, just a fleshy-nothing to fill her void. The sickness in my throat, tears trapped behind my eyes. Burning red, reeling, washing around inside me, frantic and terrible.

Despite this, I will and must continue on – but I know I can never ask her about it – it will destroy everything. For I have to have this love and all the

215

insanity and pain that comes with it. I am still mad with it and love-mad with her.

Therefore, I must hide in my delusion. Drink it away, fuck it away, until it destroys everything.

XXX

A gig before the trip to Dorset via Reading. I stand and watch the girls play with the drum and bass backing. It sounds awful. Triple-X Terry, like all promoters and other musicians, asks if we need a drummer.

I give him the standard reply: 'We're a semi-electronic band; we're not after a drummer.'

I've lost track of how many times I've had to say it to people, and each time I do there is an increment of venomousness in my tone. I'm on the verge of just telling people to fuck off.

People are also continually asking me about my hand.

'I hit a wall, I was drunk,' I tell them and try to play it down, even though I'm ill with guilt and anger about the whole thing.

I'm excited about the trip to Dorset – I haven't had a holiday for years, and the opportunity to be alone with Ariella, to heal the cracks that have appeared in our love, is important to me.

We take the train to London. I hold her hand – through her lacy fingerless black gloves, the wormy little finger poking out of the side of our amalgamated mitt.

We are alone and excitable, there is a sexual electricity bubbling up – she talks about being alone, about sucking my cock – she says she's been worried I haven't been able to pleasure myself with my broken hand. She's going to wank my cock off, suck it, and put it in her at least three times a day she promises.

Obviously, we will have to spend some time with her family too.

At Euston we change for Reading, it is only an hour on the train. It seems mad to be going back on ourselves but it was the quickest route.

Ariella's mother is German although she has lived in England for years. She and Ariella's father divorced when Ariella was ten.

'This is my mother, Helena,' Ariella introduces us.

Physically, Ariella is nothing like her mother, but I notice Alice resembles her, and I stare for a moment thinking about it before I say hello.

Along the street from the station, the canal – where the houses are islanded in the middle. Little kingdoms of their own. It is very picturesque.

'How do people get across?' I ask Helena.

'Look, darling,' she explains, pointing at the houses on the other side, her accent still thick and German, 'they all have little rowing boats to get across.'

The middle of June – real heat and the light on the pavement so bright, shadows spilling over it. I listen as Ariella and Helena talk.

Helena's curly blonde hair springing from her shoulders, blue eyes with ice-white sclera.

I watch the way they interact, and as we reach the house at the end of a terrace on a smart street, I realise I dislike Helena.

They may not be alike in appearance but they are alike in personality – and I realise I already know this.

In the house, Ariella laughing, semi-serious:

'Honestly Mother, you don't always have to be with some man to make you happy. You need to learn to not be afraid to be alone.'

'I know darling, I know.'

I stay silent. Watching the progeny and the creator, I feel like I am looking at the source that spat forth the reason for my monsters. The origin of it all, here, in the mother.

I realise this is absurd.

The thing I will never ask Ariella about: am I just a convenient fuck to keep you secure, to prevent you from being lonely? – is here in the room wearing a different though equally hideous mask.

I look at Ariella and wonder if she knows what I am thinking.

A strange look on her face.

We have dinner – the table laid out neat and nice – sandwiches, cheeses, salami, crusty bread rolls, slightly melted salty butter, sauerkraut, red wine.

Helena asks about the band, about my broken hand, about everything. I let Ariella do the talking.

Helena talks about her job teaching history at the University of Reading. I notice she has a few pagan ornaments – the Green Man hanging on the wall and Pan atop the mantelpiece.

'Alice will be at your father's house, won't she?' Helena says to Ariella.

'When? While we're there? Did she say that? She didn't tell me that.' Ariella seems concerned. 'She definitely said this week?'

'Yes, I think so.'

'Why wouldn't she tell me that?'

We go for a walk around the town and stop to have coffee in a little café. Sitting outside under parasols, I smoke a café crème, the coffee cools quickly and it's gone too fast.

We drop into a few shops. I buy a pack of vanilla incense sticks. Then I spend half an hour with my back to a wall while Ariella and her mother chinwag with some old dear.

Then it's dinner back at Helena's – soup, chicken salad, and I'm still hungry at the end. Girl's portions.

Back at the station and I'm pleased to be getting away. Then, on the train back to London to get another train to Dorset.

Watching my life spatter by through the windows.

'My mother,' Ariella says to me, 'she makes me so sad.'

From Euston to Dorset. Ariella keeps telling me the name of the village her dad lives in, but I can't seem to remember it.

'What is it? Stainbury?'

'*Stalbridge!*' she laughs.

We pass through lots of little villages on the way. Little railway houses, old stations, long fields stretching out, grass green and scorched yellow. Fields of rapeseed.

'Salisbury,' I say as we pull up at a station. 'Isn't that Stonehenge?'

'Yes,' Ariella replies, sensing my excitement, 'it isn't very exciting though when you get up close.'

'I'd still like to see it.'

Another station.

'Templecombe,' I point out to her, 'as in the Knights Templar.'

'Yes,' Ariella surprised, 'how did you know that?'

I shrug my shoulders. 'There's something about all these places, something mystical.'

'You'll get on with my dad, he's very mystical. And largely self-educated, like yourself.'

The roads of Stalbridge are narrow and wind through the village. The houses are old and have huge square chimneys poking out the top, and the sky hangs clear and beautiful blue with criss-crosses of white cloud high and visible in all directions. The footpaths are narrow or non-existent and I feel exposed walking in the road. This is pleasant, picturesque England.

We come to her father's house. It is a lovely old farmhouse – the drive is gravelled and crunchy underfoot as we approach. I'm amazed at its size and the open space surrounding it.

It must have cost a fortune, I think to myself.

A sign on the side of the house reads:

Red Fox Pottery.

We're through the dark-red front door. A shriek of delight goes up from a middle-aged woman.

'Hello, Dot,' Ariella flings her arms around this woman.

'This is Dot, my Dad's wife,' I shake her hand, the sensation of her skin on mine, her fingers soft, almost crispy.

Alice walks into the room.

'Hello, 'Arry.'

They hug for a moment and I watch. Then Alice's eyes looking at me, cold, blue-empty, her upper lip resting gently over the bottom one. Her lisp, soft and raspy, blonde curly hair. Having seen her mother, I can see the familial resemblance between them. I feel I must be mistaken, but I can sense the animosity from Alice towards me.

221

'Why didn't you tell me you were coming?' Ariella asks, sounding bemused.

'Surprise.'

Ariella looks at me confusedly.

'Where is father?' she asks.

'Having a shower, he'll be down in a moment. Cup of tea?'

'Yes,' replies Ariella firmly.

'Cup of tea?' Dot asks me.

'Yes, please.' I reply, nervously.

'Oh, what have you done to your hand?'

I'm beginning to hate people asking about it. It's becoming like a badge of my mental terrors – one for all to see, and one I can't remove. People assume that I must have fallen over or had some kind of sports accident.

I can feel Alice's eyes on me – her face like stone.

'I was drunk and punched a wall.' I tell Dot, matter of fact-like.

'Oh,' she laughs, 'I bet you regret that!'

I can see the look on her face; it is one of confusion and bewilderment. Judgement, in all of five minutes. I feel emotionally small and feeble, here in middle-class England, a northern working-class boy. All the terror of the estates of my childhood – burnt-out cars, burglaries, beatings, suicides, robberies in the street, feral dogs, drug dealers, rape, the police in the cul-de-sac every day and night – these terrors come flooding back and I'm suddenly trapped in a class nightmare. I feel like scum.

Is this Ariella? I ask myself. Have I just been blind to this little posh girl, or has she hidden it so well?

I'm smiling. Ariella is smiling. A smile that plays-down the violence of the night I broke my hand. Alice isn't smiling. She is looking at me hard, hate-filled.

My smile drops away.

The old man walks in.

'Arry!' They hug.

This is my Dad,' Ariella introduces us. I shake his hand, awkwardly with my left (as I have to do with everyone) but he keeps his eyes on his daughter.

'George,' he says still not looking at me.

He and Ariella rub noses like Eskimos.

'Nop, nop, nooey.' They say to each other in cute voices.

I raise a quizzical eyebrow.

Dot directs me to the long kitchen table and I drink my tea. They talk and I stay quiet, looking at the ornaments, pictures on the wall and hand-made pots on the shelves.

Tea finished – the old man suggests:

'Take your things up to your room, rest up for an hour and we'll make supper.'

Ariella takes me upstairs. Books line the walls, I'm carrying our suitcase, and I'm lumbering with it. The house is enormous inside, ascending – the corridors narrow. Rooms spill off either side. More books stuffed into cases. Old, yellowy paperbacks spilling out.

Our room, two single beds, but a double mattress laid out on the floor.

'Let's have a fuck,' she suggests.

'What, now?'

The quilt on the bed is thin, white – we get underneath, pulling our clothes off as we go. Then

223

she's on top of me, reverse cowgirl, my cock sliding in and out, while I stare at the scar from a minor operation to remove a mole on her back. It's still erotic, but strange with her facing the other way, and being in an unfamiliar place. She comes, but I don't. She takes my cock in her mouth – the red/pink of her lips, the way her breasts swing like heavy bags of wet sand. Some of her childhood things, toys and games on shelves, the yellowy wallpaper, sunlight through the window, the breeze that ripples across my now exposed bare skin. Gooseflesh.

I come and she swallows it all with a look of wanting to please and disgust on her face.

'Let's have a shower now,' and she takes me up a flight of stairs. We both get in and I hold her while the hot spray from the chrome showerhead spits us clean. Her lips against mine, warm, soft, wet, and rubbery.

We dress, head downstairs, supper just being served – cold meat sandwiches, cups of milky-beige tea. Alice has gone to bed. The atmosphere a little lighter. The old man talks. He is in his seventies, with a warm, funny face and silver-hair falling down the back of his head like an old clown. He dances around his words, and I wonder if he has gone a bit senile.

Later, goodnights all round. Ariella and I in bed, surrounded by the unfamiliar darkness and sounds of somewhere new:

'My poor dad,' she sighs, 'he's not who he used to be, he can't remember things anymore.'

I wake up early, five a.m., with the sun pouring in through the thin curtains. My belly is rumbling.

Ariella asleep, so I dig my book out of my bag and read it. *The Western Lands* by William S. Burroughs.

Around seven, I fall back asleep. We wake up together at eleven. We dress, then sleepily and snoozing still, we head to the kitchen. There is a note on the table telling us that everyone else has gone into town.

We eat breakfast – cornflakes, the milk cold and icy. When we're done:

'I want to show you the piano.'

Ariella takes me to the front of the house and through a door that leads into a large room.

'This used to be stables,' she informs me, 'it's my Dad's pottery shop now.'

There are pots of all kinds on shelves. They are delicate and beautiful. I want to touch one but decide not to. At the other end of the room, a large grand piano. Ariella sits in front of it and begins to play.

'I got a new song half-written,' she explains, 'see what you think.'

She plays and sings. I don't catch the words, but the piano part sounds just like our song *Turtle Dove* which in itself sounds like *Cornflake Girl* by Tori Amos.

'I'm not saying this to be mean,' I tell her, 'but you have a particular piano style, that often sounds like *Cornflake Girl*.'

Her face drops and I realise I've upset her.

'I'm not that good a pianist,' she sighs, 'I can only play what I can play.'

'Yes, you are, just try and think outside the box.'

She pauses for a moment. Then:

'You don't like *Turtle Dove*, do you?'

'Yes, I do,' I lie.

225

'I miss playing it. It makes me feel nice.'

'I'm sorry. I just don't think it fits in with our new sound.'

What I really mean is that I find it twee and a bit nauseating.

In the late afternoon, Ariella takes me for a wander around the village. A trail with a path carved by human feet. Fields filled with sheep – I stand and watch them, listening to the hum of the electric fence.

It is Saturday. 'Let's go and have a drink,' I suggest while we're sitting in the sun in a small playground.

Ariella on the swing, moving gently back and forward. 'No, there's only one pub here and I don't really want to go in there, it's full of old men and farmers.'

'We could just get some booze from the shop.'

She hesitates for a moment. 'I don't really want to drink while I'm here.' She stares blankly down at the floral shadow cast by the gate that is on the ground.

I don't say anything.

I get up from my swing and begin pushing her on hers. She is laughing, her mouth wide open as I push her as high as I can.

'Stop!' she is giggling, 'I'm going to piss myself.'

I finally relent and she stands up.

'I feel all wobbly, like a new born lamb!'

She puts her arms around me.

It feels like we are alone for the first time. So far away from everybody and everything else. I hold her and close my eyes. If I can just stay here, in this moment – but as soon as I've tried to grasp it, it has gone.

'I'm hungry,' Ariella grabs her stomach. 'Let's go to the chippy. I want a mushy pea fritter. You can only get them in Dorset.'

'A mushy pea fritter?'

We're sitting at the dining room table eating our food. The fritter is delicious, shaped like a burger with crispy batter and filled with thick green goo. It is a little bit sweet, even while being incredibly savoury.

'These are amazing,' I tell Ariella.

Half an hour later, the rest of her family return.

'Norma and John are coming for dinner on Sunday night,' Dot informs Ariella, 'I thought we'd have a roast, seeing as it is your last night here.'

'They're the neighbours,' Ariella whispers to me.

'Have you had a nice day?' I ask Alice, trying to soften the atmosphere between us.

She looks at me like a spoilt little brat. Her top lip curling over the bottom one. Cold eyed, shooting out a laser-beam-bitch-ray. She ignores me and helps Dot unpack the shopping.

My mood drops. I come over all sour and I can feel the venom filling inside. I'd like to slap the look off her face. I look at Ariella to see if she saw what happened. She did, and she looks terrified.

'Arry,' the old man interrupts our psychic exchange, 'come through to the snug, I haven't seen you all day.'

We follow him through. He sits in his armchair, floral cover over the armrest.

'Put a record on for me,' he asks Ariella.

'Which one?'

'Derek and Clive.'

'Have you heard this?' he asks me.

'No, I haven't actually. I've heard of it though, Peter Cook and Dudley Moore, isn't it?'

'That's right,' he laughs, 'from Ireland, are we?'

I'm confused at this. 'No, actually, I'm from Newcastle.'

'You sound like you're Irish.'

There isn't a trace of any Irish in my accent whatsoever.

'Nope, born and raised in Newcastle,' I tell him again.

'Hello cunt,' the record starts.

The old man laughs.

'You stupid cunt.'

'You couldn't legally buy this when it first came out,' he chuckles.

'You just bought this record, this fucking bit of vinyl,'

'In the late seventies, you had to ask for it in the record shop,'

'Here it comes, cunt.'

'Some places would tell you to go away,'

'You've thrown the fucking record out the window and smashed it.'

'Others used to keep it hidden under the counter, and you weren't allowed to tell anyone they sold it.'

We sit with him and listen. The record is funny, but the situation is weird.

'Ariella was telling me you used to be a pilot,' I say to him.

'Oh, she doesn't lie,' is his reply, and he goes back to listening to the record, chuckling all the while.

I was hoping he would have elaborated on being a pilot.

'CANCER!'

228

'Come on, let's go and see Dot,' and Ariella drags me out of the room.

I follow her, but instead tell her I'm going upstairs to lie down for a while.

Later, she comes up and I'm reading.

'You alright?' she asks.

'Yeah, but can we get out of here for a bit. I'm bored.'

'And go where? There's not much to do around here.'

'I dunno. Go for a walk?'

We have a late dinner. Alice giving me daggers all the while. She sits there, silent. I'm beginning to hate her. It's dark by the time we decide to go out.

Sky filled with stars in a way that I've never seen before, it is deathly quiet, and the air is soft, warm, and sweet. Ariella holds my hand, worm-fingers. I'm not looking where I'm going as I'm staring up at the twinkling blackness above.

'Look!' I stop and point into the sky.

A shooting star whizzes above, arching into nothing. It only takes a few seconds and then it's gone.

'Did you see it?' I ask.

'Only just.'

We stand in the darkness, in the road. It feels like the whole world has gone away. She puts her arms around me and rests them on my back. I place my chin on her head. I can feel her heart beating. I close my eyes and try to hold onto this moment. Again, it is fleeting, and I can't enjoy it for what it is, because I'm trying to squeeze every drop of existential juice from it.

'I wish we could stay like this forever,' I mutter, with

229

my lips buried in her hair.

She lifts her head up and presses her lips against mine.

'Let's go back now.'

She leads me off, but I'm walking slowly.

'What is wrong with your sister?' I ask, strangely calm.

We stop again.

'I don't know. I haven't really spoken to her since we got here. However, I suspect that she is probably scared of you. I don't want to bring it up while we're here, 'cos we're having a nice time, but you were terrifying that night. She was shaking and pale after you went for that taxi driver. I don't mean to sound like a soft, southern, little sissy girl, but we didn't grow up with violence. I'm sorry if that makes me sound stuck up or whatever, but that's the way it is.'

'I'm deeply sorry about all that.'

'I know that, and you've apologised to me, but you haven't apologised to Alice, have you?'

'No.' I pause for a second. 'I'll apologise when we get back.'

It is quiet back at the house. The light is on in Alice's room, so I knock on the door. She opens it, light spilling out. She is in her pyjamas.

'Hello, Alice. Listen, I just want to talk to you about that night, you know, the night I went crazy.'

Her eyes on me, with a fierce scrutiny.

I'm nervous and I can feel myself rambling, but I want to be sincere.

'I'm really sorry about the way I behaved. It was wrong of me to go on like that, I was drunk, and I'd just broken my hand. I was upset and angry.'

230

She stands there saying nothing.

'So I hope you accept my apology?'

'Alright,' she replies not changing her expression, 'thanks for that. Goodnight.'

She closes the door.

You fucking bitch, I think to myself. Fuck you. Fuck this place, you posh stuck-up cunts.

I bite my lip. Grind my teeth. I find Ariella in bed.

'Was she okay about it?' Ariella asks.

'Well, she *accepted* my apology, but I don't think she has, really.'

'Oh, dear. Well, you've said it now so if she wants to be a child about it, then let her.'

'Fuck her. I've had enough now, I want to go home.'

'Only one more day. It's Father's Day tomorrow, so I'd like to spend some time with my Dad.'

'Of course.'

'Do you want me to suck your cock?'

'Yes.'

Next day – Ariella brings her homemade Father's Day card down to give to him at breakfast.

'Nop, nop, nooey,' they say to each other.

I sit with my cornflakes and stare at Alice. She looks back at me. I'm trying to call her a cunt with my body language.

The sun is out, so after breakfast we sit in the massive garden.

'We're thinking of turning the paddock into an orchard,' Dot tells Ariella.

I sit on a red and white stripy deck chair and say nothing.

'Norma and John will be here for about eight,' she

231

continues, 'so we will start just after lunch, around one.'

'Alright,' Ariella replies.

'You're alright helping aren't you?' Dot turns to me.

'Helping what?'

'With making the dinner.'

'Everyone in this house contributes,' the old man chips in.

I'm flabbergasted. I open my mouth but nothing comes out. I'm thinking, so this is southern hospitality, is it? Expecting your one-armed guest to prepare and cook dinner for your fucking neighbours!

'I'm sorry,' I tell Dot as straight as possible, 'but I don't think I should, it won't be good for my hand.'

'Oh,' she laughs, 'you'll be alright peeling a few spuds and carrots.'

I grit my teeth.

I'm swallowing hard; trying to keep it all down, the venom and anger bubbling up. Sitting at the long kitchen table, slowly peeling carrots with a look of intentional pain on my face. Alice sitting opposite, scowling at me, Dot buzzing around the kitchen.

Ariella and her dad have escaped this prison-grade afternoon of food-prep fun and are still out in the garden. I'm attempting to put the flavour of hate into the carrots. I hope they all choke on it.

After a couple of hours, I'm relieved of duties when Ariella and the old man come into the kitchen to cook the food. I fuck off upstairs.

An hour later and Ariella comes into the room. I'm sitting on the bed reading my book.

'I'm sorry you had to help with the dinner.' She puts

232

her head on my shoulder.

'It's fine.'

'It's just the way they are here.'

'Everyone here is a middle-class, conservative-voting, stuck-up cunt,' I snap at her, 'and that sister of yours can get to fuck. I don't want that bitch in our house.'

'But she's my sister!'

'I don't give a fuck.'

'I don't think she would ever come to our house again anyway,' Ariella, a look of sadness spreading across her face. She sits staring at the floor, then, 'I'd better go and see if father is okay. I'll be back in a bit.'

I decide to stay in our room reading. The smell of food cooking and creeping through the door stabbing at my belly.

A long while later, Ariella comes back. It is twenty to eight.

'You okay?' she asks. 'You've been in here for ages. Do you want to come down? Norma and John are here. They want to meet you.'

I head downstairs with her. I shake hands with the neighbours, a well-to-do couple in their sixties, and after a brief hello, they go on yakking with the old man.

The dinner is food – that is, it is edible and hot and that's enough. I don't give it time to have any flavour; I just force it down my throat. Dot pours me a glass of red wine, and I gulp it down like a man dying of thirst.

'So, what do you do for a living?' Norma, sitting opposite, asks me.

'I'm a postman.'

233

She turns to her husband and scoffs at this.

I simply stare ahead at her blankly. All I can think of is standing up, walking calmly around the table, putting my hands around her throat and strangling her until her head explodes. Then grabbing her husband by the back of his head and smashing it into the table until his nose splats across his face.

I'm so furious I can't move.

I sit in silence.

'Are you okay?' Ariella asks me after a while.

I can't talk. I simply give a quick shake of my head.

'Okay, we'll talk about it later.'

Dinner is over. Alice is doing the washing up. I have to dry the fucking dishes.

The neighbours fuck off. I pretend to be busy tidying away dishes so I don't have to say goodbye.

I hope they both die of cancer. Painfully.

Later, in bed:

'Are you alright?' Ariella asks me.

'Did you see what that fucking old cow did?'

'Who? Norma?'

'Aye, when I said I was a postman she turned her head and laughed, scoffing, as if to say I'm not good enough. Sorry, I'm not a fucking doctor or whatever.'

'Oh, fuck that old bitch,' Ariella replies, 'I wouldn't worry about what that old cunt thinks. I love you for who you are, that's all that matters, right?'

'Yeah.'

'What does she know about you? Or about us?'

'Yeah.'

'So, don't worry about it, alright.'

'Alright.'

In bed in the dark, Ariella cuddled into me. I'm ill with fury. Fucking southern wankers is all I can think.

Next morning – saying goodbye. I tell Dot and the old man that it was nice to meet them and I'm thankful for their hospitality. Alice decides to stay in bed.

On the train back to London, Ariella:

'I'm sorry, that was an awful holiday for you, wasn't it?'

'We got to spend some time alone together. So, it wasn't all bad. Can we go on a proper holiday, just us?'

'Yes, it will depend on gigs and things though. You never know what we might get offered.'

I feel my reasonably good mood drop off, as if pushed gently from a cliff.

'Everything is always about the band with you, Ariella. What about *us*, you always make me feel like I'm canny low on your list of priorities.'

'That's not true,' she pauses, wounded, 'I just want us to make it, to get signed. I can't spend my whole life working in a care home.'

A long silence.

We change trains in London. A black cloud hanging over my head. Kings Cross. Waiting on the platform for the train to Newcastle.

'I want a drink,' I tell Ariella.

'The newsagent is over there,' she points.

I move closer to see what is in their fridges.

'They don't sell booze.'

'The train will be here in fifteen minutes,' a worry in her voice.

235

'I'll be quick.'

I find a shop outside the station. I buy a quarter bottle of Bells whiskey and two cans of Kestrel Super-Strength lager.

On the train, I open a can and drink half, then fill it back up with the whiskey. Within twenty minutes, I feel very drunk.

Ariella silent, just playing with her phone.

'Why aren't you talking to me?' I ask.

'Sorry,' her eyes on the phone, 'I'm just sending a message.'

'Who to?'

'Johnathan.'

'Fucking Johnathan,' I snap.

'Sorry,' she replies.

I pull the phone from her hands and throw it down the carriage.

'Get to fuck, you curly-haired faggot,' I shout.

'I can't believe you just did that!' Ariella almost in tears.

'Fuck off man. You care more about that prick than you do about me.'

'You're being so ridiculous.'

A woman in the seat in front of us turns to her friend laughing:

'Oh no, domestic.'

The red mist.

I stand up and say:

'Have you got a fucking problem, pet?'

Their faces drop, sore like smacked behinds.

'No, I was just saying it sounds like a domestic.'

I'm calm:

'It's none of your fucking business, so shut the fuck

up, bitch.'

A woman from further down the train brings Ariella's phone to her.

'Is this yours?' She hands it back to her.

I'm entertaining the thought that I'd like to murder everyone on this train. I begin to wish that it will crash and kill every fucker off.

I'm swirling, red-fury drunk. Weaving in and out of rational thought. All hate built up, bubbling inside, a manic psychosis.

Ariella, looking at her broken phone.

I, staring into the abyss.

XXXI

I wake up, cotton-mouthed and confused. The familiar surroundings of home. I'm in the bed alone, sunlight leaking through the corners of the curtains. I check the time; it is twenty to eleven.

I creep downstairs. Natalie curled up on a chair in the living room watching the TV. She looks tiny, like a toy, lost amongst the cushions.

'Where is Ariella?' I ask.

'She's gone out for the day; she said she wanted to be alone.'

I spend the day waiting for her, a sickness in my gut. I sit writing at the computer, listening to the annoying whir of the thing, and looking out of the window at the path that leads up off the road to the house, waiting for her to appear.

Late in the afternoon, the sight of her walking along the path, eyes down, sorrowful-face. The way she puts her hands in her black corduroy jacket, the sound of her boots scuffing the ground. Her face, fawn-like.

I pick up my book, jump onto the bed, and begin to read.

She shuffles into the room.

Two cold and strained 'hello's.

I'm sick – my heart is beating so fast I can feel it in my face. I'm waiting for her to say we're finished, that I've ruined everything.

'We need to talk,' her words linger, a terrible sadness.

'I know,' I reply. 'I'm so sorry about what happened on the train; that was a terrible thing to do. I feel awful about it.'

Her eyes on me now, for the first time since entering the room.

'Listen, I can't take much more of this,' she explains, 'I don't want my life to be like this, you're making me feel crazy. I'm starting to feel self-destructive, like, I might do something terrible to myself. You make me feel like utter shit sometimes, with the way you behave. And, I want you to get some help. You have a problem with how you express your anger. Normal people don't behave like that, don't you realise that?'

I sit and stare at her. I think, normal people don't need to be in a relationship just because they're afraid of being alone, but I say nothing.

'I'm sorry, I know my behaviour is wrong, but I'm not going to see a doctor or a counsellor or anything like that, they won't be able to help me.'

'Then, I've got no confidence in us anymore.'

'I promise,' I tell her, 'I promise I will stop this.'

'I'm sorry about my sister, and I'm sorry about Johnathan. You can forget about them. I love you. I'll stop talking to Johnathan, if that's what you want.'

'I don't want…' I pause feeling like an overreacting child, 'I just want us to be *us*. It's so difficult sometimes. We're never alone, that dick sends you a text every five minutes. We live with someone else. You mean everything to me, but I don't feel like you feel the same.'

'Of course I do.'

'But you're so *fair*, so bloody egalitarian.'

'I thought that would be a good thing. Besides, that's just who I am.'

'Aye, but you worry about everyone else's feelings at

the sake of us.'

A long silence. Then through a voice, cracked and audibly sorrowful, I say:

'I just want you to love me as much as I love you.'

Tears falling from her eyes now, dripping, the sound of it, rolling off her face onto her skirt.

I'm getting the cast taken off – a local anaesthetic, numb arm and hand. Good-looking female nurse, busty – cuts me free. My arm looks withered like a leafless branch on a wintering tree. It's hairy too – like a nasty looking caterpillar. Two long pins poking out of my hand, where they're holding the metacarpal bones together.

The nurse clamps a pair of pliers on one of the pins and pulls it clean out of my hand. It is a surreal sight to watch. I feel sick watching them come out, but the whole thing feels abstract, like a dream. Then half an hour of physiotherapy, gripping things, rotating the hand and so on.

'You must come back here every Wednesday for the next three weeks for further sessions,' she informs me.

It feels good to have the cast off; it had become itchy and annoying. However, I now have to go to the D.O. for a return to work review. On my way in, one of the union reps, Micky Channel-Four, grabs me. He looks like Kiefer Sutherland's non-identical twin brother who ended up with all the leftover genes.

'Don't let them bully you into coming back to work if you're not ready,' he tells me firmly.

Sure enough, that's how the meeting goes. They

want me back as soon as possible. I tell them I can't return until I've finished my physio, so another month at least.

After a bit of cajoling, we agree that I will return on light duties in the D.O. from the beginning of July. That only gives me two more weeks off.

With the cast off, I'm back to playing bass.

'Be careful with your paw, Mr Cat,' Ariella warns me as we're setting up in the music room for a rehearsal.

'Seeing as you are back now,' Natalie says, with her stiff mannerisms, 'I thought I would organise for us to play at The Cumberland. There's a guy starting up his own record company in Newcastle. He used to work for Virgin, apparently. He wants to see us play.'

'When did you find out about this?' Ariella asks, sounding both surprised and annoyed.

'Only this morning.'

My arm and hand feels a bit stiff, and I get a little bit of pain in my hand, but otherwise I'm okay, and I can play.

At The Cumberland gig, Ariella a bit drunk. Red wine lips, she's a bit giddy. We're in the corner watching the other band. They finish, then an interval. We have half an hour before our set. Ariella has a new phone. Every time she uses it, I feel guilty. She's frantically texting away.

'Who are you texting?' I ask, half-jokingly.

Her face washes white.

'I'm texting Johnathan, okay?' she snaps at me, 'not that it is any of your fucking business who I text anyway.'

'Don't fucking speak to me like that,' I tell her through gritted teeth, a hint of a threat in my voice.

'Or what? You'll fucking hit me?'

'No,' I shake my head, 'don't be fucking stupid.'

She stands up and begins ramming her fist into my face, three short punches that turn into several rapid slaps, each one becoming softer as she begins to sob.

I sit there motionless, taking it. Everyone in the pub is watching.

She runs off outside. I wait a moment, my face stinging. Then I follow her. She's sitting outside on the steps that lead up the hill, her head in her hands. I sit next to her and put my arms around her. Her face in my chest, sobs.

'I'm sorry,' she cries.

'So am I.'

A long silence. The lights from the pub behind us with voices and music spilling out. Darkness in front of us, the field with the goats and sheep. Trees dotted here and there, the long steps winding down.

'I'm sorry about what happened on the train,' I tell her.

'I know. You've apologised already.'

I feel a sudden, strange, deep sensation of hope that everything will be all right if I can stay sober. I feel for the first time that I can beat this monster, and a determination to do it.

We cuddle into each other.

'You've changed so much,' she tells me.

'I know.'

'I really admired you when you were a Buddhist, for not drinking when everyone else did. For sticking to what you believed. I thought you were such a

242

beautiful boy,' she pauses for a second, 'I still do think you are a beautiful boy.'

'I never *believed* in anything in the first place. It's all bullshit.'

'I know.'

I stand up. 'Come on, let's go for a walk,' I take her hand, kiss it and lead her off.

'I'm going to quit drinking,' I explain.

We stop and she kisses me.

We go into the garage on Shields Road. Ariella stands and browses through the porn magazines, picking them up and laughing all the while.

'Let's buy one,' and she hands me a copy of *Escort*.

Back in The Cumberland, we set up to perform. I tell Ariella to sit in front of her piano and read the jazz mag.

'It is performance art,' I laugh, and explain to Dom.

We play, and play really well, considering we haven't done so for nearly two months.

There is a sense of camaraderie after the gig. I'm sober, and being friendly and good-natured.

'This is what you used to be like,' Natalie, direct as ever, informs me.

I feel overcome with the sensation that everything will be okay, that I'm on the verge of rising above the demons inside me.

Then, I look at Ariella, and I can tell something isn't right.

I go to the toilet, and when I come back, Ariella has gone from her seat.

'Where is she?' I ask Nat.

'I think she's outside talking to Gary.'

An hour goes by and she still hasn't come back in.

243

Nat and I begin to pack the gear up off the stage.

'I'd better go and find her,' I tell Nat.

She's nowhere inside or outside of the pub.

'Where is Ariella?' I ask Dom.

'She's gone for a drive in the car with Gary.'

I feel the red mist of anger come down over my face like a wave of nauseating sickness. Mixed in with it is the green, slimy bile of jealousy. However, I'm sober and so I swallow it all back down. I send Ariella a text asking her if she is okay. She apologises and explains she felt sick and wanted to go home, which is where she was now, in bed.

Next day – Ariella in the bath. Singing, the sound of her voice secretly sweet as it reverberates around the house. To me it is saccharine. Nervously, I pick up her phone and look through her messages. She's been discussing all of our relationship problems with Gary. Every single intimate detail. I feel like smashing her phone, or throwing it into the bath with her. I feel inadequate, belittled, furious, and manic. All monsters return, raging, frothing.

I feel betrayed.

My hands, white at the knuckle, shaking, violent. I want to ram my fists into the wall. Smash all the bones, it doesn't matter anymore.

In that moment, I give into the monsters, completely. I've opened the abyss and they're laughing at me.

You fool, they say. *You can't escape from us.*

I lie on the bed feeling ill. Ariella walks in, towel around her, shivering a bit. She looks at me; she can sense something.

244

'Are you okay?'

'Yeah,' the lie is obvious.

'Are you sure? I'm sorry I disappeared last night.'

'You've apologised already,' my words served cold.

'Well, it's Saturday, so I thought maybe seeing as we were out last night, we could invite Dom and Gary over tonight.' She says, trying to warm the situation.

'Aye, why not,' I agree with the tiniest hint of sarcasm, 'I guess I'd better go and get the drinks in then.'

She laughs a little nervous titter. 'You mean for them?'

'No, I mean for me.' I stand up and pull my boots out of the cupboard.

'I thought you'd given it up?' A terrible sadness in her voice.

'I've changed my mind.'

I'm out the room, out of the house, out of my head.

XXXII

The five of us in the living room. I'm not saying much, just sitting, and drinking from my two-pint bottle of San Miguel. There are only four seats so Ariella is on the floor next to my legs. I shuffle a bit and kick her by accident.

'Sorry,' she says, 'I'm not giving you much room here am I?' and she moves over to the armchair, where Gary is sitting, resting herself against the face of the chair and his legs.

'Oh, Gary,' she laughs at his feet, 'take your shoes off, I want to paint your toenails.'

He giggles and slips them off. Ariella sits and paints his toenails, bright red pot of paint, the gingery fluff on his big toe.

Like a bomb going off – the ugly green/red monster swells up, a storm brewed up from nothing – the nightmare, tyrannical beast mushroom-clouding in my face.

I stand up and walk out of the room. I feel their heads turn to follow me. I go upstairs, into our room. On the top of the drawers a basket with her things in – I whip it off with one strike of my arm. Then her computer monitor, a swift foot brings in down onto the floor.

I hear the front door open and close again, Gary and Dom leaving.

For a moment, my senses return, and in the eye of the storm I pick the monitor up and place it back on the desk, then gather up her things and put them back in the basket. I'm trying to get my head together. Ariella walks into the room.

'What is wrong with you?' she asks, laughing.

'Nothing.'

She notices the basket – all her things rearranged.

'Look, if you're going to have a fucking paddy like a child for no reason, then throw your own stuff around, not mine.'

'Fuck off you stupid cow.' The kraken rises.

'What's wrong with you? What did I do this time to set you off?'

My words stuck in my throat. I can't say anything. I just stand there scowling at her.

'You've got serious mental health problems,' she tells me. 'Normal people don't go on like this, why can't you see that?'

I turn and look out of the window. It is still light outside.

'I really can't go on like this.' She turns to leave.

'You were flirting with Gary, right in front of my face.'

'What?'

'You sat under his legs.'

'What? No I didn't, I sat next to him, on the floor.'

'You're always flirting with everyone. Why the fuck are those lads even here? Can't you see they're just sniffing your cunt, trying to worm their way in?'

She's laughing at me. 'You're so deluded. I mean, *Gary*. He's a nice boy, I like being his friend, but don't insult me by saying I fancy him.'

I want to scream at her that I've read her text messages. I try to hold the words in my throat.

Then, they tumble out. 'You told him every fucking thing.'

'What?'

'I'm sorry, but I looked through your phone, I saw that you told him all our problems.'

'How dare you look though my private stuff?'

'You fucking disappeared with the fat cunt for hours. What was I supposed to think?'

'You know what, fuck you.'

She's out of the door and down the stairs. I grab her arm, open the front door, and push her outside. Nat stands in front of me.

'What? You're going to kung-fu chop me are you? I don't fucking think so.' I stand looking down at her.

'You're a fucking arsehole.' She turns and opens the door.

I slam it closed. Put the latch on, find my keys, and double lock it. I close all the curtains. Get another beer from the fridge, put my headphones on, and turn up the volume. There I stay for the next hour, spiralling downwards.

My phone buzzing with messages and calls. I turn it off. I go to bed. I feel like I'm drifting, half-awake/asleep. I get up at the usual time of five a.m. for work. I turn my phone back on. In the quiet of the house, I read a stream of unrelentingly angry messages.

At work, a sickness in my throat. The end is nigh, I can feel it. I want to vomit.

I get home and she's there. She won't look at me.

On my knees, 'Listen, I'm so sorry…'

'Do you even care about what happened to us last night? We had nowhere to go. We had to sleep on the floor of the office of Nat's lecturer at uni. Do you realise that if someone had found us there she could have lost her place on her PhD? Obviously not, because you don't give a fuck about anyone else. And now I have to go to work and I've had no proper fucking sleep.'

'Do you still love me?' I beg like a snivelling dog.

'What? Of course I do, but this has nothing to do with whether I love you or not.'

She's out the door. The house is quiet. I begin to pack up my things. There is no use in me staying here. I realise I am a walking disaster. I phone my mother and tell her I'm coming home.

The path outside the house lined with my things. My mother picks me up. Silence. I send Ariella a message, telling her that this is for the best.

I unpack my stuff at my mother's house. My brother has taken over my old room, so now I'm in the tiny box room. I feel awful, and strange.

I sit in silence in the living room, not knowing what to do. I watch a film. The plot going on while I'm detached from it, like watching someone else's dream.

I go to the pub with my brother. We play pool. Nothing is real. This isn't my life.

I can't sleep or eat. I miss her, and being next to her body at night. I realise I've ruined everything. She explains that she is going back to her father's house in Dorset for a week, and that I should write to her there. We decide not to text or contact each other, to try cooling things off.

I sit at the computer and type away – sad and desperate, trying to control my anger – I write down everything except that one thing I can't bring myself to say – the terror of knowing that she has to be with someone, and that I could have been anyone.

I have a sudden precognitive sensation of the future and now I'm waiting to see if it will come true.

I receive a phone call from the college inviting me to an interview for a place on the Music Production HND in the last week of July. Despite everything else that is going on, I decide to make sure I get on the course.

Ariella's reply arrives in the post:

I have just received your letter. I will have to write in response because if I speak to you, it may come out the wrong way, and you will get the wrong overall impression.

The overall impression you should get is this:

I love you and I want us to be together one day.

Of course, in bad times, my own demons come out to play, and at the back of my mind, I wonder whether this is a fucked up way of letting go of me – whether you will see if you can do without me for a while then tell me it's over.

Maybe you secretly want someone prettier or more like you, or from the same place as you, who can therefore understand you more. Maybe this is a way of testing things out. You know how good-looking you are – I have plenty of reasons to be jealous too if I set my mind off in that direction. But these are my demons, because I'm scared of being left alone one day. I have to be alert – on the lookout all the time. I have to question, probe and find out whether the ground is actually there, if it is solid enough to stand on.

I know in the front of my mind that I am wrong, and I hope that saying the above does not trigger in you the demon that likes to say "Ah – that is her way of letting you know that she

250

secretly wants rid of you."

If that demon is triggered in you — it is also wrong.
I want to be very clear about that.

I want you forever and I believe that you want me forever too.

Sorry to use the whole "demon" analogy — I know it sounds a bit Victorian — like when they believed people were possessed if they were distressed in any way. It's just that it came to hand as an expression.

I hope to make myself clear. Sorry if it's not great — but I too am quite distressed. I feel insane, but I have to organise my thoughts. I hope I write well enough to translate some of what I'm feeling.

In your letter, you talk about no one just listening to you. I am trying my best here. The things you wrote down made me inexpressibly angry and sad. If I had spoken to you — well — I couldn't have said anything. But I realise that writing is good because you have to listen to everything before you reply. I guess I'm calming down as I write.

What I want to say to you about the listening thing is that I agree with you. It is necessary for you to find someone who can listen to you without having to butt-in all the time. It sounds like you have not had that privilege in life very much — and I'm sorry for my failings in that area. I wish I could help more — I will try — but failing to listen comes with the territory of being emotionally involved. You get so desperate upon hearing what the other person is saying — and you want to reassure them that you don't think in that way — or your demons come out to play. Let's face it — most conversations are a logistical mess — a nightmare when it comes to deciphering meaning — even if they are only conversations about mundane things — they are many-layered — impossible and fluidic.

Basically, I will try my best. I will try my best to understand

251

because I love you.

This is the bit where I respond to your suspicions — so it gets a bit defensive because I'm afraid I am angry.

Maybe I am not helping you in this bit. I don't know what the right and wrong things are to say to you in order to help you. Sorry — but this bit is for my sake. Because, I need you to listen to me too. Maybe I shouldn't ask you to listen — maybe I should ask someone else. But I only want you to understand all this. Because you hurt me badly with what you wrote — even if you didn't mean to. Even though you were trying to get me to understand what was going through your mind. You said you were not trying to justify your actions — just to explain what you were thinking — and I have to believe what you say. I have to force myself to believe that you are not justifying your actions by saying all that stuff about me. You are just explaining how I make you feel. Ok. I can believe that.

Here's my response to the way you say I am making you feel:

1. *I was entirely unaware that you were feeling or thinking any of those things.*
2. *If I had known you were feeling or thinking any of those things, I would have gone mad like I am now. It is so fucking distressing to me that when it doesn't make me cry that you thought that — it makes me laugh because — well — to think — I mean — what? It's funny because it could not be further from the truth.*
3. *I don't know whether — if you had told me sooner — I would have been able to convince you otherwise — I just can't understand your mental state. I can't understand why you added things up in the way you did, or whether you will trust me now reading this, or whether*

252

you really mean it when you briefly said that you took all that stuff back about me fancying Gary. I'm afraid what you believe about me seems to be completely out of my control and I don't know what to expect in response to this – because I would have never expected many of the responses I have seen from you – particularly that one!

4. *These are the honest facts:*

- *I do not have any sexual interest in Gary.*

- *I cannot distinguish between my behaviour towards him and anyone else with whom I am friends.*

- *The gig: I disappeared with him because I thought he might cheer me up, he is a funny guy. I felt a bit funny that night and intimidated by you, so Gary is more approachable in some ways, in the casual/friendliness sense. But I never imagined it would hurt your feelings. I was trying to give you space.*

- *I had indeed sent messages to him. I am not ashamed of the messages – except for the fact that I told him about stuff you would have not wanted me to say. That is my error and I ask forgiveness for the following reason – I wanted another man's perspective on how you were behaving – I wanted some help because I felt terrible – like I couldn't understand you and couldn't help you. I thought maybe I was over-reacting to your behaviour – because that's how you make me feel – like a southern sissy bitch who doesn't understand*

253

*the bare facts of life – because her life has
been so fucking peachy. I was really disturbed
by your behaviour, and I couldn't talk to you
obviously – and I thought of Gary. I suppose
I thought of him because he seems neutral. I
wasn't trying to change their feelings towards
you, I love you, you are an excellent person –
I was trying to explain that our lives had
become hellish. I explained that your
aggression was disproportionate to causes of
it. I have never told anyone (except Nat and
Alice) about your behaviour. I have never
told anyone about the night you went for me
with the metal bar under the bed when I was
behaving badly. There is a dent in our door.
In fact the front door too. I hope we get the
deposit back.*

• *I asked him not to tell anyone I had said all
that. I wanted some kind of confirmation
that it was acceptable for me to find your
aggression too much to handle – and in fact,
I did not get that confirmation – because
those boys love you and would never want to
say anything like that. Gary was not shocked
and just told me that he didn't mind me
talking to him if I needed to. He said he
would help if you asked for it, and he agreed
that our living/playing lifestyle was a difficult
one. The thing is those boys (as I guessed
when I anticipated him being neutral) have
no interest in taking sides – they like us all
as people. They just want to help. I have had
no words of encouragement for any of my*

254

actions or responses to you from Gary. In some ways, he did not satisfy my urge – because I wanted someone to say, "It's okay Ariella – you are not being a sissy – you do not deserve this."

But no one has said that to me except myself. So if you think I should put up with it or fuck off – you are in the majority. Unlucky for me.

When we disappeared, he was saying to me that I shouldn't worry. I'm not sure I agree with him. I have been worried recently.

- *As for the leg thing and painting his nails – well what can I say, I'll have to remember not to be so provocative next time. Come on!*

- *"If I behaved that way with a girl" – I might think you had a slightly camp fascination with the art of manicure. On a more serious note, I'm sorry. Perhaps my demons would get the better of me – I'm not sure. But they never have done yet. You have spent time with Bunny, and Nat. So far I have restrained myself, I think. Time will tell.*

- *Look – I know people say I'm flirtatious. To be honest – they are just easy to please. Perhaps everyone they meet is emotionally retarded and has no lust for life. Maybe I stand out because I find small things really funny – or amazing. Maybe I'm a cretin who feeds off the appreciation of other people. Maybe I ask for it with every move I make. Maybe that's something I should work out –*

255

since – according to you – it often results in the wrong kind of attention. Sorry for any problem it causes. In my conscious mind, I distinguish between how I "flirt" with someone I like, someone I love, and want to fuck every day. YOU!

- *Let's face it – I was pretty fucking direct when I decided to be with you. If I wanted to be with anyone else, I would have done it by now (perhaps you think I have – I really don't know).*

- *But I will work on it if it's a massive problem.*

- *I can't live with violence. Even if everyone else can. It drives me mad and makes me want to self-destruct. It makes me want to finish the job off for you – to kill myself on your behalf. Your violence makes me not want to exist. It makes me want to die – that is my only way to compete with your aggression. To let myself be destroyed. If you think about it – it makes a lot of emotional sense. Because, I have some self-loathing part of me (as well as a self-loving part of course) – you provide the best excuse for self-destruction. I will self-destruct because part of you hates me and it would be easier if I didn't exist. In that moment of aggression, that side of me crystallises – all I can see is that you are right – you should destroy me. In the past my behaviour has also been bad – so I feel I deserve it even more (like the time with the*

metal bar – I had been really bolshie and childish over something or other).
But, the part of me that loves myself always wins. I don't really want to die. This is why we have to sort this out (not because you would necessarily kill me one day) but because I actually believe that neither of us deserve it.

- *You don't deserve to go through that terrible process over and again. You don't deserve the pain that makes you get like that. You are such a wonderful person – I absolutely adore you. I want you to trust me that you have no reason to feel pain or threat. I love YOU alone.*

- *The aggression is indeed associated with male things – pride, keeping control over females, frustration, threats from others, et cetera.*

- *I can't live with you until you can assure me that you have found another way to express the aggression.*

- *Unfortunately, the aggression does not scare me enough to make me obey. It just makes me want to die to get back at you. What would make me change is if you felt you could express all these things to me in words. I don't understand the language of violence. I can try to understand words.*

- *I do NOT think of you as a beast or a monster or as beneath me in any way. This is just as much of a delusion as you thinking I fancy Gary. For Christ's fucking sake! I am*

257

ME. *You know me. If that's how I make you feel – well – you are misinterpreting me. I just can't deal with a certain side of you – in the same way that you probably can't deal with numerous sides of me.*

There are some sides of me that I should probably try to diminish – like the sick – self-hurting – sides – you know. I am not perfect. I do not claim to be. Perhaps I need to change too. Do tell me how.

- *A question: how will I know when you have sorted out that side of yourself? I guess I will trust you.*

- *Thinking of you, I am fucking dying for a fuck from you. And a hug, and love. Guess that has to wait.*

- *I think I'm losing it – I should stop – how much have I written? This is getting a little pathetic. I have spent about two or three hours writing. My hand hurts. I don't suppose I have said anything useful. Bugger.*

- *Sorry for all my failings as a person and girlfriend. Forgive me if you can. I love you and want you back. But not as we are now. It's too painful.*

I love you. Don't cry. I will though. Miss you.

Love from, A.

XXXIII

I'm reeling from her letter. The truth, right there, the thing I can't bring myself to admit to fully, in black and white.

...these are my demons, because I'm scared of being left alone one day.

At the same time, I feel like I must make some kind of effort to change, so I book an appointment to discuss my anger with a doctor. Yet, on the day, I cancel, convincing myself it will be a waste of time as they won't understand or be able to help. Although, deeper – I fear bringing my shame to surface in front of someone neutral.

I entertain thoughts of going to kickboxing classes or something similar – to relieve the tension and frustration, hoping to punch the anger out, but the motivation is false, and I know I will never do it.

I mope around at my mother's house. I don't want to be there – single bed, tiny room. I spend my evenings alone, getting drunk, feeling manic. My mother carries a look of concern for me on her face.

There is a thought, born from a vision of the future – clear in my head, of what will happen. I know it – I trust in this precognition – of what Ariella will do – of what I will do. How these things will happen, I don't know. However, a morbid, terrible curiosity is taking hold of me. I'm terrified of the consequences.

The monster rears its hideous head in preparation. It is telling me:

You can't help yourself. You can't save yourself.

Lonely – empty days, shuffling through council estates delivering letters. Dog shit, dogs, snapping the post from the letter box, the smell of wet dog, the fabric of my blue postal-pants burning my inner thigh, my arse cheeks rubbing together from the eight-mile walk, an existential sickness in my head, the sound and feeling of the summer wind – warm, somehow comforting, and the trees and their leafy symphony. Into flats, and the horrible warm smell of cooking, my feet sweaty, eaten away with moisture and full of cheese-holes, the ache that runs up my calves and the repetitive strain in my right rotator-cuff. Boots worn-through, soles smooth.

I feel like I'm descending downwards, spiralling, falling. Mad thoughts rush me – I feel insane. I don't sleep for more than three hours at a time. I sustain myself on German wines and cheap cigars. I feel like if I don't talk my way out of this with another human, that soon I will explode. I have no friends. My vision of the future leads me to abandon Dom and Gary.

Then I think of Dan Thujone. I send him a text, asking if he fancies a pint, maybe. To my surprise, he agrees, and I arrange to meet him at The Goose.

A bleak Monday night. We sit, a pint of Kronenbourg each. The pub is quiet. The tables, round and small with overly large menus in the way.

'The beer in here is cack,' he tells me, 'it's definitely watered down. But it's cheap.'

Dan Thujone looks and smells like a rock star, with his professional hair, high-cheek bones, and cool, crisp shirt with three top buttons undone and a thin spaghetti-wire of hair protruding out.

'Christ,' he exclaims regarding The Goose, 'this place is like an aircraft hangar.'

I tell him my troubles, and he listens. Unlike I'd imagined I would with a doctor, I don't feel embarrassed or shamed baring my life to him.

'It's funny,' he says after listening to me moan, 'that should happen to you at this time.'

'How come?'

'Lisa secretly booked a holiday away with her mate, *Big* Lisa.'

'They're both called Lisa?'

'Aye. I didn't find out about the holiday until a week before she was going on it.'

'Shit, that's terrible. How long have you been living together?'

'About a year. Well, I wasn't too bothered about her going really, except that her mate, Big Lisa, was bringing her fella. Which my Lisa was trying to keep a secret from me.'

'Why?'

He shrugs and purses his lips, his eyes focused on the sticky table. He rips-up a beer mat.

'I dunno, but even when I found out, I wasn't allowed to go. Wouldn't you be suspicious? Her, *her* mate, and her mate's *lad,* but not *her* lad. You tell me, is that alright?'

'No, it's not. So when are they going on this holiday?'

'They're on it now, which is why I said it was funny. 'Cos I've been doing what you're doing, moping and drinking alone.'

'Well, we can be sad cunts together. Cheers.' We clink glasses.

I go home, gassy from the lager, a bit drunk, feeling like I've made a friend, an ally.

261

I read Ariella's letter over again, trying to bring myself to sanity. I feel like I've gained some unexpected perspective from talking with Dan. I write back to her, my thoughts and words ambivalent.

At Newcastle College John Marley Centre, for my HND interview. I'm sitting in the reception, feeling strange at being here again. Paul Balls walks in, a smile on his face.

'Alright?' he pokes a hand at me to shake, 'I seen your name on the application, I'm pleased you're doing the HND. I was telling Pat Daughter, that's the course leader, that you were great on your access course.'

I talk to him for a few minutes, telling him about my musical adventures since I last spoke to him. He leaves, wishing me all the best. I notice that waiting in reception is a scruffy looking bloke – beard, corduroy jacket, specs.

'Are you here for the HND?' he asks me in a thick Northern-Irish accent, having heard my conversation with Balls.

'Yes,' I stick my hand out and tell him my name.

'Liam,' he replies.

He seems suspicious of me for some reason and the situation suddenly feels strained.

Silence.

A bald, well built-man with an aquiline nose, wry smile, and laughing-eyes approaches Liam and myself. He asks who we are. We tell him in turn.

'I'm Pat Daughter, the HND Music Production course leader. If you could just follow me please guys,' his voice is nasally, his words overly pronounced in Geordie, and there is some hint of arrogance about him, 'just a few forms to fill in first,' he explains as we go into a classroom, 'then a music production and theory test.'

I wince at this; worried I am going to fail.

'Just to let you know guys,' Daughter says as we sit down, 'that from September, the HND course is moving to the Rye Hill Campus. We've got a new, purpose-built, performance academy for performing arts students to move into, with brand-new, state of the art studios, it's gonna be double-cush.'

He hands us an application form, a pen, and an exam each. 'Fill the application first guys, then, start the exam. I'll be back in an hour,' he explains.

'He seems like an absolute dick,' Liam turns to me.

I laugh at this and begin to fill out my forms. Ten minutes later and I'm onto the exam. Some of it, the technical and recording stuff, I know, and I start to get less worried about it. Some of it, especially the theory, is like a foreign language.

'You any good with theory?' I ask Liam.

'No, not really.' He laughs, and picks at his nose with a strange nervousness.

I finish the exam as best I can. Daughter returns and collects them.

'Okay guys,' he grins with his big face, and eagle-beak looming in a threatening manner, 'I'll just quickly mark your tests.'

Five minutes' horrible silence. Then:

'Well done guys, you've both passed. So, you're on the course. Liam, you got forty-three out of sixty,' he hands him his paper back. 'You got forty out of sixty,' he turns to me.

'What was the pass mark?' asks Liam, flicking a finger into his nose again.

'Forty.' Daughter smiles, almost sickly-sweet.

I just passed, I think to myself.

I'm excited about it. Not just for starting the course, but also because it means I can jack my job in at the D.O.

The course starts late in September, and all the details I can expect in the post. I have nearly two months to go until it begins; but even so, I give my manager at the D.O. my verbal notice, and I explain that one in writing will follow it once I know my exact start date.

Greg, my line manager, seems unmoved. His face, cold stone with a black beard.

'We'll be sorry to see you go.' His words emotionless. A robot in a green shirt, beer-belly, dead-eyed.

Fuck you, I think.

I start counting down the days.

XXXIV

Hello,

I started again (again) because the first two attempts were written in the wrong tone of voice.

I'm glad you are calming down and getting some space to think. It's good that you're talking to people. Talking to people is perhaps the crux of the matter in all of this — because it sounds as if that's what you often deprive yourself of when it comes to difficult situations.

I hope that however you deal with all of this — you end up feeling able to tell me and other people what you're thinking/feeling — particularly if they really hurt you in any way. That would be a relief for you — to be able to say those things — whatever the response!

It sounds as if you are approaching the aggression thing in a sensible way, and that you really want to get over it properly. Especially since you say that you want to feel change within yourself, and not just for my sake. That is definitely a good way of seeing it — because although I know that being with me is kind of an incentive in all of this — it is really important that you want to change for your own peace of mind. That will probably make all of the difference. The way I see it (and I may be wrong) is that whenever I have been aggressive — it's because I have felt so frustrated as having no control over a matter — the only thing I can control is things around me — objects, my body, etc. The aggression itself is not the problem unless it harms or effects people around me in any way — (which sometimes — it has done). The problem is the frustration itself — the feeling of helplessness or whatever it is that is getting to me. I wonder whether it's the same for you?

265

If you were alone in the jungle – you would use the aggression on the jungle, rather than on people around you. It might be used in a <u>constructive</u> way. (I know I'm getting theoretical here – but I'm trying an experiment in my mind). So this is my point – if you remove <u>me</u> from the equation – aggression <u>itself</u> is not the problem. The problem is the feeling that makes the lone wanderer feel aggressive. If he could feel less frustrated somehow, then maybe <u>his life would be better – generally speaking –</u> regardless of anyone who comes into his life in the future.

In some ways when you fail to tell me if you have a problem or a sadness, you are <u>alone</u>. That's why – although I can't wait to be back together with you again – you should mend for your own sake because you will feel better within yourself and be much happier generally.

I would still like to meet up with you and spend fun times together in the meantime when you feel you are ready to see me again. I will always be here for you. And I will wait until you feel better within yourself – and have come to terms with whatever it is that gets to you. I know you can do it. You are an intelligent man and I love you. If you ever want me to help you – I will.

It's good to approach it from all those angles – <u>kickboxing</u> (or whatever you end up doing) to channel the physical energy, <u>meditating</u> to give your mind a chance to breathe again, and <u>seeing someone</u> (I know you are reluctant – I don't know if I can trust you to carry it through to be honest because of the way you feel about all that) who is impartial and can <u>listen</u> to you. Maybe someone who has encountered cases of severe frustration before and has a lot of experience in soothing the causes of it.

At the end of the day – I know everything I have written sounds a bit old-woman-like. It's not as if I have gathered all the wisdom of the universe in my short life. You will do what you need to do – and I will live with you when I feel that it is not going to be destructive to do so. I will take a risk by trusting you – and if it goes wrong again we will have to separate again. That's the only way I can deal with it – because when you feel bad – there is nothing I can do to help – I can try – but really – your feelings seem to run deeper than that – I feel that your feelings come out in aggressive moments and they may well be aggravated by me – but run deeper than me. They seem to be about something in you – your history that is still hurting you.

Certain things you feel – that you said in your letter – that I'm the only person you have ever really cared about – and that makes you paranoid of losing me. Well – when you think about it – that's fucking sad. I absolutely adore you and naturally, worry about losing you in the same way that you worry about losing me. But, I have worried about my parents the same way in the past. It is sad for you that you never had that closeness before. Of course, any closeness I have had with my parents is kind of out-grown now. Now I am much closer to you – you know me best. But it makes me sad to think you may not have had that at some point (except maybe with your Gran). That would definitely have an effect on how safe and secure you feel in the world – how loved you have felt. Because closeness is everything to me – I can't imagine surviving without it – it must be very sad. I hope you can heal that side of yourself – so that you learn to trust that I am here for the duration because I love you. When you get used to that idea – the world will become a different place for you.

My own frustrations.

The Johnathan thing:

I know now how men are – if you had warned me that this whole "thing" as you call it was a massive problem for you for whatever reason – I may have re-considered going to see him. But, to be honest I find it really fucking annoying to be under that pressure. I lost a good friend in Johnathan. He was not right to be my lover – he was not right to be my best friend – but he was a good friend. Never mind. I guess we sacrifice things for people we love. But it's sad that such a stupid thing could upset you.

I guess – fair enough – you didn't know whether I still loved him or fancied him or whatever. So I guess that made you suspicious. Maybe I should be more sensitive to that – I probably would have been if you'd told me.

Did you really only go to see Bunny to get back at me or test me? I'm afraid I find that stupid. It's healthy for couples to have friends outside of that couple – be they male or female – and I saw you going to see Bunny – and me going to see Johnathan, in that context. That's why I never had a problem with it. So what did your test prove? That I don't love you because I didn't tell you off for going to see her?

I will try to be more sensitive next time. But I have read stories of women being cut off from their friends by possessive men. I don't think that's healthy. Ok – that fact that he was an exboyfriend – I should have been more sensitive – but I just did not anticipate a problem – I saw it in a completely different way to you.

Never mind. I have been so fearful of contacting him ever since

268

you went mad on the train at me – well – it's not an issue for you anymore. You win.

But that's not the point. I hope we can both have friends without getting mental about it. I really hope that is beyond us.

I think I would get very defensive if I felt my friendships dissuaded more and more in a gradual way by anyone. I would feel manipulated and controlled – and would resent it.

Of course if you didn't like how I was behaving towards someone, you should feel able to say it to me – and I would try to listen and respond. I do love you – and don't want to hurt you at the end of the day. Likewise – I would let you know if something you were doing made me feel particularly insecure. It's important that we be sensitive to each other at the end of the day.

I love you. I don't think I have anything more to say. I am not angry anymore (at the moment) because I have let you know what makes me angry. I hope you are beginning to feel that way too. Maybe we can speak on the phone soon. My hand is tired and scruffy.

Lots of love,

A. xxx

XXXV

After speaking on the phone, Ariella and I arrange to meet up for a chat. We have coffee at Starbucks in town – she seems apprehensive and strange, as if worn out. Afternoon in late July, shoppers buzzing about, I watch them through the window, swarming in an insect-like chaos. Two large coffee cups on the table, a thin biscotti each, the strange red print on the wrapper. The coffee cools too quickly, leaving it overly bitter and lukewarm.

'Was it good to see your dad properly?' I ask.

'Yes, although I'm worried about him. His mind isn't what it was.'

We're avoiding eye contact. I reach out and touch her hand.

'I've missed you.'

Her hand in mine – the strangeness dissolving, warmth spreading.

We finish the coffee, walk through Leazes Park. Mallard ducks, swans, seagulls, on the lake. Men fishing quietly. The rowboats tied up, paint scratched off, numbers in black.

Sitting in the gazebo, behind the trees, St James' Park behind us, the field with grass green and short – we kiss. It seems like a lifetime since we last pressed lips together. I feel it run straight to my prick.

'I want to fuck you,' she tells me, 'I've been dying to fuck you for two fucking weeks.'

'We can't go to mine, my mother will be in.'

'Oh,' she sighs, 'I don't think you should come to the house either, not just yet anyways.'

'Never mind,' I say, feeling the soggy dribble of pre-

270

cum in my pants, 'it can wait.'

'But I want it in me,' she protests, 'I've missed your long cock.'

She bursts into laughter upon hearing herself say this.

'We could go somewhere, like, in the bushes.'

'I think it might be a bit exposed round here.' She laughs.

'How about the Dene?'

'Alright,' she giggles.

We decide to wait a few hours until dark. Sitting in the Trent House – her hands tiny on the glass of red wine. I'm drinking a bottle of Budweiser, each sip a terrible guilt.

There is electricity when we touch each other – my skin ripples, gooseflesh. My hand on her leg.

'I really miss your cock,' she whispers.

'I'm sorry for everything.'

'You've apologised already.'

'I miss being next to you in bed.'

'We just have to live with it now.'

Off the Metro at Ilford Road – the row of houses all neat, hanging baskets, nicely painted doors. Around the corner and down the bank to the Dene. The summer evening fragrance of it – in the dark, streetlights dissolving behind us. The sound of the waterfall, the moonlit picnic field, eerie – the whole scene abstract.

'Where shall we do it? I'm frightened now.' Ariella, her hand tight in mine.

I put her up against a large tree, the trunk rough,

271

knobbed, and gnarly. The circumference of it is three times the size of her waist.

I reach under her long brown skirt, slip her knickers to one side, and slide my fingers in and out of her gash. She's at my zip – I flip my cock out tumescent – pre-cum pearl glistening in pale moonlight. I wedge my prick in her, thrusting, face to face against the tree. I come quickly and she says:

'Just leave it in me.'

We hold each other, long breaths in silence, her heart beating against mine, stars poking out of the canopy. She shudders as she comes – I feel it rippling against my still rigid cock, waves of it down my shaft.

Unembraced – but hand in hand, I walk her back up the hill to the road.

'I wish we could just hold each other in bed now.' She sighs.

'Maybe stay over at mine on Friday night? My mam and step-dad will be out.'

'Alright.'

On the train, back to Fawdon, the buzzing of the doors as they close, the hideous grey, black-squared pattern on the seats, fiercely bright electro-illumination of the lights – a sensation of impending doom in my heart.

Next day – a text message from Dan informing me that Triple X Terry is hosting an awards ceremony for North-East musicians at The Archer this coming Saturday, and that both Ariella and Lisa have been nominated for best female vocalist. He informs me that Lisa can't make it, so he's going in her place, and suggests meeting up with me before hand for a few drinks. I tell him yes, and we arrange to meet at The Goose. I also inform Ariella of this, and she laughs it off saying it's a bullshit popularity contest.

Friday night. Ariella arrives at my mother's house. We hide in my now tiny bedroom, watching a film, curled up on the tiny single bed. It is hot, moist, and close.

She is wearing a short blue skirt – milky snake legs hanging out of it – tattered black cardigan, her breasts partially hidden in a purple vest. I look at the moles on her skin, and wonder what picture they might make if I join them up.

I slide my hand up her skirt and twiddle her clit. Soon, my stiff length in her mouth – she's tonguing the end. I take her from behind, working it in and out until we come together. Lying in the warm night, outside of the quilt, strange precognitions playing out in my mind – that terrible vision of the future. I know implicitly that there is an impeding and certain doom on the horizon.

Next day – we go to town, sun blazing, her creamy-snake legs coming out of her blue skirt. We both with sunglasses on. People in shorts, sitting outside cafés, convertible cars appearing, fat men with shirts off. The public pathetic heat deprived desperation brought on by the British summer.

We go in and out of a few shops, holding hands, laughing at things in a childish way, making silly noises at each other – everything surreal to me.

We part.

'I will see you tonight,' she tells me. A long press of her lips against mine, then herself against me. I go off to meet Dan, a strange sadness creeping upon me.

I sit with Dan in The Goose drinking horrible pints of Kronenbourg 1664, in the goblet-shaped glasses. The faint taste of line-cleaner. I feel sugary, with a weird lager-washed sherbet sensation in my face. We're both a bit giddy, telling tales of our woes. Smoking a café crème cigar each – the baccy in my mouth, the rusty flavour of it.

At seven, we roll steaming drunk around to The Archer. Pints each. I find Ariella. She seems unhappy that I am drunk and laughing with Dan, so she sits with a face like a slapped arse.

Triple X, a phantom, cancerous-skeleton in a black denim jacket, stands on the stage dishing out awards. He reads out the nominations then the winners. Lisa wins. Dan staggers up to the stage.

'Cheers,' he says collecting the award, 'aye, she's a great fuck.'

He walks off stage. I'm doubled-up laughing. The joke is lost on Ariella.

'What the fuck is the matter with you?' I slur.

'Nothing,' she sighs.

Dan at my side. I congratulate him on his wonderful speech and shake his hand.

'I'm going to the bar. Same again?' and he goes off.

'Seriously,' I try to reason with Ariella, 'what have I done wrong?'

'Nothing.'

A horrible silence.

Dan returns and thrusts a pint at me.

I turn my back from Ariella. A moment later, Dan nudges me with his elbow, I turn to see Ariella ripping paper up and throwing it over her head.

'What are you doing?' I ask her.

'I'm getting married,' she spits the words at me.

I give a nervous laugh, unsure what is going on. 'Married who to?'

Her eyes to the floor. 'I'm fucking marring Gary.'

The rest mist. The demons, the monsters. *Zazaz zazas nasatanada zazas!*

I take my pint and throw the liquid in her face. The shock of it – she jumps, eyes wide, mouth hanging open. All heads and eyes in the pub turn to us.

'What the fuck did you do that for?' she gasps.

'You're sitting there, ignoring me, I've done fuck-all wrong, and now you're telling me you're marrying Gary?'

'I said God! I'm marrying *God!*'

'Go fuck yourself man, we're finished.' I turn and walk out of the pub.

Down the street, Dan runs to catch up with me.

'You alright man?'

We stop in the street. 'Aye, what a fucking bitch.'

'I can't understand what you did wrong.'

Suddenly, Ariella appears with some spectacled girl with long black-hair.

'If you lay a finger on this girl again I will call the police!' she declares.

'Who the fuck is this?' I ask Ariella, stunned that someone I don't even know is sticking her nose in our business.

'It doesn't matter who I am,' she snaps, 'but I know who you are and what you've been doing to this poor girl.'

'Oh fuck off man you fat, specky cunt.' I snap back with a ferocity that frightens her silent. I turn to

275

Ariella, 'So who else have you been mouthing off to about our relationship?'

She looks like a wet dog that has gotten into trouble for putting its wet muddy paw-prints all over the furniture.

'No one,' she says softly.

I turn and walk away.

'Aye, fuck off you arsehole,' the girl shouts after me.

I turn and walk back to her at a pace. I stand right in front of her, teeth gritted, raging.

'Go on,' I breathe fire, 'I fucking dare you to say that to me again, right in my face. Go on, bitch.'

She stands there, blank expression on her face. 'Aye, I didn't fucking think so.'

I turn and walk away – the catalyst of the premonition now in motion.

I get off the Metro at Fawdon. Go into the off-licence and buy a bottle of wine. The house is empty. I drink my wine in a violent silence. I go for a walk to the field at the top of the road; pluck up bunches of nettles, rub them all over my body, all over my face, hands, neck, genitals. Burning, welts coming up, agony upon agony. I stagger back home, blind with pain. Terrible visions playing out in my mind, I feel a terrible psychosis creeping upon me – monsters green and red. I open the medicine box. I consume an entire packet of paracetamol. Stand then sit under a freezing cold shower hugging myself, shaking, vision blurred. An old bottle of calamine lotion, the top all crusted, unscrew it, and smear it all over myself. In bed, sticky, burning, in and out of sleep – my phone buzzing with hate-messages.

XXXVI

In bed for a whole day. Drifting in and out of sleep. Sweaty and clammy, sensations of madness and delirium. Sunlight and noises penetrating my skull – I hide under the blanket, curled up, foetal. My mother pokes her head around the door, asking if I'm okay.

'Urticaria,' I mutter from under the blanket, 'I'm not well, my skin is bad.'

'Do you want me to bring you a sandwich?'

A while later – I wake, house quiet. Daylight outside, I guess late afternoon. On the floor, a box of cetirizine, pint of water, cheese and ham sandwich, white bread, no butter.

I take a tablet, eat the sandwich, and lie in bed looking at my phone. A thread of messages from Ariella starting with hate-filled, to sad *this is this end*, to numb, sorrow, apologetic and back to hate.

I type that I am sorry for everything. I tell her it will be best if we avoid contact for a while. My eyes brim with tears and I wonder how to continue existing.

There is a message from Dan too, asking if I am okay. I tell him not really. He explains that Lisa is doing a gig with her band, The Saints, at a pub called The Smugglers in Sunderland this Friday, and that I should come.

A sensation of giddiness, maniacal thoughts, the gut-moving madness of new experiences as I walk along Scotswood Road towards Dan and Lisa's flat in Cruddas Park. I know the flats from delivering post – the blocks loom, a little menacing, shooting up out of the earth, as if pushed up whole out of the ground

from some giant subterranean council-flat monster.
Each block named after a type of tree, and they have
a range of different reputations. One block filled with
students, one a halfway house, another private, one
ex-council, another still entirely council. I'm looking
for The Hawthorns. Dan says it's all right, most of
the time.

I find the block, inside, the concierge, behind his
plastic window, the smell of cooking from the flats –
a weird brown, warm smell. He gives me a nod. I
round the corner to the lift, which doesn't look as if it
can handle any weight, the smell of piss inside, the
buttons all crusted with spit. Yellow neon lights
buzzing. I decide to walk up the stairs next time.
Seventh floor – I find the flat. Dan opens the door, a
smile on his face.

'I've brought some cans,' I tell him, and hand him
the bag.

'Cheers, I'll put them in the fridge. Do you want a
cold one?'

The flat is small and compact, probably only meant
for single living, open kitchen and living room
combined. But the place looks rock 'n' roll; guitars
here and there, framed fetish posters, ashtrays, empty
vodka bottles. I can hear a hairdryer in the other
room. A skinny black cat asleep on the settee. I sit
next to it and stroke it.

'What's she called?' I ask Dan.

'You'll not believe this mate, but, Ariella.'

My face drops. 'You're kidding?'

'Nope.' He chuckles.

'I thought you might have mentioned it earlier.'

'I thought about telling you the other day, but then it

278

seemed weird.'

Lisa enters the room – short black skirt, red vest, legs, heels, doe-eyes, glitter eye make-up, shoulder-length black hair, painfully attractive.

'He's just found out about the cat's name.'

'I know,' Lisa's soft, quiet voice, 'I couldn't believe it when he told me your girlfriend had the same name.'

'Ex-girlfriend,' I correct her.

'Oh, sorry. Are you alright.'

'I suppose so.' I say, even though the real answer is that I'm dying inside.

'Never mind, have a few drinks, and forget about it.' She smiles.

An hour later the rest of The Saints arrive in a white van to pick us up. There's no room in the front so Dan and I are in the back, rolling around a bit drunk, with all of the gear. The drummer, Shit-Head, is making strange cat noises and in a pretend broad-Scottish accent saying:

'Donald, I've done a cack in me troosers!'

Lisa is laughing at him. I feel surreal. At The Smugglers, I help load in. Then, pints of cider.

The pub is a long and thin, dull green.

'We're right on the seafront, you know,' Dan informs me.

Punters pile in. The band starts. Rock covers, Guns n' Roses, Bon Jovi, Van Halen...

Lisa's performance blows me away – her stage presence, the strength, and power of her voice, the way she looks.

'She's fucking amazing,' I tell Dan, 'she should be signed!'

'I know,' he replies, 'I keep telling her that.'

After the gig, Dan, Lisa, and I walk down to the beach. The tide far out, the sound of it swishing off in the distance, sand – soft and wet, darkness broken with glowing lunar light.

I find a stick. I write my name in the sand. Then draw a massive elaborate penis with balls and spunk coming out the top. I run right down to the sea and lob my stick in.

I feel suddenly giddy and manic with this experience, as if I am metamorphosing into a different character. Catalysed by the beach, sea, salty air, the hanging half-moon, the emotional resonance of Lisa's performance, all these forces acting upon me – alchemically.

I take my cock out and piss in the sea.

'What are you doing?' I hear Dan's voice shouting at me from up the beach.

'I've got my cock out!' I yell back. 'I'm having a piss!'

'You dirty tramp!' Lisa's voice behind me in the distance.

'We're going back in now,' Dan shouts, 'put your tiddler away, man!'

I stand and stare at the sky, drunkenly looking at the stars that peep like secret eyes from behind murky clouds.

I am here; I am now. I exist.

I wake up, uncomfortable, cold. Still in my clothes, shoes on, unfamiliar surroundings. A skinny black cat is staring me in the face.

'Prrt,' it says to me with solicitous eyes, 'prrt, meow.'

I sit up. 'I have nothing for you, puss.' I groan.

It is six in the morning. Sunlight creeping around the curtains. The room warm, stale. I creep out of the flat, try and close the door quietly. Down the seven flights of stairs – out into the quiet morning.

Each day I tramp from door to door, sliding the letters in, numb. I have a messy goatee. I've cut my hair short and spikey. At home, I stare at my face in the mirror – my eyes look tired, staring back at myself, and I can't identify who I am. An existential pain cripples me. I drink through it. Every night, bottles of wine, or cans of lager. Sometimes Jack and Coke. Lying in bed, bathed in televisual illumination – head static, heart aching. Cathode-ray hypnosis, slipping into sleep – wake up, the television still on.

I get release on Friday night – I drop over to see Dan and Lisa. I sit down, Ariella the cat immediately is on my lap, twisting round, chirruping, arching her back, caterwauling and sticking her behind in my face.

'What is wrong with this mog?'

Lisa laughs. 'She's in heat; she wants you to fuck her.'

I twist my face in disgust as the cat tries to get its anus in my face.

'Here,' Dan hands me a biro,' just poke her a bit in the fanny with this. That will satisfy her.'

I laugh. 'What? No man.' I push the cat off me but she climbs back on.

They both laugh at my sexual harassment. I pick up the biro and poke the cat in the bum with the lid-end. She lets out a satisfied caterwaul. We fall about laughing.

281

We watch T.V. and drink.

'Have you seen this?' Dan asks, changing the channel.

A man in a rubber Michael Jackson mask, with large glasses, is walking up a street, the seat of his pants cut out, exposing his bare behind.

'No, what the fuck is this?'

'Bo' Selecta,' he cries, 'you haven't seen it, man? It's fucking hilarious.'

For the next half-hour, doubled up with laughter, tears rolling down my face.

A little drunk, I decide to break the silence and text Ariella. No contact for two weeks, I explain that a namesake cat is trying to fuck me.

She replies saying the cat is expressing her sentiments.

I explain this to Dan and Lisa.

'She wants you back,' Lisa gasps.

A glimmer of hope, I text Ariella back, asking if we should meet up soon, maybe try and work things out.

It's too soon, she replies. Still too wounded, still hurting. Things may go wrong again.

I feel bruised.

The booze runs out unexpectedly quickly, and I must have more.

'Let's get some more,' I say.

'We're skint,' Lisa pipes in.

'I'll get it, man. Where's the nearest offy?'

'Town,' Dan replies, 'but I'll walk in with you if you want to go.'

Two drunk fools – I buy a bottle of vodka, Coke, cans of cider, and bottles of Brown Ale. It costs thirty quid.

'Shit,' Dan says, 'are you sure you can afford it?'

'Aye,' and I hand my card to the bemused woman behind the counter, 'what tabs does Lisa smoke?'

'Richmond, just get ten, though.'

'Ten Richmond king size as well, please,' I say to the woman.

'Cheers, man,' Dan says as he helps me with the bags, 'we'll never get through this in one night.'

I silently disagree.

Two hours later, very drunk.

The combination of booze in my gut begins to whir and fizz and I make a dash for the toilet. Eyes bulging hot, as a wave of sick surges up my throat, I grip the bowl of the bog and spew into the pan. Bits of sick come out my nose, it is trapped in my teeth, in my nasal passages. The chemical burn of the alcohol coming back up, scraping my throat, tears running down my cheeks. I throw up again, until there's nothing left – I'm just panting and wheezing at the side of the bowl. A sense of shame and embarrassment descending upon me.

'You alright?' Dan at the door.

'Aye.' I open it.

He passes me a glass of water.

I go back through to the living room, sheepish:

'Let's order pizza,' I declare, 'I'll pay for it.'

'Are you sure, man? You look pale.' Dan laughs.

'Yeah, I'm fine.'

Dan rummages around for a menu. I make him phone and order two large meat feast pizzas. I take the money out of my wallet and give it to him.

I wake up. Grey light creeping in from behind the curtains. A cat sleeping on top of me. As soon as she realises I'm awake, her gasping puckered bum-hole in my face, a creamy dot appearing from her quivering, feline pussy.

'Get off, man,' and I gently push her away.

My head is cloudy and I feel groggy. There are pizza boxes on the floor. I stand up, woozy and uncertain, new-born lamb-like, and fetch myself some water from the kitchen. Then I go for a piss, the lingering vomit-smell reminding me in postcard flashes of the previous evening. Dan comes through in his pyjama bottoms and an Extreme t-shirt.

'Nice shirt mate,' my voice croaky, 'sorry, did I wake you up.'

'Nah, I just came through to see if you were alive.'

'Did you fuckers order pizza after I fell asleep?'

He looks at me confusedly. 'No, man, you insisted on ordering them, then fell asleep before they arrived... do you remember what happened when I tried to wake you up?'

'No,' I reply feeling confused at the tone of bemusement in his voice.

'I offered you a bit, you woke up, stuck your tongue in and out like a strange lizard-beast, made a weird-as-fuck noise, and went back to sleep.'

I laugh at this. 'What?'

'Aye, man, your eyes were all over the place, Lisa was frightened.'

I hang my head in shame. 'Sorry, mate,' I chuckle.

'Nah, its fine man. Here,' and he hands me the pizza box, 'have some breakfast.'

We sit in silence eating cold pizza together.

XXXVII

My bedroom window overlooks the road. It is opposite a narrow street of cottages that turn off vertically. At the end of the cottage cul-de-sac, the blue-green glass windows of the Rowntree's factory. A large brown telegraph pole on the corner – I'm staring at the way the many wires splinter off at the top. Ariella walks through the scene. It is like a moving picture, her five-second stride through it – my heart thumping in my chest. Nausea.

I want to bang on the window. I want to run down into the street to talk to her. I begin to wonder if I've just had an hallucination.

I text her – *I've just seen you walk past my window.*

An agonising half-hour later.

She explains that she and Natalie have moved into the spare rooms of one of Natalie's university friends, around the corner from my mother's house. She says she hopes it isn't awkward if we bump into each other.

I feel sick and yet hopeful. I draw the curtains closed, tight, shutting out the daylight.

I intend to keep them that way.

Mid-August. I am drunk always. My window a terror, too many times I catch glimpses of them, and I die inside. My mother comes in to open the curtains when I'm not there. I'm standing in the frame of the window, curtains open. Figures on the street – they look up and wave at me, Ariella's soft lamb-face. I scowl and draw the curtains, a volcanic sorrow erupting inside – all afternoon I'm sinking, rotting,

285

becoming undone. Weeks of it – a long and torturous unravelling.

Night. I go to The Discount Wine Centre and buy wine and spirits. I begin drinking. I slip my headphones on – Opeth's *Damnation*. Close my eyes, drift off, lost in it, drunk, feelings of confusion, a sensation of being unwell.

I take out my little Jack Daniels tin of silly sentimental things from our relationship – letters, photographs, ticket stubs. My ornamental knife, slid from the leather scabbard, I begin to stab violently through the flimsy tin, repeatedly. The knife isn't sharp; but it easily punctures the tin. I destroy it – pictures torn, the knife through my image. I stand up, roll down my pants, and stab myself in the thigh. It hurts, it bruises – but doesn't break the skin. I pull my pants back up – my teeth gritted – run the blunt edge of the knife down my left arm, it only scratches the skin – and so I repeat, running down the same mark, slowly breaking the skin, until the ooze of red begins to seep.

I stand up and throw the knife at the wall.

'Fuck you, you fucking bitch!' I scream.

My mother's feet bounding up the stairs, into my room.

'What are you doing?' she asks.

She sees the blood, the knife.

'My god, what have you done?'

'Nothing. Nothing, it's fine.'

She examines the wound, fetches some tissue. We sit on the bed.

'Don't hurt yourself,' she tells me.

I hold my head in my hand. Tears begin to flow, hot,

286

awful, and burning.

'You really loved that girl, didn't you?'

I nod, grief stealing my voice.

'Go to bed, you will feel better in the morning.'

I nod again. She stands up, picks the knife from the floor.

'I'm taking this; it's for your own good.'

The door closes. I cry into my pillow like a little boy.

For a month, I hide, exhausted, broken. Curtains drawn, drinking alone, sometimes meeting Dan in Trillians on a Monday for pound-a-pint night, or going to his flat at the weekend, watching Lisa perform at some random pub somewhere in the sticks.

I sit alone with my monsters. I write or make music, chewing up my existential angst, my sorrows, and a constant depressive-pain.

'Hey,' my mother shouts up the stairs, 'I've just seen Ariella across the road,' her words drilling into me. I don't reply.

Then she's at the bedroom door, telling me again.

'I know,' I say blankly.

'Why have you always got the curtains closed?'

'So I don't have to fucking look at her.'

'Oh, right.'

The window becomes a terrible thing – a portal of despair. The chocolatey smell of Fawdon – early September, Ariella's birthday. No contact with her for weeks, yet I text her happy birthday. A simple reply of thanks.

My mother has been in and opened the curtains

again – I leave them open, a morbid curiosity growing.

Natalie walks past. Then Gary and Dom, then Ariella. In a strange procession, as if something is wrong. They're all dressed up, I assume for an evening somewhere celebrating her birthday. Ariella's hair dyed – rusty like a fox, she's wearing a red-rag and black outfit, knee-boots, a gap of fishnet just before the skirt, like a strange gypsy-goth. Her face pale, Victorian. Eyes to the floor.

I close the curtains and sit alone feeling sick. I wonder if my premonition has already come true.

I go to work, counting down the days until I leave to start college. Each letter brings me closer to it. I hope for it to bring me change, to smash the depression, to move me forward, away from Ariella. Away from my shame.

Mid-September – the last letter. It plops through the letterbox, and I listen for the satisfying sound of it hitting the floor on the other side.

A day later, I pack my work uniform into the bright red postbag and dump it at the D.O.

I know I won't miss anyone, and doubt if anyone will miss me. I will, however, miss the walking, the fresh air, the gardens, the ever-changing and variable English weather and how it makes me feel, the slutty office tarts, the tips at Xmas. I will miss the twenty minutes' skive in the morning when I sit on the cold bog reading poetry, avoiding the final push on the primary, and instead letting my nuts and bum-hole grow cold, while the stench of my shit permeates the air like an accompanying fragrance.

I will miss the horrible coffee from the vending machine – the sweetness of it, and the inevitable sticky rim of the cup, my morning cigar, the smell of it on my gloves in the winter, Carol's arse – wrapped tightly in her blue pants. On my way home, I decide to have a final wank over it that night, for nostalgia's sake.

The night before my first day at college, sitting in my box-room, nailing several cans of lager.

I wake up next morning to discover my rucksack is wet and that I've knocked over a can that was on the floor, and it has spilled onto the bag, leaving it smelling of stale booze. I have no other means of carrying my stuff, so I just have to take it and smell like a wino until I can put it in the wash later that day.

On the Rye Hill Campus site, a new multi-million pound building for performance arts. It looks like a giant brown brick with windows. Through the automatic doors, a canteen, rows of benches and seats that are perfectly symmetrical oblong blocks. There is a sign for new students, directing those on the Music Production Degree to meet in the main performance hall at nine a.m. I locate it and go through the doors – people inside already, I find a seat and wait.

Nine-fifteen. Pat Daughter walks in with his nose. 'Alright guys,' his voice thinned through his beak, 'welcome to music production.'

He gives a brief lecture on the course. Then a tour of the building – the studios, practice rooms, classrooms, offices. Then a break. I bump into Liam in the canteen and we have a conversation at crossed purposes, with me failing to decipher his Northern-

Irish brogue.

'Jesus, you smell of stale beer.' He tells me bluntly.

I laugh at him. I like him, but I'm not sure if he likes me.

Liam goes outside for a smoke. I buy a coffee and sit people-watching, eyeing up skirt. I spot a familiar face that I saw during the music production lecture. I pick my coffee up and move over.

'Alright, mate?' I stick a hand out, 'Toby, isn't it? You're a drummer, aren't you? I've seen your band before.'

'Yeah,' he smiles, 'I know I've met you before, but I can't remember your name.'

I tell him.

Everyday becomes a mission – sneaking like a weasel to the Metro station, hoping to avoid both Nat and Ariella – and yet at the same time hoping I bump into Ariella, hoping that somehow there may be a fix to everything.

An automatic front is building – one that protects me – an emotional shield. A pretence that all is better now we're over, that I'm moving on, forward-march into new territory. Inside, all is crumbling – but I determine that when the time comes I eventually bump into them, I will uphold the pretence.

The mornings are colder, late September, the turn to fall – I'm getting stuck into my degree, the first assignment, the workings of the ear and how it interprets sound, is underway, and I'm focused.

My breath in front of me on the platform. Seven a.m. – I'm heading in earlier, to use the library, to work on my assignment. Nat on the platform.

An exchange of pleasantries. I feel stiff and awkward.

'You should speak to Ariella,' Nat tells me once we're on the train; 'I think she would like to be friends with you. She misses you.'

I think about this all day. A faint glimmer of hope, and yet, a precognitive sensation, something synchronistic about to happen.

That night I call her. Parents out – I pace the living room talking to her. We talk about my college course, how it's going, what it entails.

Out of the blue: 'Have you got a new girlfriend yet?' 'No, why?'

A pause. 'It's just that with all those girls at college, you must have met someone, or got your eye on someone?'

'No, it's still too soon for me.'

Another pause.

'Have you met someone?' I ask.

'Well, I've been trying to think of a way to tell you, actually, but yeah, I'm kind of seeing someone.'

'Well, I hope it works out for you.' I tell her, bluntly.

I don't even need to ask who it is – I already know. Somehow, in my distorted logic, and from a precognition I don't understand, I've known all along how things would play out. How predictable she would be. It was like game theory – human beings in certain situations will always play out the same way. Fuck you, buddy, we will always screw each other over.

A day later, out of my window, Ariella walking down

291

the street, hand in hand with Dom.

And so, I knew it – that she would jump on the nearest cock available, just like she did from Johnathan to me. Poor little girl, can't stand to be alone. Manipulating, cock-teasing. I feel a little justification for my madness, yet no one will ever see her sneaky behaviour; all they've seen are my explosions, my temper, my hurt personified. I realise I've learned a little bit about the differences between male and female – that it is easy to look like a beast when you let your emotions erupt, you say or do something violent and the whole world points a finger at you and calls you wrong. Men and women alike, look at you, blame you, and lynch you for being a monster. For feeling. And yet, somewhere in the background, unseen, unknown, play-out little bitch-games. Quiet, rotten, all sugary-saccharine, moulding and shaping things to fit inside their stinking, insecure cunt.

I close the curtains. I have to get away from all this.

LEAF III

XXXVIII

November – days falling from the calendar like autumnal leaves. Each day a battle for sleep, for peace of mind, against alcohol, against existential panic, running and hiding from myself, from thoughts of Ariella.

In the Head of Steam after college – Toby gulping down Hoegaarden, the pissy-beige liquid with scum-tide mark in a pint glass that looks like a cheap vase. Liam and myself drinking Warsteiner.

Toby's phone rings – he answers it and speaks to someone down the other end in Cantonese.

'Who were you talking to there?' Liam asks, in his usual forward manner.

'The Police,' Toby smirks.

Liam stands up on his stool, lifts his orange t-shirt up, exposing his hairy belly, and loudly sings:

'Roxanne!'

The barmaid, Rose, looks over and laughs.

'It's only half-three in the afternoon, how drunk are you guys?'

'I'm not drunk at all,' Liam responds in fact. He turns back to Toby. 'No, seriously, who were you talking to in Chinese?'

'My mam.'

'We're you born in China?'

'Aye, but we moved here when I was three.'

'You'd be pretty good at ordering a takeaway then?' Liam laughs.

'Fuck off, you racist.'

'What? I'm Irish, how can *I* be racist?'

'I've had enough Hoegaarden,' Toby drains his glass,

'let's get the tequila in.'

Tequila round one:

Liam: 'I know I haven't seen your knobs, but mine is definitely bigger. It's like a mushroom at the end.'

Tequila round two:

Liam: 'I can't handle getting a blow-job because of it, it's too much.'

Tequila round three:

Liam: 'I'm better looking that you two fellas.'

Tequila round four:

Toby: 'Orlansee.'

Liam: 'What?'

Toby: 'It's Cantonese for dribble-poo.'

Liam: 'No it's not, you're making that up. How big is your knob then?'

Someone is prodding me in the shoulder. 'You alright, mate?'

The train has stopped moving. I'm groggy and hazy – I realise I've fallen asleep. I look through the window trying to work out where I am.

'You're at the airport mate,' the man, who I realise is the driver, is telling me. 'You need to get off the train; it's going out of service. There's another one on the other platform waiting to go back the other way.'

I get up and stagger off the train, my head clouded – the taste of tequila, lime and salt in my mouth. I stand on the platform feeling confused and dizzy.

'Did you have a bag with you?' the driver asks.

I check myself. 'Fuck, yes.' I reply as I realise I've left it on the now-pulling-out-of-the-station train.

'It's going back to the depot, so someone will check the train anyway. You should be able to get your bag from the office in South Gosforth.'

I sit on the train and groan. In my pocket, I find a moist and still warm cheeseburger from Burger King that I can't remember buying. I look at the time on my phone, it's half-eight. I can't recall leaving The Steamer. At the Metro offices in South Gosforth, I weakly press the buzzer, mumble into the intercom about my bag. Someone opens the door and thrusts it at me. Luckily, all my college work is still in there.

At home, I decide to lie down forever.

Friday –

Toby asks me, 'what are you doing tonight?'

'Nothing.'

'My band is playing at Newcastle Uni, then, we're going to World Head Quarters, if you fancy it.'

'Aye, alright. Who is on at WHQ?'

'Some DJ. Mark Ronson, or something.'

'Okay.'

Evening. Fawdon is quiet, black-sky. There is a way that the sky hangs over the bungalows to the left of the road, and a strange sensation that I always feel.

In town, upstairs in the union bar – I stand and talk to Rose while the band set up. She has long, dirty-blonde hair, is thin and tall – Nordic looking, brown eyes.

'What are you studying at university?' I ask her.

'Law,' she replies, unenthusiastically. 'Did Tobes talk to you about the house?'

I shake my head.

'We're thinking of renting a house in Heaton. You're still at your mam's, aren't you?'

'Aye,' I reply with a hint of misery.

'He said he was going to ask you if you might want to move in. My friend Emily is taking a room too.'

The prospect of it goes round in my head for a moment and I mentally masticate on it. The financial reality, that I don't have a job doesn't enter my head – as I know my student loan will cover the rent for at least three months.

'Alright,' I tell Rose, 'that would be brilliant, actually.'

'That's great,' she smiles, 'we're viewing a house next week, on Rothbury Terrace.'

The band play, edging towards the NWOAHM sound – Killswitch Engage, God Forbid, Lamb of God. More drinks. Toby's drum-faces and grimaces peeking out from behind his kit.

Suddenly, a sensation of newness, new people, and experiences – the idea of moving out begins to take form in my mind.

Later – WHQ is jammed. I don't know what the music is, but I'm dancing to it anyway – although my dancing is more bumbling like a dying bee. I'm sweaty, sticky with spilt drinks.

Toby introduces me to someone. 'This is Disco,' he tells me. We shake hands.

Disco is lanky, with long thin arms and legs – he reminds me of the actor Crispin Glover.

'There's loads of fanny in here!' I shout at him over the music.

'What?' I lip read his reaction.

I shout it again.

He shouts something back in my lug.

This goes on for a few more rounds, until I give him

the thumbs up and pat him on the shoulder, pretending I've understood the conversation.

The club drawing to a close – it begins to thin out. All the females disappearing, my dancing begins to feel conspicuous.

I find Rose standing near the toilets.

'You alright?' I ask her drunkenly.

'Yeah, just bored of the loudness now. Tobes is outside talking to this girl he fancies.'

'Ah, good for him,' I slur, 'I'm looking forward to moving in with you two, you know, you both seem lovely.'

She laughs at this. 'Thanks,' she smiles, 'I think we're going back to Tobes' flat if you want to come?'

Back at the flat, cans of Strongbow, passing a joint around, I hand it to Disco, slipping the end into his thin, yellow, nicotine-stained fingers. Light of early morning creeping through the curtains.

A serious conversation in the kitchen between Toby and his new girlfriend that I can see though the open door, but I can't make out over the low rumble of music.

Then the girl – small, chestnut eyes, big smile – walks past us and out of the door.

A moment and Rose goes off into the kitchen, closing the door behind her. Another moment, she returns, picks up her bag, and begins to rummage around in it.

'You alright, Rose?' Disco asks.

'Tobes has cut himself again.'

'Shit,' Disco stands and goes into the kitchen.

Toby at the kitchen door, holding several sheets of kitchen roll to his arm – the red of his blood seeping heavily into it. He pulls the sheets away and I see the wound – it's deep and the inner flesh is exposed. I notice that up his arm he has several scars of a similar size and shape to the one he has just opened.

'I'm calling an ambulance,' Rose tells him.

'I'm alright,' Toby protests.

Disco puts his arms around Toby. 'Seriously, you need to stop hurting yourself, man.'

Rose and Toby back in the kitchen with the door closed.

'He cuts himself when he's depressed,' Disco tells me, taking a swig from his can.

A half hour later, the ambulance arrives – Toby and Rose get in it.

I sit for a while talking to Disco. Tiredness, the booze wearing off, feeling stoned, sleep creeping upon me. I feel my eyes roll, and take it as a sign to go.

Seven in the morning. As I'm leaving, I shake Disco's hand, and feel that I like him immensely – and that his vast affability is infectious. His wide smile beaming at me – I realise this man has a massive, open heart.

Bruised morning sky, clouds stretching off, low, and burning with the upcoming sun. Only a mile or so to walk home. Saturday morning – quiet roads, the sound of wood pigeons, and the pleasant emptiness of the streets. A world stirring.

It occurs to me that I am not isolated in hurt – I remember that existence is suffering, and wonder how I forgot – realise my unknowingness, trapped in my own bubble of existential despair.

A blind man – consumed with his own nightmares

300

that pull a screen down over the eyes and mind –
locked in, forgetting, severing empathic qualities. I
realise how clouded I have become – how not long
ago I was mindful. I wonder if I deliberately chose to
forget the truth of suffering, as if the burden of
compassion was too much. I wonder why, as a
species, we should bother to work towards an
emotion that I feel is not inherently natural.
Selfishness is the natural state – because to be human
is a battle against death and time. Time not enough to
conquer our own demons. I feel foolish, ignorant,
hopeless, broken. All there is is *time* to fill in, before
the ultimate truth: the void, the blackness, the eternal
emptiness.

I want to erupt, to laugh and weep at once, together.

I walk past my grandparents' house and think of my
dead Gran.

I feel absurd; life feels absurd, and existence feels
pointless and meaningless in a terrible, yet somehow
beautiful, liberating way.

XXXIX

Looking around the house on Rothbury Terrace with Rose, Toby, and Emily. High ceilings, big rooms, typical town house.

'What do you think?' Toby asks me.

'It's a house, there's a room I can live in. It's cool with me.'

I decide I want the room upstairs to the back. Emily has decided to take the one next to it. Rose has introduced us, but Emily seems shy and wary of me. Black curly hair falling down her face, slim body, green eyes that she hides.

We pay the deposit. Moving in date is 29th November.

'Drinks to celebrate?' Toby asks me.

'Aye, go on then.'

Every morning I wake up bleary-eyed, dehydrated, and emotionally shipwrecked. However, today, knowing I am moving away from Fawdon, away from the box room, the always-closed curtains, away from Ariella and Natalie, my parents. I am taking a step away from everything, and through the hangover, I feel energised, giddy, and excitable.

I arrive and Toby is already putting stuff into his room downstairs. Disco is helping unpack, making cups of tea, and rolling cigarettes on the brown rickety table in the snug/dining room.

'What time are Rose and Emily moving in?' I ask Toby as I bring my first box in from Jack's van.

'Dunno, man. I just wanna get unpacked and get the booze in.'

'Where do you want these boxes?' Jack at the door.
'Just chuck 'em in the doorway, please.'

My cardboard box mountain begins to build.

Disco notices it. 'What the fuck have you got in there?' he asks.

'Books,' I laugh. 'Fancy giving me a hand taking them upstairs?'

I get all my stuff in. Disco brings me a cuppa, sits on the bare mattress, and rolls a cigarette.

I begin to unpack, putting posters, photographs, and postcards up, setting up my computer, setting up my synth, drum machines, and guitars.

'Can I have a bash on your Korg?' he asks, pointing to the small synthesiser.

'Aye, go for it.'

He turns it on.

'The practise amp is there,' I point to the small speaker, 'and here's a jack.'

He untangles it and plugs in. The lights on the keyboard come on. He begins making all kinds of sounds, and I enjoy listening to someone else play it.

'We should have a jam sometime,' he tells me.

'Yeah, of course.' I reply.

That night – in the snug, Toby's N64 connected to the TV. Snakebites, cider shots every round while playing Mario Kart – I decide to start smoking again – thin roll-up cigarettes. The paraphernalia – filters, skins, the ritual of it.

Pokémon mini-games.

'What the fuck? This is surreal,' I say, while trying to eat sushi as a Squirtle.

'Those fucking Japs, man,' Toby laughs.

303

Disco starts to mimic the sound of the creatures on screen. I'm drunk and laughing at nothing – tears streaming down my face. Rose and Emily walk through the snug into the kitchen, bemusement on their faces.

'This is what it's going to be like, isn't it?' Rose laughs.

'Yep,' Toby nods, not taking his eyes from the screen.

'Disco,' Rose says from the kitchen while making a cup of tea, 'I'm going to bed soon, do you want to come?'

He keeps his eyes on the screen, controlling the strange monster with the massive tongue as it tries to gobble up as much sushi as possible in sixty seconds.

'Yeah,' he says in a strange half-hearted way, 'I'll be up soon.'

Half an hour later and he goes off upstairs.

'What's that about?' I ask Toby, 'are they seeing each other?'

'Fuck knows mate. I think she wants to be in a relationship with him, but I don't think he's arsed.'

'Is he shagging her?'

'I dunno, man,' he pauses looking for words, 'I love Disco, but he's beginning to get on my nerves. I moved house because he was always in my flat, he's homeless you know, and I feel sorry for him, because he's lovely, but he's just followed me here. He needs to get a job and sort his life out.'

'I didn't realise it was like that.'

Toby turns the N64 and TV off. 'I think I'm going to bed too.'

'How is your arm?' I ask, noticing him

304

unconsciously finger the wound.

'It's okay, man. Sorry you had to see that.'

'Are you alright, though?'

'Aye, it's just something I do when I'm drunk and I get frustrated. That night at Mark Ronson, I got together with Frances, then, we broke up like an hour later.'

'Have you spoken since?'

'Yeah, we're back on.' He gives me a smile and a thumbs up. 'Anyways I'll see you tomorrow. Come and give me a knock and I'll drive us to college.'

In the morning, I find Disco asleep on the rickety sofa in the snug. He is the colour of autumnal earth – his clothes are browns and oranges, chestnut eyes.

'Alreet?' he groans sleepily.

'What happened? I thought you were sleeping with Rose?'

'She kicked me out of bed because I wouldn't shag her.'

'Why not?' I ask, with a hint of incredulity.

'Because she's mental. I don't want to get involved with her.'

'Fair enough. Do you want a brew?'

'Aye.' He sits up and moves over to the table, pulls out his pouch of tobacco and starts rolling cigarettes. He hands me one and I hand him his coffee. 'I shouldn't have got into bed with her in the first place. It's just nice to be in a bed sometimes, instead of on a sofa, or down the Off-Quay.'

'Have you got a lock-up?'

'Aye, I use it with me band. We should go down one night for a jam.'

'I'm up for that.'

I finish my brew and roll-up. 'I'm off to college, but if you're about I'll catch you later?'

'I'm rehearsing tonight, but I might catch you later. If I don't sleep down the Off-Quay.'

I feel a sudden pang of sadness hearing this. 'Nah, just come here mate, you might as well sleep where it's warm and comfortable.'

He smiles. 'Cheers, man.'

I leave him and bang on Toby's door. 'Tobes, you awake man?'

There's no answer.

'Toby?'

'You'll never wake him up, mate,' Disco shouts through from the snug, 'I would just go if I were you.'

Outside – grey, cold, and wet.. Clouds hang low, sky-covering, and ominous. Cold wind scuffles empty drinks cans, leaves, crisp packets, cigarette ends together in a mini-tornado – the clatter of the can rumbling down the street.

Toby's blue Micra parked outside the house – I consider going back in to wake him up – as I have no money for the bus and now I have to walk. Not that the walking is a problem, however I realise I may be late for my lecture. I put my headphones in. I can only listen to sad songs, Björk's *Vespertine*, *Pagan Poetry*, an icy soundtrack, compliments this seasonal vista.

I arrive at college – through the automatic glass doors – Toby sitting having a coffee – bleary-eyed.

'Soz, man,' he says.

'Twat,' I laugh at him.

My face is numb and cold, but I feel awake.

306

I look at the time on my phone. We're three minutes late.

'We'd better get in there; you know what a cunt Pat Daughter is. He'll be banging on about P45s and working at McDonald's again if we're really late.'

'Fuck that hook-nosed Jew-nobber,' Toby laughs.

A routine begins to develop on most days: college until three in the afternoon, then drinks in The Head of Steam afterwards with Toby and Liam, then evening drinks of cheap cider with Disco, while Toby courts his girlfriend. On a Friday or Saturday night, I head off with Dan and Lisa to a dive somewhere in the northeast to watch Lisa perform. I wake up on their sofa, dehydrated, confused, sometimes with memories of kissing random women.

While I have paid my rent for three months, my reserve of cash from the remainder of my first student loan payment is diminishing. I realise I need part-time work. I slip into the scummy job centre and browse the machines. I find one job that looks suitable: event staff.

I make the call there and then. Interview next day, the man on the other end of the phone briefly explains the job: providing a security presence at concerts and other events, and rigging work if I want it.

I sit alone in my room some nights, waiting for Disco to drop in or sitting in a deep silence for the evening if he is rehearsing or otherwise engaged. My room is big – I light candles and sit in the darkness in front of the computer screen, writing essays while tipsy on cheap cider from the shop across the road or just typing away randomly into the online journal I've set up – recording half-remembered dreams, thoughts, images. Sadness creeping up on me in quiet times. I realise I'm chasing all my melancholy away, drinking it away. My room is eerie – massive bed left unkempt, no quilt cover, just a black sheet with a skull and crossbones on it, no pillow covers – a brown stain of grease from my head. Creaky old wooden furniture, red carpet worn down with unknown stains here and there. The ashtray filled with ends – I run out of money and tobacco, twiddling old stubs, filling a skin with flaky ash-caked bits, ripping a ticket for a roach, fingers dirty, shiny, and black-tar-stinking.

I look older – no or not much sleep most nights. An insomniac's love affair with alcohol. Dipsomaniac. There is a small cupboard under the stairs in the house, where the gas and electricity meters are – drunk out of my mind I climb inside it, poke my head out to scare the girls as they go past. Emily looks at me with a contemptuous scowl. I find her walking round the house at three in the morning, fully dressed-up, as if to go out for the evening, even though she hasn't left the house. Heels on, short skirt – I want to spunk up her back.

At the interview, my enthusiasm for working on the rigging for gigs gets me the job. It's a cash in hand, casual deal; you only work if you want it. The rigging consists of two shifts: one in the morning setting up, and one that evening, bringing the thing down again. All the gig-work is at the Arena, though they outsource to other events as well.

'Work this Saturday if you want it,' the gaffer tells

me, 'The Darkness.'

I tell him yes.

Night, frost, and winter beating against the doors and windows. Sitting with Disco playing *Super Mario 3* on Toby's old NES. Roll-ups, cheap cider.

'You know, I don't think I ever finished this game as a child,' I tell him.

'Me neither,' he replies.

'Let's stay up tonight and nail it.'

He laughs and agrees.

'How come you won't get together with Rose?' I ask him, getting a gold star at the end of a level. 'She's lovely, and attractive.'

'Yeah, aye, I know that,' he sighs, 'but she's a bit radge sometimes, man.'

'Aren't all women?'

'True, but… did Toby tell you what happened?'

'No.'

'About six months ago, my ex, Lauren, left me for this other bloke. I had my suspicions like, but even so, I didn't take it well.'

'Christ, I don't think I would have either. Why did she leave you for him?'

'I'm not one-hundred-percent sure. He's older than me,' he paused for a second; 'you and me are the same age, aren't we?'

'I'm twenty-two.'

'Aye, I thought so, me too. Well, long story short, she works with him, I think he was just more attentive, he's not a piss-head loser, like me, and he's like thirty or something and has a *real*-job. About a month after we split, one day I woke up, and I had

309

this thought, more like a sensation that came over me, that there was no hope, nothing even worth breathing for, man. So I sat on the Green in town and consumed ten boxes of paracetamol.'

'Shit.'

'Aye, so then I began to panic a bit and I phoned an ambulance.'

'What happened?'

'The ambulance was there in seconds, man, I actually walked to it and got in. Started to feel weird once I lay down though.'

'Stomach pump?'

'Aye. I passed out.'

'Did you really want to die?'

'Part of me did, but then I realised it was probably just a cry for attention. Stupid, really.'

'What's that got to do with Rose?'

'I still love Lauren.'

'Ah.'

'That's stupid as well,' he tells me, keeping his eyes on the screen while as Mario-Racoon takes a sprint that allows him to fly up into a perfect square of coins. 'What's the point of getting together with someone when you can't feel, or give them anything back, emotionally?'

'That's very wise,' I comment, pondering his deep words. 'You could still fuck her, though.'

'You man-whore.' He laughs. 'If I fuck her it would just make things worse.'

'You have more control over your knob than I do, mate.'

The conversation turns to my tale of woe with Ariella. I explain everything and he listens patiently. I feel there is a mutual understanding between us of our individual heartaches.

'You know what I think, though,' he says to me after listening to my story, 'you have to lose that first real love of your life, you can't gain anything or grow or realise a lot of the bullshit that you think about yourself or the world, and understand your mistakes, until you lose that love from your heart.'

I nod.

'Being that much in love with someone makes you mental, doesn't it?'

I nod again. 'True story, mate.'

'We're just apes,' he laughs, 'stupid apes, that can talk and who think they're intelligent, but all they want to do is drink cheap, nasty, cider, smoke rollies, and play *Super Mario 3*.'

I laugh at this.

'So don't forget,' he adds, 'you're just an ape.'

Three in the morning. Running out of lives on Bowser's ship – the last level on *Super Mario 3*.

'Bowser, you're a fucking cunt,' Disco says as a bullet with an angry face kills Mario, 'your turn, how many lives have you got left?'

'Last one.'

'Shit, come on man, you can do it.'

I'm dead within three seconds of starting the level. 'Fuck!' I cry.

'I'm on my last life now,' Disco tells me with serious determination.

He makes it past the bullet that killed him last time, only to snuff it at the hands of a hammer-throwing mole.

'Ah, piss-flaps man, I think we're destined to never

finish this stupid game.'

'Try again tomorrow?'

'Nah, fuck that man, it's a sign never to try again. It's just not meant to be.'

XL

The load in – metal scaffolds unloaded from truck after truck, boxes, and crates on wheels pushed fast down ramps, endless lengths of thick, different coloured wires. All this in a mad chaos, men running about erecting the stage, lighting and sound system – I'm not sure what I'm supposed to be doing, so I stand on the dock, helping bring in the crates on wheels. The whole thing is exciting and interesting, yet I fear for my safety – a few hours in and I've already got a bloodied gash down my arm from the corner of a crate – men are climbing up the scaffold with rigging dangling all over the place – electric drills screaming, screwing the whole thing in place. No one is wearing any safety gear.

'Can you get up there and bolt this together?' the gaffer asks me, handing me a drill.

I look at the contraption he has handed me. I climb up, one-handed, until I'm at least twenty foot off the ground – no harness, helmet, or anything. If I fall, I'm in for an injury. I'm sweating and panicking a bit; I'm useless at DIY, using tools and building things. I fumble about, trying to get the job done so I can get down.

When I finally get down, my knuckles are white and I can feel my heart pumping hard in my chest. It's cold too – and the metal of the scaffold is icy to the touch, my fingers are numb, skeletal and stuck in a rigid-grip. I can't decide if I like doing this job.

By the time the stage, lighting, and sound are set up, it's nine in the morning. I've been here since five. I have to come back at half-ten that night to

313

deconstruct and pack up the whole thing.

The light of the morning filling my eyes – walking through town, Xmas shoppers, the cold of early December – my emotions flutter about inside, that strange seasonal sensation that shifts and makes me feel odd – the way the clouds hang, how trees are bare or green – the strength of the sun.

At home – quiet, Disco sitting at the table in the snug, smoking a cigarette, reading the Metro paper.

'Did you just come in, there?' he asks looking up from the paper.

'Aye, I started that job this morning.'

'How was it?'

I tell him.

In the kitchen, I put the kettle on.

'Brew?' I ask him.

'Aye, please man.'

I set the mugs up, open the cupboard, pull out the cheap brown, crumbly coffee granules, and dump a teaspoon each into the mugs. Looking at my food stores, I realise I'm hungry. I also realise that I don't have much food, haven't been eating at all recently, and that I've lost weight. Food seems unimportant, somehow. Since not living at my mother's, all I've done to sustain myself is drink cheap and nasty cider.

'Do you want breakfast?' I ask Disco.

He thinks about it for a second. 'Aye, alright. What have you got?'

'Nowt.'

I hear him chuckling. 'Aye, I'll have that.'

'How does a bowl of pubes, belly-button fluff, dust, and crumbs sound?'

'Delicious, mate.'

I pour out the coffee and hand him a mug. He's made me a cigarette and laid it out waiting. I pick it up and examine it. It is perfectly straight, rounded, and smooth looking.

'You make amazing rollies, man,' I tell him.

'It's an art form.'

'I'm fucking starving though; all I've got in the cupboard is a packet of nine-pee prawn flavour noodles.'

'You have them, mate. I'm not arsed about breakfast.'

'I was hoping to keep them for tea.'

I watch as he rummages around in his coat pocket. He lays three coins on the table, one silver, two copper. He looks at it for a second. 'I've got seven pence.'

'Hang on,' I tell him, and I run upstairs to my room. I find the few scattered copper coins I know I have on my desk and count them on my way back down. 'I've got four pence.' I tell him, adding it to his coins.

'Eleven pence,' he says looking at the money, 'what can we get with that?'

'Does Coli-Heed sell ten pence bags of crisps?'

'Dunno, probably.'

I scoop the money up and head for the door. On my way, I have a thought, and begin to pull the cushions off the sofa. Underneath – crumbs, fluffs, a sock, and in amongst it a twenty pence piece.

'Fuck yes!' I say, picking up the coin.

'How much?' Disco asks excitedly.

I tell him.

'Fucking hell,' he laughs, 'a packet of ten pence crisps each!'

315

I go out the front door – brace myself against the cold, and into Coli's corner shop. Mr. Coli is standing behind the counter. He is five-foot five, greying, with a friendly, 'buy something then get out', smile. Looking at his wares, my brain is ticking over, trying to work out the best possible purchases for my meagre coinage. Coli watching me. I feel pressured. I spot a packet of custard creams for 21p, meaning I can purchase a packet of 10p crisps too. A packet of pickled onion Space Raiders.

Back in the house, I dump the biscuits and crisps on the table.

'Nice choices mate,' Disco nods.

We crack open the biscuits, crisps, drink some more horrible black coffee, and I smoke my cigarette.

'This is the life, eh?' Disco laughs.

I laugh too, feeling quite surreal, a mixture of fatigue, hunger and madness.

The load out – a rewind of the load in. Unbolting everything, pushing crates up ramps onto the back of HGVs. However, this time, everything is twice as manic and the gaffer is harassing everyone to be quick about it. He points out a pile of large, metal scaffolds used to rig up the lights; they need to be loaded next. I join the queue to pick one up, and I watch the method people use to haul them up. From a squat, the thing goes up and over your head, so you poke your head through the hole in the scaffold, then balance it and take the weight on your shoulders. My turn, I squat to pick one up, a shooting pain runs up my back and I can't get my breath.

'Fuck,' I wheeze out, 'my back has just gone.'

My abs contract tight and I can't straighten myself. No one says anything or is interested in helping me. I waddle off to the side like an old man. I manage to make it to a chair, sit there not knowing what to do. The gaffer comes over.

'I've hurt my back,' I tell him.

'Do you want to rest for a bit then continue?'

I shake my head.

'Get yourself away, then.' He tells me without a hint of compassion.

The three-mile walk home that I have to take now seems like a horrible marathon. Just after midnight, drunken revellers spilling in and out of pubs and clubs, puddles of sick on the pavement, hot brown bits of kebab and stringy purple salad, pizza boxes left open like gaping greasy mouths, hideous faces gurn at me like ventriloquist dummies, the smell of heavy perfumes, onions grilling, spastic guttural drunk voices, lights buzzing, neon nightmares. Orangey women, blokes in shirts, dick-head disco dancing, men clapping their hands above their heads and singing football chants. I'm hobbling, a semi-paralysed turtle. I try to make it to a point in the distance, then rest for a moment.

I arrive home two and a half hours later. I'm numb and a bit insane with cold and pain. I expect to find Disco asleep on the sofa but he's not there. In the kitchen, I rummage about looking for painkillers but there's nothing. I pour myself a pint of water. In bed, with every move I make, a whimper of pain escapes from my body.

Sunday – the house is completely silent. I can't move without a terrible pain pulsing up my back. I manage to construct a horrible "jail tab", as Disco calls it, emptying the remains of old "jail tabs" into a skin and rolling it up. It doesn't taste of tobacco; it tastes of burning and ash. The thing is so thin that no real smoke comes off it. With considerable agony, I make it downstairs and assemble a cup of tea. It is an amazing achievement. Back in bed, I decide all I can do is sleep until the pain goes away.

Drifting in and out – waking, unsure of where I am or what is going on, then the pain kicks me into reality. Early afternoon and no sign or sound of anyone. I crawl along the passage to the bathroom, lock the door, groan as I manage to turn the shower on, get in, and lie in the bath with the water licking me. I close my eyes – spots appearing in front of them. I feel mad, delirious. In my ears, I begin to hear something – a song, like a chant. It is getting gradually louder, tiny increments, until I hear it full, as real as anything I've ever heard. Native American singing, I can't make out the words, and the rhythm and structure are so hypnotic that I cannot correctly analyse the sound I am hearing. After reaching a crescendo, it fades back out – and my ability to think returns. I realise it's the most beautiful thing I've ever heard. I wonder if I've finally cracked completely, and I begin to laugh and cry at the same time. Something transcendental has happened – although it is probably just through fatigue, alcoholism, insomnia, malnutrition, and pain. I get dressed, squeaking with pain as I do so, thinking to myself – I will never tell anyone about the Native American Indians in the shower.

I creep painfully back downstairs and into the main

318

living room, flipping up the covers on the settee looking for coins. My heart flutters as I realise I've struck gold; five pound fifty!

In Coli's shop, I purchase some paracetamol, skins, a small block of golden Virginia, two 1.5 litre bottles of cheap White Storm cider, a packet of cheap custard cream biscuits, a Chomp, and several packets of cheap crisps.

I might be in agony, but I feel like king for the day.

Back home, I lock my bedroom door, take my clothes off, put on my big Pantera hoodie, tracksuit pants, and climb into bed, where I determine to stay until my back pain subsides. I neck four paracetamol, just to be sure, with cider to wash it down, set up a pile of films to watch, eat all the biscuits, filling the bed with crumbs, and smoke a roll-up.

Midday, both the bottles of cider are empty, I've had half the paracetamol, and my head is spinning. Watching *Princess Mononoke*, a reminiscence of Ariella – and a sudden, drunken lament, as a tear slips down my face, and a stupid melancholy fills my heart.

I decide to sleep – pull the grotty quilt over me, shutting out the daylight. Curled up, foetal, drunk-thoughts spiralling downwards, feeling cracked, unhinged.

I wake up – it is dark. I check my phone, six in the evening – there are noises outside my room. I need to piss. A sharp pain runs up my back, freezing me in the bed with stiff-agony. I can't move and I'm frightened. With the effort of moving a mountain, I manage to sit up. I let out a deep, guttural, groan of pain. An empty cider bottle – I aim my piss into it, hot, warm, and stinking.

Crawl back into the bed. Sleep again. Deliriums, bizarre dreams, giddy, out of body surreal thoughts – I don't know if I'm thinking, lucid-dreaming, or hallucinating. .

Knocking at my door, sometime, I'm not sure how long, later, Disco, then Toby:

'You in, man?'

'We're having a party.'

'Have you seen him today?'

'No one has.'

'Maybe he's at his mam's'

I feel bug-like. Kafkaesque. Trapped insect-upside-down on my back. Ominous terrors beyond my door.

Into the night – blasting music, shouting, a carnival of drunkenness going on, it sounds manic, girls screaming, I can hear Disco's guffaw – Toby drumming on the table, people joining in and chanting.

My eyes pop open, staring into the blackness, swirls of colour over my vision. I nail the remainder of the paracetamol. All night I drift in and out of sleep, until the noise gradually fades.

The grey-light of morning, I pull myself up, my lower back aching and stiff. No sign of anyone, I creep downstairs and make a cup of weak tea. Back in bed, I smoke a cigarette, watching the blue smoke.

I look at my phone; messages and calls from Toby wondering where I am. A message from Bunny:

Hi, I know we haven't spoken for a while, but, have you seen the news? Someone shot and killed Dimebag Darrell on stage last night. I'm not sure of the details, but I thought I would let you know, 'cos I know how much you love Pantera. Hope you

320

are okay. Gimme a call, it would be nice to speak to you.

I sit in silence, stunned at this, not believing it to be true.

It is half-eight. If Bunny is still her usual self, she will still be asleep now – but I decide to call her anyway.

Her voice on the other end, cracked and half-asleep. She reaffirms what she said in her text, then, we talk about what we've been up to since we last spoke. Twenty minutes later, I feel better for having spoken to her, yet overcome with a terrible sadness. I head downstairs. Disco sitting on the sofa in the snug, smoking a rollie.

'Have you just come downstairs?' he asks.

'Aye.'

'Were you in bed?'

'Yeah, man.'

'All night?'

'All night,' I laugh.

'We knocked on your door; we thought you must have been out.'

'No I fucked my back at work and couldn't move.'

'Shit, you alright?'

'Better than I was, just stiff.'

I head into the kitchen, flick the kettle on and make us coffee. Then back over to Disco, hand him his mug, and the block of Golden Virginia.

'There you go, man, knock up some of your super-slim snout.'

While he's rolling, I tell him about Dimebag.

'That's fucking awful,' he says, giving me my cigarette, 'what happened, exactly?'

'I don't know yet, I will have to go online to find out

321

properly.' I pause to light my roll-up, then pass the lighter to Disco. 'What are you doing today?' I add.

'I'm gonna have to go to my Mam's. I don't really want to, but I need to sleep in a bed, man. And get some clean clothes. And eat a real meal and stuff.'

'Where does your mam live?'

'Morpeth.'

'Isn't it a fuck-on to get to?'

'Aye, that's why I only go there once or twice a week. That and I hate my Mam's boyfriend.'

'How come?'

'She's ill, she's got MS. And he's just a cunt, he doesn't want me in the house. Anything and everything I do, he makes out like I'm making her life worse. So, I just try to avoid going there as much as possible.'

'Shit, sorry man.'

'I don't *live* there; I just keep some of my stuff there. Plus, like I said, it's nice to sleep in a bed now and again.'

'I understand that, man.'

'I'll be back later though.'

'Cool. I have to go and pick up my pay for my work over the weekend. Fancy going into town tonight?'

'Aye, alright.'

It's another long walk all the way to the office behind the Arena. A woman with an unhappy face makes me show her my I.D., then sign a sheet of paper to confirm who I am. Then she hands me a brown envelope, it clinks with the sound of coins. I put it in my pocket.

'More work on this weekend,' she tells me.

'I don't want to do load-ins,' I reply, 'or outs.'

'Okay, well there's steward work if you want it?'

'Yeah, alright.'

'Someone will phone you through the week to confirm.'

Outside, I open my pay and it's lousy. Realistically, there's not enough to see me though the week, not if I want to smoke and get drunk. Out of the meagre fifty pounds, I set aside twenty-five for food and twenty-five for fun. I head to Morrison's and buy as much cheap food as I can get. Nutrition is irrelevant – as long as I can fill the gnawing void of hunger, I can exist. Packets of nine pence noodles, a bag of suspicious-meat sausages, cheap peanut butter, cardboard World War I trench-style bread, tins of custard and peaches. All low budget, the trolley filled with the garish, hideous yellow of the supermarket's own brand. At home I put the shopping away, then nip back over to Coli's and buy a two-fifty gram pouch of Golden Virginia, skins, filters, two bottles of cheap White Storm, and eight cans of Red Stripe. Coli regards me with his usual, quiet eyes, and I wonder what he is thinking. I wonder if he would like to pop over and play *Super Mario 3* with Disco and me, drink cheap cider, and talk shite. He looks about sixty, but you never know.

When I go back in the house, Toby is in the kitchen, cooking.

'Alright Prick-Tits?' he says to me, affectionately.

'Aye, man.'

'Is Disco coming over today?'

'Yeah, we're going into town later. What are you up to?'

'Going over to see Frances, but we might be back here later on. Just got some weed so might have a bit of a smoke.'

'Ah aye, I'm up for that.'

'I've been meaning to talk to you about Disco,' he says putting the lid on the pan he was attending to at the hob, 'I'm getting a bit sick of him being here. He was always at my last house, you know? As I've said, it's hard because he's a lovely guy, and he's loads of fun, but he needs to sort his life out, get a job, get his own place.'

'Aye,' I nod, 'but he's got nowhere to live.'

'You don't see what's happening, man. I wanted to say this to you,' he pauses thinking about his words, 'Disco moves from one person to the next. He latches on to someone, and makes them feel sorry for him. It's not his fault, he is a lovely guy, don't get me wrong, but he needs to stand on his own feet. He's like a puppy.'

I laugh at this.

'It's true,' Toby says laughing, but serious. 'He latches on to someone, then when that person gets sick of him, he moves onto someone else.'

'First it was Jürgen, you know him, right?'

'The drummer? Yeah.'

'Then me, and now you.'

I want to say something in Disco's defence, but I know that what Toby is saying is true.

'He's good company,' I tell Toby, 'I mean, we're both trying to get over a relationship, I like him being here.'

'I know,' Toby shakes his head, 'he helped me through stuff too, but, you're going out tonight, aye?'

'Aye.'

'Aye, well, you'll end up buying all Disco's drinks and drugs. It's okay for a bit, because you want to pay for his company, because he's such a canny guy, but you'll get sick when you're skint all the time because of him.'

I nod my head, knowing that what he is saying is true, but not wanting to believe it.

Upstairs, I sit and write, then put the post up on my Live Journal. I drink black coffee and smoke cigarettes, stub them out, then put the ends into a tin reserved for emergency baccy. I follow one or two people I know on Live Journal – and through association, follow friends of friends. One journal in particular I have been reading every day is by a woman called Isola.

Isola is the saddest woman in the universe – her mother died of cancer, she writes about it beautifully, with a sadness that almost brings me to tears. She exists in a void – a void that I know myself. I write her a letter, explaining that I know what it is like to lose someone to cancer, and that even though we don't know each other, she's not alone in the world. I send it off electronically via Live Journal – then regret it a little bit, thinking that maybe I should have just minded my own business.

I take some time to find out what happened to Dimebag. Reading about it, I feel myself on the verge of tears – and I can feel all the progress I've made recently in keeping my spirits afloat crumbling a little. I begin to feel like I've lost a family member – which is ridiculous, as I never even met the man. I'm in mourning, and the loss I feel is real.

Six in the afternoon, getting ready to go out. Walking from the bathroom to my room, just a towel round my waist – Emily coming in the other direction towards the bathroom, also in just a towel. We smile at each other – then her smile turns to a scowl and she pushes past me. I wonder what she has stuck up her cunt.

Waiting for Disco to drop by – I sit drinking cider in my room. I can feel a sadness creeping up on me. I decide not to fight it, and place the first Sepia Tears demo in the CD player. I haven't listened to it for a long time.

I sit in silence, Ariella's voice filling the room – ghostly, spectral – her words haunting. Now the tears come, and I let them roll down my face. My vision blurred, mouthfuls of fizzy-cheap cider, heart aching on the verge of exploding.

Turtle Dove – the song that I can't listen to, or decipher the meaning of.

My dying dear…

I never knew who it was that was dying. She never explained what it was about – like I had discussed with Lavender, it was probably a story inspired from a book she had read. But listening to it now, something doesn't sit right with that theory – I feel as though I am listening to it with fresh ears.

On the other side of the room, the mountainous pile of books on the floor – nestled there, part of its structure, *The Dice Man*, by Luke Rhinehart.

My die–ing dear…

The words resonate – the song opens up inside me – the meaning changes, like snow melting, a new form – alchemic.

My die–ing dear…

Now I understand. I put the song on repeat, the images falling into place like a slowly completing jigsaw, and I'm amazed at myself for never realising before…

My die–ing dear…

My ribcage rattles with the thunder of a terrible remorse – hot rain of tears rolling down and off my face – pain escaping my body, drunken, foolish.

I loaned her *The Dice Man*, long before we formed our relationship – I explained how I had been inspired to use the die. It wasn't *dying*; it was *die-ing*.

My die–ing dear…

I want to laugh, however, I'm insane with this satori – this awakening, the blackness of mourning and pain keeps coming and the absurdity of this enlightenment is at once heart-breaking and depressing.

When you say I'm holding, this Rocky-Road, in bloodied hands, well you send me dancing, you send me waltzing into the dark, with broken wings… no one knows how I want you, you're beautiful… you spin me a six… and I'll be good for ever…

327

I'm amazed at myself for my inability to interpret the meaning of this song before now. Recalling the time I bumped into her and she was munching on an ice-cream – the red sauce dribbling down her hands – it seems dream-like and unreal to me – I wonder if it ever happened – if any of it ever happened.

I conclude that despite her desperation to be with someone, her fear of being alone – she wanted me long before Johnathan ever decided to leave the scene.

Sitting alone – winter beating at the window – drunk, smoky, ash-fingered, my face thin – aged with insomnia, malnutrition, dipsomania, and grief, I am a ridiculous man.

My face stiff with dried tears – the room dark save for candles burning and the light of the computer screen – I feel as if I've gone through a metamorphosis – I sit at the computer and write – a cathartic sensation, the clacking of my fingers on the keys, a deep, insane madness in my head and heart.

The sound of Disco's voice downstairs – I abandon the computer. He's in the snug. I walk in and give him the tobacco, skins, and filters.

'Filters?' he exclaims.

'Aye, roll up, mate.'

From the fridge, I get the other bottle of cider and a can of Red Stripe. I bring them and two pint glasses through.

'Snakey-time,' I tell him, pouring out the drinks.

He hands me a cigarette.

'That's the smoothest one yet,' I tell him, examining his work. 'By the way, I'm inviting Liam out tonight, I think you will get along well with him.'

'From what I've heard, you're probably right.'

The Head of Steam – Rose working behind the bar, we're drunk already when we turn up. Disco has no money – so I'm buying the drinks. However, I don't care; I'm having a good time.

The hot lights of the pub, shelves of exotic spirits, continental beers, the red smooth sofa/bench that runs around a little fenced-off and raised seating area.

'Get that table,' I tell Disco, 'I'll get the drinks.'

'Two pints of Warsteiner please, Rose.'

She begins pouring the pints then asks, 'So what are you two doing tonight? Getting drunk, by any chance?' She's laughing as she asks this.

'Of course!' I reply. 'Liam is on his way now.'

'He's bonkers,' she's still laughing, 'the more he has to drink the less I can understand him.'

Not long after, he arrives, scruffy looking, that index finger of his flicking in and out of his nose quick as lightning, he sits down, belly hanging over his belt.

'Liam, this is Disco,' I introduce them.

I'm imagining that this is a great meeting of two incredible men, two historical figures, two brilliant minds colliding. Einstein meeting Newton, Van Goethe meeting Picasso, Kirk meeting Picard, et cetera.

'What are you boys drinking?' Liam asks.

'Warsteiner,' I tell him.

'That stuff tastes like piss,' he replies.

'You were drinking it the other day,' I laugh at him.

'I know, but I thought about it afterwards, and I realised it tasted awful, you know. So I'm on the Erdinger.'

An hour later:

'So Disco, how big is your knob then?'

Another hour later:

A booze-blur, people seem to be skidding past my eyes, lights pulling from their roots, trailing incandescent neon-worms, aural-buzzing, muffled, deep whirring sensations.

A good-looking girl with soft-eyes and red-hair throws a piece of paper at Disco as she's leaving.

It reads, *I think you are gorgeous*, followed by a phone number.

'You lucky shit,' I tell him. 'She was lovely, you have to text her.'

He seems unsure. 'Nah, man, it's too much hassle.'

He crumples the paper up and throws it away.

'I can't believe you did that, I would have sent her a message. You could have fucked her!'

'She would have wanted more than that, and I can't be bothered. I just want a cup of tea and a roll-up these days.'

'And *Super Mario 3*.' I add.

'Luigi is a proper bender,' he laughs.

Rose has been giving us sneaky drinks. Left-overs, drip tray slops, cocktails from the end of bottles.

An hour later:

I realise Liam has been gone for a while. 'Did he say he was going for a piss?' I ask Disco.

'Dunno, man.'

I head downstairs looking for him. He's outside struggling to stand up. Shouting something vague and hostile at some lads across the street.

'What's happening, man?' I ask.

He mutters something and I can't understand a word he's saying, he's so drunk he can hardly stand up. He takes his belt off and begins to wrap it menacingly around his hand, while looking towards the lads across the street with a violent glare in his eyes. Then his pants fall down. He tries to haul them back up but slides onto the ground. I help him up.

'It's time to go home, matey,' I tell him.

'What?' he puts his arms around me, 'you're my baby,' he tells me.

'Come on man, its bedtime.' With effort, I turn his body towards the cab rank. 'Go on, get in a taxi. I'll see you at college tomorrow.'

I watch and wait until he climbs into the back of a cab. Then he gets back out again, looking around at the deck for something, with his hands trapped in his pockets. Then he gets back in the cab and it drives away.

As I'm coming back in, Disco is standing in the entrance smoking a *real* cigarette, not a roll-up. He hands me one.

'Real snout, where did you get these?'

'This kid wants to sell us some MDMA,' he points to a meek-looking, pale-faced student standing next to him.

'How much?' I pull all the money out of my pocket and hand it all to Disco, who does the exchange.

'Let's go and to The Happy Chip for some scran, then go home.' I tell him, while looking drunkenly at the mountain of coins in my hand.

'Nah man, I've got a better idea,' he smiles.

In The Happy Chip, I give Disco the money. 'What are you getting?'

'Just wait,' he laughs.

The Happy Chip is on the cusp of the gay scene, and

331

filled with mincers, hot and butch type lesbians, and the limp-wristed. I'm standing in the queue talking to a six-foot man in drag about what I've been up to this evening. The floor is greasy. The music is awful.

'We're just getting some food then fucking off home,' I explain in a more than is necessary, drunken way.

Disco ushers me out of the door. He has a tiny little brown bag in his hand.

'What did you get?' I ask him, confused.

He opens the bag. 'Magic mushrooms.'

'I'm hungry.'

'Eat half of these,' he tells me, 'then we'll get food, trust me.'

'Was there any change?'

He fumbles around in his pockets and then hands me a twenty-pence bit.

'We'll not get much with that.'

'Just wait, I've got a plan,' he says, grinning and stuffing the magic mushrooms in his mouth.

I nail my half of the bag, and he leads me off towards the Quayside.

On The Side – the little curving road that leads towards the underneath of the Tyne Bridge – we stop outside a little pizza shop. Just to the entrance is a bin. Disco kneels down to look inside it.

'Here we go sunshine,' he grins, as he awkwardly pulls a large pizza box from the bin. He opens it like it were a treasure chest, 'get in, only two bits missing, looks like a meat-feast, still warm as well.'

He scoops up a slice and takes a bite then offers the box to me. I take a piece – I'm hungry and there's a vague sensation of disgust as I tuck into the lukewarm doughy pizza – the cheese and meat greasy and moist.

One in the morning. We walk along the Quayside in the dark and freezing cold, passing the pizza box back and forth.

'People are greedy,' Disco tells me, 'people buy more food than they can eat when they are drunk. I realised this a while ago when I was waiting for the bus outside Subway one night. Some drunk bloke had just bought a massive sarnie. He came out the shop, opened it, and changed his mind. He said to me "Do you want this? I'm too pissed to eat it." So of course, I had it. Free scran.'

I start laughing at this story, even though it isn't funny. Pizza in my mouth and it is muffling my giggles.

'What are you laughing at?' he asks me, also now laughing.

'Orlansee,' I burst in to full guffaw.

'Ah nah, dribble-poo,' Disco is creasing-up, 'has Toby been teaching you his made up Cantonese words?'

'I think the mushrooms are kicking in,' I tell him, still laughing.

An hour later and the quiet streets of Heaton. Second Avenue – Disco spots someone down the street, 'Rob!' he shouts.

The figure turns round in the street. We jog up after them.

'Alreet?' Disco asks the man.

Disco introduces me to a skinny, curly-head man with a face that looks like it belongs in the seventies.

'I'm going to a house party if yous want to come?' he invites us.

333

Further up the street. A random house filled with people I don't know. Disco gets the MDMA out, finger-lick, dab, run around the gums.

Half an hour later, sitting on a sofa – reeling forward, a living room, unknown faces, music inaudible save for the murmur of bass through the floor.

'I'm so pleased you came into my life, mate,' I'm telling Disco, 'even if we are just apes, you're making me forget about all the horrible shit that happened this year.'

'Me too, man,' he puts his arm around my shoulders, 'fuck women, man, all we need is to have a nice cuppa, a roll-up, and play *Super Mario 3*. What else do you need in life?'

'Fuck Mario, the cunt,' I say seriously.

Disco is laughing. 'Aye, Luigi, the fucking bender.'

'I reckon we should invite Coli-Heed over to play, 'cos we will never finish the stupid game ourselves.'

At around four, I decide to leave. 'I'm fucked, man,' I tell Disco.

'No worries, I'll be around later this morning.'

The short walk home through the dark, empty streets of Heaton. My mind whirring and buzzing – a sad moment where I wish I was heading home to Ariella's warmth in bed.

Instead, I crawl into my own crusty bed with my clothes still on, and pass out.

As if in the blink of my insane eye – I'm awake again. Nine o'clock. A terror of dehydration at my throat, I head down to the snug, head rushing, reeling – colours and spots in my vision. Coffee – I look through my pockets and realise Disco has the

334

tobacco, skins, and filters. I have twenty-pence, and walk over to Coli's, boggle-eyed and stinking. I buy some green Rizla skins. Back home – empty out some dumps from the emergency tin – black-fingered, not caring, I knock up a jail-tab.

Smoking, more coffee – trying to gain control of my head. My phone ringing. An unknown number.

'Hello?'

'Alreet? It's Disco. Just seeing if you are awake.'

'Aye.'

We start laughing down the phone at each other; it goes on for a few minutes, chuckling at nothing like idiots.

'Have you got the baccy?' I ask him, 'I've had to have a jail-tab.'

'Hang on,' he replies, while searching himself, 'aye it's in me pocket. I'll be round in a minute, I'll knock us up some extra-smooth Disco specials.'

'Reet, I'll brew up.'

Ten minutes later and we're sitting in front of the TV in the snug – more coffee, roll-ups. Disco's face is red, his eyes glazed and he has a look of manic hilariousness about him.

'I feel fucked,' he's laughing.

'I was lying in bed before, and I think I had a lucid dream,' I tell him, 'I was imagining David Blunkett and Stevie Wonder sharing a council flat in Elswick. It was like a situation comedy, they're both blind, David is the serious one, while Stevie is the fun one.'

Disco is laughing hard. 'What would it be called?'

'Blunkett and Wonder.'

'That's hilarious. You're a fucking weird guy, but I love you,' he's laughing still.

335

Toby walks through, sleepy-eyed. 'What happened to you fuckers? I thought you were coming back here for a smoke last night?'

'Sorry man, we ended up at a house party.' I tell him.

He goes through to his room – then comes back with a bong and a bag of weed. He nestles himself on the end of the sofa, takes a toke, then passes it along.

'I'm guessing we're not going to college today then?' I ask him.

'Fuck that,' he replies coughing and smiling at the same time.

XLII

I log into my Live Journal – a message from Isola. A thank you for my concern and her phone number, telling me that if I ever need to talk, I can call or message her. I look at the number on the screen wondering what to do. I've been talking to her for a month or so on Live Journal and MSN messenger – there is a deep distance to her, as if she is lost somewhere in the world. I'm curious about her – the sadness in her words endears her to me in a beautifully depressing way. I think it is the understanding of isolation, melancholy, sadness, and existential angst that she expresses that I understand on an empirical level.

I send her a text and ask if she wants to go for a drink. I feel a sense of regret after sending it, thinking that it could be awkward.

Ten minutes later – she replies, saying she would like to meet up. She points out that it's not a date or anything; she's not interested in anything romantic. I say that's fine – and I convince myself that it is, although there's a little bit of disappointment floating around in me.

That night in The Head of Steam – Xmas lights up around the bar – a warm festive atmosphere. Isola is already there when I arrive. She has a distant look on her face, a smile that is soft, and looks like an effort to wear. Her eyes are brown and I stare straight into them as I sit down next to her with my drink. Her hair is dyed-black, a little fringe over her forehead, and tied up at the back. I think she is pretty, in an odd, confusing way.

We small talk for a while. I tell her that I think her writing is beautiful, how touched I am by it, by her thoughts on her mother's death. When Isola talks, she has an aura of spiritual-sadness about her. Her words are soft and small, and I feel she has to struggle to be present, as if some unknown thought is pulling her away.

'I'm worried I'm going to be homeless soon,' she explains, 'I can't work, I'm ill with depression. My flat mates don't understand. I'm so far behind with my rent. They don't even speak to me half the time. I didn't have anything to eat for three days the other week, a friend of mine, Duncan, brought me a care-package, which was sweet because I think he didn't have much food himself.'

Moments of silence as we look at each other, smiling, in between inhalations of blue smoke from cigarettes. All around, the buzz of the people in the pub – yet, here we are, this strange meeting, a black-bubble. I can't help but stare at her.

'Have you heard The Chronos Quartet?' she asks me.

I tell her I haven't. She says I should.

Then the words run out, like a tap shutting off, a dryness creeping in.

'I'm gonna head off,' she tells me.

We've managed two hours, not bad for meeting up with someone you don't know.

Outside, in the dark, the bitter nip of mid-December. Bundling-up, hats scarves, gloves.

'Can we meet up again?' she asks.

'Of course, I would like that a lot,' smiles spreading across our faces.

A hug – the first warmth from a female body for so long.

I walk home, bracing against the cold, not sure what I feel.

Next day – overcome with a blankness, a sensation of unreality. Snow falling outside my window – I look out over the yard, at the white of the sky, the roofs covered, crispy-white. Almost a week to Xmas. I haven't bought anyone any presents – I don't care, there's no capacity in me to give or receive or pretend I enjoy the bullshit festival of a religion that makes me want to puke.

College finished for winter holidays. Losing my grip with it – no focus, no purpose – despair creeps in, out of a blackness, a drunkenness, Jekyll and Hyde – flicking on and off like a light switch.

Lying in bed forever – the crumbs in the sheets, smell of stale tobacco and booze – a sensation of existential angst, tight in my throat – a terrible pain of living that comes on against my skin – the cold rubbing me – frosted-hives explode all over my body. With the sounds of weather, the feel of it, the sensation of it, the way trees make music in the wind, how the air feels as I breathe it in – all this and I know I am alive, yet the meaninglessness of being grips and strangles me. I am here, thus – I exist, I feel, and it is awful. There is a beautiful despair in the endless void of the self that persists in wanting to make sense of nothingness, and a hilarity and surrealist absurdity that comes with it.

I feel this and see it everywhere. In Isola, in her eyes, the distance. I want to look at her – that smile that breaks her heart to put on her face.

I send her a message. I tell her I enjoyed talking to her. Can we meet again – maybe at the weekend?

A reply straight away – but it is Ariella. A bizarre feeling looking at her name appear on my phone – I have a panic thinking I have sent the message intended for Isola to her by mistake. I check, and I haven't – Ariella wants to know how I am, how I am doing.

A conversation begins – small talk, she's moved house, now living in Shieldfield. She bumped into my mam the other week before she moved, heard I was living with friends – was I making music, was I happy, and so on.

I lie and tell her I'm great, everything is good, new friends, moving on. I close the conversation down as quickly as possible – a sickness rising in me, I don't want it to consume me, to let thoughts of her take residence in my head.

Later – Isola replies. She would love to meet up again. I tell her I have work that weekend. Maybe meet on Sunday.

I decide never to do the load-ins or outs for fear my back will give in again. So, I'm working as a security guard/steward at events in the Arena. Andrea Bocelli – I know his name because my Grandad likes his music. I'm supposed to be watching the audience – but the music is so beautiful that I can't keep my eyes off the stage. A version of Rodrigo's *Concierto de Aranjuez* – one of my favourite pieces of classical music – I want to reel over, I feel every note in my body, my eyes brim uncontrollably with tears, I try to remain composed, but my skin creeps with electricity – I can't breathe. I wonder why I feel like this. Sometimes I'm so numb and empty – and yet, art, writing, music, fill the void of my existential emptiness – it is nourishment, art is all I can live for, to create, to express, to make sense of the suffering of being.

'Keep your eyes on the audience,' one of the senior stewards tells me.

I turn my head towards the rows of people sitting in the dark, but my heart and ears are fully on the music.

I meet Isola at The Head of Steam again; sitting in the same seat – she's wearing the same lost expression on her face, that same sad smile.

We're a bit more relaxed with each other – more small talk; her family, my family, her English Literature degree, music, her mother's death.

I can feel a strange mixture of event-related emotions sloshing together inside me – an alchemical mistake consisting of alcoholism, malnutrition, depression, Dimebag's death, Disco's suicide attempt, the death of Isola's mother, Toby's self-harm, Ariella. Circumstance. The human sickness, my existential angst.

Time reeling forward. Drunk now – the pub buzzing with people as usual. Isola laughs at my silly jokes – giddy, eyes and mouth crushed under her laughter. Somehow, our hands have linked together under the table – fingers locked together like secret pink-sausages.

'I'm skint now,' she tells me, 'but I've got wine in the house. Do you want to come to mine for a drink?'

341

'Yes, of course.'

We decide to walk it, bracing against the cold and light rain. Her arm in mine, shivering, up Arthur's Hill.

'What are you doing for Xmas?' I ask her.

'Going to visit my sister in Durham, I don't really want to; I don't get on with my family all that well.'

'I know the feeling.'

'Except for my Dad, and he will be there. He's been in France for six months. He builds studios.'

'Music studios?'

'Yes, you'd get on with him I think. He's into all that psychoacoustic-stuff, how sound works and whatnot.'

In her flat – we're both soggy and cold.

'I hope my flat mates aren't in,' she says as she hands me a glass of red wine, 'do you want something to eat?'

'I'm okay, thanks,' I tell her.

'Are you sure? I haven't got much, but we could have toast.'

'Alright then, thanks.'

Upstairs in her small room, darkness save for the light of a laptop and a small lamp. Skull and crossbones flag up on the wall, little ornaments and trinkets here and there; a strange hint of sadness is enchanted in them. A photo of her as a little girl with her mother.

'Should I put some music on?' she asks, 'I'll put Clint Mansell and The Kronos Quartet on for you. This is called *Requiem for a Dream*, I think it's really beautiful.'

I sit and listen to the music. It is beautiful, and full of agonising tension. I can't move while I'm listening to it. She sits next to me – drinking wine, I feel explosively strange, out of context, unreal.

The last note fades. 'Did you like it?' she asks.

'I loved it,' I reply.

'It's from a film, also called *Requiem for a Dream*. Have you seen it?'

'No.'

'Let's watch it together sometime.'

I look at her – those brown eyes melting, that sadness that permeates her every action.

I lean over and kiss her lips – she moans, as if I've sucked the breath from her lungs – she's kissing me back, mouths drunken, and twisting together.

Clothes come off in a fabric tornado – her teeth and warmth on my cock, my fingers inside her. On top of her, inside her – her orgasm, my orgasm. A moment severed away from everything – for a second removed from *here* and the pointlessness of now.

'You made me come,' she tells me.

Cuddled into each other, strange bed, odd sensations.

'Do you want me to go?' I ask her.

'No, you can stay,' she tells me with a smile. 'I want you to stay.'

I melt into the bed, into her, with a sorrow and melancholy that burns under my eyelids. I think that we could be anyone here; two empty people in need of connection, in need of human warmth. Does it matter who we are at this moment? How much hurt and pain float to the surface with defences down. Existential terrors always at my throat. I feel small and insignificant. Little lost boy, forever.

Waking up under the covers – a big marshmallow of

343

a bed, lost in there, confused about where I am. Her body next to mine.

'You snore,' she tells me, sleepily, 'I've been awake all night.'

I feel embarrassed. 'I'm sorry, I didn't realise.'

'It's okay,' she kisses me.

The day in her bed – coffee, cigarettes, watching the films *Big Fish* and *Requiem for a Dream,* feeling strange. Kisses, embraces, long drawn-out sex.

'Do you want a line of Prozac?' she asks me.

'A line?'

'Yeah, it's better than just swallowing it.'

The pink crumbly dust of it on her bedside table.

Late afternoon, I'm at the door about to leave. The cold and the low-sun, grey sky, the light in my eyes and a surreal feeling inside me.

'I'll see you again soon,' she smiles.

'Of course, I'll text you.'

A kiss and a long embrace.

I walk home a step ahead of myself.

XLIII

Two days to Xmas. I bring Isola to the house and introduce her to Disco and Toby.

'Don't trust him,' Toby jokes referring to me, 'he's a fucking Nazi, and he likes it up the hoop.'

In my room, I light candles and we drink red wine in the semi-dark, listening to Damien Rice's *O*. We're looking at each like other starry-eyed idiots.

'Here,' she says handing me a cassette tape, 'I don't have any money to buy you a Xmas present, but I made you a mix tape.'

'A tape?' I laugh, 'this isn't the nineties, it's a good job I still have a tape player.'

'Bollocks to you then,' she laughs, 'they're all a bit depressing, the songs, I don't really like happy music.'

'It's great,' I tell her, 'thank you very much. Should I put it on?'

'No, just save it for when you are alone. I want you to fuck me now.'

Afterwards, she's holding me so tight, that I almost can't breathe.

'Your housemates seem canny,' she tells me.

'Aye, I love living with them.'

'I can't stay tonight; my sister is picking me up first thing.'

'I'll miss you.'

Later – I'm a bizarre mixture of happy and sad, a terrible ambivalence that is pulling me apart. Isola leaves. I sit with Disco watching *Blazing Saddles* in the snug.

'Did you watch *Rainbow* when you were a kid?' he

asks me.

'Yeah, why? What made you think of that?'

'Did you ever notice that Bungle never wore clothes, but wore pyjamas for bed?'

I start laughing. 'What the fuck man.'

'Also, why the fuck did Zippy have no eyelids?'

'Didn't he used to sleep with his hands over his eyes?'

'Yes, exactly. George had eyelids though. It didn't make any sense.'

'I think you've been thinking about it too much.'

Xmas Eve. Everyone is dispersing. I head to my mother's house. My gifts for everyone are meagre. I feel empty here, lost, not right. This home, the cupboards full, and their lives working correctly, I feel like a disease infecting it.

I stay up all night – my brother and I watching the telly in silence. I'm drinking cans of weak lager – the light of the TV; I'm numb in cathode ray worship.

I think of Isola, Ariella, Disco, Toby, Liam, Dan, Lisa.

My brother goes to bed. I look at the Xmas tree, the presents, the decorations. I feel sick here, out of place. I belong in the dirt, from where I came. The materialism of Xmas makes me want to puke. I boot up my mother's computer – log into my Live Journal. Isola has posted a picture of me on her page. Underneath it reads *he is mine.*

Xmas Day. No sleep – opening presents, I want to throw it all away. Stuff, endless, useless things that don't matter. I feel ungrateful and awful about it. Quickly drunk. Grey cardboard dinner, I'm not here for it, I'm transparent, interdimensional. I don't care; this is not where I want to be.

Early evening. Drained of all energy. Head home in a taxi. Take my things upstairs. The house is empty. I have it to myself. Lie in bed – total darkness. Sleep off some of the fatigue – a dream of Ariella, I wake up with tears rolling down my face. My phone rings.

Disco:

'Are you in?'

'Yeah, why?'

'I'm getting a lift back to Newcastle.'

He arrives. We have the house to ourselves.

'Look at this,' I show him the big bottle of Jack Daniels that I got for Xmas.

'Fucking hell mate, I got socks.'

'Let's drink this shit.'

An hour later, Disco:

'Have you ever had a fight in the nip?'

'What?'

'Rose and Emily will be back soon, imagine they walk in the house, and find us bollock-naked and having a fight.'

It takes a moment for my brain to process what he is saying. Then I start laughing.

'What?' I ask him again.

'Naked boxing. Ha'way man, it'll be hilarious.'

'How are we going to time it right?'

'Rose said she would be back about nine-ish. What time is it now?'

'Half-eight.'

'Right, let's have another large drink, get naked, and then wait until we hear the door.'

Ten minutes and two straight and large treble JDs

later and we're both in our under kegs, giggling asininely.

Another ten minutes, another large drink, and we're very drunk and a bit cold.

The sound of the door.

'Right this is it!' Disco nudges me, leaping to his feet. We both get into faux-boxers stances. The door to the snug opens and Rose and Emily trot in.

'What on earth are you two doing?' Rose laughs, 'actually I'm not surprised at anything yous might do anymore. Nice undies, though.'

I turn my head to look at her, then turn back just in time to catch a right from Disco in my eye-socket.

'Ah! Fuck!' I yelp, covering my eye.

'Shit, I'm sorry man,' Disco is laughing his head off and drunkenly gripping my shoulder while trying to remain upright.

'I can't open my eye.'

'Hit me now,' he tells me, 'go on, anywhere you like.'

The girls are standing watching.

'No I don't want to hit you. I'm blind in one eye.'

'Go on, man, just do it.'

I stand up right, relaxed, trying to open my throbbing eye.

'Listen,' I say calmly, before jabbing Disco in the nose with a sharp left.

He holds his nose and crumples to the ground.

'Shit, you alright, mate?'

'Aye, aye,' he gets up, blood in his hands.

Rose fetches him some kitchen roll and he mops up his face.

'It's not broken, is it?' I ask concerned.

'Nah its fine. Let's have some more booze.'

'Do you girls want to join us for drinks in your pants?'

They both laugh. 'No, no thanks.' Rose giggles.

'You're missing out.' I sigh, pouring out drinks for Disco and myself.

Next morning:

Coffee, roll-ups, cardboard toast. A pretty black eye. A bloodied nose.

'Put the telly on,' I tell Disco.

He powers up the old brown TV – the news on.

I half-hear what is being said, then ask Disco to turn the volume up.

The news is reporting that a massive earthquake-induced tsunami has hit parts of Asia and Indonesia, killing thousands, destroying villages, towns, and coastlines.

'This is fucking terrible,' Disco gasps.

Eyes glued to the television all day, watching the news. Polishing off the JD.

A week of stupid drinking games begins, including revised rule naked boxing, slaps and shots, one-card-cheap-cider-slam, joker-shots, and several games of *Pokémon* on Toby's N64 with shots for the loser.

I'm giddy with merriment – and the highs are so great that I'm crashing hard with the lows. I decide to throw a party on New Year's Eve, yet once I've invited all the immediate people around me – I realise that most of them can't come, as they have decided to do other things.

I also have work on NYE.

Standing in the middle of the street next to Northumbria University, trying to redirect people off this street and onto another, on account of the New Year firework display that is due to go off at seven p.m.

A family – a man, woman and two small kids – barge past me.

'Excuse me,' I ask politely, 'could you use the other path please?'

'Don't tell me what path to use,' he snaps at me and continues along the cordoned off street.

I'm wearing a massive yellow coat with "EVENT COVER" written on the back. I'm amazed it hasn't suggested some sort of authority to this moron and that I'm redirecting people for a reason.

I secretly hope that he gets a firework in the face. I watch as he tries to uncouple the metal cordon at the end of the street, realises he can't, climbs over it onto the road with cars going past, and gets his missus to pass the kids over before climbing over herself.

I've never been the most egalitarian of people, but these doylums deserve to be run over/have fireworks shot at them, declassified as a subspecies, and made to work in underground mines. Like Morlocks.

I get home feeling dejected and pissed off about the ignorant bloke – Disco is in the snug reading the Metro paper.

'So, who's coming to this party then?'

'Me, you, Isola, Dan, and Lisa.'

'Is that it?'

'Yeah, but once Toby is finished work he will bring everyone back from The Cluny.'

'I don't think he will be finished until two in the

morning or something.'

Everyone arrives and asks me the same question: 'Is this it?'

Isola looks distant and unhappy. She's quiet and doesn't want to talk to me. Rose is heading out – she pops her head into the living room and hands Disco a bottle of vodka.

Ten p.m. – Dan and Lisa leave.

'We're going to Gotham Town. Don't you want to come?'

'Nah, man I just want to stay at home. Town will be full of dicks.'

They leave and it's just the three of us – Isola looks uncomfortable.

'Sorry, this is a shit party,' I tell her, 'you can just go if you want.'

She shakes her head and smiles.

Disco opens the vodka. 'Have you ever made a t-shirt out of a Morrison's bag?'

We both laugh at him.

He disappears and I cuddle up to Isola – her touch feels empty – I kiss her and she breaks it off short. I wonder if I'm imagining this coldness.

Disco returns wearing a Morrison's bag as a t-shirt. He poses in it and I take a photograph with my camera.

The way he has made it is both genius and idiotic and I'm crying with laughter. Ten minutes later:

'Vodka shots?' he asks me, waving the bottle in my face.

I accept but Isola declines.

'I'll get some glasses,' I tell him.

'Nah man, just use the bottle cap,' and he pours me

351

a measure into it.

I nail it, and it burns my throat and chest.

Several shots later and Disco asks to use my phone. I give it to him and he disappears off with it.

An awful silence, and I realise it's not my imagination.

'You okay?' I ask.

'Yeah,' she smiles but I can hear the lie in her voice.

Fifteen cold minutes later and Disco returns. 'I've just been in the yard talking to the neighbour over the fence. She's canny fit like, must be well into her forties. She asked me what I was studying and I said I was training to be a vet. Specifically one that put horses to sleep after they've mangled themselves during races.'

'What? Did she believe you?'

'Dunno, but she looked at my Morrison's t-shirt and didn't say anything.'

'You're an ape,' I tell him.

'That's right!' he replies in a mock Michael Jackson-*Bo-Selecta* voice.

More vodka shots in quick succession and I start to feel ill. My guts begin to fizz and I suddenly feel spew shooting up my gullet. I sprint upstairs to the toilet – grip the pan and blow chunks onto the yellow-white bowl. Isola comes up to see if I'm okay. My eyes are bleary and I suddenly feel unsteady and very drunk.

'I want to go to bed,' I tell her.

'Bed? But it's only eleven o'clock.'

'I know. But I need to lie down, and maybe listen to Opeth.'

'Opeth?'

'Yeah.'

I shove the CD in the player, lie on the bed – the room is spinning, and the music starts to play. I moan along with the words – the blurred-watery outline of Isola looking at me.

'Move out the way,' I tell her, 'and I lean over and spew again straight onto the carpet.

She jumps back in disgust.

'Are you getting into bed?' I ask her.

'What? No way, you need to clean that up.'

'I'll do it tomorrow.'

I black out for a moment – wake up to see Isola scrubbing the floor.

'I can't believe I'm cleaning up sick on New Year's Eve,' she says, sounding very unhappy.

'Now will you get into bed?' I ask.

'No, it smells of sick, I'm going home. You're drunk anyways so we can't even fuck. I'll see you later.'

'I love you,' I tell her.

'You don't love me; we've only been seeing each other for two weeks, you're just drunk.'

'But I do love you…' I murmur.

'I'll speak to you tomorrow.'

In the dark – alone with the sound of Opeth's *Deliverance*. Tears rolling down my face. Slipping out of consciousness.

XLIV

The stench of my sick. I'm confused and dehydrated. Crawl along the corridor to the bathroom – head under the tap drinking icy-cold water that is numbing my mouth.

A mission back to bed. Falling in and out of sleep and feeling unwell.

Finally roused and it's eleven a.m. – I'm starving, stomach growling, empty.

Disco in the snug looking chirpy and upbeat as usual.

'You alright? Happy New Year.'

'I feel like cack. Sorry I went to bed. What did you do?'

'I went to a house party. I only came back here an hour ago.'

'Did Toby let you in?'

'No, it was what's-her-face. Misery, upstairs.'

'Emily. She's odd, isn't she?'

'The other night she came downstairs at three in the morning fully dressed up as if to go out. I said, "You been out somewhere nice?" she said, "No, I've been in all night." She had heels on and a little skirt and full-on make up all over her face.'

'I'd like to spunk in her mouth,' I say, matter of fact.

'You would, you man-whore.'

'I'm hungry. Do you want some breakfast and coffee?'

'If you're offering.'

I look through the cupboards and there's nothing much, as usual. 'Soup and a slice of bread?' I shout through to Disco.

'Yeah, go on then.'

We sit in silence eating, then coffee and jail-tabs in front of the telly.

'What's the plan today?' he asks me.

'Fuck knows. More booze?' I say with determination.

He laughs at this. 'That's the spirit, mate.'

Toby joins us in the snug wearing Bermuda shorts, a t-shirt, and flip-flops as if it were the middle of summer. 'Alright, fuckers?' he smiles, a waft of stale alcohol coming off him.

'We're discussing drinks today,' I tell him. 'You in?'

'Fuck aye. What's the plan?'

'Dunno, what do you reckon?'

'Fancy town? The Head of Steam is open.'

A gaggle of us drunk in the quiet streets of town, early evening, cool sun disappearing behind grey buildings. Toby drops his pants and tucks his cock between his legs.

'Check out my mangina!' he laughs.

Noticing a large puddle in the street, he squats and dips his arse in it, scooping water up, and washing his bare cheeks.

I can't see or breathe for laughing so much.

'I've got arse-filth,' he claims.

I can feel myself becoming mentally and physically exhausted. Isola, who hasn't said much since she met up with us earlier, is quietly drinking a glass of red wine. I've apologised for getting drunk and being sick.

She said it was okay. However, I can see something isn't okay, and I can't work out what that is.

Pubs closing early. Everyone heading back to ours.

Isola:

'I'm going home. Do you want to come to mine?'

I say, 'Yes, of course,' although I would really like to go home for more silly behaviour and merriment.

Later:

In her room – she's riding my cock. I'm not mentally there – I can't get involved. A sadness has gripped me – there's an awkwardness – I can't get comfortable. I remain tumescent until she has come – then she's tugging me so hard I'm worried she will snap my cock off. Then my prick in her mouth, and she's all teeth. I stop her.

'I've had too much to drink,' I tell her. 'I can't come.'

Marshmallow bed – infinite mattress, lost in fabric. Wrapped in melancholy.

A new year – the day hangs grey, expanding out in front of me, a bleak and infinite coldness. Standing at Chillingham Road Metro station with Isola. From her flat to my house, then back to her flat – because she said my bed still reeks of puke.

The sound of the live train cables – a low hum – graffiti along the lower walls of the platform – grey concrete, the yellow and black of the Metro logo – like a dangerous animal showing its colours to prove it is poisonous.

Nothing feels right.

Another security job – this one working at a new music venue in Gateshead – The Sage. Nestled on the banks of the Tyne, it looks like a giant glass slug. I'm

356

told I have two full days work – and by full, that means eighteen hour shifts.

Saturday. A walkie-talkie and a yellow jacket. Local media have informed the public that The Sage is opening today which is incorrect, as it is the following day.

Standing in front of a glass door – turning annoyed people away.

'But the paper said it was opening today,' some old middle-class couple bark at me.

'I'm sorry, sir, but it isn't,' I politely reply.

'Well, we'll see about that,' and he marches inside.

A man in a suit inside the building tells him he's wrong and they skulk off, cursing.

As the day picks up, the hordes of people increase, to the point that while trying to deal with one group of annoyed punters, another group are trying to get into the building. The design of the glass doors makes it look like they aren't there – like you can just walk through, and is preventing people from getting in. Unluckily, several people have walked straight into them and an elderly man is now lying on the floor with a broken schnozzle.

I have ten hours of this. Then, I get a break for an hour. I haven't brought any food, and only have fifty pence on me. I find a shop. My little belly is grumbling. I opt for a bottle of water.

I feel my phone vibrating in my pocket. It is Ariella. A strained conversation – she's asking if I'm okay, have I met someone new, and what is she like? I wonder why she is asking me this – something about it feels strange, like she's poking her nose in my business, sniffing for clues about my new relationship

– I wonder if she or someone she knows has seen me somewhere with Isola.

A sudden feeling of being so far away from Ariella, the remembrance of our relationship now so far out to sea. The sensation of it in my gut – how abstract it feels.

'Isola is great,' I try to say without sounding like gloating, 'she's like my Prozac-queen, she's keeping me afloat.'

'Oh, that's good, I'm pleased for you,' a detectable unhappiness in her voice.

Once she has found out what she wants to know, she ties up the conversation in a sad knot.

'Bye-bye,' her voice fading and cracked with sorrow.

After my break, I move to the back door to keep an eye on vehicles coming in and out of the building. Here I stand in silence like a statue until two in the morning. Walk home in the dark. Thinking about the phone call. Sleep for three hours. Get up, I have no food in the house, so I squirt a mouthful of Rose's weird mushroom paste into my mouth, and cook a bowlful of Toby's rice. Then I walk back to The Sage. In my mind, I'm convinced that working shifts in quick succession is illegal – but I'm not trying to think about it.

In a carpark round the back of The Sage. Where I stand, from seven in the morning, until eleven at night. Four cars come to park here. Only two of them contain people visiting The Sage. At four in the afternoon, someone comes to relieve me so I can have an hour's break. I've kept my bottle of water that I refilled at home, and I sit alone on a cold stone wall and drink it.

Back at work. I'm supposed to stand still – yet, I'm so bored that I play a pacing game with myself – timing how many times I can pace back and forth between two points in a minute. Night creeps in – I feel forgotten about. No cars have even driven past for three hours. At eleven, when someone finally comes and rescues me, I feel like I've been through a spiritual ordeal – left out in the wilderness to find myself. However, all I've found is my usual gnawing hunger, isolation, depression, exhaustion, and existential angst.

I spend the rest of the night until two in the morning in the big carpark in front of the building. The gaffer looks at me and tells me to get away now. My aching feet and brain cry relief.

A long trudge home. I check some bins along the Quayside for food – I find a half-eaten bag of chips that are lukewarm and disgusting, but I eat them anyway.

In bed and I'm floating downwards – the smell of sick, bleach, stale cigarettes and booze lingering in the air. I'm going to sleep, I tell myself as I lay motionless, broken with malnutrition and fatigue. I'm going to sleep for as long as possible – a whole day maybe.

I'm cold, and try to hug myself, and in doing so feel my ribs protruding out – I realise I have almost no fat on my body – I am wraith-like, I wonder if it is possible to just fade away into nothing – become ethereal, simply be a sensation, a consciousness without a voice, beyond flesh.

Ariella's voice repeating in my head. *Bye-bye, bye-bye, bye-bye, bye-bye….*

January, a cold porridge of a month – dreary, gloopy, bullied by chilled-wind, and debris scuttling around the pavements, trees-naked, a grimness.

College is a struggle – I wake up in the mornings and bang on Toby's door – most days he doesn't answer; he's either unconscious with excessive Hoegaarden consumption or sleeping at Frances's house. So I have to walk to college – I don't know how I'm getting through it, I'm handing the work in but none of it seems legit – as if a ghost, somewhere deep in the flesh-machine that is me, is writing these essays, recording these songs, playing these instruments. I'm scraping by with passes for my assignments – I don't know how.

In the dark of my room, I'm drunk and waiting for Isola to come over. When she arrives – parks herself tentatively on the edge of the bed and looks uncomfortable.

'I have to tell you something,' she says softly.

My heart hammering in my chest. 'What?'

'I got drunk with my friend Kevin last night, and we ended up going to bed.'

'Oh,' I reply, my heart retreating to its normal rhythm.

'You're not pissed off? I thought you would be.'

'I thought you were going to say you were pregnant,' I explain.

'What? No, of course not.'

A horrible silence. She's looking at me, as if she's waiting for me to say or do something.

I'm numb. I don't feel anything.

'So, you're alright with the fact that I've slept with someone else?'

'If that's what you want to do,' I tell her, suddenly feeling the need to lie down.

I lie facing the wall, sinking down, slipping off, a drunken-satori opening up, too empty and dead from existential ruminations to feel what she wants me to feel.

'So you're not angry then?' her voice at my shoulder.

'I can't be bothered to be angry,' I explain, 'not anymore. What's the point?'

'I thought you would go mental,' she tells me.

I think:

You wanted me to go mental. 'Cos you want out of this relationship.

'Well, I'm gonna go now, so I'll speak to you later, okay?'

'Okay,' I say softly, not moving from my position.

The door closes. The light from the hall snapping off, returning my crypt of ashtrays and empty cider bottles to its full gloom. I sink down into the bed – now letting emotions come on – a soft existential nausea, slowly crushing sadness, and the out of kilter feeling of *being*.

Ariella saying *bye-bye* in my head like an endlessly repeating mantra, all night, maybe for eternity, until the words lose all meaning and only the sound of it remains.

XLV

A few days of no contact with Isola, then, a message from her asking if I'm okay – I say yes for the sake of ease, then I ask if we are finished.

Of course we are; she slept with someone else, she points out.

Suddenly a hideous rejection strangling me and I try to swallow it all, so I don't have to taste the slowly emerging flavour of anger – but it never comes. Just a sour sensation on my tongue and in the sides of my throat. I sit and think about my anger – and wonder why not so long ago I would have thrown something through a window, but not now – now I only feel defeated and lack the energy to care.

Collecting all the old newspapers that are lying round the house – I spread them out on the floor and cut out the interesting larger words from the headlines and articles. Then I begin mounting them along the big right-side wall in my room. Starting at the top, I begin to build sentences, a strange, irrational magic emerging – and meaning begins to bleed through the nonsense. I exhaust all the useful words from the old papers, building up a gibberish poem.

It reads:

A granny dessert-ed after feeding bonkers casseroles said,
'Rio's face laced with can when he saw it.'
She put it the chance cheesecakes, on him.
Pies which Rio had to get with neighbours cleaned.
Deported criminals an ideal world there'd be a failure of hot
for everyone.
Illegal immigrants who left the country racist, it's realistic.

The home office long before we see chief constables blast.

But our country, abused called again convicted and deported, cannabis worth should simply not be.

Jamaican drug dealers at Newcastle into granting them visas. Grandma eats since walked back in.

But I reckon Jamaican drug dealers few porkies.

A secret colleges.

Sony BMG with supplying crack below left, teleported and 148 went on.

Prop up everyone should simply not be here for a better country.

The government force smashed a scam game but done little Jamaican drug dealers.

Whether we'll see into granting them visas means what he says.

148 went on endless numbers.

She was let and it was a ploy to caution.

But CD was sold out by called again text song hit the shops cannabis worth chance of a No.1.

Grandma eats ups are not possible.

A granny returning to the UK has after feeding other control. Grey-haired offences.

Boss then force smashed a scam effects lasted Jamaican drug dealers she used it in granting them visas.

She put it in colleges.

Cheesecakes, with supplying crack pies.

Even though it makes no sense, I find an interesting rhythm in it, and as Burroughs said, "*When you cut into the present, the future leaks out.*"

And so I keep staring at the words, looking for an irrational connection somewhere in the real world. The whole exercise is time consuming but the bizarre

sounding rhythm of some of the phrases is rewarding.
Grey-haired offences.

Sitting in the snug with Disco.

'I've split up with Isola.'

'Shit. Sorry mate, you okay?'

'Aye, it was never gonna work. Besides, she fucked someone else.'

'What? Honestly? That's fucking shit, man.'

I shrug my shoulders.

'Well,' he says, rummaging around in his pocket, 'let's have a smoke and some cups of tea and a chat.'

I laugh, and he begins rolling-up.

I tell him about my cut-up project, and about how Burroughs and Gysin discovered the technique.

'There's a fuck-load of old newspapers in that cupboard.' He says, pointing at the lacquered-brown, rectangular unit.

'Is there? I never looked in there.'

I open the cupboard to find the stack.

'I could live in this cupboard, it's just the right size for me to squeeze in.' I shout to Disco.

I dump the pile of newspapers on the table in the snug, dig out two pairs of scissors, some card, and glue. We sit for the afternoon, cutting up words from articles and pasting together sentences.

'I fucking love craft time,' Disco laughs with a roll-up hanging from his lips.

'This is how Bowie used to get some of his lyrics.'

'Is it?'

'Aye, not sure which ones though.'

'What a bender,' Disco laughs to himself.

After a while, the piece of card looks like this:

Researchers also king them down with reversed hypertrophy at polling stations.

Muslims in power. By millions of men all Islamist website to cure impotence.

Dilated and weakened at polling stations researchers also blew up Baghdad.

Impossible popularity has rocketed every voter.

Candidates were needed. And those who vote consult their Jordanian drug.

Is nothing less by posters put up by cultural shift.

Many times you blew up a polling station still a shock to Baghdad.

Secretary's report popularity stakes in American world without the development of finesse.

We have always erection. Therefore we publish in the journal such remarks.

Now they are the anthems on the drug.

He dismissed the blanket statement that psychological orthodox Jews take more risks. Clear examples of road safety.

Ument says a peace look set to start by Britain with capital Helsinki this many is in the bree Aceh movement.

International fighting for cynics.

A ceasefire to cure impotence.

Cynics will say I was vital to allow aid help Tony Blaired victims.

Endangering the meanwhile.

Logical the Tsunami struck. Don't think this is foreign media into a foreign ministry of 4 million people attention on forgotten war.

Jack Strawed by Millions of men.

Smoking seriously harms you to the highest standards of quality.

The sound of Disco's laugh as he is highly amused by some of these phrases.

'A ceasefire to cure impotence,' he laughs, 'these are mint song titles. We should make music for these. Fancy coming down the Off-Quay tonight? I don't think anyone rehearses on a Thursday so we should be okay.'

Later. The Off-Quay is a workspace unit, mainly used as rehearsal space for bands. After a certain time at night, you can feel a vibration of sound emanating from the building. Disco's band *Skywalker* rent this room and share the coverage of the rent with Toby's band.

'It's a canny size,' I say as I'm setting up my keyboard and bass, 'you could live here if you wanted to.'

'I've slept here on many occasions,' he replies. 'Here's the Electribe,' and he shows me a square bit of musical machinery with red-illuminated flashing soft-buttons and several dials and knobs.

'We'll build some beats on this,' he explains. 'Then build the songs around them. We should wait until later on, then see what is on the radio, and find some weird samples.'

'Can you record directly into it?'

'Aye, man. We'll put Radio 4 on, there's always weird shit on there.'

After midnight – Disco tunes in the radio. He presses record at random and captures a soft, delicate, southern female voice, "*And he took, half a step toward me, and as I looked up, half a drop of mercury slid down my spine.*"

366

'See what I mean?' he smiles, that's mint.

The songs begin to take shape, and by six in the next morning, there are four rough tracks. Disco opens his vocals, singing over the deep-grooves. I'm playing bass over the beats, and under his guitar. I swap to keys here and there.

Disco sings, '*Your heart's like a bonfire, no one can see you there. Open your eyes and breathe it in. There's no need to conspire, no one can see you there. Open your eyes and breathe it in. It's a place you go. It's all fire, this world pulls you under, this world pulls you under, this night-fire is all mine. It's a place you go.*'

The deep-groove, in sleepy rhythm, the swirl of the music – a nocturnal-audio, heads nodding, I feel like we're making something incredible. The sound of electro-drums snapping, rolling kicks, heavy beats dropping on and off. Samples of strings, bleeps, breaks, funk. A driving musical-melancholy.

Working on the tracks in a frenzy over the course of a week; staying up all night, sleeping on the rickety sofas, cups of black tea, endless amounts of thin roll-up cigarettes.

Disco has had a look through my CD collection and pulled out some discs he thinks might have some interesting samples on. He's also brought a CD of mine called *20 Sci-Fi Film Classics*, which contains muzak versions of sci-fi TV and film themes.

'Where did you get this?' he asks, laughing at how terrible it sounds.

'Found it in a charity shop.'

'Ah, yes!' he exclaims as he skips a few tracks on. The theme to *Quantum Leap* begins to play and he turns the volume up to full blast – the music is coming through the PA – so it is deafening. Disco breaks into a gangly-legged dance and minces round the room in time to the music. I can't see for tears of hilarity blurring my vision.

Mission to the all-night garage at four in the morning. The tyranny of early hours in winter, huddled up in our thin coats, both emaciated, existing on *creating*. We have 27p. It is 15p for a Chomp.

'We need three pence,' Disco points out, then we can have one each.

'Wow!' I say sarcastically.

'You won't say that when you're eating it. A Chomp is the food of kings.'

Both our sets of eyes are scanning the floor for coins. Up the steep stairs past The Cumberland, the three pence, waiting for us.

In the garage, the attendant through the little hole.

'Two Chomps,' Disco asks while pushing the horde of coins under the gap.

When you are hungry, eternally hungry, the flavours of anything are so intense that it is often too much. The meagre meal that is a Chomp, a thin slice of chocolate and fudge – this will be all I will eat until tonight, when I crawl home from college and eat a packet of nine-pee noodles. My eyes black and twitching with tiredness. My *being* burning alive with *art*.

'All I want to do in life is create,' I tell Disco while savouring my little chocolate bar and walking back to the Off-Quay.

'It doesn't matter what the government does, it doesn't matter what anyone does to me, they can take away everything, but you can always create. Even if just in your head, you can imagine and make things and tell yourself stories. Nothing in this life can remove that. You can live, be anywhere, have nothing, and do great things because you are making sense of existence through creation.'

'That's what makes life worthwhile, man,' he agrees. 'The less I have, the richer I feel.'

The weekend.

'We need to go out tonight,' I explain to Disco. 'It's been two weeks since I split up with Isola, I think I should try and fuck someone to get over it.'

'There's a new rock night on,' he tells me, 'in Legends.'

That night. The sticky floor of the club. Bumbling around – stealing half-finished drinks from tables and making bizarre cocktails.

Disco is dancing with a woman. I'm standing to the side, looking at a red-haired girl with big, bright, red-lips.

Three a.m. Kick-out time. Disco at my ear, 'I'm going back to this lass's house to fuck her.'

I rummage in my pocket; I have eight pounds that I have saved for a taxi. I give him half.

The sweaty masses leaving the club. I spot the red-haired girl. Her eyes meet mine.

'I think you are gorgeous,' I shout at her.

She says something back, I'm not sure what, but then we're kissing. Then in a taxi, back to mine. I don't have enough to get all the way there – and so pretend to stop the taxi near a shop, around the corner from the house, pretending that this is the best place to get out.

In my bed. Her pink nipples. She is nineteen. Those red lips rubbing over the end of my cock, the taste of her – she is ample, not fat, rounded, curvaceous – boozy kisses, ashtray tongues.

'What's your name?'

'Annabelle-Leigh.'

Her bag on the floor – the contents spilled out, lipsticks, a pocket mirror with a picture of The Beatles on the reverse, keys, money, cigarettes.

My cock thick, tumescent, in and out of her sopping slit, both drunk and unable to come. Fucking – the sound of my thighs slapping against her, teeth-gritted, lungs heaving.

I run out of thrust.

'Have you come?' she asks.

'I can't,' I tell her exhausted, 'I'm too drunk.'

She tugs away at my cock, yanking it furiously.

'Stop. It's okay. You're beautiful,' I tell her.

Lay down – world spinning, my arm across this foreign body. Weirdness. Falling asleep.

Wake up three hours later. Sit up, groan, the mental gasp as a pack of flashing images of last night reel through my brain. A lump of human flesh in my bed. I head downstairs and bring up two pints of water. I hand one to Annabelle – her make-up smeared all over her face, ginger-wire hair mangled up. She looks like Jack Nicholson as The Joker. I realise I've been seriously beer-goggled.

I get back into bed with her, work my cock up her snatch, and pump until I blow my load. Now a terrible feeling – that I want her to leave. But the rigmarole of small talk begins.

An hour of chat, drinking coffee, smoking in bed. She sucks my cock and makes me come again. The smell of her cunt-juices, perfume, and sweat in the sheets. It's heady; you can't smell it unless you breathe it in.

'Do you have a girlfriend?' she asks, sounding young and naive.

'No.'

'I don't have a boyfriend, either.'

'I think I'm broken,' I tell her. 'I don't do relationships anymore.'

She gets dressed. 'Where am I again?' she asks laughing.

'Heaton.'

'I have to get back to Sunderland,' she tells me while scooping all her belongs from the floor into her bag. 'Could you order me a taxi?'

'Aye of course,' I tell her.

Five minutes later, she leaves. I still feel drunk and sit in front of the TV – watching the news, listening to the emerging stories from survivors of the Tsunami.

A knock at the front door – Disco looking tired, drunk, a bit fragile.

'I need tea, and a rolly, and a chat.' He laughs.

I knock us up a brew each and we scrape together two roll-ups from the dumpers in the emergency jail-tab tin.

'Did you have a good time?' I ask him.

'She was a bit mental, she wouldn't let me fuck her, because we didn't have any condoms, but she wanked me off. What about you?'

371

'She was fat and ginger. So, great.' I laugh.

He laughs too. 'You love it, you man-whore.'

'Fat, ginger women need love too. What is pleasing to the hand is different to what is pleasing to the eye, my friend,' I nod, smile, and wink.

XLVI

Isola, for a very short time, muted the memories of
Ariella – now they switch back on, even more
intensely than before. A little, horrible thought in my
head: I still love Ariella. These words bring down my
walls, all defences crumble. I let it come, let myself
mourn – steaming drunk, in the early hours,
staggering around Shieldfield flats where I know she
now lives – I'm singing our songs in a drunken,
spastic voice. Looking up at the tower blocks
wondering which one she lives in, scanning the lights
in the windows.

I feel blank at times – empty, except for a terrible
sensation of being unloved. In drunkenness, late at
night, bombarding Ariella with messages, saying I still
love her, miss her. No reply. Except from Dom,
suggesting I leave her alone.

I delete her number from my phone. Try to get a
grip on myself, only to circle back to this terrible
sensation of lost-love. I remind myself that existence
is suffering. That suffering arises because of craving
to be free from suffering, and that this endless
rumination on what is, what has been, and what I
have done will make no difference other than to make
me ill. Even though I realise this, and rationalise my
actions and thoughts, they go on. Like the never-
ending winter, the greyness, and the narrow and
cobbled back streets of Heaton that stretch out
forever behind the avenues, my thoughts of Ariella
extend out into a relentless future. It exhausts and
frustrates me.

I tramp these city alleyways, pissing behind wheeliebins in the middle of the night, lost, roaming, looking for coins on the ground, eating old food off the floor, feeling like dirt personified, the slime of existence made flesh. I'm alone in a godless universe; no purpose, or meaning to anything. Absurdity in all I think and do, my words a waste of time and effort, all thoughts cripple me – relentless existential nightmares. I'm so thin and gaunt, and I don't care if I live or die sometimes. I feel like I'm waiting to dampen out of the universe, quickly snuffed.

Then I spend time with Disco, Toby, Liam, Dan, and Lisa – and I revive just enough. People who have come into my life and are giving me breath, giving me tiny bits of emotional nourishment to keep on going. Little gasps of air in a world of smog.

Disco at his usual spot at the table in the snug – late January. I put my Polaroid digital camera down in front of him.

'Let's make a cut up film,' I suggest.

'A film?'

'Yeah, we'll read out the cut-ups we made the other week, and then scramble them up on Toby's computer.'

He chuckles at this in his usual way and agrees. We smoke a joint made from several leftover ones and then in different locations around the house (in the yard, in the kitchen, in my bed, on the toilet, in the shower) and changing/swapping clothes, and levels of nakedness, we read out the lines of cuts repeatedly. Then import the clips into Movie Maker and begin to scramble them up in an arbitrary manner, speed up, slow down, flip, reverse, cut-in, and out. The film begins to become increasingly manic and hilarious. Images of myself and Disco popping in and out of the same space-time location like magic. It becomes so funny that I can't see, breathe, or speak.

Another night working on music in the Off-Quay. One song is particularly tight so we record and mix it on my old tape four track. It's a very rough mix, but it demos the song quite well.

'Should we do a gig?' I ask him.

'We're not ready.'

'Yeah, but if I book it for a month in advance?'

'Who with?'

'I'll ask Triple-X Terry.'

'Alright then,' he agrees 'the only problem is the wire for the Electribe is dodgy. If you knock it, the power goes off. I'll have to find a way of keeping it from falling out.'

Next day – I phone around and book a gig with Triple-X for the end of February. He wants to know what happened to Sepia Tears – I directly avoid answering him.

'I thought those two were a bit stuck-up anyways,' he gurgles down the phone, expecting me to agree.

'It was complicated,' I say flatly.

Sitting on the snug settee, drunk, alone in silence. Eight p.m.; a weeknight in the middle of nowhere. House empty, save for external noises reverberating through the walls and floors. I've run out of booze, money, cigarettes, so I've consumed a whole packet

375

of paracetamol and now I'm fuzz-brained, and half-awake.

That little pocket on the front of my jeans, above the normal pocket – the one that has no use – not the right size to fit anything in, I poke my finger in it. Something in there, I slip it out. A fiver. I study it with excitement, noticing that it has battled with the washing machine a few times by the look of it. I waste no time and head straight to Coli's for tobacco, skins, and cheap cider.

Sitting on the sofa, king for a day. Emily walks in, done up, little skirt, full make-up. I can barely speak. She is all legs that end in heels. I want to lick her.

'You always look lovely,' I tell her.

'She doesn't say anything,' but smiles at me like I'm her pet.

For a moment I have a half-thought of just being blunt and asking if she wants a rough fuck. But I'm too drunk and damaged – and I crawl off to my bed, lying in the dark wanking myself off, imagining shooting my hot spunk all over her face.

An unconscious sleep. Next day. I wake up, three in the afternoon. In the bathroom, pale light. I look at my face in the mirror. I don't know who this person is – all I feel is existential sickness. I feel like a scab, hanging off, waiting to flick off into the wind. Dirt personified – I ache just through being, everything so out of kilter, nothing ever fits where it should.

I take my electric razor and start to shave my hair off, right down to the bone. I want to see who is there – what's underneath. I want to cleanse myself somehow, purge – lift myself from the murkiness and fog of not knowing who I am, of who and what I am supposed to be in this life.

Skinhead. Hollow-eyes, black rings, gaunt, thinned, and malnourished. This ascetic figure in front of me. Self-destructive, degenerating. This head-shaving ritual – it does give a newness, but I feel further submerged, not lifted – but pushed deeper, darker, foggier. The person underneath is a beast, and not human, but animal. All sex and violence, monstrous, explosive, exhausted by existence.

Disco's voice in my head saying: *you're just an ape*.

I knock on Toby's door. He opens it and his face explodes, big cheeky grin.

'Fucking hell,' he laughs, 'you fucking Nazi skinhead.'

I go into his room, where Disco and Frances are sitting on the bed passing a bong back and forth.

They take turns rubbing my bald head.

'It suits you,' Frances says, her eyes glowing and round.

I take a lung-full of smoke from the bong and we watch the cut-up film on the computer. My face hurts from laughing so much.

I feel manic and insane.

'I'm just an ape,' I tell Disco.

'Ow! That's right,' he agrees in a mock Michael Jackson, *Bo Selecta* voice, 'you're a fucking skinhead ape, mother-fuckkay! Ow! That's right. You know that's right, right?'

I wake up in bed the next day, wrapped up in toilet roll like a mummy. I start laughing, trying to struggle free.

377

'Disco, you twat,' I laugh, as I manage to untangle myself.

I check my face in the mirror just to make sure I have no marker-pen doodles on my face, or have had my eyebrows shaved off. I'm fine; I'm still just a bald-ape.

'What am I supposed to do with all this bog paper?' I ask Disco, who is sitting in the snug watching the news.

He laughs and throws a roll-up at me. 'Wipe your arse on it, man.'

XLVII

Early February. My birthday, turning twenty-three. I don't want to celebrate it; I think to celebrate the ridiculousness of my existence is stupid. I phone Bunny.

'I know it's out of the blue, and we haven't spoken much recently, but could I come to visit you for my birthday? I need to get out of Newcastle for a bit.'

'Of course,' she squeaks down the phone, 'it will be fun.'

The strange and at once familiar, exciting, feeling of pulling out of Gallowgate bus station.

Pulling into Golders Green – the temperature always a little higher than up north. Bunny meets me off the bus.

'What happened to your hair?' she asks.

It feels like a long time since we last saw each other. I dump my bag at her house and talk to her parents for a while – the same lingering smell of cat urine permeating my nostrils – the expensive pottery books on the lower shelves all still lined in cellophane to protect against feline piss.

London at night, drunk, slurring, mumbling, over the Thames via the Millennium Bridge, the looming London eye lit up. Hot-white lights everywhere, unfamiliar sounds of traffic and cockney-accents. I run out of cash, the overdraft in the red, now hammering my credit card, I no longer care, Bunny has no money – I buy all the drinks, the food. We move on to Camden, a dank pub, a gibberish conversation with a strange man – my limbs flailing, I'm incoherent, drunk, mad, northern.

Laying on Bunny's bed – I kiss her.

'What are you doing?' she gasps.

'It's just a fuck.' I drool.

'Oh, is it now?' she laughs.

'Come on, how long has it been since you had your fanny licked?'

She laughs. 'Fair enough then.'

I stand up in front of her and insert my stiff cock into her mouth. She jerks and sucks on it until I go off in her cheeks. She spits the load out onto the floor in disgust.

'You know I hate come in my mouth, you horrible shit,' she says sounding sick.

The blob of spit and semen on the floor – white globule, creamy with bubbles. I look at it for a second, nestled amongst the chaos and mess of her attic room.

I lick her cunt – same old knickers, same old taste, wiry pubes caught in my throat. Spreading the lips and tonguing the nub. I find a strand of pink Xmas tinsel lodged in her lips. Is it the same one? How many times has this happened? Did I dream any of this? A fleeting moment of absurd déjà vu.

'You've got tinsel in your fanny,' I tell her, pulling the strand out and showing her.

'What? Don't stop, I'm nearly there.'

Her short orgasm, shuddering body.

I wake up next to her feet. Dehydrated, confused.

My birthday on a bus. Six hours crawl back north – eyes, rolling heavy with exhaustion. I keep looking at my phone, wondering if Ariella will send me a happy birthday.

Valentine's Day. In the snug with Disco.

'My valentine this year is White Storm cider,' I declare.

'Mine too, I love booze.'

'I love booze too, wanna go out tonight?'

'I would but I haven't got a stitch to wear.'

'What?'

'Nowt, aye let's go out.'

'Have you read *The Dice Man*?' I ask.

'No, why?'

I explain the premise of the book, then head upstairs and find my dice.

Back in the snug:

'Here's the game,' I tell him, 'One die dictates the drink, the other the location.'

He's laughing at this.

'Six drinks, six locations.'

'Okay, what are the drinks?'

'Lager, cider, house vodka, house whiskey, water and...' I pause thinking about it.

'Something horrible?'

'Aye. Taboo?'

'Okay,' he giggles at this.

'What are the pubs?'

'Steamer, Dog and Parrot, Gotham, what else is near there?'

'North bar?'

'Aye North bar, The Telegraph and Tokyo? Maybe?'

'Okay, write all this down though.'

Several hours later, and I'm drinking a pint of water while disco struggles with a measure of house whiskey.

'My phone has been cut off,' I tell him.

'When?'

'This morning. I can receive calls, but can't make them. My credit card has been cancelled as well.'

'Shit man, you shouldn't be paying for these drinks tonight.'

'It's fine. My mother gave me twenty-quid because she said I looked like I wasn't eating enough.'

'And now you're drinking it?'

'Yes. Fuck food.'

Strange looks as we walk in and out of bars, rolling the die on the counter and ordering random drinks. After several hours of this, Disco says:

'I think we should abandon the dice game now. I'm starting to feel sick from that last vodka.'

Standing in Tokyo like two tramps while long-legged stunning women prance around. The smell of limes and mint while people drink mojitos. My eyes everywhere, skirts, heels.

I check the time. 'It's half-nine man, let's go to Legends.'

He agrees.

Later, staggering around, sticky-floor, the sound of Rob Zombie blasting, cheap disco lights, smoke machines, vile alcopops.

Annabelle-Leigh.

'Hi again,' she says.

My lips on hers, her red lipstick all over my face.

She is wearing a tight black dress that clings to her body, revealing her curves and fat.

382

'I want to fuck you,' she shouts in my ear.

I dance with her for a drunken eternity – idiotic robotic-sleaze-sex dancing, spastic flailing of limbs, falling in and out of rubbery kisses. Mentally blank, empty-brained, doylum-dancing morons.

The club ends – I can't find Disco. I stand outside for ten minutes in the freezing cold, Annabelle cuddled into me.

'Fuck it, he must have gone already.'

'We're going to have to walk mind,' I tell her.

'Walk, how far?'

'Two miles.'

'I can't walk two miles, not in these shoes, anyways.'

I put my hand in my pocket and pull out seventy-four pence and some fluff.

'I'll pay for it,' she tells me.

We get in a taxi.

In my bed – complicated sex-moves, getting her ginger fanny out of parachute knickers. I lick her quim all over as if it is the most delicious thing I've ever tasted. I put my cock inside her and pump away. She's enjoying it, but I become mentally detached, drift off, something not right here, a sorrow creeps upon me. There is no love, only flesh. Only this: I am void, a black hole. I am not the universe incarnate – I am the universe incorporeal – a collection of dirt that arrogantly thinks of itself as aware.

I am unaware, unenlightened. In the emptiness of the moment – I see my ridiculous self, the fool that I am. Grinding away at this vagina, at this ridiculous life. In a flash, I see all that I say and do as surreal.

My cock in her mouth. She sucks and tugs it, cups my balls and caresses them. Works it roughly – I don't feel anything sexual, just a vague drunkenness and an attack from a terrible existential phantom.

Then the rising tingle up my shaft, frantic wanking – tonguing the tip – erupting hot white creamy spunk all over her breasts. Pink nipples like shocked albino eyes.

Her bag spilt all over the floor and bed again.

Rehearsing for our gig. The cold of the Off-Quay, the low, muffled rumble of other bands playing elsewhere in the building.

'Listen, man,' I tell Disco, 'Toby is talking about how he is sick of you sleeping at our house again. I was at Event Cover today; they're looking for staff. If you get some work for them, he might back off a bit.'

'I doubt it,' he replies, 'I know I'm taking the piss.'

'I don't think you are. I like having you at the house.'

'I know, cheers man.'

'Anyway, fancy it? There's a rugby game on in Scotland and they need more people.'

'Will I have to sign off?'

'Dunno, probably not, if you can get away with it.'

'Alright, then.'

On a bus to Edinburgh for Scotland vs Italy in the 2005 Rugby World Cup.

'Did you get the baccy?' Disco asks.

'Aye, did you bring lunch?'

He opens a carrier bag and shows me two thin-looking peanut butter sandwiches.

'One each, man.'

I realise my belly is going to growl today, not that it doesn't most days.

The bus has been organised by Event Cover and is full of staff. We involuntarily have to listen to people talking amongst themselves.

'This is torture,' Disco says to me, an hour into the journey, 'listen to these morons, people jabbering on about *Coronation Street*, and what they ate at McDonald's yesterday. Like these are the important things in life.'

Aye, they've obviously never sat smoking jail tabs while cutting words out of the Metro paper to make poems with.'

He laughs at this. 'That's art, that is.'

At a motorway services. Standing with huge, illuminous yellow jackets on. Smoking thin rollies. The brown-green Scottish countryside, rolling fog.

'People will let you do anything if you are wearing a jacket like this,' Disco suggests. 'We could dig up that road and no one would say anything.'

'Because of the jacket?'

'Of course. It demands some sort of authority, doesn't it? We could direct the fucking traffic if we wanted to. All people see is the jacket. It's like a bizzie's uniform; you don't see the man underneath, just the authority in the outfit.'

At the rugby match, standing by a stairwell, walking up and down the stairs. Feeling drained, looking at the crowd but not taking anything in. This place could set on fire and I wouldn't do anything about it – I wouldn't stop anyone from doing anything.

Second half – Disco comes round the corner.

'I've escaped,' he tells me, 'come on, let's go for a smoke.'

'Aye, fuck it.'

We find a corner to hide behind. 'Take your jacket off,' Disco tells me while taking his off.

'What? It's freezing, man.'

'Aye, but if we get spotted no one will know who we're working for, there's that many people here, none of the Event Cover doylums will have a clue.'

'This is shit, isn't it?' I ask rhetorically, with little jittery-jumping movements to keep myself warm.

'I'd rather be at home with a cuppa having a chat,' he replies through shivering, nattering teeth.

I laugh at this. 'Me too, man.'

Back on the bus, night creeping in. Peanut butter sandwich. It's so dry that I can't chew it.

'Did you bring anything to drink?' I ask Disco.

'Here,' he hands me small bottle of water.

I take a swig and pass it back, bits of peanut butter and white bread floating in it.

Someone down the bus starts singing *The Wheels on the Bus*.

Everyone joins in. Except for Disco and me.

'What the fuck, man?' he shudders. 'I'm trapped on a bus with a pack of spastics.'

The childish singing continues.

'I don't think I want to work for these cunts anymore,' I suggest to Disco.

'Aye, fuck this like.' He takes his headphones and iPod Shuffle out of his pocket. He plugs the phones into his lugs, and turns to look out the window.

The black road and night gushing past, strips of fleeting cat's eyes, rumble of the wheels on the road. I catch sight of a sign that says "Berwick".

386

I close my eyes and try to disconnect as a hideous chorus begins to sing the theme tune to *Home and Away*.

XLVIII

The gig – many people have turned up, including the two girls from my college course, Hannah and Elizabeth.

We blast through our five songs, watch the other bands – then I spend some time talking to Dan and Lisa – while Disco is getting cosy with Hannah. Hannah has sunshine-blonde hair, blue-eyes, wide smile, white-teeth. She is very attractive. Elizabeth is dark-haired, cheeky-looking, mouthy, and equally attractive.

End of the night – Elizabeth offers to drive us home with our gear – Disco and me in the back of the car, drunk, giving wrong directions. Hannah in the front, flirting in the mirror with Disco.

At home, I cook a chicken and BBQ pizza – dump it on the table, and cut it into bits with scissors.

'You're cutting your pizza up with scissors?' Elizabeth laughs.

'Fuck, aye, it's easier than using a blunt knife.'

The girls decline to have any so Disco and me sit and munch through the whole thing.

'Come on, Han,' Elizabeth tells her, 'let's go.'

'Actually, I might stay for a bit, if that's okay?'

'How are you going to get back?'

'Taxi.'

'You can stay if you want,' I tell Elizabeth, 'have a drink?'

I'm hoping she will say yes and some alcoholic lubrication will loosen her knickers.

'No, I have to walk my dog.'

Elizabeth leaves. Disco leads Hannah off into the front room. I go to bed.

Next morning. I'm in the snug eating a slice of toast. The relentless tsunami news, still going on.

Rose walks though the kitchen, face like stone, cheeks like a bairn's smacked arse, ignores me. Then she's out the door, nearly taking the thing off its hinges with the force of her slam.

Disco, sheepish, walks into the snug followed by Hannah.

'She is fucking mental,' he shakes his head.

'Who?'

'Rose, man. She came into the front room this morning and kicked me in the fucking head.'

'Hard?'

'Aye, look at the side of me nappa.' He shows me his head, where there is a bright red mark.

'I don't know who that fucking bitch is calling me a slut, either,' Hannah barks, 'she'd better watch herself because I will fucking kick her all over.'

'Thanks for last night,' she kisses Disco on the cheek, 'as she's leaving.'

'What happened, exactly?' I ask him.

'We were asleep on the settee together, Rose walks in, and kicks me in the face while I'm asleep. She's deranged, man; she seems to think we're in a relationship or something. That mad bitch Emily was standing there too.'

I head upstairs to have a shower and change clothes – in the bathroom, my toothbrush snaps.

Back downstairs, Disco is talking to Emily, a horrible atmosphere in the house.

389

'Listen, man,' I say to Disco, 'I'm going for a walk to buy a new toothbrush. You coming? I've got my camera; I thought we could make a stupid film in the park.'

Emily's bitch-slapped face as we leave.

Along the greyness of Rothbury Terrace – towards Heaton Park.

'That Emily just needs a hard cock up her cunt,' I tell Disco.

'Yeah,' he agrees, 'let's go two's-in on a bastard.'

I point the camera at a group of crows that all take off at once.

'Did you get that?' he asks.

Through the park, the empty branches of the trees, no sign of spring, grass short, thick brown streaks of mud – a weekday in the middle of the universe – time irrelevant, we are nowhere.

Filming random pockets of existence, clips of each other saying surreal things, making absurd gestures, noises, the joy and hollowness of our atheistic lives.

'Making a film about going to buy a toothbrush. These are the best days of our lives,' I say to Disco while filming him.

He laughs and pulls a stupid face into the camera.

Rehills – I buy the toothbrush – and with it, the memory of all the times I came here with Ariella. These invasive pockets of sadness, they pop up without warning, emotional landmines.

Back through Heaton park, via the Shoe Tree. At the end of their time at university in Newcastle, all the graduates throw a pair of shoes up into the tree before leaving.

'Look,' Disco points up the tree, 'a new pair of fucking Converse up the tree! I'm having them.'

I film him lobbing sticks up the tree trying to bring them down. After several attempts, he's wheezing and exhausted.

'You try,' he tells me.

I give him the camera and try chucking sticks up towards the shoes. I bring down a pair of manky old brown leather boots. I throw them back up, the laces twisting round the branches.

I give up, exhausted too.

'They're not coming down, man,' I say breathing heavily, 'you'll have to climb up.'

'Fuck that shit!' he says into the camera in a silly *Bo-Selecta*-Michael Jackson voice, 'I may be an ape, but I ain't climbing no mother-fucking tree, that's right, ow!'

That night at home, I'm accosted by Toby, Rose, and Emily.

Listen man,' says Toby, 'we've decided Disco can't stay here anymore, it isn't fair on us, on you, he doesn't pay any rent, and by letting him practically live here, we aren't helping him sort himself out.'

I stare at the carpet and try to find words. What Toby is saying is right, but I don't want to hear it. I look at Rose.

'I don't want him bringing his cheap sluts here either,' she snaps.

'She's a girl on our collage course,' I say bewildered at Rose, 'she's actually really canny.'

391

'Regardless,' Toby continues, 'he can't sleep here anymore, and as you're the only one that doesn't mind it….'

'I don't mind at all,' I interrupt him.

'You should tell him he can't stay.'

A morning trying to put my speech together. I'm angry about it, but I can't do anything about it now.

That evening, I meet Disco down The Off-Quay.

'I need to talk to you, mate. Everyone else at the house is telling me that you can't sleep there anymore.'

'Ah, right. It's okay, man.' He smiles.

'Obviously not me though, I don't mind you staying at all.'

'It's cool man, these things happen. I can just crash here, and go back to my mam's when I have to.'

Next day – I meet Disco at the library where he is sitting at a table, lining up bus tickets.

'Here's my plan,' he tells me, 'I've got all these bus tickets, right? So, I'm going to scan them into a computer and cut out the numbers from the tickets. Then I can rearrange them on the screen, and change the date so I can have a free weekly bus pass.'

'What? How?'

'I'll show you.'

We sit at the computer while he arranges the numbers over a ticket with blanked out information.

'Are you just doing this in Paint?'

'Aye, man. I had the idea the other day when I was on the bus. There were loads of tickets in the bin so I collected them all.'

We sit and look at the fake ticket on the screen.

'I dunno man, it looks dodgy.'

'Wait until it is printed out, man,' he smiles, 'oh by the way, have you got ten pence for the machine?'

'Aye, sure,' I dig around in my pocket and hand him the coin.

'Right, I'm sending it now, remember this number, this is the print job.'

He reads me the number. At the printer, he collects his work. It looks real.

'Fucking hell, man. You'll totally get away with that,' I tell him.

He asks a woman at the desk for a pair of scissors, cuts out his ticket, and slides it into the plastic wallet they give out on the bus when you buy a weekly pass.

'Look at it, man,' he holds it in front of me, 'you'd never know it was fake.'

'Fuck me, man! It looks real. You genius.'

'This means I can kip at the Off-Quay, and nip back to me mam's through the day.'

'Fair enough.'

On my way home, I look at my bank account at the machine on Chillingham Road to see what I already know: that I'm at my overdraft limit. I put my PIN in, the machine whirs, and then consumes my card. *Please contact your bank,* it tells me in green digital writing.

'Fuck,' I shout.

I take my credit card out, knowing that I won't get anything out of it either, but out of desperation it is worth a look.

The machine gobbles up my card.

'Fuck!' I shout again.

At home, I look through the cupboards, fridge, and freezer. I have no food, nothing, not a crumb. I have no tobacco or alcohol. I look under the cushions on both settees. Nothing. In my room I lift up my bed, check all my pockets, all empty of coin. Back in the kitchen, I flip up the lid of the bin, poke around looking for leftover food. There's nothing there. I wash my hands, thinking about what to do. I realise I've hit bottom. I have nothing. No money or food. No work lined up. My student loan isn't for another week, and then that will have to cover the overdraft and then rent, bringing me back into the overdraft. I go upstairs and look in the cupboard, staring at my DVD collection. I pull them out and put them into a plastic bag.

On Chillingham Road, Blockbuster Video, I wait while the cashier scans my collection, one box at a time. There must be two-hundred pounds worth there.

'Right, so fifteen pounds forty-nine, for all these,' she tells me.

My heart sinks. I feel morbidly depressed. 'Yeah, okay then,' I tell her with a sigh.

However, to a desperately poor man, this is a fortune. It will keep my demons at bay for at least another day. I decide to worry about tomorrow when tomorrow comes.

I buy battered sausage and chips from Gills. White Storm, Golden Virginia, Rizla, Swan Filters from Coli's.

In the cocoon of my room. I lock the door. Sit alone, staring at the high ceiling. A coldness, an infinite quiet, save for the wind rattling at the window.

XLIX

The house empty – no Disco in the snug in the morning anymore. I sit alone at the table staring at my mug of cheap Morrison's coffee, feeling sad about it all.

The sound of the house phone ringing, eerily sonically discordant and aggressive-sounding in the quiet house.

Disco:

'I can't get to Newcastle today, man, I got caught on the bus with my fake pass.'

'How?'

'The driver said some of the numbers didn't match up.'

'Did you put the wrong date on?'

'No I mean, like, serial numbers or something.'

'Oh, shit man.'

'He tried to keep me on the bus, said he was going keep me on until an inspector arrived. I said "you can't fucking do that, mate" and I pulled the lever for the emergency door release and legged it.'

I laugh down the phone at him. 'You mad bastard.'

'Anyway, I can't get there until I get me dole. Getting a bus pass is going to cost me thirteen quid a week that I haven't got. I have to go, man, 'cos I'm in a phone box.'

March. Signs of spring, little openings in the sky of lingering sun – it is fleeting, ghostly, prickles the skin with hope.

Rehearsing down the Off-Quay, the Electribe keeps cutting out.

'What are we going to do about this?' I ask Disco.

'I dunno, I think we should cancel our gig next week, it will look bad if it keeps cutting out during the set.'

'Is it the power cable?'

'No, it's the connection to the power on the thing itself. It's been funny for a while. It will have to be repaired properly before we can continue.'

'What about the gig?'

We cancel the gig. We stop rehearsing.

My final rent for the house in the form of a cheque that I know will bounce. Only three months left of the contract.

Toby:

'What are you going to do when the contract runs out?'

'I dunno, what are you doing?'

'I'm not sure, man. I think I'm going to move back to my mam's over the summer until college starts again in September. I need to save some cash. I'm so broke.'

Days thinking about it. I realise I have no option but to move back into my mam's house. I have exhausted myself here – financially, mentally, and physically. The fun has stopped – now just a persistent existential angst.

My phone cut off, so I haven't received any job offers from Event Cover. I decide I won't work for them again. I borrow an old phone from my brother – walk eight miles there and back to collect it – no money for the bus, shoes worn, feet aching. My head swimming in despair. While at my mother's, I rob the cupboards of food – stuff she won't miss, old tins of soup that have been at the back of the cupboard for months –

out-of-date stuff, things that have been in the freezer since the last ice-age. It doesn't matter what it is – so long as it sustains me through to another empty day.

Walk back past the old house – looking up at the window, thinking about Ariella. Through the Dene – haunting echoes of her laugh – the smell of her perfume, caught in my nose for a second – I try to bring it back but can't grasp it again.

No contact with Disco for a week. I ask Rose if she has seen or heard from him.

'I think he's staying at Baz's house.'

'Who the fuck is Baz?'

'You know Baz? He lives on Tenth Avenue. He's in a band. He works with Toby.'

Tenth Avenue is three streets away. I wonder why he would be round the corner, but not contact me. That night I ask Toby the same question.

'Yeah, he's staying at Baz's. I'm sorry, man. I told you, he latches on to people that give him a free meal, he can't stay here anymore, so he's staying at Baz's. I tried to warn Baz, but he wouldn't listen, just like you wouldn't listen.'

'Sorry, man.'

'It's understandable. Disco is lots of fun, he's a good laugh, but he's like a puppy. He makes people feel sorry for him, so he can stay with them. Baz will get sick eventually, too.'

I lie on my bed and think, but *I* didn't get sick of Disco.

Day later. I get Baz's number from Toby. I phone him and ask to speak to Disco.

'Do you want to go into to town for drinks?' I ask him.

He's busy doing stuff with Baz.

Next day. I phone again.

'Fancy some cans in the park? The sun is out.'

He's busy with Baz again.

And so I get the picture; Toby was right.

April. Spring banging on the door. No more Disco. I feel like I understand his reasons, and there's no hurt or hate, even though I feel there should be. This is how Toby feels about it too; Disco isn't a bad guy at all – he's just lost, like the rest of us. I spend time at the weekends at Dan and Lisa's flat or drinking horrible watered-down pints at the Trillians pound night.

I knuckle down and catch up with college work. Days roll on, Emily has moved out early, even though she's paid all her rent. Rose is never in the house either; she has a new boyfriend and spends all her time at his flat. Toby is either always at work or at Frances' house. I sit alone in the big empty house. It feels enormous. My heart so heavy, I lock my bedroom door – hide away for days on end. Lost in myself – drifting. The infinite quiet, I can hear my internal organs struggling to keep me alive – and the terrible bleakness of my being thumping, relentlessly in the eye of my mind.

Days of endless solitude. I feel like I'm tiny in the massive room, massive house, curled up in the corner of my bed with a vast expanse of space around me. No contact with anyone – I watch the contents of my mind swim around all my existential terrors, the past, Ariella. My monsters and demons – their ugly faces in memories.

May. A letter on the doormat. The landlord has sold the house. Even though the tenancy is not over for another four weeks, the new landlord will take ownership of the house immediately.

Sitting alone in the snug. Eight in the morning, toast, coffee, cigarette.

A middle-aged woman, flanked by two teenagers, enters the house.

In a horrible Aussie accent: 'I'm the new landlord. We need to put some stuff in here now so we're putting it in this front room. Okay?'

I sit and stare at her.

'Sure.' I reply. Although I'm thinking, you can shove it up your arse for all I care, pet.

End of the college year. Somehow, I've managed to pass. Two weeks left of the tenancy. My mother and step-dad going on holiday. I decide to start moving home. I pack up all my essentials and leave the stuff I can't manage until they get back and I can get a lift with it in the car.

There's no point staying in the house any longer – a feeling of sadness as I leave.

At my mother's, I eat myself stupid for two weeks. Back in the tiny box room, drinking myself blind, in bed with bottles of Black Tower – a nice sensation of not having to worry about food or bills.

An empty afternoon, out of the window – Natalie and Ariella. I stare solidly, my heart thumping, I can't move – they walk past and don't look up.

I sit on my single bed, skin alive with gooseflesh. Sadness and agony all over me.

400

My mam and step-dad return. Early morning – I head over to the house to pack up the rest of my stuff. It is raining and windy – in the dead house, the window in the toilet open. I lean over the toilet to close it and look down into the yard. I'm not sure I believe what I see; the drain has exploded – grey/green slimy shit oozing out all over the yard – and the smell that confirms it.

I phone Toby:

'Toby, man, have you been in the house recently?'

'No, man, no one is living there anymore, even though the tenancy isn't up for another couple of weeks. Did you meet that Australian bitch? What a cunt. I moved out last week 'cos she kept coming round, trying to tell me what to do. Stupid cow.'

'Yes, I met her. Listen, I popped back today to get the rest of my stuff and the fucking drains have exploded out the back – there is, like, a river of cack out there. It fucking stinks.'

'What?' He's laughing down the phone, 'I'm just at Frances' house. I'll be round in a minute.'

A few minutes later, he's knocking on the door.

'Did you hand your keys in?' I ask him.

'Yeah man, I didn't think I was gonna be coming back.'

We open the back door at stare at the lake of shit, covering our noses with our hands.

'Oh my god,' Toby laughs, 'this is the most disgusting thing I've ever seen.'

'Orlansee,' I tell him.

He laughs hard at this. 'Major fucking orlansee this is, man.'

'What are we going to do about it?' I ask him. 'Do you want to wash your bum in it?'

He laughs some more. 'Nothing, we don't live here anymore.'

'Aye, but we can't leave that, it's a health hazard. Plus, the neighbours will be able to smell it too.'

'Alright, you're right, man. I'll phone the wicked witch and tell her about it.'

An hour later, I load my stuff into my mam's car. Shut the door of the house, lock it, and poke the keys through the letterbox. Strange, mixed feelings of sadness and joy as we pull away.

Living at my mother's: I eat, but don't sleep. Fatten-up a little, try to repair my malnourished body, and damaged mind – but there is the necessity of booze, the liquid painkiller, the need to numb myself.

The long mirror in the hall at the top of the stairs, I look at myself, I don't know who I am.

Months later, a pilgrimage:

Standing, looking at the tree I fucked Ariella against in the Dene.

I think to myself:

The leaves come and go. They cycle, year after year, photosynthesise and give life to the tree. Then they die, wither, and fall. When they fall, they fall indiscriminately, scattered about the foot of the massive trunk of the tree.

Now spring. The green of the new leaves.

I think of the leaves that have fallen from *my* tree – how they have given me life. How they have fed *my* existence, kept me going, nourished me. How their falling was necessary for me to grow.

After autumn and winter – no matter if it seems like forever, spring always comes round.

26376697R00223

Printed in Great Britain
by Amazon